FRENZIED

Brandon Massey

Dark Corner Publishing

ATLANTA, GEORGIA

W hen her son didn't answer the first time she called his name, Beth Turner wasn't concerned. Ryan was a student at the University of Georgia, home for summer break. He loved to stream music on his iPhone and play the Xbox in the media room in the basement. If he were doing any of those things, Beth doubted he would have heard a pressure cooker explode in the kitchen.

Besides, when she had texted him earlier that afternoon, during their layover in Denver, he'd remarked that he wasn't feeling well, that he had a headache and might lie down for a while. She wasn't feeling too hot, either. She and Howard had just arrived home from a seven-day Hawaiian cruise to celebrate their twenty-fifth wedding anniversary. Although it was only six-thirty in the evening, she was jetlagged and looking forward to getting some sleep.

Silence greeted them in the entry hall of their house. All the lights were off, too, the thick shadows relieved only by a few stripes of sunshine filtering around the front blinds.

The house felt empty, but when the Uber driver had dropped them off she had noted that Ryan's Prius was parked in the driveway on the side of the house. Ryan rarely went anywhere on his own without driving his beloved car, even though their community, South Haven, was designed for walking and cycling.

"Doesn't look like he had any wild parties while we were gone," Howard said, and snickered. He switched on a hallway lamp and ambled down the hall, hands on his ample waist. Dressed in an authentic

Hawaiian shirt and khaki cargo shorts, Howard was as well-tanned from their vacation as he had ever been, and she'd always envied his ability to get bronzed. She was a redhead, and had to lather on the sunscreen and manage her exposure to the sun.

"Everything's in one piece," Howard said.

Beth had never been worried about Ryan throwing a party, but while they were away, Howard had joked about such a possibility. She suspected that Howard had *wanted* to return home to chaos, that he was disappointed their youngest child wasn't the keg-tapping frat-boy that Howard had been in his college days at UGA, or that his older brother had been. He was a studious kid.

She set down her luggage and shuffled to the end of the entry hall, her flip-flops clapping across the hardwood floor. Their two-story, six-bedroom home was built in a Colonial style, like many of the residences in South Haven, but the interiors featured modern design: free-flowing spaces, arched doorways, lots of windows to let in natural light. They had lived there for nine years and had filled the place with furniture and interesting souvenirs from their many travels abroad. A glance around confirmed that nothing was out of place.

"Any sign of Charlie?" Beth asked. Charlie was their four-year-old tabby.

"Haven't seen him," Howard said with a shrug of his wide shoulders. "You know how he is, could be anywhere."

That was when she heard the noise: a thumping on the ceiling, which would have come from something going on upstairs, in the approximate region of her son's room.

"Did you hear that?" Beth asked, head cocked.

"Huh?" Howard was in the kitchen leafing through a pile of mail stacked on the counter. "Hear what?"

"Ryan?" she said, almost yelling.

As she spoke, she was heading to the staircase. Tension clenched her stomach in a vise.

"Hang on, Beth . . . Jesus." Puffing, Howard shuffled after her.

She ignored her husband and hurried up the stairs, taking them two risers at a time. It was mother's intuition, singing like electricity in her veins. Something was wrong with her son.

Another thump, from the end of the second-floor hallway, behind Ryan's closed bedroom door. She slammed into the room without knocking, though she knew Ryan hated for her to barge in on him, but her anxiety was at a fever pitch and nothing was going to keep her from her seeing her baby.

The room was shadowed, every curtain fastened across the windows, no lights on. But she saw Ryan on his bed. He wore only a pair of dark boxers. Lying atop the bed sheets, cradling his head, he thrashed so violently that the entire bed rocked, banging against the floor. He moaned in pain, but mumbled words escaped him.

"God . . . oh . . . so hurts . . . bad . . ."

Terror spiked Beth's heart, but she tamped it down as the maternal urge kicked in, and jumped into action. She flipped the light switch near the doorway.

"Fucking out get!" Ryan screamed.

Beth froze, stunned not only by her son's garbled stream of angry words but how he looked. His eyes were inflamed, outlined with crusty crimson whorls, his pupils dilated. Similar red lesions spotted his face, back, and arms. Blood trickled from his nostrils.

He's sick, Beth thought. *But with what?*

"Holy shit, son." Howard moved into the room ahead of Beth. His normally booming voice was almost a whisper. "What happened, buddy?"

"Out fucking get!" His voice was ragged. Ryan clenched one hand into a fist, and Beth saw the back of his hand was marked with the strange lesions, too. Spittle had foamed in the corners of his mouth. "Out . . . get . . . now."

Something's wrong with his mind, Beth thought. She was a real estate agent, with no medical background whatsoever, but she thought he may have been suffering from some kind of fever, or virus, that had brought on a state of delirium. She didn't know what else it could be.

But she was afraid to get too close to him. The idea jarred her. He was her youngest of two children, but she had always secretly thought of Ryan as hers; and Howard had claimed their oldest, Eric, as his. It had been an unspoken agreement between her and Howard, and the kids had known it, too.

But Beth's survival instinct overpowered her maternal inclinations. She was afraid to get any closer to her baby.

"Listen to me, buddy, you're not well, we're getting you to the hospital," Howard said in a gentle but firm *father knows best* tone. He went to put his hand on Ryan's arm.

"Don't touch him," Beth started to tell her husband, but too late.

Howard touching Ryan was like setting off a detonator on an explosive device. Ryan snarled and punched his dad in the face. Howard was a sizable man, six feet and two hundred something pounds, while Ryan was significantly smaller in stature, but the blow came with such force and speed that Howard staggered backward and crashed into the dresser. A clock, some old woodworking project of Ryan's from his middle school days, clattered to the floor.

Beth broke her paralysis and stepped to Howard. A flower of blood had bloomed on his face. He blinked, stupefied.

"He hit me?" Howard asked.

"We've got to call the paramedics," Beth said.

Ryan leaped off the bed, blinking against the light. Beth feared he was going to attack them, though that was such a crazy thought— Ryan, her quiet, somewhat introverted son, who had never displayed any violent impulses whatsoever. He didn't run at them. He scrambled to the other side of the bedroom, moving with a sort of bug-like, twitchy speed.

When Beth realized what Ryan was going to get, she grabbed a fistful of Howard's Hawaiian shirt and whispered: "We've got to get out of here and call for help. Now."

Howard wiped his nose and looked at the blood on his hand. He still looked dazed.

"Now!" Beth said, and tried to haul him upright, peeling back one of her manicured nails.

Throughout the room, Ryan had hung and shelved artifacts of their family's travels over the years. There was the beer stein from a pub in Munich. A pair of maracas he'd gotten in Puerto Rico. The painted wooden mask from South Africa.

And the machete from last year's visit to Brazil.

"Ryan, no!" Beth screamed. "Please!"

Muttering an incoherent stream of words, Ryan snatched the machete off its display hook on the wall.

By then, Howard had finally struggled to his feet. Beth bolted out of the bedroom, and Howard followed close behind, nearly knocking her over, but he had the presence of mind to slam the door shut behind him. It would grant them only the briefest reprieve.

The doorknob rattled. Ryan roared with rage.

Our son wants to kill us, Beth thought. *God in heaven, how is this happening?*

She dashed to their bedroom at the end of the shadowed hallway. One of her flip flops came loose and went flying. Shambling like a man caught in a bad dream, Howard knocked over a table in the hall, and an expensive Lalique vase hit the floor and smashed to pieces.

A pair of French doors granted entry to the master bedroom. She and Howard hustled inside and were swinging the doors shut when Ryan exploded out of his room. He gripped the machete. His swollen eyes seethed.

"Mommy . . . Daddy . . . pieces . . . hack you . . ."

Beth shut the door, locked it. Howard grabbed the back of a nearby upholstered chair and dragged it in front of the door. Then he clutched his chest, grimacing.

Beth had been going to get the telephone but stopped in midstride. "Howard? What's wrong?"

"I'll be okay." Blood from his busted nose trickled over his lips. He sounded out of breath. "Just palpitations."

She doubted his diagnosis. Howard was on a statin and had been advised by his physician numerous times to lose weight, exercise, and eat better, but he went on drinking his beloved tequila and eating whatever he wanted, and his exercise usually amounted to no more than strolling across a golf course with business clients. He was a prime suspect for a heart event, especially then.

"I'm calling 911." She punched on the telephone handset. She could barely make out the buttons on the phone, and realized it was because tears had flooded her eyes.

"Beth, they'll kill him," Howard said.

"What? He's sick."

"They see our son with a machete, they're going to kill him," Howard said matter of factly. He shook his head. "I don't know what's happening, but he'll attack them. And they'll kill him."

Outside the room, Ryan bellowed. The French doors buckled inward as he rammed against them. He was screaming something. Beth couldn't understand him.

She half-believed she was still asleep on the airplane, that all of this was only a terrible nightmare from which she would soon awaken with great relief. It was tempting to lie down on the bed, pull the covers over her head, close her eyes . . . and hopefully wake up back in the world she knew and understood.

Howard switched on a lamp on the nightstand on his side of the bed. He dug into the nightstand drawer and removed the .357 revolver.

Crime never had been an issue in South Haven. It was a gated live-work-play community patrolled by a private security force. But Howard had been raised in an old-fashioned Georgia family that counted hunting and gun collecting as favorite past times. Heck, when Beth had met Howard's dad for the first time and demonstrated she knew how to hold a rifle, the old guy had winked at his son and cracked, s*he's a keeper, son.*

"What are you doing with that?" she asked.

"Protecting us." Hands shaking, he checked the chamber for ammunition.

"He's our son. He's just sick, dammit, clearly. You're going to shoot him?"

"He'll try to take us out, Beth." Howard snapped the cylinder into place. "I don't want to hurt him, Lord knows I don't, but I've got to protect us."

The machete cleaved through the door, eighteen inches of gleaming, sharpened steel.

"Ryan, stop it!" Beth screamed.

But Ryan slashed at the door with the machete. Wood fragments flew.

"Go into the bathroom, lock yourself in there, call help," Howard said. "I'll stay out here and try to slow him down."

"Don't you dare hurt him, Howard. I swear to God I will never forgive you if you do."

"He's my son, too." Swallowing, Howard wiped sweat from his brow with the back of his hand. "Go on, hon."

Beth hurried into the bathroom, locked the door and flipped on lights. A short scream escaped her.

She had found Charlie.

The cat lay on the travertine tile floor, head twisted around a full one-hundred-eighty degrees, lips parted in a frozen cry, green eyes gazing at the ceiling.

The sweet-natured tabby was a rescue. He'd loved to curl up in her lap while she caught up on her favorite shows, would purr with pleasure whenever she scratched behind his ears, and liked to nap on the sofa beside the front windows.

Ryan had loved the cat, too. She couldn't believe he had snapped the animal's neck.

"Oh, Charlie," she said in a broken voice. Kneeling, she covered the cat's corpse with a bath towel. "I'm so sorry."

As she rose, she caught a glimpse of herself in the huge mirror that hung above the dual vanity. Her hair was wild and her mascara was smeared by tears. She looked like hell, which was appropriate, because once they had walked through the front door, she had been plunged into hell on earth. The Hawaiian cruise, seven days of sunny paradise, felt like a vague memory from the distant past.

She dialed 9-1-1.

A woman answered. Beth struggled to explain to the operator what was going on, but managed to describe that her son was sick and was "behaving erratically." She didn't tell the operator that Ryan had evidently murdered the family cat and was presently hacking his way into their bedroom with a machete. She couldn't say such things—the police would come here guns blazing if she told them those details. The operator assured her that authorities were being dispatched and cautioned her to stay in a safe place if she felt endangered.

"No, no, we're okay," she said, and just as she spoke the words she heard a loud *crack* of rupturing wood, and Howard yelled.

"Ryan, dammit, stop right there!"

"Hurry, please," Beth said, and ended the call. She dropped the handset on the vanity and wrung her hands. She worried that she had given the operator too much information, or that the woman had overheard too much background noise and was already conveying to the cops, *suspect is armed and dangerous, go get him, boys.*

Howard let out a choked cry, like a wounded animal. Something crashed against the floor with enough force to rattle the tiles on which Beth stood.

Her pounding heart felt as if it had crawled into her windpipe. Slowly, she stepped to the door, unlocked it, cracked it open an inch.

Ryan stood over his father at the foot of the bed. He swung the machete in wide, powerful arcs, like a diligent laborer clearing underbrush in a jungle. Blood covered the blade, the walls, the bed sheets, and most of all, Ryan's own body, gore splashed like war paint on his face and chest. Howard wasn't moving.

Beth screamed.

Ryan's head ratcheted in her direction as if his neck pivoted on a pole. His swollen eyes simmered with inhuman fury.

"Mommy . . . you . . . hack . . ."

He loped after her, running across the bed, his bare feet leaving bloody footprints on the sheets. She pulled the door shut, fumbled to lock it for whatever good that might do, and retreated from the doorway. She scanned the vanity for something to use to protect herself, grabbed an aerosol can of hairspray and twisted off the cap, the cap clattering to the floor and spinning away.

Ryan kicked the door open as if it were constructed of cardboard. He lunged inside.

Beth directed a jet of hairspray right into his inflamed eyes, the fragrant mist filling the air. Ryan howled and staggered into the bathtub like a blind man tumbling into a swimming pool.

She took no pleasure from his pain, she'd wanted only to slow him down until she could get somewhere safe. She turned the lock on the doorknob and hustled out of the bathroom, slamming the door behind her.

She was hyperventilating, and felt light-headed. She looked around her own bedroom as if she had never seen it before.

There was so much blood.

Howard's blood.

Slightly dizzy, she moved through the room, feeling as though she were floating. Blood everywhere, and there, near the bed, lay Howard, chopped into a random assortment of pieces.

Before she realized what she was doing, she was kneeling to touch her husband's head, which had been mostly severed from his neck. Blood smeared his face, and her fingers came away dipped in crimson.

"Oh, dear God." Vomit surged up her throat. Forcing herself to look away, she stumbled out of the room.

Behind her, the bathroom door rattled in its frame.

She also heard, distantly, the familiar and comforting warble of sirens.

Got to . . . get out . . . .

From there, it was as if she were seeing everything unwind through a series of jump-cut scenes in a found footage film. Running out of the house into the evening sunshine. Three Roswell police cruisers converging in front of their residence, light bars swirling. Her nosy neighbor, Miss Eleanor, coming up to wrap an arm around her and pull her aside. Ryan scrambling outdoors, nearly unrecognizable in his suit of spilled blood, but still armed with the machete, and still snarling with fury . . . and finding a new target in the group of police officers hurrying out of their vehicles with guns drawn.

It took twenty-seven rounds of ammunition to take him down.

It was only the beginning.

Chapter 2

I n Mark Deacon's dream, an enormous monster stalked him through dark corridors, intent upon tearing out his heart.

As he raced through the darkness, armed only with a flickering flashlight, he heard the creature shambling after him. No matter how fast he ran, no matter how many twists he followed in the shadowed tunnels, he could never put much distance between himself and the predator. Panting, he hit another turn, and in the illogical way of dreams, the monster was suddenly in his face: a towering beast with simmering red eyes, a wide mouth full of long, pointed teeth, and curved claws as sharp as surgical scalpels. Roaring, it swiped a massive claw across his chest. He collapsed to the ground, his flesh torn away as if made of crepe paper, exposing his pulsating heart. He lay helpless while the creature crawled on top of him and devoured his heart as it still throbbed . . .

He erupted out of sleep with a cry on his lips.

The bedroom was dark, the only sounds the hum of the whirling ceiling fan and his jagged breathing.

Bolting upright, snatching away damp bedsheets, Deacon put his hand against his chest. His heart was still there, of course—knocking at a rapid pace thanks to that crazy nightmare.

He sucked in deep breaths. As his pulse slowed, he pulled his fingers away from the puckered scar on his chest.

According to his cardiologist, it wasn't safe for him to get overly excited. His heart, damaged by a gunman's hollow-point bullet, no longer functioned at peak capacity, and never would unless Deacon consented to a heart transplant. He had no interest in a life constrained by an unending diet of immunosuppressive medications and a heightened risk of cancer. He had chosen to adapt to his new reality.

The bedside clock read half past six. He hadn't slept well—grim thoughts and bad dreams had cycled through his mind all night—but it was time to rise. He would soon need to commence his morning rounds.

A warm shower blasted him fully into wakefulness. Standing in front of the mirror, he dressed in his uniform.

He was forty-two-years-old, six-foot-one, a hundred and ninety pounds. He had a milk chocolate complexion and wore his facial hair in a goatee that had lately begun to display flecks of grey hair.

Some women said he bore a strong resemblance to the actor, Idris Elba. Deacon liked the actor so the comparison didn't bother him.

He went to check on his father, who shared the two-bedroom apartment with him.

Pops was already awake. He sat in his wheelchair beside the neatly made bed. He wore a plaid shirt and khakis.

Although his father's eyes were open, he was so still that he looked like a mannequin—or a dead man.

That was one of Deacon's fears. Walking in and finding his father dead. One day it would happen, and such a time was probably not that distant. Pops was seventy-six. Considering that the average life expectancy of an African-American male was seventy-two, Pops was already living on borrowed time.

His mother hadn't come close to reaching her life expectancy. Ovarian cancer had taken her at the age of forty-six, when Deacon was still a teenager. Pops had raised him and his baby sister and done a pretty fair job, at least with his sister. She was an attorney out in Los Angeles with a doting husband and two adorable kids.

Meanwhile, I'm stuck living with this grouchy old man, Deacon thought, and smiled at his father.

"Morning, old fella," Deacon said.

"They're going to be talking about this all day." Pops motioned to the flat screen TV mounted on the wall. "But I guess no one expects *you* to do anything about it, huh?"

Sighing, Deacon glanced at the TV screen. It was a local metro Atlanta news program, and the news crew appeared to be on site there in South Haven, sticking microphones in the face of any resident they could find who had an opinion about yesterday's gruesome murder.

Deacon plucked the remote from his father's lap and switched the channel.

"Hey!" Pops said. "Turn back, dammit."

"Watch something useful." Deacon flipped to an infomercial about male sexual enhancement supplements. "Here you go. This is what you need to get those geriatric juices flowing."

"Hah, at least I've got myself a woman." Pops checked his wrist-watch and cracked a smile. "She'll be here shortly. Who you got, son?"

"Anita is not your woman. She's your nurse."

"Stop player hating," Pops said.

"No one uses that slang anymore," Deacon said. "You make your-self sound old when you talk like that."

"Don't hate the player, hate the game."

Deacon only shook his head. "So outdated."

"What the hell do they say then?" Pops asked.

Deacon started to speak, realized he didn't know how to reply, and just shrugged. "I don't know."

"Now who sounds old?" Pops said and laughed.

Deacon laughed with him. He hung out with his father a short while longer, bantering with him about whatever topics came to mind, until Anita arrived at seven o'clock sharp.

Initially, Pops had resisted the idea that he needed in-home nurse care. Both of his legs had been amputated above the knee, due to complications from type-two diabetes. Prosthetics had been installed on both limbs, and while he had basic mobility, Pops often grew frustrated and settled back into his wheelchair. Then his kidneys had gone bad, and he needed dialysis sessions . . . the nurse helped him stay active, got him to and from the dialysis clinic, coaxed him to take his medication. Pops' resistance had eventually thawed, and when the new nurse, Anita, had been assigned his case, he had instantly fallen in love.

Anita was in her early fifties but easily could have passed for a woman in her mid-thirties. She was Jamaican, with smooth skin the color of mahogany, dark curly hair, and a smile that made Pops melt.

"Pops is in high spirits this morning," Deacon said to her as she entered the apartment. "Be careful."

"Oh, I can handle him." She chuckled. "How are you doing, my friend? I've seen the news, such a terrible thing to have happened to that family. Was the boy on drugs? Or sick?"

"No one knows anything conclusively yet." Deacon said.

"Well, you be careful out there, honey, in case it's catching."

"I'm not a cop any more, Anita," he said. "I'm just a security guard."

She offered a small smile, her copper eyes twinkling. "So you say."

***

Deacon enjoyed carting around South Haven in the mornings.

He drove an electric-powered golf cart with the words "South Haven Security" inscribed in blocky black text on both sides of the vehicle. The cart reached a maximum speed of about twenty-five miles per hour, but in the enclosed community, there had never been a reason to drive any faster.

As he'd reminded Anita, he was just a security guard. He carried a walkie-talkie, a Taser, and a tactical flashlight, the tools attached to his duty belt. Although he was licensed to carry a firearm, he didn't bring it. There had never been any need. Not yet, anyway.

While the early-morning sun painted the sky in pinkish hues, Deacon drove the cart from the guard headquarters, located near the main entrance gate, to the commercial section of the community located in the heart of the development. South Haven had been designed around the central theme of "old-fashioned living with a modern flair," a shining example of the New Urbanism trend that had swept the country in the past couple of decades. The town square was home to the business district, lined by a pedestrian-friendly thoroughfare imaginatively called "Main Street."

Only a few national retail chains were allowed to set up shop in South Haven. Commerce was mostly homegrown small businesses: Jilly's Bakery, which served great coffee and pastries; a corner grocery that specialized in organic goods; a hair salon, medical clinic, barre studio, frozen yogurt shop, book store, and various restaurants that offered everything from pizza to grass-fed beef.

A water fountain dominated the center of the town square, amidst a few acres of freshly manicured grass crisped with morning dew. On summer nights, the South Haven Cinema hosted a free "Screen on the Green," event, an evening broadcast of family friendly films. Last week, they had screened *The Goonies*.

The town square was mostly vacant as Deacon rolled through. One of the only businesses open at that early hour was the bakery—his destination. He parked the cart in one of the numerous "Reserved for Electric Vehicle" slots along Main Street.

Inside, Jilly's Bakery was brightly lit, with a gleaming walnut-topped counter that ran the length of the restaurant, and a large glass display case full of donuts, croissants, muffins, cupcakes, and other pastries. The delicious aromas of roasted coffee beans and freshly baked bread wafted on the cool air. A chalkboard menu posted on the back wall advertised a summer special on their artisanal cold-brew coffee.

Music piped from the bakery's sound system: a classic Eagles track that Deacon recognized, *Hotel California.*

There was only one customer sitting on a leather stool at the counter. He hunched over a cup of coffee and a half-eaten blueberry muffin. Deacon settled on the stool next to the man and clapped him on the shoulder.

"Hey, Jim," Deacon said. "Good morning."

"Is it?" Jim grunted.

Jim Copeland was his second in command. He was as stout as a wrestler, white-haired, with a ruddy complexion. He wore wire-rim glasses that framed his cool blue eyes. His thick, long beard brought to mind the wizard character of Gandalf from the *Lord of the Rings* films.

Like Deacon, Jim had used to be a cop. Unlike Deacon, he had retired from the force after a long career, let his beard grow, and joined the security firm to pursue something productive and low-key to do during his retirement.

"I saw what that kid did." Jim sipped coffee, grimaced as if it tasted too bitter. "I was with the Marietta PD for thirty-five years. I saw a lot of bad shit. I *never* saw anything like that, the rage in his eyes. It was inhuman."

"A tragedy for sure," Deacon said.

"Inhuman." Jim crumpled a napkin in his fist. His blue eyes, normally sparkling with mirth, were haunted. "I couldn't sleep last night. I kept seeing those damned eyes of his."

Deacon didn't know what to say. Although he and Jim had worked together for two years, he'd never seen him in such a somber mood and didn't know how to pull him out of it.

The owner of the bakery, Jilly, emerged from the back of the shop. She was a tall, raven-haired woman in her mid-thirties, with a silver nose piercing and multiple tattoos along the length of her muscular arms. She wore a black apron and an Atlanta Braves baseball cap.

"The usual?" she asked Deacon.

"Please." He indicated the shop with a sweep of his arm. "Slow morning?"

"Been that way, yeah." She poured hot water into a paper cup, dropped in a bag of non-caffeinated herbal tea, applied a lid, and slid it across the counter to him. "Two of my staff called out sick, too. Both of them said they had migraines, which is kinda weird, but whatever. I'm the only one here holding down the fort. Strange morning."

"Let's hope things pick up," Deacon said. "I'd like to see life get back to normal here."

"After last night?" Jilly barked a humorless laugh. "No shit. I knew the father, Howard Turner. He used to come in a couple times a week and grab a cheese Danish and hot chocolate. He was a nice guy."

"Their kid was a college student, was on the dean's list," Jim said. "But what I saw in his eyes . . ."

"My theory is, he was on bath salts, or something like it," Jilly said. "Remember that dude in Florida, the Miami zombie? He was on those drugs, too."

"I remember the case," Deacon said.

"Look, I'm nobody's schoolmarm," Jilly said, "I like to vape my weed and chill on my days off. But I don't mess with that synthetic crap. Way too dangerous."

Deacon checked his tea, saw it had steeped long enough. He removed the bag and rose off the stool. "Ready to roll, Jim?"

Grunting in reply, Jim followed him outdoors and settled into the passenger seat of the golf cart. Deacon secured his tea in one of the cart's twin cup-holders and pushed the ignition button. The engine hummed to life.

"Let's do it," Deacon said, and commenced their morning rounds.

In silence, they drove out of the business district and entered the residential area. South Haven featured a wide variety of architectural styles: Colonial, Victorian, Craftsman, Tudor, Italianate, even Art Deco. Overall, the community contained nearly seven hundred residences. Many of the homes were quite large but stood on modest-sized lots; no one was isolated from their neighbors. Most of the detached garages stood on the rear of the residential lots, accessible via a network of alleys.

Mature elms and maples flanked the roads, providing abundant shade. Every street had sidewalks on both sides, to encourage walking. No one lived more than a ten-minute walk from the town square.

The single-family residences were priced well above Deacon's financial resources, but he admired them nonetheless. This was no cookie-cutter subdivision, the likes of which had proliferated throughout metro Atlanta. No two homes in South Haven were identical. In spite of the divergent styles, there was a sense of order, community. He would have loved to purchase a home there someday. If he won the lottery.

A few cars buzzed past them, residents beginning their morning commutes.

"Folks are driving to work," Jim said, finally speaking. He stroked his beard. "But no one is out jogging or walking. Did you notice that?"

"You're right," Deacon said. "And it's a warm morning, sunny, a perfect time to be outdoors."

"People are shell-shocked after last night. Can't believe something like that happened here. South Haven's supposed to be like an oasis from real crime."

In the two years that Deacon had worked security there, there had never been a homicide. A handful of break-ins, a few assaults, several cases of auto theft—but never a murder.

"You might be right," Deacon said. "Or they don't want to be waylaid by a TV news crew."

He spotted a van ahead, antennae bristling from its roof and people clustered around it. He made a sharp turn at the next intersection, taking them away from the group.

"Thanks," Jim said with visible relief. "I'm in no mood to chat with those vultures. They feed on human misery, thrive on it."

"No argument from me on that," Deacon said.

Ahead, Deacon saw a familiar figure wandering along the sidewalk: an elderly lady who lived alone in a Victorian-style cottage. Beckwith, that was her name. He vaguely remembered that her husband had passed away last year, but she continued to live in the house with her dog.

Ms. Beckwith wore only a pink nightgown and slippers. A red leash dangled from her hand.

"What do we have here?" Jim muttered. "Canine rescue?"

"All in a day's work," Deacon said. "I love my job."

Ms. Beckwith noticed them drawing near, and waved them toward her. Deacon veered to the curb.

"Jake is gone." Her eyes were reddened from tears. Her face looked as if she had tried to apply make-up and lipstick, but she had missed several spots, which gave her the unfortunate appearance of a deranged clown.

"Jake?" Deacon asked. "Your dog?"

"I took him out to poop last night, and he slipped his leash, I don't know what I was thinking. I must have been distracted thinking about that awful murder that happened here. I called for Jake but he didn't come back. I was certain he would have come back by this morning. He seemed ill . . . . I can't believe he's run away. He's never done this."

"What breed of dog is Jake, ma'am?" Jim asked. He had taken out his pen and a steno pad.

"He's a St. Bernard, of course," she snapped.

"All right, I only wanted to be sure," Jim said. "You aren't the only one who lives here who has a dog, you know."

"Any idea where Jake might have gone?" Deacon asked, jumping in quickly. "Does he have any favorite places here, for example?"

"Lord, I don't know." She blew her nose with a pink handkerchief. "Sometimes, I take him walking on the trails . . . he loves it over there. I was going to go look there, too, but my arthritis is awful this morning. I'll have to drive."

Deacon glanced at Jim. Jim nodded, reluctantly.

"We'll take a look," Deacon said.

Chapter 3

The South Haven Greenway was on the eastern side of South Haven, approximately one hundred acres of cultivated green space, the trails paved expressly for walking, running, and biking. Part of the land curved around a shimmering lake that was deep enough to swim in.

Deacon brought the golf cart to a halt at the greenway's wide entrance. The wrought-iron gates had already been opened; one of his graveyard shift colleagues had unlocked them at six o'clock that morning, per the posted hours of operation.

A thick, cool mist hung over the woods. Deacon heard birds chirping and the wind soughing through trees, but not much else.

"Looking for that dog in here is a wild goose chase," Jim said. "Especially if it's sick. He probably laid down somewhere back in here and died. Poor bastard."

"We promised to search," Deacon said. "A dog that size, if he's wandering around in these woods, we've got a reasonable chance to spot him."

"How far do you want to go?" Jim asked.

"We'll make one circuit of the entire trail. If we don't see him, we've done our duty and call it quits."

"Fair enough."

They rolled through the entrance, onto the paved path. Deacon drove slowly, scanning the forestland on both sides of the trail.

One man jogged past. Deeply tanned, he wore a black muscle shirt and shorts, ear buds nested in his ears. He nodded at them as he raced by.

"Christ, it's deserted back here," Jim said. "We'd normally have passed a dozen folks by now."

"Unusual," Deacon said. An uncomfortable tightness had spread across his gut. It was a familiar feeling; intuition warning him that he was treading into a potentially troublesome situation. As a cop, he had grown intimately familiar with such feelings, as it had been his duty to put himself in harm's way. Although he was only a security guard and no one really expected him to put his life on the line, his sense of duty still held sway over him.

Protect and serve, he thought. Even when one was only looking for a lost dog.

"You give any more thought to what we talked about the other day?" Jim asked.

"I did." Deacon nodded, not taking his gaze away from the surrounding woods. "Not interested."

"You could at least meet the woman. What harm is there in that?"

Jim and his wife, Linda, had been determined to set him up on a date with Linda's colleague. Both of them were of the mind that a single man over the age of forty *needed* a woman in his life, a wife, whether he wanted one or not.

But Deacon had done the marriage thing, twice. Once when he was just twenty-four; again when he was an older but apparently not much wiser thirty-six. Neither had lasted longer than two years. He accepted that he had an innate knack for getting involved in relationships that were destined to implode, and his only consolation was that he hadn't fathered any children that could have been wounded by the collateral damage.

"I don't need anyone's help getting dates, Jim," Deacon said. "All I do is pull up an app on my phone, swipe through a few photos, click which woman I want, and boom, I've got a hot date that night."

Jim chuckled. "Those aren't dates, those are booty calls. And I don't believe you actually do that. You're too old-fashioned."

"You don't know what I do, man," Deacon said.

"Hey, do you want to see a picture of Linda's friend? Linda sent me one."

"Nope."

"Why the hell not? She's gorgeous."

"Doesn't matter what she looks like. She could be Halle Berry's long-lost identical twin. Still not interested."

Jim was about to respond when a scream shattered the morning's stillness. A woman's scream. It came from somewhere ahead, not far, but beyond their view.

"Oh, shit." Jim bolted upright, pushed up his glasses.

Deacon had already mashed the accelerator. The golf cart bounced over bumps on the path, and wind buffeted his face and threatened to snatch his cap off his head. Beside him, Jim was speaking into his walkie-talkie, warning the guard on duty at HQ of the potential situation they were approaching.

They careened around a curve in the trail, and that was when they saw it: The St. Bernard. The bearish dog had pinned a struggling young woman to the pavement. The dog was snarling, and Deacon saw the flash of teeth, the spray of blood.

I thought these dogs were supposed to be friendly, Deacon thought. *Gentle giants. What's going on?*

Hands tightening on the steering wheel, Deacon brought the golf cart to a stop about thirty feet away. He shifted the gears into Park.

Jim barked into his walkie-talkie that HQ needed to get the police, and paramedics.

The dog continued to maul the woman, so consumed with its attack it didn't notice their arrival. Flailing, trying uselessly to get from underneath the massive hound, the woman let out short screams of agony, terror.

"Jesus, that fuckin' dog is huge." Jim had drawn his Taser, but grimaced. "I could use my old Glock 9mm right about now. Or a rifle."

Deacon had drawn his Taser, too. He realized he had never used the stun weapon in a live situation, only during training.

His heart slammed. He was supposed to carefully manage his heart rate, per doctor's orders, but at that moment it felt as if it were knocking two hundred beats per minute.

"What's the play?" Jim asked.

"I'll draw his attention," Deacon said. "I'll try to lead him away from the woman. You take care of her."

"Got it." Jim extended the Taser, gripping it in both hands, as they had been trained.

Deacon blasted the golf cart's horn, twice, and yelled: "Jake!"

The dog lifted its head and swung in their direction.

Both of its eyes were inflamed, crusted with red sores and oozing a mucous-like substance. Blood dribbled from its snout. A foamy, pinkish mixture of saliva and blood seeped from its mouth.

"Rabies," Deacon said. "Has to be rabies."

Jim moved away from the golf cart. Deacon edged to the left. Chest heaving, the St. Bernard looked from one of them, to the other.

"I'm your man, Jake," Deacon said, and the dog's attention locked in on him. Deacon stepped off the paved trail, shoes crunching over grass. "You watch me, Jake."

He hoped using the dog's name would snap it out of attack mode, would trigger some latent memory of being a friendly house dog, recollections of belly rubs and warm nights in a loving home. He could only imagine how Ms. Beckwith had spoiled the canine. The dog undoubtedly had enjoyed more creature comforts than half the people on the planet, and even in its diseased state of mind, it had to remember something of that charmed life.

"You're a good dog, Jake," Deacon said. "I know it, Jake. I know you are, boy."

The St. Bernard growled. Deacon's grip tightened on the Taser. He dug his heels into the grass.

"He's coming for you," Jim said. "Get ready."

"Take care of the woman," Deacon said, though from a quick glance in her direction, the woman wasn't moving at all.

The dog rushed him.

The animal had to weigh close to two hundred pounds, about as much as Deacon actually weighed, and it was *fast*. Spittle flying, snarling, the canine thundered toward him. Deacon held his breath, steadied his aim, and when the dog was within a range of ten feet, so close Deacon could smell his hot, rancid breath, he fired the Taser.

The stun gun crackled, compressed nitrogen launching the twin metal probes from the barrel in a silver blur. The probes attached to the dog's massive neck. Fifty thousand volts of electricity surged through the wires and into the animal.

It should have brought the dog down.

It would have brought virtually anyone down.

But the canine slammed into Deacon with a roar. For Deacon, it was like being hit by a linebacker running at full speed. The Taser flipped out of his grasp. He hit the ground on his back, the impact rattling his teeth. The dog was on his chest, and this close, it seemed even bigger, like a grizzly bear. Foamy saliva sprayed over Deacon's face, and Deacon brought up his arm to protect his neck, because the animal's sharp, blood-streaked teeth were going straight for his jugular.

Is this how it ends for me? Deacon thought, dimly.

There was the crackle of another Taser being discharged, Jim's, and then the dog was suddenly off his chest. Probes attached to its flank, the animal wobbled drunkenly, and smashed into a tree. But like a prize fighter that refused to quit, the dog did not go down.

"This is unbelievable," Jim muttered, and looked at the stun weapon in his hand as if convinced it must be defective.

By then, Deacon had gotten to his feet. He was woozy, his chest ached, and blood spattered his face, but he had escaped the dog's bite.

The stumbling canine tore free of the probes. Drooling, it staggered away into the woods.

Both Deacon and Jim hurried to check on the woman. Before they reached her, Deacon knew what they would find.

She was dead.

Deacon lowered his head.

"We got here too late," he said. "It was over by the time we rolled up."

"That dog." Shaking his head, Jim wiped away tears. "It looked just like that kid I saw last night, I swear. Those eyes. What the hell is going on?"

Chapter 4

Emily Taylor administered the home pregnancy test for the third time that morning. She re-read the instructions. She Googled it. She watched a YouTube video demonstrating its use. She was a student at Emory Medical School and a former high school valedictorian—she knew she could figure out how to do this properly.

But she received, again, the same result she had gotten from the prior two tests.

It was positive.

She was pregnant.

She dropped the test stick on the edge of the vanity, flipped down the lid of the commode, and collapsed on it. She hugged herself, though the bathroom was warm. She couldn't stop trembling.

I can't be pregnant, she thought. *That is not part of the plan.*

But she had missed her period, and while that had been alarming, she had needed to validate it by giving herself the early pregnancy test. Perhaps it would be wise to visit her gynecologist and have blood drawn and tested, too. Just to be absolutely sure.

Because this revelation was going to totally wreck her parents.

Emily's father was a plastic surgeon with a thriving practice in Alpharetta. Her mother was an anesthesiologist with offices in Dunwoody. They were both, to put it lightly, overachievers, and they expected only the best from her, their third and youngest child. Her mother's expectations were particularly high. Her mother, the daughter of a Chinese immigrant, was a so-called "tiger mom."

For Emily's entire life, her mother had enforced a strict code of discipline and a relentless focus on achievement. Private tutoring, as preparation for preschool, began when Emily was three. Piano lessons commenced at age five. She had attended an exclusive private academy from kindergarten through high school, and one of her earliest academic memories was bringing home a math test on which she had scored a ninety-eight percent, an accomplishment of which she was proud, and her mother frowning at the paper and remarking, in a voice thick with disappointment, "Why not a one hundred percent? You did not study hard enough. I expect better. Go to your room."

For her mom, failure was never an option.

And in her mother's world, getting pregnant while still a med school student was failure of the most reckless kind. She could imagine her mother kicking her out of the house and actually refusing to speak to her again. *My daughter? Yes, such a disappointment, a true embarrassment to our family. I haven't spoken to her in years.*

Tears spilled down Emily's cheeks. She snatched a fistful of tissues out of the container on the vanity, mopped her eyes and face. Rising unsteadily, she used her fingers to comb her dark hair out of her eyes.

She needed to speak to her boyfriend, Zack.

She and Zack had been dating for about a year and a half. He was a grad school student at Georgia Tech, majoring in mathematics; his choice of major was probably the only reason her mother had approved of her dating him at all. They'd had sex, of course (though not as much as Zack wanted), and had always been so careful about using protection, and she was taking birth control, too. She didn't understand how this could have happened. Had she somehow missed a day or two of taking the pill, in spite of all her precautions?

Zack lived in South Haven, too, with his parents. She sent him a text message on her iPhone, saying they needed to talk, face to face. He didn't reply immediately, but if she knew him, he was either at home, or at work. During the summers, he worked as a part-time instructor at a math tutoring center located on site in the community, helping those ambitious students who wanted to get ahead when school kicked off again later in the fall.

Another message came through on her phone: it was from her best friend, Megan.

Update, Em?

Megan was the only soul on the planet with whom Emily had shared her situation. They'd been close friends since third grade, and after high school graduation, Megan had gone to Julliard in New York, to study drama. She currently was in-between theatre productions on Broadway, but even in the midst of her most hectic performance schedules, she and Emily managed to connect for a few text messages every day, and Emily looked forward to visiting her in Manhattan before the summer ended.

Emily sighed, responded: *Round three: positive.*

So sorry. Any chance of false positive?

Don't think so. I had nausea this morning.

Ugh. Sorry. Proof then.

Yeah. Probably.

Are you going to tell Zack?

He needs to know. This is a face to face chat.

He's going to shit himself.

We both have plans. This isn't part of it.

I know. You aren't telling your mom?

She would disown me.

Sad but true. I'm here for you, Em. Whatever happens.

Emily swiped to see if Zack had replied, and found no response. She would have to go find him, then.

Before leaving, she stuffed all three of the home pregnancy kits deep into a plastic grocery bag, and disposed of the bag in the trash bin standing inside the wooden carrel on the side of their house. It would not do for her mother to stumble across any evidence of what was going on. She could imagine how *that* would have played out.

Her family lived in an embarrassingly opulent, six-bedroom Tudor-style home on Magnolia Way. It had a detached three-car garage located at the rear of the property, and each slot was occupied; her parents were away on a seven-day vacation in the Greek isles.

She hopped onto her bike and rolled out of the paved driveway, into the adjacent gravel alley. She owned a Honda Civic, but for getting around South Haven she preferred to ride her bicycle. It was a bike-friendly community, one of the big perks of living there. The weather was sunny with a cool breeze, and not yet too humid.

She sucked in deep breaths as she swerved out of the alley and onto the street. She enjoyed the contractions of her pumping muscles, the sizzle of simmering adrenaline, the wind blowing through her hair. Cycling was only of the only activities she pursued simply for the thrill of it, and as she pedaled and swerved, her mind roamed beyond the stressful concerns of the day.

She noted that the roads, however, were curiously vacant. She would have expected to see young mothers out pushing babies in strollers, someone walking a dog, or out cultivating a flower bed. But it looked as if all of the residents were indoors, or simply not home.

Something to do with last night's murder? She had known that guy, Ryan, sort of. He was a little younger than she was but she had seen him at neighborhood gatherings. He seemed like the studious type, which is why it was so incredible that people were saying he'd been on drugs and had gone psycho on his family.

Zack and his folks lived in a two-story Craftsman-style home painted forest-green, with black trim. She braked to a stop at the end of their faux-cobblestone walkway.

She checked her phone again. He hadn't yet responded to her text message. She was about to get off her bike and go ring the doorbell when she heard something metallic grinding against pavement.

She looked over shoulder and saw Zack's neighbor, Mr. Pinto. He was a Latino man, perhaps in his late-sixties, and lived with his wife in the residence across the street. Emily had been seeing him for years during her bike rides through the community, and he always paid her a wave as she zipped past.

Mr. Pinto carried a garden hoe, dragging the business end of the tool along the street as he lumbered toward her.

"Sir?" she asked.

There was something wrong with his face. His eyes were red with inflammation, and the flesh around the sockets appeared to have been cauterized. Dark veins mapped his brown-skinned complexion. Blister-like lesions marked his cheeks and forehead, as if he were leprous. A trickle of blood dribbled from his nose and collected in his thick grey mustache.

What the heck is wrong with him?

The budding physician in her wanted to examine, to treat, to help. But the skin at the nape of her neck had tightened.

She balanced her right foot on the bike pedal, her thigh muscles coiling.

Mr. Pinto spoke in a garbled stream of barely intelligible words, spittle spraying from his swollen lips.

"Flowers . . . roses . . . lilies . . . ruined flowers, the boy did . . ."

Drawing closer to Emily, he lifted the garden hoe. Instinct compelled her to act before conscious thought could issue the command. She surged forward on her bike.

Mr. Pinto swung the hoe, the blade whistling through the space she had just vacated.

"Ruined flowers!" he screamed. "Boy ruined them he did!"

Chilled to the core, Emily pedaled away. She risked a look over her shoulder and saw Mr. Pinto running after her, clutching the garden hoe in his hands like a sword. His sneakers were untied, laces flopping. He was fleet-footed for a man of his age, blistered face taut with savage resolve.

"Ruined flowers! Roses! Lilies!"

She couldn't believe this was happening. A flurry of questions spun through her mind. What had she done to provoke the attack? Had Mr. Pinto gone insane? What was the matter with him?

She pedaled as fast as she could. She was a petite woman, only five-feet-one, but her legs were strong from regular exercise. She lowered her head and forced herself to go faster. When she looked behind her again she saw she had put some distance between herself and Mr. Pinto.

But he was still coming. One of his shoes had flown off, and he kept on after her, limbs swinging as mechanically as a machine, and though she had a good lead she worried that he would outlast her. He had the look of a man who would never tire, who would run and run and run and eventually overtake her as she ran out of gas, and swipe that hoe across her throat—

A large, dark object suddenly clipped her front tire.

"Score!" someone yelled.

Emily swerved, almost lost her balance, but course corrected before she flew over the handlebars. Slowing, she looked around. A boy who looked to be about twelve was outdoors, in the yard of the property on her right. He was bending to pick up one of the stone pavers that lined the large bed of petunias at the front of the house. From the distance, she could see the redness outlining his eyes, the lesions spotting his face.

Did he just hurl one of those stones at me?

Her bike's front tire was damaged, several of the spokes warped out of shape. A paver lay on the street a few feet away from her, dirt along its edge, like a tooth torn from the root.

Jesus. The boy is digging stones out of the ground and throwing them at me. For no reason whatsoever.

Behind her, Mr. Pinto was gaining on her, feet slapping against concrete.

She couldn't believe her predicament. Had the entire world gone mad overnight?

Belting out a yelp of joy, the kid heaved another stone in her direction, but by then she had started forward again. The paver hurtled through the air and smashed into Mr. Pinto's head with a sickening thud. The old man dropped to the street, the garden hoe spinning out of his hands.

"Score!" the kid shouted again.

Grinding forward on the bike, Emily gritted her teeth. She had to suppress the almost overpowering compulsion to go check on the man and try to assist him. She focused solely on escape. The damaged front tire wobbled, slowing her, but it was still faster than she could have traveled on foot.

She had to get somewhere safe and figure out what the heck was going on.

Her lungs ached from exertion, and perspiration had matted her hair against her face. She swung around to look behind her and saw that Mr. Pinto was on his feet again, blood covering his face like a port wine stain.

But he wasn't alone. The boy was at his side, an armful of stones clutched against his chest. Both of them ran after her. The kid drew back his arm and heaved a paver after her, like a quarterback flinging a Hail Mary. The stone missed her by several feet, but smashed into the rear window of a Lexus sedan parked at the curb. The car alarm blared.

"Score!" the kid cried.

If I don't get away from them, they're going to kill me.

It was a perfectly illogical idea, the notion that residents in her upper-class neighborhood would be hell-bent on murdering her only because she had happened to pedal by on her bicycle. But in the new age of terror, when boarding an airplane could be the equivalent of climbing into a mass grave, when going to college could result in you getting gunned down by a stranger, when going to a street festival could put you in the path of a madman wielding his car like a weapon, perhaps it wasn't so crazy after all.

At the next intersection, Emily veered left. Pedaling as hard as she could, bent over, heart pounding and sweat seeping into her eyes, she rode away from the madness, but deep down, worried that things were only going to get worse.

Chapter 5

A lex Vasquez didn't like the man who sat in his shop.

Alex was a franchisee of Bimi's Frozen Yogurt. His store was located in a prime retail spot in South Haven, smack dab in the middle of the action on Main Street. At eleven-thirty in the morning on that Friday, business was unusually slow for a sultry July day. The only people in the store were Alex, a teenage trainee named Chloe, and the man at the corner table, their only customer since they had opened half an hour ago.

From the safety of the management office in the back of the shop, Alex watched the guy via a closed-circuit, color security monitor.

The man was Latino, like Alex, maybe in his mid-forties, also like Alex. He was huge: easily six feet five, perhaps two hundred and fifty pounds, and Alex was willing to bet that much of his bulk was composed of lean muscle. He wore a two-piece, charcoal-grey suit and a white shirt, and an expensive-looking watch with a gold band. His dark hair was trimmed in a buzz cut and he was clean-shaven. He had deep-set brown eyes that took in everything, and gave nothing in return.

In anyone else's opinion, the guy might have been a wealthy owner of a string of strip clubs or seedy bars, someone who'd started in the business as a bouncer and worked his way up the ranks through cunning and ruthless efficiency. But Alex saw him differently. Although the stranger sat calmly at a table, methodically eating frozen yogurt from a cup, occasionally glancing at his cell phone, Alex had pegged him as hired muscle. He noticed the bulge in the man's jacket, the unmistakable shape of a concealed weapon.

But hired by whom, and for what purpose?

Alex had his suspicions.

Perhaps, after he'd been on the run for eight years, the Sinaloa Cartel had finally located him.

Alex had long suspected this day would come. Outside of exiting this world for good, few people truly escaped such insidious, far-reaching organizations. You enjoyed only a measure of temporary freedom.

He had begun to believe, after eight years, that he might have been one of the lucky ones. He had built a new identity in metro Atlanta, married a wonderful woman who loved him in spite of his sordid past, and opened a business that had no ties to his prior infamy. Life had never been sweeter.

He stared at the man on his monitor. His eyes narrowed.

If this was the end for him, he would not go quietly.

Alex unlocked the bottom right drawer of his desk, slid it open. The Beretta nine millimeter resting inside was already loaded, and lay alongside an extra clip of ammunition.

Rising, Alex nested the gun at the small of his back.

"Umm, is everything okay?"

Startled, Alex turned. The teenage blonde, Chloe, stood at the threshold of the doorway. Her blue eyes were wide with alarm. She had seen the gun, he realized.

"What is it?" he asked.

"The customer out front, he like, said he wanted to talk to you?" she said.

"Why? He appears to have thoroughly enjoyed his dessert." Alex indicated the security monitor. The man was scraping the last traces of yogurt from the cup.

She shrugged. "He didn't say. I'm sorry. I guess I should have asked?"

Chloe had the odd habit of phrasing most of her statements as questions, as if afraid to state her thoughts forthrightly.

"It's okay." He motioned to a chair. "Why don't you wait back here while I speak to him?"

He offered her a smile he hoped was reassuring, but she nervously twirled a strand of her hair.

"Do you, like, know that guy?" she asked.

"I've no idea who he is. I'm only going to speak to him. Please wait here."

Twisting her hair, she settled into the chair. After this frightening encounter with her boss, the girl would probably submit her resignation.

He left the office, shoes whispering on the tile floor. The Beretta felt good at his back, like the steadying hand of an old friend.

When he emerged from the corridor, the customer—Alex told himself to keep thinking of the man as merely a customer until he learned otherwise—was already focused on him from across the room. Intensely. Alex could recognize the cold gaze of a killer. He was certain that many had died at the hands of this man.

The shop was built around a self-serve design concept. Twelve dispensers arranged along the circular-shaped wall provided a range of frozen yogurt flavors: standards such as vanilla, strawberry, and chocolate, and more adventurous selections such as mango-banana and salted caramel vanilla swirl. A separate stainless steel station offered all manner of dessert toppings. Once customers had created their frozen treat to their liking, they brought the cup to a digital scale at the checkout counter in the middle of the store and paid for their purchase based on a per ounce price.

It was a simple, profitable business that ran virtually on autopilot, especially during the sweltering Georgia summers. It required only one employee on most days, someone to keep the toppings refreshed, refill the yogurt dispensers, ensure the basic cleanliness of the facility, and contact Alex if machinery malfunctioned. Alex would be saddened to give up this dream of an enterprise, and hoped he was wrong about this man's identity.

"I'm the manager, Alex," Alex said. He approached the table, but remained just out of reach of the customer's muscular arms. "Thank you for visiting our store today. How may I help you?"

The man grinned. His teeth were perfectly white. He may have been a hitman, but he certainly believed in cosmetic dentistry, bespoke clothing . . . even manicures, it appeared.

"The yogurt here is fantastic, my friend." The man raised his empty cup. He had an unexpectedly soft voice, like a choir boy, with the faint accent of one who hailed from Culiacan, Alex's hometown and the base of the cartel. "Everywhere I travel, and I travel frequently, I make it my mission to locate a frozen yogurt establishment. I believe this is the best I've had yet."

"Thank you, we appreciate the compliment," Alex said. "Are you in town on business?"

"Yes, always business." His eyes glimmered darkly. "But I've learned how to mingle my business with small pleasures such as a delicious cup of frozen yogurt."

"How did you find us?" Alex asked.

"Oh, I've a knack for locating things that I want," the man said, and offered a small chuckle. "My friends, they call me *El Sabueso*."

Alex had to smile at that revelation. El Sabueso. The Bloodhound. He believed he had heard of this man, though he had never seen a photograph of him. He had developed quite a reputation in the organization. He should have expected they would dispatch an assassin of his renown to track him down. Alex was, after all, no ordinary defector.

He had not merely left the cartel. He had turned traitor, leaked incriminating information to the Federales—a select few individuals not already on the cartel's payroll—and stolen from them, too, using those funds to bankroll his new life in America. A betrayer such as he would have earned the attentions of their best.

For a breathless moment, the two men watched each other, neither of them speaking. The Bloodhound's large hands rested on the gleaming table, thick fingers splayed. Hands at his sides, Alex waited next to the self-serve station.

Make a move if you dare, Alex thought. His fingers tingled.

The Bloodhound finally smiled, but it was the expression that might as well have been painted on a mannequin, as his eyes reflected only cold calculation.

"Adios, my friend," the Bloodhound said. "Hasta que nos encontremos de nuevo."

Alex nodded, thinking, *We will indeed meet again.*

Moving with the casual grace of a dancer, the Bloodhound rose from the chair and exited the shop.

Alex exhaled. He stepped around the table and went to the doors. He locked them.

Chloe rushed out of the back office, eyes flashing with anxiety.

"What happened?" she asked.

"I'll pay you for your entire shift now," he said. "We're closing for the day."

He had to get to his wife, and he didn't have much time.

***

Alex lived in South Haven. Four years ago, he and his wife, Melissa, had purchased the five-bedroom contemporary home, intending to fill it with children and life. The children had yet to come, and they had recently begun to discuss adoption.

Considering recent developments, Alex was relieved that they didn't have kids. It would have been terrible to subject a child to the experience that loomed on the horizon.

It was time to activate Plan de Escape.

Alex parked his Toyota Tacoma truck in the driveway. After he shut off the motor, he sat there clutching the steering wheel, teeth gritted in a grimace.

I cannot do this, he thought. *I've sacrificed too much to get here to leave it all behind.*

Sweat trickled into his eyes. His hands shook on the wheel. He felt charged with so much emotion that if he had tried, he thought he could have ripped the wheel out of the steering column and hurled it like a Frisbee through the window.

The Escape Plan, as disruptive as it was, was the only plan that would allow them to find peace. If the Bloodhound failed to kill him, the cartel bosses would dispatch more assassins, in endless waves, until the streets of South Haven resembled the blood-soaked grounds of the San Fernando massacre. Innocent people could die in the crossfire.

Alex couldn't allow that to happen.

He had tried to contact his wife via her cell phone, and when that failed, the house landline. She had responded to neither. He was concerned. While she had remained in bed that morning, suffering from a migraine that prevented her from going to work at her hair salon, his worries had nothing to do with her illness.

He got out of the truck. Before getting in the vehicle back at his store, he had searched it for explosive devices, and found none. That did not surprise him. From what he recalled of the Bloodhound, the man preferred to eliminate his targets up close, with a trench knife driven deep into in the abdomen and twisted through the innards, granting a painful death underneath the Bloodhound's impassive gaze. Only in an extreme circumstance would a man of his fearsome reputation have deployed a car bomb.

But Alex could not afford to take any risks. He would have to use the Toyota until they reached their other vehicle, stored at an offsite location.

He scanned the surrounding street, paying attention to vehicles parked alongside the curb. He did not notice anything out of order, but that meant nothing. The Bloodhound was surely watching. Perfect concealment was one of his skills.

He hurried inside the house.

"Melissa!" he called. "We've got to talk, it's important."

The first level of the house was full of deep shadows. He checked each room but didn't see her. He raced up the staircase.

"Melissa?" he asked. "Are you still lying down?"

Melissa had endured migraine headaches before, and her doctor had given her a powerful prescription of triptan to alleviate the pain. When he had left her four hours ago, she had taken some of her medication and laid down to rest. He would have expected she would be feeling better by then.

Unless the Bloodhound had already paid her a visit . . . .

The door to their master bedroom was shut. He knocked. When he got no answer, he turned the knob.

Shadows filled the room. All of the blinds were closed. Alex had left them that way, per Melissa's request. She said the sunlight intensified her headaches.

The bedsheets lay in a tangled knot on the floor, pillows askew on the mattress. The bed was empty.

He heard an unexpected but familiar noise. A mechanical buzzing, coming from the attached bathroom. Hair clippers?

The bathroom door was closed. He opened it and paused on the threshold.

He couldn't believe what he was seeing.

Melissa stood in the darkened bathroom, using the clippers to cut her hair. She had been a professional hair stylist for over fifteen years, had scads of loyal clients who drove many miles to sit in her chair, but she was buzzing the clippers across her scalp with no apparent regard for the final result. Layers of her lovely black locks littered the vanity and the tile floor. Several sections of her scalp were bald and glistened with red razor blade marks.

"Mel?" His voice was soft with shock. "What's wrong, honey?"

She swung in his direction. That was when he got a good look at her face, though her features were partially obscured by hanging strands of hair. He noticed her reddened eyes, the flesh of her sockets puckered. Blood dribbled from her nostrils. Pinkish blisters spotted her cheeks and forehead.

"Down . . . down get to the dirty roots." Drool trickled from the corners of her mouth. She laughed. Her hysterical laughter was like chalk screeching across a blackboard, sending a chill deep into his marrow.

"The dirty, dirty roots!" she cried.

The clippers slipped out of her fingers and into the sink. The device continued buzzing, flopping around like a beached fish in the wash basin.

Melissa seized another hair cutting tool that lay in the stylist's kit on the vanity: a long pair of stainless steel scissors with needle-sharp points. She studied the blades with a dull gaze, as if unsure of their purpose.

"Melissa, please," Alex said. He stepped forward, one hand raised. He had a lurid vision of her driving the scissors into her eyes while cackling. Some strange illness had taken hold of her, and he could not be certain that she wouldn't injure herself.

With a screech, she slashed at him. The scissors streaked across the palm of his extended hand. Pain seared his flesh. He bit back a cry of pain, drew backward.

Melissa advanced on him. She swiped the blades back and forth through the air, steel glimmering. "Get dirty roots!"

Alex spun around to run.

That was when he saw The Bloodhound standing in the bedroom doorway, wearing a grin of anticipation and brandishing his infamous trench knife.

Chapter 6

"Come on!" Emily said. She shook the doors of the math tutoring center where her boyfriend worked. They didn't open, and when she cupped her hands around her face and peered through the glass, she saw only a darkened, empty office space full of desks, chairs, and monitors.

Closed, she thought. *Perfect.* Although according to the operating hours posted on the front door, the center should have been open. But that morning, nothing was as it should have been.

It had required the bike ride of her life to elude the crazed Mr. Pinto and the stone-throwing teenager. When she finally got away for good—after taking several gut-turning turns on various streets, powering up steep hills, and even cutting paths between houses a couple of times—she needed several minutes to catch her breath and rest her burning thigh muscles. She was almost convinced the duo would track her down regardless of where she went, half-believed they could locate her by her scent alone, like a pair of wild animals.

It had been that kind of morning.

Once she had found safety, she had called the police, of course, and reported the bizarre assault. The police shared that they already had units on site in South Haven, and wanted her to go home and wait until an officer came to see her—though they could not give her any idea when that might happen. She wasn't willing to sit at home cooling her heels, not without doing everything she could to find Zack. Her boyfriend's silence was alarming.

And if he wasn't answering his phone, wasn't at home, and wasn't at work, it was easy to fear the worst. Something damned strange was going on in South Haven, and she feared that Zack had fallen victim to it. Whatever *it* happened to be.

"They're closed, too?" a male voice said behind her. "Bummer."

She turned. It was a man she recognized; he worked at the South Haven Cinema. Tall and gangly, he wore chunky black glasses and a black vest, blue jeans, and Van sneakers. He had a pile of unruly brown hair that looked as if he'd taken it off a mop head. A tattoo of Princess Leia adorned his left forearm. He sipped a cherry Icee through a red straw.

"I'm looking for my boyfriend," she said. "He works here. He wasn't home, either. He's not answering his phone. I need to talk to him."

She caught herself before she said, *"I need to talk to him about my pregnancy."* She didn't know why she was sharing so many details with someone who was a relative stranger to her. It wasn't in her nature to be forthcoming about her personal life with anyone except close friends and family. Her growing sense of uneasiness had knocked her off balance.

"Maybe he's got the sickness," the man said. He indicated the rolled-up poster he carried. "Was going to put out this new poster for the Screen on the Green, you know we have it every Friday night in the summer, but I think I'm gonna cancel. No one's gonna show up for it anyway. Not even worth switching out posters. I was gonna show *Forrest Gump* but whatever."

"Hold on a minute, please. You mentioned 'the sickness.' What sickness are you talking about, exactly?"

He shrugged. "I think it's like a summer flu or something. Two of my guys called out sick and said they have headaches." He pointed with the tip of the poster. "I walked around to some of the shops here. A lot of 'em are closed. The ones that are open, I talked to people on duty and they all said they've got someone who called out sick."

Emily scanned both sides of Main Street. He was right. The hair salon, the frozen yogurt shop, the pizzeria, the florist . . . all of them appeared to be closed, which was unusual for mid- morning on a Friday. The corner grocery store was open, and notably, so was the medical clinic.

It was called the Take Care Clinic, and it appeared to be doing brisk business. She noticed people gathered outside the doors; they sat on plastic folding chairs in the shade of the awning, and they had the weary look of those expecting long waits. She was acquainted with the physician who worked there, Dr. Britt. Years ago, Dr. Britt had encouraged Emily's medical school aspirations. Could the physician possibly know what was going on?

Just thinking about it, Emily wondered if there was any connection between this summer flu the man had described, and Mr. Pinto and the stone-thrower teenager. It was quite a leap of logic to connect the two together—someone with ordinary flu symptoms didn't evolve into a crazed killer—but the strangeness of both had set the gears of her imagination churning.

The movie theater guy was hanging near her, blue eyes dancing behind his lenses.

"It's gonna get a lot worse before it gets any better," he said.

"Why do you say that?"

"It's like that in the movies, right? A lot more people are gonna get sick with this virus. Probably the CDC will get called in. They might bring down quarantine, too. Don't you like, watch sci-fi movies?"

"I'm going to talk to a doctor," Emily said. "I've seen other . . . incidents, too. It might all be connected."

"Really? Like what?" His eyes looked hungry for some extra titillating tidbit, a bit of gossip.

"Just be careful," she said. "I've seen people who aren't behaving like themselves."

He stared at her as if waiting for the punchline, but she turned away from him without going into further detail. She hurried across the street to the medical clinic.

***

Emily literally had to step over people in order to get inside.

People of all ages occupied every available spot in the confined waiting area. It was a basic clinic for a live-work-play community, not a level one trauma hospital serving a major city, and as such, had less than a dozen seats. Folks went there for common colds, flus, tummy aches, and school immunizations. It was never designed to fight an epidemic.

But as Emily stood on a small section of open carpet in the middle of the office and scanned the worried faces of the residents, many of whom she recognized, she couldn't help thinking that they were in the midst of a mess far more serious than she had feared.

She didn't notice anyone who shared the symptoms that had marked the stone-thrower or Mr. Pinto: no inflamed eyes or nostrils dripping blood. The folks she saw just looked miserable. They cradled their heads in their hands and slumped. One patient, a child of about six, was teary-eyed and clutching his mother.

Emily's heart twisted.

She eased through the knots of gathered people and reached the reception desk. A young black woman who looked to be at her wits end snapped up from filling out paperwork and offered a sad smile.

"Sorry, but it's going to be a long wait," she said. Her nametag read, Rita. "You see how busy it is here, right?"

"Is Dr. Britt in?" Emily asked.

Rita shook her head. "She's out sick, too. We've just got our nurse on duty, Jennifer, and me the office manager. You might be better off going to an emergency room at the closest hospital."

"Excuse me, did you say *one* nurse to serve all these people?" Emily asked.

"We're doing the best we can here, miss."

Emily sucked in her bottom lip. "What symptoms is everyone reporting?"

"Are you a doctor?" Rita asked.

Emily drummed her fingers on the counter. "I'm in medical school. I just completed my second year, at Emory. Maybe . . . maybe I can help."

The woman's eyes brightened.

"We need all the help we can get. Come to the door over there and I'll let you in back and you can talk to Jennifer."

***

The nurse, Jennifer, was a blonde-haired, green-eyed young woman who looked no older than Emily. As petite as an elf, she wore blue scrubs and sneakers, and she was scrambling out of one of the patient rooms as the officer manager was guiding Emily down the hallway.

"This lady says she can help us out," Rita said. "She's in medical school."

Jennifer thrust her slender hand toward Emily and offered a quick smile. "Appreciate it, honey. You got a name?"

Emily told her.

"Call me Jenn," she said. "How much experience do you have with patient care?"

"Well, I finished my second year last month, so honestly, not much. But I'll do my best."

Jenn waved her off. "It doesn't matter. Heck, we're so stretched I'm not turning down anyone who offers to help. Grab some scrubs, please. They're in the supply closet at the end of the hallway. Then wash your hands and meet me in room three in five minutes. You'll get filled in on everything while I meet with a patient."

Jenn whirled away before Emily could ask any questions. The officer manager deserted her, too. Emily paused for a beat, and then walked down the carpeted corridor to the supply closet.

This had to be the weirdest day of her entire life. She'd gone from a positive pregnancy test, to fleeing a couple of crazed residents, to volunteering in a community medical clinic overburdened with patients suffering from the flu. Her life had become like a wacky reality TV show.

The narrow closet contained boxes of latex gloves and surgical masks, and several sets of scrubs hanging on hooks. She found a set that fit reasonably well, pulled them over her shorts and tank top. She took some gloves and a mask for good measure.

As she was washing her hands in the restroom, a choked scream pieced the clinic. The source was close—very close.

She quickly dried her hands with a paper towel and hurried outside. Jenn was rushing into room three. Emily followed close behind.

Inside, they discovered a scene out of a nightmare. A woman was sprawled on the floor next to the examination table, blood smeared across her tanned face. Her son, a boy of perhaps ten, gripped an iPad and had wedged the edge of the device across his mother's neck. He leaned all of his weight against it, using it to systematically crush her windpipe.

"Play it I can!" he shouted, spittle spraying. "Whenever want it play!"

Emily saw the red crust around his inflamed eyes, the stream of blood dripping from his nose. Like Mr. Pinto and the stone-thrower boy, she realized.

The mother's eyes bulged, her face turning blue.

"Help me get him off her!" Jenn said.

The nurse hooked her hands underneath the boy's armpits and lifted him up. She was a small lady, barely larger than the boy, but she was much stronger than she looked. As she dragged him away, the boy snarled like a captured beast. He flailed his arms and legs, over-turning a chair.

Emily got her arms around his wriggling legs, noticing that crimson lesions marked his flesh at several points. Together, she and Jenn hauled the kid onto the exam table, the protective sheet of paper crinkling underneath the thrashing child.

The boy unleashed a string of obscenities that made Emily's face turn red: "Cunts . . . bitches . . . fucking play it . . . can play it . . . cunts . . . play it . . ."

He's completely out of his mind, Emily thought, and the budding physician in her was racing through a memorized catalogue of illnesses and diseases that could explain these symptoms, but she didn't hit upon anything—this was outside her limited experience and knowledge.

On the floor, the mother was sitting up, hands at her neck and gagging.

The boy continued to fight like a bucking bronco. Veins stood in stark relief on his face and neck, interspersed with the ugly lesions.

"I need to sedate him," Jenn said. "We've got some Propofol on hand, but only I can unlock the cabinet."

"Ma'am, we need your help," Emily said to the mother. "We're going to sedate your son to help him feel better, but I need you to help us keep him under control."

The mom slowly got to her feet, grabbing the edge of a desk to help her stand.

"He said . . . he said he just had a headache," she said weakly. She appeared to be dazed. She looked at her writhing child on the exam table as if she didn't recognize him. "He was running a fever . . . I thought he had the flu . . ."

As she contemplated the woman's muttered comments, Emily felt a chill settle deep in her marrow.

"Help me hold him, ma'am," Emily said.

Nodding vaguely, the mother replaced Jenn at the table, and Jenn scrambled out of the room. When she returned and administered the injection in his neck, the boy's struggles subsided a bit, but he continued to mumble incoherently, and his mother still needed to hold him.

Both Jenn and Emily stepped away and huddled together in the corridor outside the room.

"That dosage should have knocked him out," Jenn said. She ran her fingers through her hair, shook her head. "I don't understand how he's still alert."

"I've seen these symptoms before, this morning, in other people who live here," Emily said. "A man I actually know, and a boy. They attacked me. They were shouting unintelligibly, like the child here, and they had all the same symptoms: the inflammation around their eyes, the lesions on their face."

"His mother brought him in because she thought he had the flu." Jenn grimaced. "We aren't staffed or equipped to handle this situation."

Emily knew that she and the nurse were of the same accord: they had an entire waiting room of people afflicted with the same symptoms. How long until they became violent?

"I have an idea," Emily said.

Chapter 7

Between The Bloodhound standing in the bedroom doorway, and his crazed wife coming at him with a pair of scissors, Alex didn't know which threat to fear the most.

Raw instinct took over.

He dipped to the floor and drew his Beretta, his scissor-sliced, bleeding palm making him wince. He squeezed off a shot at The Bloodhound.

The gun's report was jarring. Seeing Alex draw the weapon, the hitman had slid out of the doorway and taken cover. The gunfire struck a landscape painting hanging on the hallway wall outside the bedroom, a vista of a sun-kissed Mexican beach. The artwork crashed to the carpet.

Melissa was running out of the room, partially shorn hair flapping like feathers from her scalp. She swung the scissors in a wild arc.

"Mel, wait!" Alex said.

In his mind, he could envision what would unfold next. The Bloodhound would easily disarm her. He would balance his trench knife against her throat and demand that Alex drop his weapon. Then he would slowly kill both Melissa and Alex, prolonging their suffering while his eyes gleamed with pleasure.

That wasn't what happened.

The Bloodhound re-appeared in the doorway as Melissa was dashing out of the room. Perhaps it was her appearance—the inflamed eyes, the chopped up hair—but indecision flickered in his gaze. At that moment of hesitation, Melissa launched herself at him, literally leapt onto his chest like a giddy child leaping into a parent's embrace. She jabbed the scissors deep into his ear.

The Bloodhound screamed. It had been many years since Alex had heard a man scream like that, and it was a sound he had hoped never to hear again.

"Dirty roots!" Melissa cried, and went to stab him again.

But The Bloodhound, in a fit of agony and rage, tried to fling her off him. She slashed his face, blades tearing across his eye. Howling, face stained in blood, he finally managed to heave her off him. She hurtled against a dresser.

By then, Alex had opened a bedroom window and kicked out the screen. Warm, flower-scented air sifted inside.

Holding one hand against his ruined eye, moaning, the Bloodhound staggered out of the room. He was wounded, but not dead. A man such as him would never walk away, not even from a blood bath.

"Dirty roots . . . down them to . . . dirty . . . dirty . . ."

Melissa was on her feet again. She was coming at Alex. High on manic energy.

Although armed, he couldn't fire at his wife. She was sick, out of her mind with an illness he couldn't begin to comprehend. She need-ed help, but there was nothing he could do for her then. He would have to get to safety and return with health professionals who could get her under control and give her the medical assistance she needed.

He climbed out of the window and let go of the ledge. He dropped about fifteen feet. A thick row of hedges at the front of the house cushioned his fall, prickly leaves brushing against his skin.

Dizzy, rattled, he stumbled out of the flowerbed and looked up.

Melissa jumped out of the window.

"No!" he said.

But she dove headfirst, like a swimmer leaping off a diving board, with no apparent regard for her own safety. She flew in an arc that took her beyond the hedges and landed her in the rosebush at the edge of the flowerbed, and Alex heard the sickening crunch of breaking bones as she hit the earth in a violent tangle of limbs. She didn't even scream.

Dios mio, he thought, breathing hard. He wiped sweat from his brow with the back of his hand.

Melissa wasn't moving. She lay in the roses—roses she had carefully planted and tended since they had moved into the house—her body contorted in an impossible position, skin punctured by a multitude of thorns.

His knees were weak. But he went to her.

Her head had been twisted around almost a full one hundred and eighty degrees. Her green eyes were open, but were as empty as a doll's.

No, no, no . . .

Hot tears streamed down his face. He threw his head back and shouted at the summer sky, a garbled, anguished stream of Spanish and English. He shouted until his throat felt raw and his voice finally faltered and broke into a ragged whisper.

Then he carefully extricated his wife's limp body from the roses, and carried her inside the house.

The Bloodhound might have been waiting for him, could have regained his bearings and been planning a new ambush, but Alex didn't care. At that moment, if death came for him, he might have welcomed it.

Without Melissa, he had nothing to live for anyway.

He laid his wife across the cushions of the leather sofa in the family room, underneath a large, framed photo taken on their wedding day. They'd had a destination wedding in the Dominican Republic. They stood on a glorious beach, smiling for the photographer, confident of the happiness they believed was their destiny.

It was never supposed to end like this. In a matter of minutes, everything they had worked for had fallen apart, blown away like a sandcastle under breaking waves.

He needed to call an ambulance, but there was time for that; there was nothing they could do for his wife any more.

He wanted to cover her with a blanket. He couldn't find one in the family room. Wiping his eyes, he got up, went into the hallway.

Dark drops of blood speckled the hardwood floor. The trail led to the back of the house, all the way to the double doors that opened onto the wooden deck.

Alex felt a hunger stirring in him that he had not felt for many years. The base of his spine tingled, a pleasant sensation.

First, duty, he told himself.

He found a blanket for his wife and gently covered her. He kissed her forehead, brushed her hair away from her eyes.

Now, revenge.

He drew his gun, and followed the blood trail.

Chapter 8

There was plenty more bloodshed and mayhem that day in South Haven.

Pete Staples was getting to the good part with his mistress, Ashley. Pete was a golf pro, employed by the South Haven Country Club, and he also lived in the community. His PGA tour winnings and a handsome trust fund ensured a comfortable lifestyle, and working at the country club put him in frequent contact with the bored, gorgeous housewives who often came in seeking to improve their swing.

Ashley was his latest conquest, a stay-at-home-mom, and she had dropped off her kids at her parents' house for the day. Pete's own wife was doing lunch and a movie with her friends and wouldn't get back home for hours.

What Pete hadn't counted on was Ashley's husband, Rick, coming home early. The douchebag was some kind of ad salesman, supposedly out all day trying to close a deal with a potential client downtown.

Pete had Ashley propped up on the cherry-oak dresser in her bedroom. Her long, tanned legs were wrapped around his waist. The dresser and attached mirror rocked as he thrust into her.

Grunting, waves of pleasure cascading over him, Pete happened to glance in that mirror and saw the reflection of her husband Rick standing in the bedroom doorway holding a golf club.

His erection wilted like a punctured balloon. He pulled out of Ashley.

"What is it?" she asked, and then she looked over his shoulder and covered her mouth, a scream escaping her fingers.

As Pete spun around, snatching up his shorts, Rick thundered toward him with the club. There was something seriously wrong with the guy's face. His eyes looked as if they had been soaked in corrosive acid. Weird blisters dotted his pale complexion. A fat vein pulsed like a malignant worm in the middle of his forehead.

"Hey, man." Pete said, raising his hands.

Rick swung the golf club at him. As it whistled toward him, Pete couldn't help noticing that it was a nine-iron.

This is gonna hurt like hell, he thought.

The crack of the club head against his skull was like an explosion. As Pete collapsed to the floor, Ashley ran past them, naked as the day she was born, and Pete's last coherent thought was: *Run, girl. Run for your life . . . .*

***

Ty came out of his house late that morning to retrieve the bundled newspapers dropped at the end of his walkway. A self-employed day trader, Ty subscribed to paper editions of *The Wall Street Journal, The Financial Times, Baron's,* and other periodicals that covered the fast-changing world of finance. Each publication offered a digital edition, but he preferred to read the hard copies. Skimming them on his lunch break gave his eyes a respite from the bank of flashing screens and the Bloomberg terminal in his home office.

When Ty strolled out of his residence and glanced at his neighbor's house across the street, he had to wonder if his eyes were failing him.

Layla was in her front yard watering her roses, and she was bare-chested.

He rubbed his eyes with the back of his hand, pinched the bridge of his nose as if to clarify his vision.

Layla was a retiree and lived with her husband. She had to be in her mid-sixties, at least thirty years older than he was, but you wouldn't have guessed it from her every day appearance. She was fit and always looked fashionable. Ty also believed she'd gotten some work done: she had some of the most incredible boobs he had ever seen on a woman of any age, a sheer marvel of cosmetic surgery. A few months ago, she had invited Ty and his wife over to her house for wine and cheese, and between sips of pinot noir he had kept sneaking peeks at her amazing cleavage. She had caught him looking once, and winked, obviously aware of the mesmerizing effect she'd had on him, and well-pleased with his attentions.

Those perfect breasts of hers were on full display as she swept the spray nozzle back and forth across her bed of multi-colored roses. He was convinced she had to be wearing a bra but she wasn't. She wore only a pair of khaki shorts.

Watching her, Ty swallowed, his newspapers forgotten.

Was this a joke?

He looked back and forth across the street, saw no one else out on his block. It was only he and Layla.

He began to cross the street. "Good morning, Layla!"

The woman ignored him. She was intent on her flowers, sweeping the water nozzle back and forth, back and forth. The roses were thoroughly soaked, and he noticed that the runoff from the flower bed was streaming across the front walkway, trickling onto the curb, and running into the storm drain.

Is something wrong with her? It's as though she's in a trance.

"Layla!" he said again, advancing onto the walkway. His flip-flops squished through water. "Hey, good morning!"

Finally, she turned.

Oh, Jesus, look at her face . . .

She snarled at him, like a dog interrupted while chewing a bone.

"Back . . . get!" she screamed.

"I'm sorry, I was worried."

Layla flipped a switch on the spray nozzle—and turned the jet spray on him. The powerful stream caught him full in the face.

It was like being punched by an icy fist. Ty spluttered, gagged, staggered backward and lost his balance. He fell to the ground, smacking his tailbone hard against the pavement.

Layla stalked forward, continuing to spray him. Blinded by the cold water, he struggled to his feet, turned, and stumbled across the street. The jet of water hit him in the back of his head, and he nearly fell down again.

Dripping wet, he hurried back to his house. When he reached the region of his own property, Layla turned away.

She returned to her flower bed and resumed watering her roses.

She's out of her goddamn mind, Ty thought.

He was going to call the police. Her attack on him qualified as an assault, and from the look of her face, something was deeply wrong with her.

But first, he went inside and locked the door.

***

"Girl, get your lazy ass up and fix me some breakfast."

Clint was starving, and it was his girlfriend's responsibility to do something about it. That was how he'd been raised. His daddy had been a hardworking man, and when he'd come home after pulling his shift at the old Ford auto plan, dinner had damn sure better be on the table, hot and delicious, or else someone's ass was gonna get whooped. Usually that someone had been Clint's mama.

You gotta train up these women, son, Daddy had taught him. *Spare the rod, spoil the woman, that's what I say.*

It all made perfect sense to Clint. But evidently he and his lady, Sara, were still in the training phase. He'd pulled an all-night shift on his road construction gig and come back to their apartment in South

Haven expecting a hot breakfast. Was that too much for a hard-working man to ask for? He was so hungry he could have eaten a whole damn hog.

But as he stood in the bedroom doorway, looking into the shadowed room, he saw Sara was still in bed, wrapped under the sheets. If it weren't for the lick of blonde hair curling over the edge of the sheet, he wouldn't have known she was under there at all.

"Hey!" he said, and kicked the door. "Get your ass outta bed!"

She stirred, but made no effort to get up.

Clint grunted. He couldn't believe she was ignoring him. Actually, he could. It was this goddamn neighborhood they lived in. It was full of rich bitches that stayed home tanning by the pool while their men earned all the money; these woman weren't required to cook, clean, or even take care of their own goddamn kids. Clint saw them roaming around South Haven all the time, prancing around in their tennis skirts and sipping expensive coffee drinks.

Sara most likely had fallen in with some of that moneyed crowd and picked up their pretentious attitude. But they weren't like those people and never would be. He'd allowed her to choose this apartment, and let her stay home while he worked, but he'd be damned if she wasn't going to fulfill her responsibilities as a woman.

He stomped into the room, his dusty work boots leaving crumbs of dirt across the carpet. Unbuckling his leather belt, he approached the bed.

"Training time," he said, wrapping one end of the belt around his hand.

Clint popped the tip of the belt against the shape of her rump.

Sara shrieked, squirming underneath the covers like an agitated sack of snakes.

"I told you to get up!" Clint snatched away the bedsheets.

Sara snarled at him. There was stuff on her face, as if she had chicken pox, and though the room was dim, he could nonetheless see something was deeply wrong with her eyes, too.

Involuntarily, he took a step backward.

Shrieking, Sara sprang like a spider off the bed. She leaped onto him, wrapped her legs around his waist and bit his face.

***

Pernell Jackson worked as a mail carrier for the US Postal Service, and the highlight of his work day was delivering mail through South Haven. Due to the design of the community, he couldn't stay in his mail truck, winding his way down the side of the road and depositing letters in mailboxes posted at the curb. No one had curbside mailboxes in South Haven.

There, he had to get out of his truck and walk from one residence to the next, inserting the day's mail in either a slot at the front door, or in a box posted beside the entrance. It was old school delivery, and Pernell enjoyed every minute of it.

That morning, he parked his mail truck at the usual beginning of his residential route, at the intersection of Gold Road and Mill Street. He gathered all of the pieces for delivery in his big canvas mail satchel, climbed out of his truck, adjusted the bag across his shoulders, and kicked off his route.

He had covered half the block when he spotted the dogs.

There were four of them, of varying sizes and breeds. A Golden Retriever, a Collie, a beagle, and some kind of terrier. In his twenty-two years working as a mail carrier, he'd had numerous encounters with all kinds of canines, been barked at, chased, and had to blast a few with his pepper spray. None of these was the kind of dog that typically would have concerned Pernell. A Golden, in particular, was usually one of the sweetest dogs he'd ever seen.

But the animals' behavior was damned strange. They had emerged from the backyard of a home across the street, traveling in a pack, and something looked . . . *wrong* about them. Their eyes were inflamed, and they were drooling.

Rabies, Pernell thought. He had never personally seen a rabid canine but he knew the symptoms. His hand quickly went to the canister of pepper spray riding his hip.

As he reached for the spray, the dogs snarled, and charged.

"Oh, shit," he said. His heart leaped. Although armed with a powerful deterrent, he didn't like his chances fighting four vicious hounds. He raced along the sidewalk, heading back the way he'd come. The mail satchel slipped off his shoulders and crashed to the ground, letters and circulars fluttering everywhere. Pernell pumped his arms and forced his legs to move, move, *move.*

He barely made it to his truck in time. One of the dogs, the beagle, leaped toward the open window, and if Pernell didn't have the pepper spray still in hand he would have been breakfast. He blasted the snapping dog in the face. The beagle yelped and dropped off the window ledge.

Pernell rolled up the glass. The other dogs surrounded the mail truck. They barked and snarled.

Sweet Jesus, what is going on? Pernell thought. He felt as if he'd been dropped into an old Stephen King movie.

He fumbled out his cell phone and called the police.

***

Manuel arrived at the job site precisely on time, at eleven thirty in the morning. He was a carpenter, specializing in custom cabinetry and woodwork; he took pride in punctuality, in doing an outstanding job and leaving his clients satisfied that they had hired him. When he rang the doorbell of the Craftsman home on Merriam Lane in South Haven, where he was slated to resume work on a job in the kitchen, he anticipated another opportunity to complete a project that exceeded his client's expectations.

No one came to the door. But Manuel heard several people talking inside. Their voices were so loud that he assumed they hadn't heard him ring the doorbell. He mashed the button again, and waited.

Still, no one answered. Strange.

Access to the home was controlled via a numeric keypad posted next to the door. The homeowner had given Manual a temporary passcode, allowing him to let himself in and out as needed throughout the duration of the project. Manuel had pressed the doorbell out of courtesy and habit, but he urgently needed to get inside and resume working. He pulled up the notepad app on his phone where he had stored the passcode, used the six-digit code to unlock the door.

As he pushed the door open, the sounds hit him like a sonic blast.

"If Clemson wants a chance to beat Alabama in this football game, they've got to discover more offense in the second half . . ."

Manuel realized what he was hearing. It was a recorded television broadcast of a college football game.

Personally, Manuel was more of a *futbol* fan. He found the American game to be overly violent and slow-paced. But from his understanding, the homeowner, a retired lawyer, was an ardent fan of Clemson football, and had decorated his house with team memorabilia.

To each his own. But for the guy to be re-watching the game at a decibel level that could ensure permanent hearing loss was damned weird.

Manuel advanced along the entry hall. The hardwood floor thrummed in tune with the sounds of the broadcast.

"This stout Alabama defense is the toughest challenge the Clemson Tigers have faced all season . . ."

An arched doorway led to the spacious family room. A seventy-five inch, flat-screen television dominated the wall that faced the hallway. It was the largest TV Manuel had ever seen in someone's home, and would have been more appropriate in a sports bar.

The homeowner, Mr. Allen, sat on a leather sectional sofa, his back facing Manuel. Manuel didn't recognize him at first because of what the man was wearing: he had on a football helmet with the Clemson Tigers insignia, and a jersey, too, as if he were a member of the squad waiting on the coach to sub him into the game.

Warily, Manuel entered the room. "Mr. Allen?"

Mr. Allen ignored him. He was fixated on the screen, where it looked as if play had resumed.

"Sir?" Manuel said. "I only wanted to let you know that I'm here to resume the job."

"Asshole . . . tear 'em a new one!" Mr. Allen shouted at the television.

Manuel noticed that Mr. Allen cradled a leather football in his lap. He also noticed that there were crimson blisters on the man's hands.

"Mr. Allen, are you okay?" Manuel asked.

As he asked the question, he stepped in front of Mr. Allen, blocking the view of the television. It seemed the only way to get his attention.

When Manuel saw Mr. Allen's eyes, simmering in the shadowed depths of that helmet, he realized something was very wrong with this man.

Mr. Allen screamed at him.

"TV . . . goddamn . . . move!"

Mr. Allen flung the football at Manuel. The ball smashed into Manuel's nose. Crying out, Manuel stumbled backward and crashed into a table.

His nose bled, and it hurt terribly. It might have been broken.

Mr. Allen retrieved his football from the floor and settled back on the sofa as if nothing had happened. He yelled at the screen again, something unintelligible.

Keeping close to the floor, blood dripping from his nostrils, Manuel crawled out of the room and fled the house.

He saw a police cruiser veering around the corner, lights flashing, followed closely by another squad car. He heard an ambulance warbling, too.

I'm getting out of here, he thought. *The people here have gone totally loco . . .*

Chapter 9

S outh Haven was a gated live-work-play community, but the developer of South Haven, Ronald Falcon, lived behind an additional set of gates, on a wooded, five-acre parcel of land at the southern edge of the community property. Deacon parked the golf cart at the wide entrance and pressed the buzzer.

The boss man had sent him a text message. He'd demanded a face-to-face meeting with Deacon, immediately.

After they'd witnessed the mauling of the young woman, he and Jim had spent some time searching for the dog, this time with the assistance of a Fulton County Animal Control officer armed with a powerful tranquilizer, and a Roswell PD cop armed with a rifle. Although they were adequately prepared for another battle with the St. Bernard, their search of the greenway proved fruitless. The canine had given them the slip.

But the dog was still out there, somewhere. It was just the beginning of what had become an epically bad day.

Deacon waited outside the gate, fingers drumming the steering wheel. He could anticipate the purpose of his employer's unexpected summoning, and he wasn't looking forward to this discussion.

The ornately designed entrance gates were nearly ten feet high. An "F" as big as Deacon's head was carved in the center of the gates; a rendering of a giant falcon in mid-flight stood at the top of the entrance. There were security cameras posted throughout the community, all of which Deacon's team could access on closed circuit televisions. A security camera was posted at the entrance to the Falcon property as well, standing atop a tall wrought-iron pole bristling with lights—but no one except Mr. Falcon could access the feed.

A buzzer sounded. The electric-powered gates parted silently.

He drove down a long, winding driveway flanked with tall elms on both sides. Soon, the trees cleared and the residence came into view.

South Haven was full of large, stately homes, but even the biggest of those was like a studio apartment when compared to the Falcon estate. It looked like a mansion that had been transported from the French countryside. Once, Deacon had been granted a tour of the sprawling residence, and recalled that it boasted something like fifteen thousand square feet of living space. You literally needed a map to navigate the place.

He parked the golf cart underneath the porte-cochere, and walked to the front entrance. Another gigantic "F" was carved in the expensive polished oak of the door.

A wooden box was attached to the brick beside the doorway. Deacon slipped his hand underneath and withdrew a pair of disposable shoe covers.

All outside visitors were required to wear shoe covers when entering the Falcon home. Mr. Falcon had an aversion to dirt, germs, and filth of any kind.

Shoe covers installed over his Rockports, Deacon was about to ring the bell when the door opened.

"Bless my heart, if it isn't Mark Deacon," a thick Southern accent announced. "How're you doing, darling? It's so nice to see you again."

Deacon smiled at the woman, but inwardly, he groaned. He had been hoping that Falcon's daughter wouldn't be home. But Angie Falcon seemed to have a sixth sense that enabled her to predict his visits.

"Hey, Miss Falcon," Deacon said.

"It's Angie, sweetheart," she said and giggled. "How many times have I told you that? Now get your handsome behind in here and give me a hug."

He estimated Angie Falcon was in her early thirties. It was hard to tell exactly due to the amount of makeup she wore and the extensive cosmetic surgery she'd had done. She wore a clinging blue sundress that left little to the imagination, and displayed her deeply tanned, voluptuous body to the fullest. Her straight blond hair flowed over her shoulders in luxurious waves. Her eyes, the color of aquamarine, twinkled with mischief.

One of Deacon's colleagues told him that Angie previously had been a Playboy Playmate. He called her "Miss January." It was a joke that Deacon didn't dare share outside of HQ, though he believed the rumor was probably true.

The fact was, Angie Falcon made him as uncomfortable as hell.

She spread her arms to pull him into an embrace, and as he bent to give her a brief, one-armed hug, she pulled him tightly against her, pressing her large breasts into his chest. She wore too much perfume, as if she'd bathed in the stuff, and the scent of it made him slightly dizzy.

"Why don't you come see me anymore?" she whispered hotly into his ear. "We never finished what we started, sweetheart."

"You know why, Miss Falcon," he said, and gently extricated himself from her arms.

"You know what they say about a woman scorned," she said, but her pouty, red-painted lips drew into a teasing smile. "She might have to take matters into her own hands."

Three months ago, Angie had called Deacon to the estate, claiming that she needed assistance with a light fixture, and that no one else on staff was present and her father was out of town on business. Reluctantly, suspecting a set-up, Deacon had come. Angie answered the door wearing a form-fitting silk kimono, and had led him to their lavishly appointed spa. There was no issue with the lighting, of course—

she had set a dozen scented candles aglow in the chamber. Deacon had immediately turned to leave, but not before Angie stepped in front of him and let her kimono drop to the marble floor. He couldn't help staring. Her body was magnificent.

I knew you wanted me, she had said, and grinned with triumph. *It's all over your face, sweetheart. You're drooling like a dog.*

She'd placed her hand on his crotch and gently squeezed, clearly pleased at his growing erection, and an involuntary groan had escaped him. But he didn't touch her, though every fiber in his being wanted to give in to lust. He'd silently stepped aside, opened the door, and left without looking back.

The memory of her body had lingered with him . . . but the truth was, he believed she was toying with him, that Mr. Falcon had put her up to the seduction attempt as a test of his loyalty. Falcon was the kind of man who thrived on such insidious head games, and had no compunctions about using his daughter for such purposes. As proof of Deacon's suspicions, a week after the incident, Mr. Falcon had called him and said he was giving him a ten percent raise, effectively immediately, as a reward for his "loyal service."

"Daddy's in his office," Angie said.

Deacon nodded. "Thanks, I know the way."

"Hmph. Don't be a stranger, honey." She grinned. "I'd better get ready for my yoga class. I'm so *incredibly* flexible now. Maybe I'll show you some of my moves the next time I see you."

Deacon only shook his head, bid her good-bye, and turned away.

His covered shoes whispered along the polished marble floors. The Falcon residence was more of a museum than a house. Expensive artwork adorned the walls, and sculptures stood on pedestals. Gigantic television screens hung in every room, and all of the sets were on, though all of the rooms he passed were vacant.

A year or so ago, Deacon had read an article about Falcon in *Forbes* magazine. Falcon had a net worth in the high nine figure range, and developed properties all over the world. He'd also heard that Falcon's father, the founder of the company, had recently died. Upon learning the news Deacon had dropped off a card offering his condolences.

"Hi, Mr. Deacon."

Deacon turned in mid-stride. Falcon's teenage son, Caleb, had appeared behind him. The kid was fifteen or sixteen, tall like his father, and shared some of his father's facial features, but their personalities were dramatically different. He'd never exchanged more than a simple greeting with the boy, and sensed that he was painfully shy. From what he'd heard from Angie, her younger brother was a mathematics prodigy, already attending college-level courses via an online program.

"Hi, Caleb. How are you doing?"

The boy looked as if he wanted to speak, but he only pressed his lips together, and disappeared back into a nearby room. Deacon shrugged, and continued on.

Falcon's office was located in the west wing of the estate, at the end of a long corridor. Passing by the other, smaller offices that belonged to Falcon's staff, Deacon noted that all of them were dark, empty. Had everyone called out sick there, too?

A bronze bust of Ronald Falcon stood prominently in an alcove near the door to his office, in a pool of golden light. Deacon had seen at least ten different sculptures of the man, organized in various locations of the estate. There was a large sculpture of Falcon on Main Street too, as if he were a national war hero.

Bracing for a storm, Deacon knocked on the door.

***

Falcon didn't answer Deacon's knock. Frowning, Deacon turned the knob. The door floated open.

The office was enormous, easily a thousand square feet. The lights were dimmed, and the blinds were drawn, too. The only illumination in the room issued from a bank of monitors hanging on the wall behind Falcon's battleship of a desk.

Mr. Falcon had his back to Deacon. He was studying the screens, large hands clasped behind his back. He wore a dark, tailored suit. Deacon had never seen the man wearing casual clothes.

Deacon cleared his throat. "You wanted to see me, Mr. Falcon?"

"South Haven," Mr. Falcon said softly. "Let's consider that name. South Haven. *Haven.* What's a haven, Mr. Deacon?"

"A safe place?" Deacon asked.

"A safe place, indeed. A place of refuge. A shelter."

Deacon said nothing. He stood and waited. Falcon was the kind of man who liked to take his time making his points, especially when delivering a harsh message.

"My family used to run a gold mine on this property," Falcon said. "We'd purchased over two thousand acres and had the largest mining operation in Georgia, outside of what they were doing farther north in Dahlonega. The mining business went defunct decades ago and my father had the idea of re-opening the mine for tours. I had the better idea of building a community that reminded me of my childhood: a haven, Mr. Deacon. Fashioned on the ideals of a better time, but including the modern amenities people expect."

Deacon remained silent. It wasn't the first he'd heard of the old gold mine. He'd seen the entrance himself once: it was nestled deep within the South Haven Greenway, isolated behind a seven-foot-high fence bristling with barbed wire.

"Would you please stand with me, Mr. Deacon?" Falcon asked.

Pulling in a breath, Deacon joined him at the bank of monitors.

Deacon was six-feet-one, and Falcon still towered over him. Although the developer was in his mid-sixties, he had the physique of a bodybuilder. He kept his head shaved completely bald; his frosty white eyebrows were his only facial hair.

Mr. Falcon glanced at Deacon. His piercing blue eyes were the color of gas flames.

"What do you see, Mr. Deacon?" he asked. "Look closely, please."

Falcon rarely raised his voice, spoke usually in sotto voce. Like a kindly grandfather sharing a treasured secret.

"I see different sections of South Haven that you've got under surveillance," Deacon said. "There are some cops here today. We've had a number of incidents."

"Incidents," Mr. Falcon said. Shifting away from the monitors to face Deacon, he pursed his thin lips. "Hmm, yes. I dislike incidents."

"I don't like them either, but no one seems to know what's going on. People are turning on one another for no apparent reason."

"No apparent reason?" Falcon asked.

"The root cause has yet to be determined, sir."

"How have you gone about determining this root cause, as you call it?" Falcon's gaze was laser-like.

"I've been supporting the residents as needed, but the actual investigation into these crimes is in the hands of the Roswell Police Department."

Mr. Falcon laughed. He rarely laughed. The laughter came from a place deep in his massive chest. The man was genuinely amused.

Deacon didn't laugh. He felt as if he'd stepped off a cliff and was about to hit the hard earth below.

"What kind of work did you do before I hired you, Mr. Deacon?" Falcon asked.

"I was a cop with the Atlanta PD. Sixteen years on the force. I primarily worked narcotics and homicide." Falcon knew all these details about Deacon's background, probably knew things about Deacon's career that Deacon himself had forgotten, but Deacon repeated his resume highlights anyway.

"It sounds like you were an experienced cop, Mr. Deacon. Yes?"

"Absolutely, one of the best."

"Perhaps better than these officers in South Haven right now?"

"I'm sure I'd compare favorably to any of them," Deacon said.

"But you haven't been helping them," Falcon said. "I'm certain they could use your assistance determining *root cause*."

Deacon paused. "With all due respect, Mr. Falcon, I'm not a police officer any more. You didn't hire me to be a cop. You hired me to be the head of security, and that's the job I'm going to do. Nothing more, nothing less."

Falcon went silent. Deacon waited a beat, and then turned to walk to the door. He had gotten halfway across the room when Falcon cleared his throat.

"You aren't dismissed, Mr. Deacon."

"If you're telling me to work like a cop, we've got nothing else to discuss . . . sir," Deacon said.

"Do you remember the terms of our contract?"

"Of course I do."

"I don't think you do. Have you reviewed it recently? There's a clause that states that you will perform all the standard duties of a private security specialist, in addition to *other responsibilities, as determined by Ronald Falcon*."

Shit, Deacon thought, his jaws clenching.

"How's your father doing?" Falcon asked. "Is the nurse taking good care of him?"

Falcon paid for his father's nursing services. He allowed Deacon and his father to live in the apartment rent-free, too. But as Deacon knew too well, nothing was ever free.

"Excellent care, sure. He's doing well."

"I'm pleased to hear that, Mr. Deacon. May I remind you that if I sue you for breach of contract, which I most certainly would since I love to avail myself of my legal rights, you will be fiscally responsible for all sums paid to date for private nursing services."

Deacon didn't respond.

"The subsidized rent for your two-bedroom apartment," Falcon continued, "or let's simply call it free housing, because that's what it is. You would owe me back rent at market rates."

Deacon was still silent, tension building in his chest.

"I'm not quite the math prodigy that my son happens to be, but I believe that combined, nursing and rent, well . . . the sum would surely exceed six figures. Plus legal fees, of course."

"All right, you've made your point," Deacon said. "But you do remember that I have some health issues here? There's a reason why I'm not still Atlanta PD."

"If I wanted a mindless brute with a gun, I would have hired one. I hired you because you have the intellectual capacity to be effective in spite of your physical limitations."

"My team will have to be involved," Deacon said. "I can't do it alone."

"So be it. I want you to put the *haven* back into South Haven, Mr. Deacon."

Deacon nodded crisply. "But if the police question my interference?"

"This is my world, Mr. Deacon." His eyes darkened. "In spite of what others may think. I built this community. Not my late father—may he rest in peace. Certainly not my brother. I alone created this wonderful place for others to enjoy. They aren't enjoying it now. You will make sure they enjoy it again."

"Understood, Mr. Falcon."

Nodding, Falcon turned away from him. That was Deacon's cue that the discussion was over. Deacon walked out of the office and left the mansion, thankful that he didn't run into Angie again.

His responsibility was clear: he had to do everything in his power to restore order to South Haven. If that meant stepping on some toes, so be it.

He switched on the golf cart and settled behind the wheel.

A rich man like Falcon might have been confident in his own powers, but Deacon didn't share his sense of self-assurance. Act like a cop again? He'd left the force three years ago, and it hadn't been an amicable departure.

He started driving the golf cart, unsure of his destination.

***

Although he had driven without a clear end-point in mind, Deacon found himself traveling back to his apartment.

He pulled the golf cart into the parking lot of the apartment complex. There were two Roswell PD squad cars angled in the center of the lot, light bars swirling. An ambulance was on the scene, too.

Cops and meat wagons. They had become a common sight in South Haven that day. Deacon didn't know all of the specifics of what was going on, as he wasn't the one getting the calls for officer assistance, but in his many offhand conversations with rubbernecking residents, a common theme emerged, as he'd told Falcon: people were going bat shit crazy.

Like that kid from last night who'd hacked up his dad with a machete.

Like the St. Bernard that had mauled a woman that morning and nearly eaten him, too.

But the sight of the cops so close to home set him on edge. After shutting off the golf cart, he hurried to the ground-level unit that he shared with his dad.

Pops sat at the kitchen table eating a fruit salad and sipping iced tea while he paged through the *Atlanta Journal-Constitution*. In an age of digital media, Pops insisted on daily delivery of an old-fashioned hardcopy of the newspaper.

He looked up at Deacon's entrance.

"Back already?" He cracked a grin. "Or did they fire you for gross misconduct?"

"Hey, Pops." Deacon looked around. "Where's Anita?"

"She's out on the patio making a phone call. What's the deal, son? You ran in here looking like you needed to piss like a racehorse."

"It's nothing." Deacon sighed, opened the refrigerator. He grabbed a cup of Greek yogurt off a shelf.

"That's mine, boy. Get your own."

Deacon ignored him. Leaning against the counter, he peeled the foil lid off the yogurt and stirred the contents with a spoon. It was strawberry flavored, with the fruit at the bottom, and the sight of the red chunks brought back the vivid memory of the woman's throat, ripped to shreds by the rabid dog.

He grimaced, forced himself to eat a spoonful of the blend. As a cop working Atlanta's Old Fourth Ward, he had seen much worse, and had learned to move forward with life in spite of the things he'd viewed. But that didn't mean it was easy. The memories often haunted your dreams and waking hours.

"I've been watching the news," Pops said. "Overnight, South Haven has become the murder capital of the whole damn country."

"Falcon wants me to get involved."

"Of course he does." Pops chuckled. "What the hell else you got to do? Rescue cats from trees? Play ball with the neighborhood kids?"

"You know what I was hired to do here, Pops. I wasn't hired to be a cop."

"Why don't you take me out to the courtyard to get some fresh air?" Pops asked. "After you fetch my piece?"

Deacon stepped to the patio. Anita stood at the wrought-iron railing, deep in conversation on her cell phone. He lip-synced to her that he was taking his dad out for a bit, and she nodded distractedly.

"Where's my piece?" Pops asked when Deacon returned.

"I've got mine," Deacon said, which was true. After the incident with the dog, he had returned to HQ and strapped on his Glock 17.

Deacon edged his father's wheelchair outside the unit, and onto the paved walkway that ran the length of the building. He wheeled his dad to the courtyard, parking the chair beside a stone bench that sat in the shade of a magnolia tree in full bloom. Deacon settled on the bench next to his dad.

For a couple of minutes, they sat in companionable silence. Insects buzzed past. A cool breeze tempered the cloying heat.

"We could leave this damn place, you know," Pops finally said. "My sister would take us in for a few days until shit cools off here."

"Aunt Carol can barely tolerate your presence for a few minutes, much less a few days."

"Might have a point there." Pops chuckled softly. "Then a hotel?"

"Not for me." Deacon shook his head. "You know I can't go AWOL, Pops. I've got an obligation."

"Damn contract," Pops said.

"Falcon pointedly reminded me of that when he demanded I get involved here. He's a cold-blooded bastard."

"Rich man like him demands a return on his investment." He spat. "Ain't nothing free, son. That man tells you to jump you'd better ask how high. Ask you to dance and you'd better start stepping and finger popping."

"I'm not a cop anymore." Deacon clasped his hands in his lap. "I don't know if I can handle that sort of thing again, physically. My heart . . ."

"Your heart's a lot more than that thing beating in your chest, son," Pops said. Extending his long arm, he poked Deacon in the chest with his gnarled index finger. "That right there, it's just muscle, blood, tissue, whatever." Pop clenched his hand into a trembling fist. "Grit ain't just what's in your chest. It's in the spirit, the soul. I should know."

Indeed, Pops would know, Deacon thought. His father had served in the Marine Corps during the Vietnam War, had been awarded the Silver Star Medal for gallantry. Upon returning home, he had been an Atlanta cop, just like Deacon, and had retired from the force after a long, historic career.

"You can do this," Pops said. "Stop whining and get your ass out there and do what you do. Damn, you're starting to embarrass me."

"What about you?" Deacon said. "*You* really could leave. I could make arrangements for you to get to Aunt Carol's."

"I was only kidding about leaving. I don't retreat, ever." Pops paused. "But I need my piece."

A helicopter thumped past. Deacon heard the craft but couldn't see it from where he sat. He surmised it was either a news media chopper, or the police were rolling out the war machines. Neither was a welcome development.

His father stared at the sky, squinting. "Shit's getting real, son. You ready for it?"

"Born ready."

"That's my boy. Now take me back inside and give me my god-damn gun."

He rolled his father back inside. Deacon reluctantly took the Smith & Wesson .38 out of his gun safe and handed it over to his dad. He didn't know when he would return, and if Pops insisted on staying home, he deserved the ability to defend himself.

"I'll keep in touch," Deacon said.

"Don't worry about me. Go out there and get on the grind. You're wasting time."

"Good talk, Pops." Deacon bent and kissed a shiny bald spot on his father's head. "I'm on it."

Chapter 10

Alex followed the assassin's blood trail.

The droplets of blood led out of his house via the French door that opened onto their deck. The hitman had left a comma of blood on the doorknob; the doors were partly open, admitting waves of the day's relentless heat.

Beretta drawn, Alex stepped outside and pulled the door shut behind him.

He heard the warble of an ambulance in the distance. The sound brought to mind his wife. Help was coming for someone, but it would have come too late for her. She'd never had a chance.

Can't think about that right now.

He studied the wooden planks underneath his feet. Blood droplets trailed across the pine wood deck and led into the recently trimmed Bermuda grass.

They didn't have a fence. The perimeter of their backyard was delineated by a row of shoulder-height, wintergreen boxwood shrubs. Other residences stood on all sides of his house.

Alex moved to the shrubs directly across from the deck. In one section, the boxwood had been tamped down, branches snapped, and some of the small oval leaves glistened with crimson.

He briefly considered ending his hunt. Judging by the quantity of blood loss, the assassin was badly wounded, and might bleed out in due time. Alex could cease his search and let the man die, wherever he had wound up.

The new Alex, the responsible business owner and devoted husband, would have dropped it, would have shied away from any additional bloodshed. But the old Alex, who had spent almost his entire adult life performing cartel dirty work, never would have left such a job incomplete, no matter how unpleasant.

In his time, he had done far worse than execute a hired killer. Twenty years ago, there had been the old man in Mexicali, a retired cop who had taken it upon himself to disrupt the cartel's operations in the Mexicali plaza. Alex had personally managed the man's immersion in a seething vat of sodium hydroxide, while his crew filmed video of the act as a warning for any self-appointed heroes. Sometimes, in the dead of night, Alex still heard the old man's garbled screams.

He tightened his grip of the Beretta, his lips drawing into a firm line.

Old Alex was needed here, as this was all about settling cartel business.

He threaded his way through the shrubs, which put him in his neighbor's spacious backyard. His neighbors had a large wooden deck attached to their home, a gas grill sitting on the deck, sunlight shimmering on the stainless steel surface.

They also had a huge children's tower playset, fashioned from wood and plastic, standing in the middle of their yard. It stood about fifteen feet high, and the dominant feature was the castle-style tower that included a small elevated clubhouse, the tower capped with a red peaked roof. A green slide stretched from the clubhouse to the grass. A set of monkey bars, a couple of swings, and a fireman pole completed the playset.

An almost crippling spasm of grief ripped through Alex. He and Melissa had talked of one day purchasing a similar set for their own children. They'd had so many plans for their future. He found it difficult to accept that all of it had been wiped away in a matter of minutes.

The clubhouse was empty, but Alex's gaze was drawn to the shadowed niche at the base of the tower. It was a space large enough to accommodate a man.

Alex noticed a few more droplets of blood on the grass, but he no longer needed to follow them. He crossed the lawn to the playset.

He found the Bloodhound huddled in the darkness of the tower base. He was still alive. Sitting on the grass, long, thick legs splayed in front of him, he had torn away part of his shirt, and pressed a knot of the fabric against his left eye. The material was mostly soaked through with blood. Copious rivulets of blood streamed from his wounded ear.

The hitman merely sighed at Alex's arrival, as if he welcomed the inevitable outcome, an end to his suffering.

"Your wife . . . blinded me," he said in a ragged voice. He indicated his ear. "Terrible damage . . . she is . . . la monstruo."

Alex could not disagree with the assassin calling his wife a monster. He didn't understand what had become of her. This day would haunt him for the rest of his life.

"Have others been dispatched?" Alex asked. "Or is it only you?"

The hitman grinned at him through his pain, blood on his teeth. Forever defiant.

"Su destino está en manos de Dios," Alex said.

He shot the Bloodhound twice in the head.

***

Alex returned to his dead wife. He knelt next to the sofa on which he had laid her body, dug underneath the blanket covering her, and found her hands. He clasped them, lowering his head.

Her flesh still retained some warmth, but the cooling process had begun.

Speaking in a whisper, he prayed. He had been raised Catholic, and though he had forsaken his faith for many years and hadn't returned to it even after he had left the organization—perhaps he had been too ashamed—he beseeched God with a fervor that he hadn't known since his youth.

Guide my footsteps, oh Lord, he prayed. *Order my hands to execute your will.*

After some time, alerted by a noise, Alex lifted his head. Rising, he wiped tears from his eyes with the back of his hand. He hurried to the door.

Outside, someone was shooting.

Chapter 11

It was a gorgeous day to be out boating on Lake Lanier, but Dr. Hannah Bailey wished she were anywhere but there.

Early that Friday afternoon, she was stuck on a rented pontoon boat with three of her friends. Well, two of them were her friends. The third guy was her date for the afternoon, a real winner named Craig.

They had a cooler full of beer and bottled water, and another cooler packed with sandwiches and snacks. A Bluetooth speaker blasted out pop music hits. Right then, a Bruno Mars song was playing, "That's What I Like."

"Call me a traditional kind of guy if you must, okay, but I've always believed a woman's place is in the home," Craig said. Leaning against the boat rail, he took a swig of his Corona, his third beer in less than an hour. "I make enough money as a tax lawyer to comfortably support a wife and a few rug rats. I do quite well, honestly, quite well." He paused, the lip of the bottle balanced on the edge of his cleft chin. "The truth is, any wife of mine would be happy to stay home, pop out the kids, and take care of my castle."

"Pop out the kids, huh?" Hannah asked. "Sort of like a toaster."

Craig grinned. He was a physically attractive guy, tall and handsome and well-built. It saddened her, because she knew some unfortunate woman was going to consider his looks, and his career, and eagerly take his bait, in spite of his outdated views on the roles of women.

"I think we're really clicking here," Craig said. "I'm surprised by that, really I am. When Tom told me that his wife had a single friend who was a doctor, I was convinced you'd be smart, but probably butt ugly. Smart chicks are usually homely as hell, and fat."

Hannah only stared at him.

"But you aren't ugly, and you aren't fat," Craig said. He burped, and assessed her from head to toe as if she were a vehicle he was considering for purchase. Hannah wore a green halter top and Bermuda shorts, but in front of this man, she felt as if she were wearing nothing at all. "You're actually really hot, a total babe. You've got a cute face, and your body is like, wow. Has anyone ever told you that you look like Kerry Washington, that black chick from that show, *Scandal*?"

That black chick? Seriously?

"I've heard it mentioned before," Hannah said.

"You work out a lot, too, I can tell, you've got good muscle tone." Gazing at her bare arms, he nodded. "I approve of that. Any wife of mine would have to stay in shape. It's mandatory. I don't care how many babies you have, you'd better stay fit, or it's out the door you go. But I bet that wouldn't be a problem with you."

"I have career ambitions," Hannah said. "That's a serious knock against me, don't you think?"

"Oh, yeah, you'd have to quit your job, for sure." He chuckled. "But women don't really enjoy working anyway. I mean, you guys do it for a while because it's sort of expected, but deep down, you want a man to take care of you so you can stay home and have babies. It's in your genes. Admit it!"

"You understand women so well," Hannah said. "It's truly amazing."

"Isn't it?" He laughed. "Wow, we're really connecting here. This is awesome."

"Excuse me." Hannah caught the eye of her girlfriend on the other side of the boat. "I'll be back."

As she walked away, Craig whistled. *Jesus, what a creep.* Hannah tapped Ashley's shoulder and peeled her friend away from Tom.

"Girl talk time," Hannah said with a sweet smile. Tom shrugged and ambled over to Craig.

Once Tom and Craig were out of earshot, Hannah's smile faded away.

"Uh oh," Ashley said. "I know that look."

"How soon until we dock?" Hannah said. "Because every molecule in my body wants to strangle this guy."

"What's wrong with him?" Ashley asked. "Tom said he was a good guy. He seems decent."

"Where do I start? He's offended me so many times I don't know where to begin. He did say I'd have to quit my job when I marry him because apparently women don't actually want to work."

"Gosh, I'm so sorry." Ashley's face reddened, and she glanced at her iPhone. "We've got another hour or so before we have to turn the boat in."

"Ash, I'd rather get a colonoscopy than speak to him again."

"Ouch. Sounds like I totally blew this one."

"At least it's a nice day to be out on the water." Hannah gazed at the sun rays reflected off the rippling lake. "I seriously needed some R&R."

Hannah was employed as an Epidemic Intelligence Services Officer for the Centers for Disease Control and Prevention. Or, as people in her role were commonly known in popular culture: a "disease detective." It was a two-year fellowship, and she was nearing the end of her second year in the program. Her responsibility was to literally serve on the front lines of investigating a potential public health crisis. During her fellowship, her work had taken her across the globe: Brazil, Ethiopia, Nigeria, and Mexico were just a few of the spots she had visited.

It was exciting, vitally important work, but she had to keep her bag packed virtually at all times. At a moment's notice, she could be summoned to travel halfway across the globe. Needless to say, her career left no time for a full social life.

"All work and no play makes Jill a dull girl," Ashley said. "That's what my mom used to tell me, anyway."

"Mine, too, in so many words. I'm about three years behind in my duty to deliver her some grand babies."

Hannah was thirty-three years old. Her dad didn't want her to rush into marriage and children, wanted her to wait until she was in a place where she was ready for those life-changing decisions, but her mom, a die-hard traditionalist, kept pressing her to "move on to the next stage" of her life. It was tough to convince her mom that she actually loved her current stage and was in no hurry to move on to anything else.

She had only agreed to meet this Craig character because some of her longtime college friends, like Ashley, insisted on hooking her up with men. She was in no rush to find a husband, or even a committed boyfriend. She didn't mind having companions—guys to occasionally meet for dinner, a movie, or some other interesting activity—but in her mother's opinion, such behavior would invariably lead to Hannah's becoming an old childless spinster, living out the balance of her days in misery with a houseful of cats.

Hannah glanced at Craig. He was drawing yet another beer out of the cooler. He winked at her.

Ugh, she thought. *Lord, rescue me, please.*

On cue, her cell phone—her *work* cell phone—chirped in her purse.

Hannah's heart rate accelerated. If someone was calling on her day off, that meant something important was going on.

"Is that your job?" Ashley asked, lips puckered in a sour expression.

"Sorry, I've got to take this." Hannah pulled the phone out of her purse.

It was her boss, CDC Director Dr. Ross Klein. His voice was grim, as always.

"Hannah, we have a situation."

Chapter 12

D rawn by the sound of gunfire, Alex carefully moved outside his house.

Someone else, a safety-minded resident with a family to protect, might have remained inside their home, closed the blinds and hunkered down to avoid notice. But Alex's wife was dead, ravaged by some bizarre sickness, and he had just killed a man with two shots to the head.

He had no reason to play it safe.

He had nothing at all to live for any more. His meticulously prepared Escape Plan was meaningless without Melissa at his side. Why not wade into whatever mess was going on, mix it up and get his hands dirty? Perhaps he'd be fortunate and get killed in the fracas— and spare himself the agony of trying to figure out what to do next with his life.

It didn't really matter anymore.

Beretta at his side, he crept behind the shrubbery in their flower bed. Concealed in cover, he surveyed the street.

A black Ford F-150 was angled across the middle of the road. A leathery-faced man that Alex didn't recognize had taken shelter on the side of the truck, shoulder leaning against the front tire. He wore a black cowboy hat adorned with a red feather. He appeared to be holding a rifle.

One of the truck's rear tires was flat, Alex noticed. He wondered if the flat had anything to do with the shots he'd heard.

Another burst of gunfire rang out and pinged against the pickup's side panel. Alex looked back and forth along the street, and spotted the source of the gunshots: another man, perhaps in his forties, dressed in military fatigues. The soldier walked along the middle of the road. He carried a rifle, too.

"Al Qaeda . . . fuckin' insurgents . . . kill!" the soldier shouted. "All . . . kill 'em!"

What the hell is going on? Alex wondered. *Has everyone here lost their minds?*

He felt as though he had dropped acid and spun away on a bad trip, and it had started with the Bloodhound appearing in his yogurt shop. Nothing that had happened since then had made any sense whatsoever, and he wanted to know when he would awaken back into his predictably normal life.

"Insurgents . . . go get 'em, boys!" the soldier screamed. "Ah yeah!"

Alex couldn't know for sure who was the aggressor in this situation, the cowboy sheltered behind the truck or the soldier, but his money was on the soldier. The guy's incoherent shouts brought to mind Melissa's nonsensical rant about dirty hair.

The soldier fired again, and the pickup's passenger-side window shattered. Glass tinkled to the pavement with a sound like discordant music.

"Smell insurgents!" the soldier said. "Smell 'em!"

Alex estimated that the soldier was within twenty feet of the truck. The cowboy remained hunkered down in cover, waiting for something, maybe for the guy to deplete his ammo, or for the opportunity to take him by surprise.

Alex's heart knocked. What he was about to do was reckless. But his nerves jangled with anticipation.

He holstered his gun.

He sucked in a breath, and burst from behind the shrubs and ran pell-mell toward the soldier.

As he drew closer to the man, he saw the inflammation around his eyes, the swollen lesions marring his face. Those were the same symptoms that had marked his wife, and in the back of his mind, Alex realized there was a bigger problem roaring through their community, but he'd seen no one there to help, just ordinary people out here killing one another, and it was up to people like him to take matters into their own hands to restore order.

The guy was focused on his quarry hiding behind the pickup truck, and he didn't notice Alex in his peripheral vision until Alex was upon him.

Leading with his shoulder, Alex smashed into the soldier at full speed, and to an onlooker, it would have looked like a football game in which the quarterback was blindsided by a crafty defensive end. The hit lifted the soldier off his feet, his head snapping back from the force of the impact. A soft *"uhhh"* escaped him. The rifle popped out of his grasp.

Alex hit the ground too, but he was prepared for the impact, and rolled when he met the pavement. He was back on his feet within a couple of seconds.

The soldier lay spread-eagle in the middle of the street. His crimson-rimmed eyes were open but he wasn't moving. He looked dazed.

"Don't kill him!" someone shouted from behind Alex. "I don't want the boy hurt."

In the process of drawing his pistol, Alex paused. The cowboy hustled around the truck and approached. He wore leather western boots, too. The soles clicked against the concrete.

"He was gonna kill you," Alex said.

The cowboy squinted at Alex. He had haunted green eyes—the eyes of a man who had witnessed many terrible things. Alex put the man's age in the mid-fifties. He smelled of tobacco, leather, and sweat.

Shaking his head, the cowboy spat. "He's my neighbor's son, goddammit. He's out of his everlovin' mind."

"Like my wife," Alex said.

The cowboy's eyes widened a bit. "Sorry. It's spreading fast. The end of days is nigh, hombre."

Alex blinked at the remark. *End of days?*

The soldier began to stir. Sitting up, he unsheathed a combat knife from his belt. The cowboy shook his head grimly, aimed his rifle at the soldier, and squeezed off a shot with a soft pop, firing some sort of small dart that punctured the soldier's neck.

"Tranquilizer," the cowboy said. "Meant for horses. Still ain't gonna put him to sleep like it ought to, but it'll let us hogtie him and toss him in the truck till we get him somewhere safe."

The cowboy drew a pair of plastic handcuffs from a utility pouch he wore around his waist. The soldier slumped to the ground, eyes open, lips parted in a slack-jawed expression. His arms twitched slightly, an involuntary reflex. He kept whispering the word *insurgents* over and over, in a madman's mantra.

"What's he talking about?" Alex asked.

"He had tours in Iraq, Afghanistan," the cowboy said. "Ain't been right since he came home, and then *this* shit right here happened."

"What happened, exactly?" Alex asked. "Some kind of sickness going around?"

The cowboy shot him a skeptical look. "Some uninformed folk might call it a sickness, yeah. Ain't how I see it, though." Kneeling, the cowboy rolled the soldier over onto his stomach. The guy started to struggle when the cowboy attempted to cuff his hands. "Help me out here, will you? Keep the boy from kicking the hell outta me."

Alex gripped each of the solder's calves and attempted to pin them to the pavement. It was like trying to contain a pair of furious snakes. The soldier's legs kept writhing, boots barking against the concrete.

As Alex struggled to hold him down, sweat dampened the back of his neck and trickled along his spine. What struck Alex the most about the incident was that no one intervened. They were out there in broad daylight on a hot summer day, subduing a man in the middle of the street, and he noticed no passerby or curious residents. His was normally a quiet street, but the sense of isolation that had taken over the neighborhood was downright eerie.

The cowboy secured the soldier's wrists with the plastic handcuffs. He got another pair of zip ties around his ankles.

"Let's get him in the truck," the cowboy said.

"You've got a flat tire." Alex nodded toward the sagging wheel.

"Yeah, that was the next thing I was gonna tackle." The man extended a large, strong hand toward Alex. "Name's Wayne Purdue. I could sure use your help if you're willing to lend it. We got work to do, and I need a man who knows how to get things done. You knocking the kid here ass over teakettle tells me you ain't afraid to get your hands dirty."

Alex glanced toward his house. His heart kicked as he thought about his dead wife inside, lying on the sofa underneath a blanket. The wave of grief was too powerful for him to confront, and he forced himself to look away and meet his new friend's steady gaze.

"Alex Vasquez," he said. "I'm happy to help."

Chapter 13

The police weren't interested in Deacon's help.

After leaving his father, Deacon had resolved to connect with the cops on-site in South Haven, to assist their investigation and try to get more details on exactly what was going on. He had located a phalanx of officers stationed near the community's large playground. An ambulance was nearby, too, paramedics loading a muttering older man into the vehicle. Nylon restraints secured him to the gurney; a vicious bloody laceration marked his forehead.

Probably he tried to attack the cops, too, Deacon thought. *After he'd assaulted someone else.*

Deacon approached the officers, gave a quick summary of his law enforcement background and current role. He was immediately rebuffed.

We've got it under control, buddy. You want to help? Be our eyes and ears and call us with whatever you see.

But what are you guys seeing? Deacon had asked. *There's been a string of violent incidents here. What's causing it?*

What are you, a media guy? I can't tell you any of that shit.

I can help.

We don't need your help. We need you to stand aside and let us do our jobs. Get the hell out of here.

It was the disrespect for his position, Deacon realized. A security guard typically was mocked as a toy cop, and even though he explained his previous experience in the Atlanta PD, the officers regarded him with unmasked skepticism.

It pissed him off but he understood it, because he'd used to have the same attitude. There were so many wanna-be cops out there who studied cop lingo, who used police scanners to tune into department chatter, who sometimes went so far as to dress in uniforms and pass themselves off as cops (particularly when wanting to impress women). Nothing he could say was going to convince them to trust him. He was wasting his time.

Deacon returned to his command center to regroup.

The South Haven Security team headquarters was located near the entrance to the community, just past the manned gates. The building was artfully designed, with a stucco exterior, stacked stone accents, and a flat roof. Potted ferns and beds of petunias flanked the building. From the outside, it looked more like a place that might be featured in *Architectural Digest* than a fully functioning security center.

A bank of parking spaces provided electric charging stations for the fleet of golf carts, all of them branded with the "South Haven Security" identifier. A late-model Ford Expedition, painted black and with the community's insignia emblazoned on both sides, was parked near the glass doors. The vehicle was intended for Deacon's use but he rarely drove it.

Inside, the HQ had plenty of modern touches, too. Multiple flat screen televisions broadcast up to sixty-seven security feeds from cameras positioned throughout South Haven. The cameras were stationed on Main Street, where they provided a clear view of every inch of the business district; in the lavishly appointed community clubhouse; the dedicated greenspace; and they covered each residential block, too. It wasn't an exaggeration to state that *any* incident that occurred outside of a resident's home in South Haven was going to be captured on camera.

"What's happening, Jim?" Deacon rounded the front desk.

Jim was on duty at the front desk, leaving Lisa, the only other guard working a shift at that hour, at the community gates. Eventually, their night-shift guy would arrive for duty.

"I've got a front row seat at the apocalypse." Jim indicated the wall of monitors with a wave of his hand. "It's hell out there."

"We're about to leave the seats and jump onto the stage," Deacon said. He told him about his conversation with Falcon.

"Unbelievable," Jim said, shaking his head. "What a fucking prick."

"I can't force any of you to assist me here," Deacon said. "You aren't employed under the same terms that I am. You can just keep on doing your job and I'll . . . I'll figure out what I've got to do."

"That's bull crap. We're partners."

"You didn't sign up to play cop again," Deacon said. "Hell, you're retired, man."

"I may be retired but I'm not dead. I'm with you on this. So what's the plan?"

Deacon smiled. "Okay, I got nowhere with the cops. Maybe that's okay because I get the impression they don't know what's going on, either, they're just reacting as things unfold, providing damage control. But from what we've seen with the off-the-wall behavior of these residents, it's as though they're infected from rabies, or something like it. That dog, Jake, had it too."

"A virus," Jim was nodding. "It's in the eyes, like I've been saying."

"We need to talk to a doctor," Deacon said.

"We've got a medical clinic on site," Jim said. He accessed the computer at his desk. "We've got Dr. Britt, at the Take Care Clinic on Main Street."

"Call her," Deacon said.

Jim used the office phone system to place the call, putting it on speaker so both of them could listen. The line rang and rang, and after several rings it went to voice mail, asking them to leave a message to have their call returned and advising the caller to contact 911 in case of an emergency.

Jim ended the call and looked at the monitors. "I think I've seen folks coming out of there, though I don't see any one now. I wasn't paying much attention but I'm pretty sure I saw them open for patients."

"They might be busy," Deacon said. "Let's pay them a visit."

"Right with you, chief." Jim rose from his chair. He picked up his Mossberg pump-action shotgun and grinned. "I'll ride shotgun."

***

Although it was a short drive to the medical clinic on Main Street, less than a mile, Deacon opted to take the Ford SUV. With all the craziness going on, he felt too vulnerable in the golf cart. If Mr. Falcon wanted them to play cops, they would have to be equipped like legit officers.

Deacon had already been carrying his Glock 17 in a holster clipped to his duty belt. He took an AR-15 rifle from the command post's private arsenal and stowed it in the vehicle's overhead weapon rack. He and Jim had both slipped on Kevlar vests, also taken from the arsenal. The vests were so new that the purchase tags were still on them.

"This feels like old times," Jim said, getting settled in the SUV's passenger seat. "I'm ready to go on a narc raid."

Deacon smiled, pleased that his heart continued to beat at a moderate pace. After the dog attack that morning, he'd been worried that his heartbeat would soar into the red zone, but he felt good. Steady. In control.

Perhaps, he was back where he belonged.

He shifted into Drive and rolled away from the command center.

Soon into their journey, they passed a squad of police cruisers clustered around a house, and near them, yet another news crew gathered like a pack of coyotes waiting for a piece of meat to drop. At Deacon's last count, half a dozen newsworthy incidents had taken in South Haven since that morning, but the news media wasn't interested in speaking to the security guards who patrolled the community. No one gave a damn about Deacon and his team.

He was itching to make fools of them all. He wanted to bust this thing wide open. His interactions with the cops had wounded his pride, made him question why he'd ever thought becoming a security guard—a toy cop!—was a good idea, and he wanted to prove to everyone, himself most of all, that he could still deliver the goods. He could still make a difference. He wasn't some has-been cop gone out to seed. He was a—

Someone rear-ended them.

Deacon rocked forward in his seat, the harness tightening across his torso. Jim, in the process of raising a bottle of water to his lips, lost his grip on it and the bottle flipped onto the floor, water spraying everywhere.

"What the hell was that?" Jim asked.

Deacon twisted around in his seat. A flame-red Dodge Ram pickup jacked up with a suspension lift kit had struck them. The truck's cabin was raised so high off the ground that from Deacon's vantage point, he was unable to see the driver.

Deacon thought he recognized the vehicle as belonging to a resident, though he had never made the acquaintance of the owner. Thinking it was only a friendly accident, he went to open his door—but stopped when the pickup's engine revved. The truck rolled backward several feet. The customized chrome grille resembled a malicious grin.

It's one of them, Deacon thought, though he still couldn't see the driver.

"Oh, shit," Jim said.

The truck bore down on them again.

He braced himself for the collision. The pickup hammered against the Expedition's rear bumper, harder than before. Metal shrieked and popped. Deacon felt his teeth snap together painfully, and he nearly bit his tongue by reflex.

"Get out of here!" Jim said.

But Deacon was already mashing the gas pedal. The SUV surged forward. They were in a commercial section of the community, passing by a YMCA and a credit union, both of the parking lots virtually empty. Deacon spun the wheel hard to the left and veered toward the YMCA.

In his rearview, he saw the pickup sitting in the middle of the road. The driver was doing a burnout, engine thundering as the tires spun, artificially created blood-red smoke churning from the spinning wheels. The vehicle's windows were so darkly tinted it was impossible to see the occupants, and as the lurid red smoke swirled around the truck, gave the impression that the pickup was a supernatural vehicle materialized from some hellish nether realm.

Deacon braked in the middle of the YMCA's vast parking lot.

"What's the play?" Jim asked. Perspiration had collected on his brow.

Deacon searched the console, flipped on the Expedition's light bar. The vehicle was equipped with a radio, the system tuned to a frequency they used for their team's walkie-talkies, but he had been hoping it included a megaphone so he could broadcast a warning to the pickup's driver. No such luck. He wasn't sure whether it would have mattered anyway.

"If he keeps coming after us, it's game on," Deacon said. "He's crossed the line. At this point we've got the green light to hit back." He added: "To disable, not kill."

"You don't need to tell me that, chief." Jim snatched his shotgun from the overhead gun rack. He rolled down his window.

Clutching the steering wheel, Deacon brought the Expedition around to face the pickup. Perhaps a couple hundred feet separated the two vehicles. Deacon's heart raced, normally a danger sign, but a fresh infusion of adrenaline had given him heightened strength and focus.

Jim had levered the firearm outside the passenger window, using the doorframe to help balance the weapon against his shoulder. He and Deacon had visited the gun range many times. Jim might have been retired, but he retained the skills of an experienced marksman.

"Come on," Deacon said softly.

With a roar, the Dodge truck burst out of the web of smoke.

Deacon tensed. The pickup bounced over the curb. It was coming directly at them.

Deacon couldn't believe it. It was suicide. What the hell was the matter with this guy?

"I'm hitting him," Jim said.

Deacon swallowed. "Do it."

When the truck reached a range of about forty yards, Jim squeezed the trigger. The shotgun boomed, the harsh noise making Deacon's ears ring.

Double-aught buckshot sprayed the truck, shattering the windshield, but the driver kept coming, didn't veer away.

"Son of a bitch." Jim pumped the Mossberg. He fired again. The spray hit one of the truck's front tires. Rubber popped and flew in tattered black shreds.

But the driver kept coming. Closing in fast.

"Hang on!" Deacon said. Slamming the gears into Reverse, he floored the accelerator.

The SUV rocketed backward with a screech of tires. Deacon wrestled the wheel to the right, taking them out of the pickup's path, but the Dodge still clipped their front end, spinning the SUV around several feet and tossing Deacon and Jim in their seats.

Roaring past, the pickup smashed into the brick exterior of the YMCA building. The front end crumpled like a ball of aluminum foil. The tires, still spinning, spat out serpents of red smoke.

Glasses askew, Jim started to climb out of the vehicle. Deacon stopped him with a hand on his arm.

"It's not over yet," Deacon said. "Stay in here, let's take out those rear tires."

Jim nodded, his narrowed eyes like chips of ice. As he positioned himself at the window, Deacon shifted to Drive and fed the gas.

The Dodge started to move, too, as if the driver finally realized that he was unable to plow through the YMCA's brick wall. Deacon got them within a safe range before the driver could straighten out, and Jim let fly with another spray of buckshot. One of the truck's rear tires exploded into useless scraps of rubber, but the vehicle continued to roll, orange sparks sputtering from the exposed rims grinding across concrete.

"Christ, he's still coming," Jim said.

"Not for long," Deacon said. "Let's see how he likes this."

He drove the Expedition directly into the pickup, their front ends almost perfectly aligned, the pickup's damaged grille looking like a mouthful of shattered teeth. Deacon knew the SUV was much heavier than the pickup, with greater horsepower. They shoved the pickup across the parking lot, and though the driver of the Dodge had the accelerator married to the floor, the engine wailing, with two ruined tires, the pickup couldn't gain purchase, couldn't resist.

Deacon drove the pickup all the way back against the brick wall and pinned it there like a bug trapped under a boot heel. He shifted to Park and engaged the parking brake for good measure.

"Now," he said. "Let's arrest this asshole."

He was going to open the door when Jim grabbed his arm. "Wait, chief. I think the guy is coming out."

Someone jumped onto their front end. The person wore jeans and a red hoodie, the hood drawn over his head. Deacon knew the SUV was outfitted with bulletproof glass, but out of reflex, he prepared to take cover, as he fully expected the insane driver was going to draw a gun and fire at them through the windshield.

The driver mashed his face against the glass. He spoke in a garbled stream.

"Crush . . . fuckin smash 'em to bits . . . crush . . . fuckin' smash . . ."

Deacon reeled back in his seat. The man's eyes were crusted over with horribly inflamed flesh, and dark lesions spotted his face. Blood dribbled from his nose. Saliva sprayed from his blistered lips.

Shotgun gripped across his chest, Jim stared, too.

The man head-butted the windshield with enough force to make the SUV's frame tremble. The reinforced glass held tight. He mashed his head against the glass again. And again. And again.

"Crush . . . fuckin' smash 'em . . ."

Blood covered his face and smeared the windshield in messy streaks, but he continued to pound away relentlessly. Deacon had seen some terrible things during his law enforcement career, including acts of suicide and self-mutilation that had made him lose his lunch— but he didn't think this guy was trying to mutilate himself, wasn't engaging in a pointless exercise of self-punishment.

"He literally is trying to kill us," Jim said in a stunned voice. "By banging his goddamn head against the windshield."

"Frenzy," Deacon said. "He's in a state of total frenzy."

"I don't know what to call it. But we've got to stop this. Knock him out and get some cuffs on him."

"Any normal person would have been knocked out after sustaining this much damage to his brain," Deacon said. "These sick people . . . they don't have normal limits. I don't know how it's possible but that's what's happening. Remember the dog?"

Jim nodded grimly. "We'll have to subdue him. Somehow."

Deacon removed the AR-15 from the overhead weapon rack. Jim readied the shotgun.

"On three," Deacon said. "One. Two. Three."

Both of them flung open their doors. At that same moment, as he was scrambling out of the SUV, Deacon heard the crack of a rifle. Dangerously close.

Instinctively, he ducked for cover.

The SUV's side mirror, on the driver's side, broke into pieces above his head, bits of glass spraying him.

"Back in the truck!" Deacon shouted. He dove onto his seat.

Jim hustled back inside the Expedition, confusion stamped on his face. Deacon slammed his door.

"There's a sniper," Deacon said. "Nearly took my head off."

"Seriously?" Jim asked. "This keeps getting better doesn't it?"

On the hood, the man continued to bang his head uselessly against the windshield. Bone was exposed. Deacon had to pull away his gaze from the sheer gruesomeness of it.

Another rifle crack. The bullet struck the rear windshield. Luckily, it was bullet-proof.

"Fuck." Jim scooted down in his seat.

"Let's get out of here," Deacon said.

He shifted into Reverse and fed the accelerator, while twisting the wheel to the right. The sudden movement had the predictable effect of flinging the guy off their vehicle. He tumbled off the hood like a crash test dummy, his blood-drenched face painting a crimson smear across the glass.

Deacon drove the SUV forward. Their first attacker staggered to his feet and tried to catch up with them, but they easily left him behind. The sniper fired again, and Deacon heard something at the back of the SUV shatter—probably a tail light.

Deacon ran the windshield wipers for a minute or so to clear away all of the blood. When they were finally in the clear, cruising through a residential area, Deacon glanced over at Jim. Jim still clutched his shotgun against his chest and had a shell-shocked expression: lips parted slightly, eyes glazed behind his lenses.

"You look how I feel," Deacon said, breaking the silence.

Jim blinked, swallowed.

"We really need to have a chat with that doctor, chief. I need someone to make sense of this for me. Because it feels as though we've dropped straight down into hell."

***

They reached the Take Care Medical Clinic without another incident.

Deacon parked in front of the facility. A large "Closed" sign hung in the window. A handwritten note was taped to the front door, too.

"You've gotta be shittin' me," Jim said. "Closed?"

"Hang on a sec." Deacon unfolded a community map that he had brought from HQ. Using a pen, he circled the area on the map in which they'd been attacked by the driver and the sniper. Identifying those danger zones might prove useful later.

"Keep an eye out, I'll check the note," Deacon said.

Shotgun held at the ready, Jim stood watch near the SUV while Deacon approached the clinic's front door. A small wooden table stood outside the door, and held only a stack of index cards and a couple of ink pens. The note was taped to the inside of the glass door, black text on white paper.

Closed until further notice!
If you have flu symptoms, please put your name, address,
and phone number on the index card, and slide it under the door.
For your own safety, please return to your home. Drink plenty of
fluids, and rest. A medical professional will contact you soon.

Deacon studied the bottom of the doorway. Several index cards had been slid underneath the door.

"What's it say?" Jim asked.

Deacon told him. Then added: "There's staff hidden inside. Or else, why tell folks to leave cards?"

"They're not letting anyone in 'cause it's too dangerous."

"My guess, too."

Deacon plucked an index card off the table, filled it out with a message, and slid it underneath the door.

"Let's wait in the truck," Deacon said.

They had waited for about ten minutes when a slim, dark-haired young woman appeared in the doorway and knelt to gather the cards on the floor. In the shadows, she might have been a visiting ghost.

She appeared to vacillate over her next move for a moment, and then, she unlatched the door and beckoned them inside.

Chapter 14

The young lady who let them inside the clinic was named Emily. She looked familiar to Deacon. He believed he had seen
her riding a bicycle around the community in days past. He
made it his business to know most of South Haven's residents, if not
by name, then at least by sight.

After locking the door behind them, Emily led them through the
empty, darkened waiting room and down the clinic's main corridor.
Dim, recessed lighting illuminated the hallway. She spoke rapidly,
but precisely. Deacon wasn't sure if she were anxious or if that was
merely her nature.

"Officially, I don't work here," she said. "I'm not a physician or
even a nurse. I'm a medical school student. I'm a *volunteer*, for lack
of a better term." She laughed, seemed embarrassed. "I had come
here to talk to Dr. Britt, who didn't come in today, coincidentally."

"She's sick, too?" Jim asked. "Well, just shoot me now, crap."

"That's what I've heard," Emily said.

"Then who's here?" Deacon asked.

"Only the three of us. Here we are." Emily opened an office door.
Two other women were inside, huddled around a desk. Both of them
wore the shell-shocked expression that Deacon had grown accustomed
to seeing that day, and he wondered about what they had witnessed.

They did quick introductions. The ladies seemed pleased that Deacon and Jim had arrived, noticeably well-armed and equipped for
conflict, and that gave Deacon a sense of satisfaction. At least someone appreciated his private security team. Although he estimated that

this trio had been doing a pretty good job of keeping things afloat on their own.

Emily seemed to be in charge of their little group, though she was clearly the youngest. In spite of her age, she radiated fierce intelligence and competence. She might have only been a med school student, but whenever she wrapped that up, in Deacon's opinion she was going to be one hell of a doctor.

"We came because we were hoping someone could tell us exactly what we're dealing with here," Deacon said. "I've talked to the cops, and they either don't have a clue or they aren't telling us."

"They wouldn't know," Emily said.

Deacon went on: "We've seen random people losing their minds and attacking folks, and there doesn't seem to be any rhyme or reason to it. On the way here, a guy tried to run us down with his truck, and then someone else shot at us."

"And a dog mauled a woman this morning," Jim added. "It attacked us, too, when we tried to help her. This illness, this virus or whatever the hell it is, it's not limited to people. We need to remember that."

"We've contacted the CDC," all three women said, almost in unison.

"Centers for Disease Control?" Deacon asked. "Just so we're clear."

"Centers for Disease Control and Prevention," Emily said. "But yes, the federal agency that investigates outbreaks. It was my idea. We had a call with them over an hour ago. They're sending a team here."

"Not sure how I feel about that," Deacon said, thinking about how Mr. Falcon would view this new development. "But you all got any ideas on how people catch this virus? I'd say all of us have already been exposed, wouldn't you say?"

"If it's transmitted like a typical flu virus, yes," Emily said. "The flu is highly contagious and gets passed through talking, sneezing, coughing. It's likely that all of us have already been exposed."

"How long until we start getting sick?" Jim asked. "If we're infected?"

"We don't know," Jenn said. "But usually for the flu, symptoms start showing up between day one and day four of you contracting the virus."

"Among other things, the CDC told us to keep a list of names, all the people who've come here seeking medical attention, as well as any others we've observed." Emily indicated a stack of index cards gathered on the desk. "We've got forty-seven potential patients so far. Several more have come since we contacted the CDC."

"That's not counting all of the frenzied I've seen out there." Deacon pointed behind them. "The ones out there wandering the community, I mean."

"What did you call them?" Emily asked.

"The frenzied." Deacon shrugged. "It just popped into my head."

"They're crazy as wood lizards, the name fits," Jim said.

"They're sick, let's all remember to keep that in mind," Jenn said. "Classifying them as monsters doesn't help our cause. They need to be hospitalized."

"Point taken," Deacon said. "But they're out of their minds, in a *frenzy*, and that makes them extremely dangerous. Your job is to treat the ill, and I can respect that. But *my* job is to protect the residents of this community." Deacon looked around the room at each of them. "For starters, none of you ladies are armed, and you need to be."

"Why?" Jenn asked. "We're going to wait here for the CDC and then support them when they arrive. We're here to heal, not harm."

"Anything could happen," Emily said. "It might be a good idea to be prepared."

"I can give you my Taser, if you'd like," Deacon said. "I'm sure Jim wouldn't mind handing over his if you ask nicely."

"I'll take one," Emily said, as he'd expected she would.

The officer manager, Rita, also agreed to accept a stun weapon. Jim demonstrated how to use the Taser.

"It's only going to slow them down," Jim said. "From what we've seen, it won't incapacitate them. I don't know how it's medically possible for damn near fifty thousand volts of electricity to only make someone stumble, but that's what we're dealing with here, gals."

"So now we're *gals*," Jenn said with an exaggerated roll of her eyes. "What's next? Will we have to go to the kitchen and rustle up a hot meal for you hardworking menfolk?"

Jim's cheeks bloomed fire-engine red. "Sorry about that, miss. Old, bad habit of mine."

Deacon's walkie-talkie beeped. It was Lisa, the security guard on duty at the front entrance.

"The CDC is here," Deacon said.

***

Deacon wasn't sure what to expect with the arrival of the CDC. He had never interacted with the agency in person, had only seen them portrayed on TV and in Hollywood films such as *Outbreak* and *Contagion*. In those portrayals, they wore hazmat suits and ordered quarantines, directing the military to round up people like cattle and confine them against their will while they conducted cruel experiments.

Perhaps his assumptions were off-base, stemming from nothing more than pure fiction, but he was worried, especially about his father. The ornery old man would pitch an epic fit if someone tried to corral him. While they waited for the CDC to show up at the clinic, Deacon stepped inside an empty patient room and called his dad's nurse on his cell phone.

"Your father is doing well," Anita said. "He's napping right now. He dozed off watching reruns of that old show that he likes."

"*The Rifleman*," Deacon said. "It's always been his favorite program."

"That one, yes."

"He doesn't seem sick?" Deacon asked. "Like he's got the flu or a headache or anything?"

"He's been fine. Why do you ask?"

"Just heard about a nasty bug going around. How are *you* feeling?"

"Oh, I'm all right," Anita said, and he could imagine her quizzical expression. "Is there something you aren't sharing with me?"

"I've got to go, but I'll be in touch," he said. "Call me if anything comes up, and *please*, keep my dad inside."

He hung up before she could question him further. He hated to be short with her, but he didn't want to incite a panic.

As he was leaving the room, Emily met him in the hallway. She was alone.

"Can I talk to you about something?" she asked. "Privately?"

"Step into my office." He beckoned her into the room behind him and closed the door after them. "What's up?"

"I feel a little silly talking about this," Emily said. She twirled a lock of hair around her finger in what Deacon recognized as a nervous gesture. "But I've been trying to reach my boyfriend all morning. He lives here. His name is Zack Thompson. It's important that I talk to him."

"He hasn't been answering his phone?" Deacon asked.

She shook her head. Distress twisted her features. Deacon guessed that whatever her reason for wanting to talk to the guy, it went beyond mere concern for his welfare. But he wasn't going to press.

"Where are your folks?" Deacon asked.

"They're out of town on vacation and won't be back until next week. I sent my mom a text and she told me to leave South Haven—I suppose I'm stubborn because I'm still here. Anyway, what do my parents have to do with anything?"

"Just getting a full picture of things." Deacon shrugged. "Your guy live here with his parents, too?"

"I don't think they're home, either. I don't know how to get in touch with them."

"Your guy, he could be on site in South Haven. Or not. There are plenty of reasons for why a young man might not answer his phone."

"He's not cheating on me," she said, steel in her gaze. "He's not like that. I think something else has happened to him."

"You think he's sick?" Deacon asked.

Emily grimaced at the suggestion. He could tell that the possibility had been haunting her.

"I need to find him, like I said, it's important," Emily said.

"Let's see where things stand after the CDC crew gets settled in here," Deacon said. "Then if there's anything my team can do to help, we'll do it."

She nodded tightly.

There was a sudden, loud knocking at the front of the clinic.

"Must be our esteemed guests," Deacon said.

* * *

The CDC team had arrived in three white cargo vans, accompanied by a Roswell Police Department squad car. Each of the agency's vehicles had the blue and white "Centers for Disease Control and Prevention" logo displayed on the side panels. With this obvious marker, Deacon wondered how they had kept the news crews at bay, and assumed that some of the other police department cars on site in South Haven had been ordered to hold back the reporters. The federal agency had enough juice to kick the media copters out of the community's airspace, too.

Standing on the sidewalk outside the medical clinic with Jim, Emily, and the others, Deacon figured he ought to call Falcon and tell him what was going on. The CDC's arrival at South Haven was about the most significant piece of news imaginable. But Deacon had no desire to talk to the rich developer again anytime soon. Falcon had security cameras embedded everywhere and could see what was unfolding, and he hadn't requested regular status updates from Deacon anyway.

Screw him, Deacon thought. *I may have to follow his orders but I'll do that however I want.*

"You ever felt just totally out of place?" Jim asked, beside Deacon. "That's how I'm feeling right now, chief. Like I shouldn't have gotten my crusty ass out of bed this morning and come to work."

"You can still go home," Deacon said. "No one's keeping you here against your will." He added: "Not yet."

"Someone's got to stay and watch your back," Jim said. "I gave the wife the heads up that I might not be home tonight."

The people climbing out of the CDC vehicles *looked* like scientists and medical professionals to Deacon. They had that intense, hyper-alert look about them, as if no detail escaped their attention. They wore navy-blue uniforms with the CDC insignia on the breast pocket, and they carried laptop bags and other equipment.

Then Deacon saw the woman, and he sucked in a sharp breath.

"She's with the CDC?" he whispered to Jim. "Damn, I should have studied harder in school."

"Down, boy." Jim winked at Deacon.

The woman was one of the last to exit the vans, and she wore the same uniform as the others. She chatted with her team for a moment, and then broke from the cluster of scientists and approached their group. Deacon realized that she was actually in charge.

She looks like a model, he thought. As soon as the thought crossed his mind, he chastised himself. With her looks, she probably had a difficult time getting people to take her seriously. He had dated his share of beautiful women before, had heard their accounts of how good looks brought benefits, but could be a double-edged sword when it came to the work world. As tough as it would be, he would have to view this woman solely from a professional perspective.

"I'm Dr. Hannah Bailey, and I'm the lead EIS officer here," she said. "You all are? Your name and role, please."

Each of them introduced themselves. She repeated what each of them said, as if committing each face and name to memory, and shook everyone's hand with a firm grip, her own hands already protected by latex gloves.

"I'll give you an overview of how this investigation will proceed," Dr. Bailey said, her gaze sweeping across them. "Primarily, at this point, our objective is to gather information. Each of you has an important perspective. We'll interview and examine each of you, and then we'll talk to and examine those who are displaying symptoms of illness. From there, we'll form an initial diagnosis and determine next steps."

"Are we allowed to leave?" Rita asked. "I have a toddler in daycare. I've got to be there to pick him up this evening."

"For public safety reasons, no one should leave until we know, definitively, what we're dealing with." Dr. Bailey softened her words with a smile. "However, we can't detain you here against your will. There's no quarantine order, if that's what you're concerned about. I'd greatly appreciate if you would stay and help us until we've reached a diagnosis. After we get set up, we can assist you with making arrangements for your children or other family members."

"I'm sorry, but I can't stay," Rita said, shaking her head. "I just can't."

"So much for sacrificing for the greater good," Jim said.

"Mind your business, old man." Rita's eyes were black bullets.

"All right, let's stay respectful of one another," Deacon said. "Like the doctor said, everyone still has the right to leave. If you gotta go, you gotta go."

"If you're going to go, ma'am, we'd like to get some contact information from you first," Dr. Bailey said. "And examine you and draw some blood. You came in direct contact with patients who visited the clinic."

"Fine, but I'm not staying here," Rita said, arms crossed over her chest.

"We'll need to set up an operations hub, somewhere with plenty of enclosed spaces, preferably," Dr. Bailey said. She looked at Deacon. She had beautiful hazel eyes, Deacon noted. Eyes he could have dipped in like oceans.

Focus, man, he chided himself.

"On the way here, I reviewed a map of this community," she continued. "The clubhouse seems like it would serve well."

"It's perfect," Deacon said. "It has the ballroom, the restaurant, meeting rooms . . . there's plenty of square footage there. I can help your team with logistics."

"I'm with him," Jim said. "Whatever you need us to do." He glanced at Rita. "We're all about the greater good."

Rita muttered under her breath.

"I'd appreciate that, sirs," Dr. Bailey said, and offered a brief smile. She clasped her hands together. "We need to move quickly now. Until we know exactly what we're dealing with, time is of the essence."

Chapter 15

After he helped to change the ruined tire on Wayne Purdue's pickup, Alex and his new friend rode back to Wayne's house. As they drove through South Haven, Alex could hear the soldier writhing and muttering in the flatbed like a man in the throes of a serious fever.

Wayne didn't speak during the short drive, and that was fine with Alex. He was still processing the day's events, trying to cope with that sense of unreality that had taken hold of him.

Besides, what did you talk about when both of you had just dealt with something from out of a horror film?

What Alex didn't allow himself to do was think about Melissa. The grief would cripple him. He wanted to keep moving forward, stay in motion, in the hope that sheer momentum would enable him to find his footing in this strange new reality. He would help this man, Wayne—who seemed to know more than he did about what was unfolding—until he regained his equilibrium.

Wayne pulled into his driveway.

He lived on the opposite side of South Haven, in a large white Craftsman with red trim. It had an attached two-car garage. A purple and gold LSU flag fluttered from the porch. The landscaping was meticulously maintained: petunias, lilies, and hibiscus thrived in the flowerbeds.

It didn't look like the home of a man who talked about the end of the world with a casual earnestness that Alex found downright bizarre.

"Nice house," Alex said.

Wayne grunted. "Lived here three years. Moved here when my daughter got her vet practice going. We decided to put our practices together. I'm an equine vet."

"Horses?" Alex asked.

Wayne nodded. "I handle the large animals, she takes care of the little ones. Was working out fine until this morning." Wayne's face darkened.

Alex didn't want to ask what happened that morning, but he could imagine it had something to do with Wayne's daughter. Perhaps he and this man were drawn together by tragedy.

Wayne opened his door and squinted at him. "You coming? We gotta get this boy squared away."

"What's his name?" Alex asked.

"Huh?"

"The soldier. What's his name?"

"Clay," Wayne said. He nodded at a house across the street. "Clay Kenmore. Lives over there with his mama. She ain't home so we gotta take care of him. Agree with that, hombre?"

"No problem," Alex said. "Let's do it."

***

They carried Clay inside through the garage. Bound at wrists and ankles, the guy was probably only half-conscious due to the tranquilizer, but nonetheless furious at being restrained: he called them insurgents and promised to decapitate them, speaking in that nearly incoherent scramble of words that Alex was getting accustomed to hearing. Alex tuned him out.

A silver Toyota Highlander occupied one of the garage parking slots. A bumper sticker designed like an animal's paw print was stuck to the SUV's rear cargo door, the words "Purdue Vet Clinic" underneath the paw in red text.

His daughter's vehicle, Alex thought. She must have been home.

Inside, the house was fastidiously clean. Alex spotted modern appliances, fabric furniture in mellow earth tones, photographs of animals hanging on the walls. A flat-screen TV in the kitchen broadcast local news, and caused Alex to do a double-take; it looked as if the news crew was right there in South Haven. That might have explained the helicopters he had heard.

Wayne opened the basement door, off the end of the kitchen. They took the soldier down a wide flight of wooden steps, and into a dimly-lit sitting area outfitted with a sectional sofa.

"Let's set him down here," Wayne said, indicating the couch. "I'll be right back."

Wayne left through a door that led to another area of the basement, using a key to unlock the door. The soldier lay on his back across the cushions, mumbling to himself and struggling half-heartedly.

Alex looked around.

This section of the basement was completely finished. The area had laminate flooring designed to look like hardwood, the large L-shaped sofa, a massive flat-screen television, and a wooden coffee table that appeared as if it had been carved by hand from a tree stump. Framed LSU sports memorabilia hung on the brick walls. A mini-refrigerator standing in the corner hummed quietly. It looked like nothing more than the well-appointed man cave of a proud college fan.

But Alex's stomach had tightened into a knot. He knew virtually nothing about this man. Yet he was there, sitting in his house with someone they had essentially taken prisoner, waiting for . . . what, exactly?

Just roll with it. What difference does it make anymore?

Indeed. His wife was dead. And he had killed a man. A life on the run was his only viable future. This detour to Wayne's residence was merely a temporary stop on his journey, which offered perhaps the opportunity to do some good.

He settled on a sofa cushion across from the soldier. Out of habit, he checked his iPhone, and immediately regretted it: the screensaver was a recent photo of him and Melissa on vacation in Florida, wrapped in each other's arms while the surf broke on the beach around them, grinning as if they would be young and in love forever.

Exhaling, he put the phone away.

Across the room, the door swung open. Wayne stepped through the doorway.

He had changed into black scrubs, and he wore a surgical mask that covered his mouth and nose. He had taken off the cowboy hat and slid on a protective cap. He wore gloves, too.

"Let's bring him back here," he said, voice muffled.

"Do I need to wear some kind of protection, too?" Alex asked.

"Not yet. Let's move him."

"What's back there?" Alex rose.

"You'll see for yourself when we get him situated. Come on, now."

Wayne hooked his hands in the soldier's armpits, and Alex grabbed him by the ankles. Together, they carried the man into a darkened corridor with three more doors branching off from it; a door at the end of the hall hung open, yellowish light spilling from within.

Alex thought he heard a groan issue from the room beyond, followed by a stream of delirious sounding giggles.

"What is that?" Alex asked.

"Keep moving," Wayne said. "Head right on back into that room at the end."

Gooseflesh had pimpled Alex's arms. But he maintained his hold on the soldier and edged ahead.

When they crossed the threshold, Alex blinked in surprise. It was a narrow room, light streaming from a naked bulb overhead. A table stood in the corner, lined with vials and other metallic medical instruments.

Several wire crates were arranged against the wall, of varying sizes. Three of them were spacious enough to contain large animals.

One of them already held a young woman.

She wore a t-shirt and grey sweatpants. She was barefoot. Like the other people Alex had seen displaying violent, bizarre behavior, redness outlined her swollen eyes, and lesions spotted her pale arms.

Wayne's daughter?

The woman mashed her face against the cage and snapped her teeth at them. Spittle sprayed from her lips.

"Come to me pretties . . ." she said, in a voice edged with madness. She tried to thrust her hand between the cage grates, but the openings were too small. She wriggled her fingers at them in a come-hither gesture. "Me pretties."

"Don't pay her no mind," Wayne said tightly. "She's just sick. Let's get this boy in the other crate there."

The cage door already hung open, and was barely wide enough for them to squeeze through the soldier. Clay cursed them.

Once they had pushed him in, Wayne said, "Latch the door."

Alex bent to secure the cage door. As he snapped the lock into place, he felt a sting at the back of his neck. He swung around.

Wayne held some sort of syringe gun. He backed away from Alex.

"Sorry, hombre," he said. "But I gotta run some tests on you."

Alex reached for his holstered pistol, but it felt as though he were moving while submerged underwater. What had Wayne given him? He couldn't get his hands to cooperate with what he wanted them to do.

His legs weakening, he slumped to the floor.

Wayne took his Beretta as easily as one plucking a toy from the possession of an infant.

"It's for a good cause," Wayne said.

Unable to resist, Alex could only scream weakly as Wayne dragged him into the last empty cage.

Chapter 16

Thunderclouds darkened the sky, plunging the early afternoon into a state of gloom. Lightning danced on the horizon. An unseasonably cold wind shook the trees.

Deacon squinted at the fermenting sky as he climbed out of the SUV. The approaching storm worried him. A severe storm could knock out electricity. Although South Haven Security HQ had a back-up generator, he was unsure about the alternative power capabilities of the other community buildings. Under ordinary circumstances he would've taken such a development in stride, but they needed every advantage in their column at this point in the game.

Add it to the expanding tally of items that he needed to worry about.

Their five-vehicle caravan had drawn to a stop in the large parking lot outside the clubhouse: Deacon's SUV, the three CDC vans (the ladies from the clinic rode with the science team), and a Roswell police cruiser that brought up the rear. The cop had initially escorted the CDC into South Haven, and he demanded to come with them. Deacon agreed because they needed the extra support in case something went south, but he prayed the cop didn't try to take charge and force Deacon to play his executive orders card via Mr. Falcon.

Sitting atop a slight rise, the clubhouse was designed in the style of an 18th century English manor. The exterior was a blend of stacked stone, brick, and stucco, and the entire facility offered almost fifty thousand square feet of space: it included a ballroom, two private dining rooms, a board room, meeting rooms, a restaurant, and a bar. It was, from Deacon's understanding, a popular venue for weddings and other large-scale events, and also served as the headquarters for the community's members-only golf club.

"My daughter wanted to have her reception here," Jim said, coming beside Deacon. He spat on the ground. "We couldn't afford the place."

"Don't you get an employee discount?" Deacon asked.

"This was before I worked here, but when I got hired on, I looked into it. Turns out no one gets a discount on the venue, not even employees. Greedy bastard."

Deacon swept his gaze around the parking lot, which had a scattering of vehicles parked in the staff slots. "I'm trying to figure out why no one answered the phone when I called on the way over here. Looks like some employees are on site."

"They could be like the others." Jim's gaze narrowed, and he clutched his shotgun. "The frenzied."

The Roswell cop approached them. He was tall, lanky, red-haired, and, to Deacon, hopelessly young, maybe twenty-four at the oldest. At that age, all he could offer Deacon was a pain in the ass. He had avoided interacting with the cop while back at the medical clinic but he couldn't ignore him any longer.

"Logan McBride," the cop said. "*Officer*, Logan McBride. You gentlemen are just private security, huh?"

Jim's face reddened.

"Both of us are former cops," Deacon said. "We've over fifty years' experience between the two of us."

"Old timers," McBride said, with an exaggerated roll of his green eyes. He cleared his throat. "But I'm sorry to inform you: you're not cops anymore. Far from it. The Roswell Police Department is assisting the CDC in this investigation."

"We're not going to argue about jurisdiction," Jim said. "Hell, kid, I've got shoes older than you."

"You can make jokes about my age but the joke is on you, old timer. The police department is in charge here. Stand down."

"What's the hold up, gentlemen?" Dr. Bailey asked, breaking into their circle.

Deacon and the other two men looked at the doctor, and their red-faced embarrassment matched his own. He felt as if he were a member of a group of misbehaving youth that had been called out by the teacher.

"Just a friendly little pissing contest, ma'am," Deacon said.

Bailey's lips puckered as if she'd sipped sour milk.

"I need to get my team set up in this clubhouse, stat," she said. "Can we go in, please?"

"Let the three of us check it out, first," Deacon said. He added: "Just as a precaution."

"I appreciate that, but I have to insist on accompanying you," Bailey said. "One of my top priorities for this case is to gather information. I need to see everything you see."

She held his gaze as she spoke, and he knew she wouldn't back down. The lady had spunk. He couldn't suppress a smile.

"So that's how it's going to be then," he said. "Well, all right."

"I'm going, too," Emily said. She shrugged. "In for a penny, in for a pound, right?"

Deacon led the group to the front entrance. There was a handwritten sign taped to the interior of the glass double doors:

Closed Until Further Notice!

He pulled the door handles. Locked.

"Does someone have a key?" Bailey asked.

"One step ahead of you." Deacon unhooked the hoop of keys from his duty belt. "We've got keys to all of the community amenities."

He located the key labeled "Clubhouse – Front" and was about to insert it in the lock when he noticed something going on inside the building. He put his face to the glass pane.

"What is it?" Jim asked.

"I thought I saw someone going into the ballroom,"   Deacon said.

"Is that music playing?" Emily asked. She had placed her ear to the glass. "It sounds like a piano."

"If they're inside listening to music, I'd say we're in the clear," Officer McBride said. "Let's get on in there."

Deacon's lips tightened. He didn't share the cop's confidence. Nevertheless, he unlocked the doors.

He led the group inside.

***

The interior of the clubhouse was lavishly appointed. Mahogany paneling. Crystal chandeliers.   Silk wall coverings. Ornate, handmade Persian carpets blanketed large swaths of the marble floors.

All of the lights had been shut off. The foyer and areas beyond were dense with shadows.

Although Deacon didn't see any staff, piano music filtered from the partly opened ballroom doors, across the wide expanse of the foyer. The music was almost comically off-key. It jangled Deacon's nerves.

"That's a terrible rendition of *Moonlight Sonata*," Emily said. "Speaking as someone forced to master it at the age of ten. It sounds like whoever's playing has had way too much to drink."

Deacon noticed that Dr. Bailey was holding some sort of recording device, the gadget about the size of a deck of cards. Her eyes were wide and alert.

"We're wasting time," Officer McBride said. He strode away from their group and approached the ballroom doorway. "It's only some staff getting drunk, no doubt. I'm going in there to bust up these shenanigans."

"Hang on, kid," Jim said, but the officer ignored him.

Deacon hung back, and the rest of the group kept their distance, too.

Badge in hand, Officer McBride stood on the ballroom's threshold and shouted: "Roswell Police Department! Identify yourselves!"

Deacon had to hand it to the kid, he had balls. He'd been like that, too, during his rookie days on the force, and even for some time after, until he'd had the experience that sharpened his awareness of his own mortality. A bullet clipping your heart tended to shift your perspective.

But as if a switch had been flicked in the ballroom, the music instantly ceased. Deacon waited for someone to speak, in the meek tones that ordinary citizens used when addressing the police, but he heard only scattered gibberish. It raised the hackles at the back of his neck.

"*. . . playing keep . . . playing keep . . . playing keep . . .*"

"*. . . cops for us coming . . . for us cops . . .*"

"*. . . not our kind . . . not our . . .*"

Something inside the ballroom screeched. It was a sound a wild animal might have produced, and it wasn't a cry of fear, or retreat. It was a shriek of primal rage, and hearing it made Deacon want to turn tail and flee the building, but he stood firm.

"What the heck is that?" Dr. Bailey asked.

The piano music resumed. Playing at a more frenetic cadence but no less sloppy, keys being struck carelessly.

"That's it!" Officer McBride drew his service revolver and plunged inside.

"Dammit, kid," Jim said, and went after him.

Drawing his Glock, Deacon moved forward, too. His heart whammed, undoubtedly on the brink of exceeding the safe zone his cardiologist had advised, but a rush of adrenaline powered his muscles.

He arrived at the threshold of the ballroom and squinted into the shadows.

The area was huge, and a couple dozen round tables and lots of chairs had been arranged in preparation for some upcoming affair. On the other side of the room, opposite the doorway, Deacon glimpsed the grand piano, and its seated player: it looked like the clubhouse manager, a middle-aged woman he'd met many times. She had a quick smile and was always gracious with his team.

She was hunched over the piano keys playing as if her existence depended on it, faster and faster.

There were others present, too.

Three people were gathered on the square, middle section of the ballroom set aside for dancing—and they *were* dancing. Two of them, a man and a woman, were performing a strange dance that had a vague relation to a classic waltz. It was difficult for him to know what exactly they were doing because he was distracted by the spectacle of both of them being entirely naked.

"What the fuck?" Jim asked, in a whisper.

The third member, a petite young woman with long jet-black hair, wore a tight red dress. Barefoot, elevated on her toes like ballerina practicing pointe technique, she spun in a circle on the corner of the dance floor. Spinning, spinning, spinning, hair wreathing her face. An ordinary person might have lost their balance, but the woman whirled with the practiced grace of a dancer or gymnast.

She *is* a gymnast, Deacon realized. He recognized the young lady's face. A year or so ago she had participated in the trials for the Olympics, and the community had made a big deal about it, had held viewing parties and draped a congratulatory banner across Main Street.

No one was safe from the scourge tearing through South Haven.

He and Jim edged forward into the room, Bailey and Emily close behind.

"Infected," Deacon said in a low voice to Bailey. "Every one of them. They've got the red eyes, the inflammation. The wacky behavior."

Nodding, Bailey continued to record, sweeping her device across her field of vision.

"What the heck is this?" Officer McBride moved toward the trio. "Cease this foolishness and identify yourselves!"

The gymnast screamed, head thrown back, mouth wide. It was the same nerve-shredding howl as before, and Deacon wanted to clap his hands over his ears.

But then things got really crazy.

The gymnast stopped her revolutions. She rushed Officer McBride, moving in a crimson flash. The startled cop went to raise his gun, but she vaulted off the floor and leaped onto the shelf of his shoulders, locking her muscular legs around his neck and grabbing his head in her hands.

McBride let out a choked cry of surprise and tried to pry her off. Screaming, she twisted his head with savage force. Deacon heard bones crack as the man's neck snapped like a pretzel.

A weak cry bubbling in his throat, McBride sank to the floor.

Jim yelled and started firing the Mossberg.

The woman did a somersault onto a nearby table with breathtaking agility. Glasses crashed and shattered against the floor. The woman did a backflip onto another table. She crouched like a tigress and regarded them with wild eyes, the blisters on her face seeming to glow like embers.

"Out . . . out . . . out!" she screamed.

She leapt again, and snagged the chandelier. She swung on it as if it were an uneven bar, dress rippling through the air.

"Get under the tables!" Deacon yelled, but both Emily and Bailey had already taken cover under a nearby table, the tablecloth partially hiding them from view.

The waltzing couple was charging them, too. They snarled like rabid beasts.

The manager continued to play the piano, fingers flying.

Deacon grabbed a nearby chair and hurled it at the naked dancers. It hit them full on, breaking their charge, and they staggered back drunkenly.

Jim fired at the gymnast. She flipped away from the chandelier, spinning through the air and landing on another table. As the shotgun boomed, chips of plaster rained down over them, but the woman scrambled so rapidly from one table to the next that he couldn't hit her. Issuing that blood-curdling scream, she bounded out of the ballroom and vanished in the shadowed foyer.

"Shit!" Jim shouted.

The dancing couple swung around and dashed in the opposite direction. They broke through a set of double doors at the other end of the room.

The manager kept playing the piano, oblivious to the abandonment by her pack mates.

"Can we secure her?" Dr. Bailey asked, indicating the woman.

Deacon glanced at Jim, who nodded, bits of plaster in his beard.

They cautiously approached the woman. Deacon withdrew the pair of plastic handcuffs from his belt.

"Ma'am," he said, slowly. "Please come with us. We don't want to hurt you."

She didn't even look in their direction. She bent over the keyboard and muttered her gibberish mantra, her hair in her eyes. Her fingers were a blur on the keys.

"Playing keep . . . playing keep . . . playing keep . . ."

"We need you to come with us," Deacon said. "You aren't well. We'll help you."

"Playing keep!"

When Deacon touched her arm, she snarled and snapped at him like a feral cat, and he pulled away his hand just in time to avoid getting bitten.

"Christ, we should let her keep playing the damned thing," Jim said. "She's not going anywhere and she isn't violent like the others."

"What do you say, doc?" Deacon asked Bailey. "This is your show."

"We can keep her under observation in here, so long as she doesn't try to hurt anyone and she lets us take a blood sample." She glanced around the room. "I'll need to establish negative pressure. Since there were three other infected individuals in this area there could be contaminants in the air."

Deacon wished he had been wearing a dust mask. "Fair enough."

"Maybe I can persuade this lady to play a different, easier song," Emily said. She chuckled, half-heartedly. "She's been butchering Beethoven."

Deacon, Jim at his side, went to check on the young cop. McBride lay sprawled between a couple of chairs, head twisted at an ugly angle, dead eyes staring at the ceiling.

"Just a kid," Jim said. "Fuck."

Deacon knelt beside the body, and closed the dead man's eyes.

It wasn't the first corpse they had seen that day, and his gut told him that more were coming.

A lot more.

Chapter 17

D r. Hannah Bailey was in, to put it mildly, unfamiliar territory.

What she had witnessed in the clubhouse ballroom defied all of her training and experience. As a woman of science, she was as bewildered as she would have been if someone had given her irrefutable proof that the world was truly flat, Bigfoot really was roaming in the Rocky Mountains, and Elvis Presley was alive and working as a pit boss at a casino in Tupelo, Mississippi.

But she didn't have the luxury of withdrawing into quiet contemplation while she re-oriented herself to this bizarre new reality. Although she was thrown badly off balance by what she'd seen, she still had a job to do, and every minute mattered.

Deacon and Jim had searched the rest of the clubhouse and verified that the sick, violent individuals who had attacked them had vanished. No less than ten minutes later, Hannah had gathered her team in a clubhouse conference room, and they began setting up their equipment and making plans for their investigation. None of them had witnessed what she had seen in the ballroom, which probably worked to her advantage, for the moment. They could focus on following standard procedure and not worry about whether they were losing their grip on their sanity.

As the lead EIS officer, her main priority was to methodically walk her team through a critical series of steps. None was more important than the first one.

Step one: determine an outbreak is occurring.

It was an obvious step, but she couldn't go any further, couldn't build a case definition, until they had addressed a long list of questions and effectively verified the diagnosis. The questions they had to answer, primarily, were: Who? What? Where? When? Why?

They had some basic assumptions about the answers to each of those questions, some more detailed than others. Who? Well, from what they had learned thus far, the residents of South Haven were impacted. What? They were still working on that, but it seemed to be an infection that caused flulike symptoms, which gradually evolved into deranged, obsessive, frequently homicidal, behavior, which clearly meant adverse neurological impacts. The exact nature of the infection and how it was transmitted were still unknowns. Where? Since South Haven residents were infected, the source most likely would be found somewhere on the community grounds. When? Within the past twenty-four hours.

Why?

No freakin' clue.

But they were going to find out. They would start with the woman they had under observation in the ballroom, who had continued to play the piano in an off-key cadence since their arrival. Hannah had directed her team to establish negative room pressure in the ballroom as best they could, to prevent possibly contaminated air from escaping and guard against cross contaminations from room to room in the clubhouse.

"You seem to be holding up okay," Deacon said, approaching her after she had assigned various tasks to her team. "Looks like you've given everyone their marching orders."

The security guard commander impressed her. In spite of the real-life horror show they had been sucked into only a short while ago, he had never lost his composure. She wondered about his background. He didn't fit the profile of what she'd expected when she learned he was a security guard. She had expected him to be only minimally helpful, but he had taken charge of the situation and kept them safe.

She'd have to keep him around as long as he was willing to help. It sure didn't hurt that he was easy on the eyes, too. Under any other circumstances . . . she pushed the thought away and focused on the business at hand.

"I've learned in these investigations that it's important to stay focused and keep moving forward." She began striding back to the ballroom; Deacon kept pace with her. "We've got to go through all of our protocols, check all of our boxes. We can't afford to ignore anything or we risk missing a crucial detail."

"How long have you been doing this sort of work?" he asked.

Hannah had learned that with some people, such questions were a means of attempting to subtly discredit her, to highlight what they assumed was her youth and inexperience. With Deacon, however, she sensed that he was genuinely interested in learning about her background.

"Twenty-two months," she said. "The EIS post is a two-year fellowship program."

"Helluva way to wrap things up."

She offered a brief smile. "Tell me about it."

"You have any theories yet?" he asked.

"I've never seen anything like it, never read of anything like it," she said. "But we've got only minimal data at this stage. As we research we'll build our case and I'm confident we'll get a handle on it."

She sounded more confident than she felt, and she wondered if Deacon was going to call her bluff. But he only leveled his head in the direction of the police officer's corpse, which two members of her team wheeled on a gurney down the clubhouse corridor. Per her instructions they would transport the body to their isolated, ad-hoc lab in the clubhouse to draw blood and perform other testing.

"I don't know what the hell I'm going to tell that kid's boss. Or what we'll tell his family."

"I know this isn't easy." Hannah shook her head. "But we can't tell them anything right now. Except that he's gone. We have to assume that physical contact with the woman who attacked him may have transmitted the infection. We can't release his remains and obviously we can't share any information yet on exactly what happened."

"Right," Deacon said. He bunched his fists on his waist. "Jim and I got your team here and you're getting down to business, which is great. What else can we do to help?"

She paused for only a beat.

"I shouldn't say this now," she said, "but don't allow anyone else into South Haven. And don't let anyone leave."

"Oh?" he asked, eyebrows lifted. "We discussed this before but it was only between our little group. Are we talking about an official quarantine now?"

"I think we're moving to that point," she said. "I'll have to call my director and he'll have to run it up the ladder—there are local, state, and federal officials that have to sign off. I've never been personally involved in a case that requires quarantine, but it's a serious step. I think we've got sufficient cause to implement it here. With what little we already know it's clear that we're dealing with something that poses a major threat to public safety, and we've got to contain it."

"Folks aren't going to like it," Deacon said. He pursed his lips. "Nope. This is the Deep South. People buck against the government telling them what to do. You aren't from here, are you?"

"I'm from New Jersey," she said. "Camden."

"I thought I caught a Jersey accent. Well, I've been here my whole life. You tell these folks they can't go anywhere and you'll have a fight on your hands. What you're saying makes sense to me, of course, but it's gonna lead to trouble."

"It's for the good of everyone. If you can loop in your staff at the gates and ask them to start gently recommending that people stay put, or stay out, that'll be the start, until we can get an official order in place."

"I can do that, and one better," Deacon said. "South Haven has an emergency broadcasting system. We call it Code Red. We can broadcast a recorded message to every residence and business in the community. Text messages, too. You record the message, I'll get it sent out to folks."

"That's perfect," she said.

"When we get to the official quarantine order, what comes with that?"

"I would expect military enforcement," she said. "The National Guard, maybe? It's not my decision, and honestly, it's rare for a case to require such extreme measures."

He nodded. "What else can I do?"

"I've got to take a closer look at our piano player in there, draw some blood and run other tests," she said. She gave him a small, quick smile that felt more flirtatious than she had intended. "Mind watching my back?"

If he had thought she was flirting with him, he didn't let on.

"Let's do it," he said.

***

Deacon hung nearby while Dr. Bailey examined the clubhouse manager. He tried not to show it, but he was pleased that the doctor had requested his company, and he got the feeling that she wanted to keep him around as this ordeal played out.

He was more than happy to oblige. He couldn't remember the last time he had met a woman like her.

Stay focused on the task at hand, he reminded himself. *This isn't a date by a longshot.*

Both he and the doctor had slipped on surgical masks, gloves, and shoe covers. Meanwhile, the manager continued to play the piano, oblivious to their presence. Deacon wasn't sure of the song, but it sounded like some classical tune, badly botched. Was she going to keep playing until she passed out from exhaustion?

Dr. Bailey had yet to touch the woman, but she had edged closer to her. She was taking photographs with a small camera.

"The appearance of her skin," Dr. Bailey said. "Reminds me of Stevens-Johnson syndrome."

"The marks on her?" Deacon asked.

"Yes, the lesions. SJS is a form of toxic epidermal necrolysis. Typically it's caused by medications, certain antibiotics. I'm doubtful that's the case here, but it's something I'll have to consider."

"No stone unturned," Deacon said.

"SJS doesn't have any adverse effect on neurological function," Dr. Bailey said. "It's primarily a skin condition. That's why I have my doubts."

"Some kind of rabies, maybe?" Deacon asked. "Jim and I had a run in with a dog this morning, he looked rabid."

Dr. Bailey unclipped a pen light from her pocket. Inching closer to the woman, she shone the light in the woman's eyes.

The manager hissed like an agitated cat, lips pulled back and displaying her teeth. Dr. Bailey flinched, and Deacon touched the butt of his Glock.

"Okay, I'll put it away," Dr. Bailey said, and flicked off the light. The woman resumed her song.

"Sensitive, isn't she?" Deacon said.

"I need to get a blood sample next." Dr. Bailey brandished a small syringe. "I don't think she's going to like it one bit."

"Let me call in Jim. We'll hold her down if necessary. All in the service of science, right?"

***

Emily was grateful to assist the CDC team. There was so much to do, and they needed as many helping hands as they could find. Working with Dr. Bailey and the others on a crisis situation that affected hundreds, perhaps thousands, of community residents was a worthwhile distraction from her own personal issues.

She still hadn't heard from her boyfriend, Zack.

She still hadn't told anyone, outside of her best friend, that she was pregnant.

She had been in touch with her parents, both of them on vacation in Greece, and while they were frantic with concern for her and wanted her to leave South Haven immediately, she hadn't disclosed her pregnancy. It was her little secret.

She feared the worst about Zack, considering everything else going on in the community, and she refused to dwell on it too long. She forced herself to stay busy.

The South Haven clubhouse had been transformed into a CDC command center. The CDC had brought in a lot of equipment from their vans, most of which had been set up in the largest meeting room the clubhouse offered: electronics and medical equipment primarily.

Under Dr. Bailey's direction, Emily and the clinic nurse, Jenn, had set up a station at one of the conference room tables and were reaching out via phone to the residents who had come to the clinic earlier that day seeking care. They had compiled a list of nearly fifty such patients, including contact information, and Dr. Bailey had supplied a series of interview questions for them to pose to each resident.

The interviews weren't going well. Most people didn't pick up the phone, presumably because they either didn't recognize the caller or were incapable of answering. In that case, Emily and Jenn left detailed voice mail messages with requests for a callback. Only a handful of people actually took their calls, and they were mostly incoherent, rambling unintelligibly—suffering from the symptoms Emily and the others had seen in the infected.

Only one of the residents who answered their call was willing—or able—to speak. She spoke in a whisper, but confided that she had brought her husband to the clinic that morning, due to flu-like symptoms. She said he had begun to behave obsessively, and she pleaded for someone to come there to help. She was afraid to speak too long for worry that her husband would overhear the conversation and "fly into another rage," as she put it.

Emily assured the woman they would be in touch soon, and hurried to relay the details of the call to Dr. Bailey. Bailey was coming out of the ballroom with the security guys, Deacon and Jim flanking her, and it looked like she had blood samples in a plastic bag.

"So we go see them," Bailey said when Emily had finished recounting the details of the phone call. Bailey pulled her surgical mask down to her chin. "We complete the interview in person. That's ideal anyway."

"That could be dangerous," Deacon said. "I'd strongly recommend that you not go anywhere out there without armed back-up."

"I'm in," Jim said, eyes shining eagerly.

"I promised her that someone would come right away," Emily said. "She sounded really scared, but willing to tell us everything she knows."

"Let me get this blood sample over to my team," Bailey said. "Then let's head out."

Chapter 18

W hen Alex awoke, he was caged.

He wasn't sure how long he had been unconscious. The room had no windows, and the light bulb that had been aglow earlier had been shut off. A weak slice of brightness came from underneath the closed door on the far side of the room; otherwise the chamber was dark.

He felt for his wristwatch and found it gone. The warm, damp air caressed his skin. He realized that all of his clothes had been re- moved.

Wayne had stripped him completely naked. A thin polyester blan- ket was the only material that separated his bare skin from the cold metal bars of his small prison.

As his eyes slowly adjusted to the gloom, he strained to see if the others, those sick people, the soldier and Wayne's daughter, were still imprisoned in their own cages. The other enclosures appeared to be empty. He didn't hear anyone else breathing or shifting around. He heard only his own pounding heart.

What had Wayne done with the others?

What was he planning to do to him?

A memory surfaced in Alex's thoughts, like a fragment of a dream . . .

I need to draw some of your blood, Wayne said, gazing at Alex from outside the bars of the cage. His voice was muffled by the surgi- cal mask pulled over his mouth and nose. Gonna run a biopsy, too. I think you're healthy, but I need to see how you're different than the infected folks.

A spasm of coughing wracked Wayne's rangy frame, and he brought his hand against his own forehead, on which had appeared trickles of perspiration.

Shit on a stick, Wayne said. I'll be damned if I'm not sick, too . . .

Alex's memory of the incident faded into blackness. He traced his fingers across his arms. He felt a bandage taped to his inner left forearm, and another on the inner part of his right bicep. The one on his right arm hurt the most; that was where Wayne had taken his biopsy, he realized. The wound on his forearm must have been from the blood sample.

But there was another dime-sized bandage on the inside of his upper right thigh. It ached slightly. Alex didn't know what Wayne might have done to him there. Another blood draw? Or something else?

Wayne was treating him no better than a lab monkey, pricking him with a multitude of needles, and for that disrespect, Alex wanted to punish him. He might have willingly agreed to such tests if Wayne had clearly explained his intent, but to do this without Alex's consent deserved a hurtful consequence.

He just had to get out of this box.

Alex tried to sit up and banged his head against the roof of the cage. Fresh pain traveled through his muscles, which already ached from being contorted in a cramped space.

Alex grabbed the narrow metal bars and shook them. The kennel rattled, but held firm.

"Let me out of here!" he yelled, and his voice came out hoarse. He shook the cage again. "Wayne, damn you! Let me out! Wayne!"

No one came to the door.

But when he'd shaken his prison, he had heard the faint slosh of water, nearby. His ran his fingers across the bars. He felt the shape of a plastic bottle, attached to the outer wall of the cage. A metal dispenser jutted from the bottom of the bottle.

Alex tapped the end of it with his fingertip, and felt a trickle of cool water. Wayne had attached a water distribution system to the enclosure.

Bending and twisting, the movement sending jolts of pain across his back muscles, Alex maneuvered his lips to the dispenser, and licked greedily. Water had never tasted so good. The sweltering heat in the room had dehydrated him.

When he'd had his fill of the water, he lowered his head, his fingers clutching the cage bars. He was trembling.

He was furious, partly at Wayne, but mostly at himself, for winding up in this predicament. After eight years of evading the Cartel, here he was in a cage, every bit a prisoner that he would have been if the Cartel leadership had their way with him and had left him to rot in a private prison cell.

And he was alone.

No one, including the few acquaintances he'd gained over the past several years since he'd fled to Atlanta, had any idea that he was trapped in this man's basement. Such things had happened before to people trapped in cellars, in the bellies of homes standing in seemingly ordinary neighborhoods, and no one had ever suspected the cruelties taking place in those dark, hidden places.

Shouting, he punched the wall of the cage. It had only the effect of sending a spasm of agony across his knuckles.

He slumped against the rear wall, breathing hard.

It would be easy to drift back into unconsciousness. Traces of the sedative lingered in his blood. The remnants of the drug, combined with the layers of warm air in the room, had a sleep-inducing effect.

No.

He forced himself to sit upright. He shook his head as if clearing away dust.

"Think, Alex," he whispered to himself.

The cage had a door; the door had a lock. He could either pick the lock (unlikely without an appropriate tool) or bypass it somehow.

He reached for the section of the enclosure that he thought served as the door. He discovered a small hinge.

A sound reached him: footsteps, in the corridor outside the room. Quick, feather-light, and approaching the door.

His heart clutched.

He wasn't sure whether to celebrate this development, or fear what might happen next. Was it someone who had come to help him, or further abuse him?

The door creaked open.

Alex went still. He held his breath.

The visitor let out a low ripple of giggles.

It sounded like a woman who'd had one too many drinks.

Wayne's daughter, he thought, a wave of coldness trickling along his spine.

Why had Wayne set her loose? What had happened to Wayne?

Alex edged away from the door of the cage.

A shadowed shape entered the room. A slim figure. It was too dark for Alex to discern the details of her appearance, but he remembered what he'd seen of her earlier: thick dark hair, blue eyes, olive-skinned complexion. She might have been an attractive young woman had she not been afflicted by the mystery illness.

"Come to me pretties . . ." she said, in a hot whisper. She giggled. "Me pretties . . ."

He had no idea what she was talking about. He doubted that she did, either. Her mind was blasted, her words no more coherent than the babbling of an infant.

She approached the cage.

Alex cocked his leg as far as he could. He was prepared to drive his heel into her face if she tried to attack him.

She sniffed around the edges of the enclosure, like a canine questing for his scent.

Another giggle. "Me pretties."

A jingle of a key. A lock clicked. She opened the door of his cage, the hinges creaking.

Alex tensed. His muscles tingled in anticipation.

Giggling, she retreated from the room. Her footsteps receded along the outside corridor; a door opened and slammed.

He couldn't believe it. She had set him free.

Why? he wondered. *What was her agenda?*

Nevertheless, he scrambled out of the kennel.

***

Alex found the light switch and flicked it on.

The room looked as he remembered before Wayne had drugged him. Several large kennels lined the wall, all of them empty. A small wooden table stood against the far wall, the surface covered with medical instruments and vials. A swivel chair was paired with the table.

All of Alex's possessions were piled on the chair: clothes, shoes, wristwatch, wallet, cell phone, gun. Nothing was missing; even the cash in his wallet remained.

According to his watch, it was a ten minutes past five o'clock in the afternoon. He had been confined for several hours. It had felt like days.

There was also a text message and a voice mail on his cell phone. The text came from an unfamiliar number, but it was some kind of community alert: people were being asked to remain in their homes due to a medical emergency, and more info would be forthcoming. When Alex listened to the voice mail, a young woman was saying essentially the same thing.

So this really is some kind of widespread problem, Alex thought. Perhaps the right people were finally involved in fixing it.

After he dressed, he reviewed the assorted items gathered on the desk table.

There was a syringe, and vials of blood standing in a tray. An empty IV bag, too, the tube trailing from it; it appeared to have been used.

Alex wasn't a medical professional and had little knowledge of such things, but he knew that IV bags were used to administer fluids, and if this one had been recently employed, the logical conclusion was that it had been used to give something to *him*.

He gritted his teeth, anger tightening his chest.

He didn't find any notes, and didn't see any useful labels on the materials that gave him any indication of what Wayne had been doing. He would have to locate the man and demand answers.

The Beretta was loaded, and he still had the spare magazine. He didn't want to hurt anyone, but he had a right to know what the hell Wayne had done to him.

Gun in hand, Alex crept out of the room, into the corridor.

The hallway was dimly lit. To his left, it ended at the door that led to the entertainment area. On his right, there were two more doors, not including the one through which he had just exited.

He didn't see any indication of where his surprise rescuer, Wayne's daughter, had gone.

He opened the first one. It was a large storage area, the walls lined with wire shelving. All of the shelves were full of provisions: canned goods, paper towels, soaps, batteries, and more.

He also saw several containers of freeze dried meals, too, sealed in large black plastic tubs with the words, "Emergency Food Supply" printed on the front.

Wayne was one of those doomsday preparation guys, Alex realized. He could understand having provisions on hand for a few months, but Wayne had enough stocked away in here to sustain himself for *years*.

But hadn't Wayne himself developed symptoms of whatever mystery illness had plagued residents? All of that preparation he'd done might have been for naught.

Alex backed out of the room. He tried the other door.

It was locked.

Shrugging, Alex turned. He stepped along the hallway and opened the door at the far end, to enter the main area of the basement and the rest of the house.

It was steeped in shadows. The only light filtered from the hallway behind him.

"Is anyone home?" Alex asked. "Hello!"

No response. He heard just the hum of a refrigerator, and the soft patter of what sounded like rain.

The woman had to still be there, somewhere in the house, but considering her damaged state of mind, he couldn't expect a reply. He wasn't sure that he wanted to speak to her, either. Although she had set him free for some reason, her behavior was disturbing.

And what had happened to Clay, the soldier? Was he roaming free again? Muttering about insurgents and shooting people?

Alex searched the remainder of the basement, and found nothing out of place, and nothing that told him where anyone had gone. He headed upstairs.

No one was in the kitchen.

"Hello?" he said, and received no reply.

He looked out the front window. The world was awash in rain, the sky dark with thunderclouds.

He noted that Wayne's F-150 was no longer parked in the driveway. He checked in the garage. The Toyota Highlander was still stored inside.

Wayne apparently had gone, but where? Was he out there capturing more people to cage and pump with mystery fluids?

Alex searched the rest of the house. Even the young woman had left, and she had been there only a short while before. Had she been waiting for Alex to wake so she could free him?

Nothing made sense to him anymore.

He walked out of the house via the front door, onto the covered veranda. The pine-floored porch included a couple of Adirondack chairs fashioned from weathered teak.

Alex settled onto one of the chairs and checked his cell phone, which had recently buzzed. Someone had sent him another text message. It was a local phone number that he didn't recognize, but the message apparently had been sent to a list of mobile phone numbers.

> *govt is here we need 2 stick together*
> *meet at sanctuary book 7p back door*
> *tell only those u trust*
> *we cant let them kill us*

Alex frowned at the message.

The earlier messages had made it clear that some official agency was involved in handling the wave of illnesses that was sweeping through the community. Was that a bad thing if it meant people were getting treatment?

Perhaps it depended on what the government was actually doing.

He understood the meeting location: Sanctuary Book Shop. It was a cozy little bookstore not far from his frozen yogurt franchise on Main Street. He and Melissa had visited many times. The owners were a nice, elderly couple, former teachers from what he recalled.

We cant let them kill us . . .

That statement worried him.

He felt like the title character in "Rip Van Winkle." He had gone to sleep and awakened into a world he no longer recognized.

But one thing was clear: he knew where he was going next.

Chapter 19

The four of them loaded up in Deacon's Ford Expedition: Deacon, Jim, Dr. Bailey, and Emily. Deacon hoped for a non-eventful drive to their interviewee's residence, but upon consulting his marked-up community map, found that that home was located in a region that he hadn't yet tagged as a danger zone, or a safe area.

In other words, he had no idea what might happen.

The worst of the thunderstorm had passed, but heavy rain clouds hung in the sky, continuing to shed a persistent drizzle, pushing the late afternoon into a premature twilight. The ornately designed lamps outside the clubhouse had kicked on. Based solely on outward appearances, it looked like a normal Friday there—except for the complete absence of any residents visiting the facility.

Dr. Bailey's plan for the "soft" quarantine appeared to be working. Using their community broadcast system, Deacon's staff had transmitted Bailey's message urging residents to remain in their homes, and promising that more information would be forthcoming soon. Folks were either staying put or had left already.

Deacon was concerned about how Mr. Falcon would react to such a precautionary measure—the man had yet to summon him again—but he was more worried about Pops. The ornery old man had refused to leave, and his nurse's shift ended at seven o'clock that evening; Anita was a dedicated professional but she had let Deacon know in no uncertain terms that she was going home that night. He respected her decision, but that meant Pops would be alone in the apartment. Pops was moderately independent, and a damned good marksman, but Deacon still had concerns about his father being there on his own with so much uncertainty about what was really going on.

Putting the thoughts out of mind, he pulled the SUV out of the clubhouse parking lot.

"What normally happens in South Haven on a Friday night in the summer?" Dr. Bailey asked from the back seat. "This seems like such a well-planned community I'd imagine there are some organized social activities."

"A lot, actually," Deacon said. "There's a movie theater, several restaurants and bars. It gets pretty busy."

"Friday's are usually Screen on the Green, too," Emily said, beside Bailey. "That's on Main Street on the big lawn."

"Screen on the Green?" Bailey asked. "Is that a movie showing?"

"Popular movies," Jim said. "Family-friendly fare, of course. Think *Shrek, Ghost Busters, Back to the Future*. My wife and I usually go—she comes for the movies but I like the cheap food."

"He's a diehard cheapskate," Deacon said, inclining his head toward Jim. "But yeah, there're always some interesting food trucks on site running specials. Good stuff."

"It sounds like a cool place to live," Bailey said, gazing out the passenger window. "Such beautiful homes and landscaping, too. It's like something out of a magazine."

"It was, until recently," Emily said.

They were cruising through the residential neighborhoods, which, to Deacon's relief, had been empty. He slowed the SUV at a four-way intersection and checked both ways. Nothing on his right, but to his left, about a hundred yards away, he noticed a pack of perhaps a dozen dogs, of various breeds and sizes. The canines were trotting into a forested area. They moved with purpose, and that was when he saw the man bringing up the rear of the pack.

He recognized the guy, though he couldn't recall his name. Shaggy-haired and burly, he was in his twenties, lived in one of the residences with his affluent parents, and often did odd jobs around the community: including dog walking.

The guy was naked, and appeared to have leashes dangling from around his neck, like crude necklaces. None of the dogs was on leash but they trotted in step with him all the same.

One of them was a St. Bernard. *Jake,* Deacon thought, remembering the name of the dog that had mauled a young woman to death that morning and been just an inch from ripping out his throat. No doubt, it was the same dog. A chill spiked his spine.

"Dogs over there," Deacon said to the others. "I bet you dollars to donuts that every one of them is infected. And the guy, too."

"Jesus, someone out walking wouldn't stand a chance," Jim said.

"I'd like to examine one of the dogs, if we can get our hands on one," Bailey said. "We need to confirm whether the symptoms are exactly the same, if the bloodwork matches."

"If we can get our hands on one, sure," Deacon said. "But we're not messing with that pack."

The dogs and the walker disappeared from view. Deacon inched the vehicle through the intersection.

"And no one has seen any cats today?" Bailey asked. "I'm curious whether they are susceptible to what's happening."

"Haven't seen one," Deacon said. He added: "Yet. But you know cats, they're a lot more stealthy than dogs."

In the next block, Deacon spotted something ahead: a group of four individuals huddled in the middle of the street. Three men, one woman. They clustered in a circle, hands linked, heads bowed, as if performing a group prayer. One of the men was completely naked, while the others were in various stages of undress. The rain had plastered their hair to their heads, but they appeared oblivious to the inclement weather.

"What the hell is this?" Jim asked.

Deacon braked while they were still a safe distance from the group.

"We can take another route," Deacon said. "Avoid a dust up."

"No matter which way we go, we might run into some of these people," Emily said.

Deacon drummed the steering wheel for a few seconds. The only sound in the vehicle was the metronomic thump of the windshield wipers, the patter of rain, and the low hum of the air conditioner.

Emily, of course, had a perfectly sensible point. These people, the frenzied, lived in South Haven, and they weren't following the suggestion to stay indoors, because they didn't seem to comprehend spoken English any more. Yet somehow they communicated just fine with others afflicted with the same condition, perhaps by non-verbal means. Deacon didn't understand it and he didn't think Dr. Bailey did, either.

"Let's move." He pressed the accelerator, urging the SUV forward.

The group huddled in the middle of the street, and didn't turn at their approaching vehicle. As Deacon neared, he edged the vehicle to the right of them, giving them as wide a berth as possible. One of the Ford's right tires climbed over the curb.

"Oh, shit," Jim said.

Deacon mashed the gas pedal.

The naked man had spun to face them. He had something in his hand. Eyes wild and inflamed, he lobbed the object at them like a crazed bomb thrower.

Something smacked against the windshield. In the back seat, Emily screamed. The wipers stuttered to a halt as they hit the obstruction on the glass, and in spite of the obscuring rain Deacon thought he knew exactly what it was.

"It's a heart," he said. "They must have ripped it out of something. Or someone."

"Dear God," Dr. Bailey said in a hollow voice.

"Don't look behind us, guys," Jim said, though he had spun around in the seat, face twisted with terror. "But whatever that heart belonged to, they're on the ground with it now, *feeding*."

Deacon didn't want to look, but he couldn't resist a glance in the rearview mirror. His stomach clenched.

Are there any limits to this madness? he wondered. *Can this really get any worse?*

The wipers swept the bloody organ off the glass, leaving behind a crimson arc and bits of flesh.

***

Dunkirk, read the scrolling text underneath the ornately designed mailbox.

Deacon had brought the vehicle to a stop near the driveway of the residence. It was a two-story, contemporary Tudor-inspired home, complete with the steep pitch lines and decorative half-timbering. Deacon had passed the house many times while making his rounds through South Haven, and though he had never met the homeowners, had long admired the design of the residence.

All of the lights in the Dunkirk home appeared to be blazing. But the surrounding houses were dark, and Deacon didn't see anyone— human or canine—wandering outdoors.

"The wife's name is Patricia," Emily read from an index card. "The husband is sick; his name is Robert. She told us to come to the back door. I've got to text her now and let her know that we're here."

"What's the deal with the husband?" Jim asked. He gripped his shotgun across his chest.

"She wouldn't tell us," Dr. Bailey asked. "But she's clearly concerned about him finding out that strangers are in his house."

"Do all of us need to go in?" Deacon asked. "If we need to keep things quiet, maybe some of us should stay in the truck here and keep watch from afar."

"I can pull backup duty," Jim said. He tapped his walkie-talkie. "You get me on the radio if you need me, chief."

"I'll stay here, too," Emily said. "Dr. Bailey's the one who really needs to speak to her. By the way, she just texted me back. She says to come around back now. And not to knock on the door. She'll be looking for you. The gate is open."

Deacon checked to ensure his Glock was loaded, glanced at Bailey in the rearview mirror. She nodded at him and slung her leather bag across her shoulder.

"Be careful, you two," Jim said.

They got out of the SUV, and quietly shut the doors. Rain dripped off the bill of Deacon's cap.

Walking side by side, keeping along the perimeter of the damp front lawn, Deacon and Bailey approached the house.

A dog at the Craftsman-style house next door popped up like a jack-in-the-box in the front windows and started yapping, bouncing wildly on a sofa. It was a white Pomeranian, and from what Deacon could see the dog looked utterly normal. It was making a helluva racket, though, and he and Bailey increased their pace and reached the edge of the Dunkirk home, outside the canine's field of vision. The dog finally fell silent.

"I hope that didn't blow our cover," Bailey said, frowning behind them.

"Let's just keep moving."

A six-foot-high wooden fence encircled the back yard, and as the wife had promised, the gate was open. Deacon pulled aside the gate and let Bailey enter ahead of him. He left it open behind them.

A large deck fashioned from pine dominated the back yard. It was full of outdoor furniture, a gas barbecue grill, and an umbrella. A stone fire pit flanked by chairs stood farther away. A green tool shed occupied a far corner of the property.

Bailey approached the deck while Deacon hung back, hand resting on his pistol. He disliked that they had no idea what was going on with the husband. It was possible the man was relatively harmless, engaged in some pointless obsessive compulsive behavior like their pianist back at the clubhouse—or he could be a powder keg of violence waiting to explode.

As Bailey crossed the deck, the back door whispered open. A slim, red-haired woman, perhaps in her mid-thirties, emerged from inside. She wore a brown flannel blanket around her shoulders, like a shawl.

She closed the back door slowly, quietly. She looked terrified, but grateful that they had arrived. Her gaze traveled from Bailey, to Deacon, and when she spoke, she kept her voice at a whisper, even though she was outside her home.

"Let's go inside the tool shed," she said. "We can talk there."

***

Emily was stunned.

Her boyfriend, Zack, had finally responded to her numerous text messages.

Sitting in the back seat of the SUV, she stared at the glowing phone display and read his reply again.

hay watsup u cum 2 pool wanna talk 2 u k

His response perplexed her. Zack often sent texts using shorthand and emojis, but nothing like this messy jumble of words. She wondered what was going on with him.

Was he sick, like the others? Unable to express a clear thought?

In the front passenger seat, the other security guard, Jim, was talking on his cell phone. Emily didn't like to eavesdrop, but sitting in such close proximity to the man, it was impossible not to overhear his conversation. It sounded as if he were in a heated discussion with his wife, who wanted him to come home, and Jim kept insisting he had to stay because of his obligation to his fellow officers and the community.

Emily sympathized with the man's wife. Feeling an almost painful surge of longing, she called Zack. The phone rang and rang, and then dropped into the well of voice mail.

How could he not have answered the phone if he had texted her only a couple of minutes ago?

A disturbing image sprang to mind: an infected Zack fumbling with the cell phone as if it were a foreign object, unable to figure out the correct series of actions to accept an incoming call.

She called him again, and once again, received no answer. She had only his almost illegible text about coming to the pool.

She knew which swimming pool he meant. It was located at the South Haven water park, and was a favorite hangout of his during the summer months. She couldn't imagine the facility was open to residents in light of what was taking place in the community.

But he had clearly requested for her to join him there. And she ached to tell him, and only him, about her pregnancy.

She gazed out the SUV's rain-smeared passenger window. The darkening world was quiet, at the moment.

Her hand slithered to the door handle as if it had a purpose of its own. Her fingers tingled.

Don't be a dummy, a voice said in her mind, not surprisingly, her mother's stern voice. *You go out there alone and you'll die, like a dummy, and no one will feel sorry for you.*

With a deep sigh, Emily pulled her hand away from the door.

***

"I thought Rob had caught only a flu bug," Patricia said. "When he woke up this morning he said he had a headache, and it was so intense, like a migraine, that he didn't go to the office. He was running a fever, too, about a hundred and two. He felt really awful."

The three of them had gathered in the tool shed. A single, battery-powered light bulb glowed overhead. Lawn equipment hung from hooks fastened to the unpainted walls: a leaf blower, garden shears, shovel, rake, and other implements. There was nowhere to sit. Deacon leaned against the doorway, and had kept the door ajar, giving him a truncated view of the rain-drizzled world outside.

Bailey was using her digital voice recorder to capture their conversation. She led Patricia through all of the questions which, by then, had become commonplace to the situation: what triggered the onset of symptoms? Had her husband taken any medications to fight the flu? What sort of unusual behavior was he demonstrating? When exactly had it begun?

Tears came to Patricia's eyes as she continued to speak: "Rob, he's a DIY sort of guy, he loves woodworking and home improvement projects. I mean, he subscribes to a bunch of magazines, reads blogs, goes to The Home Depot every weekend, the whole kit and caboodle. He's got it into his head today that he's going to remodel the interior of the house. *All of it.* Today. He's been demolishing everything with a sledgehammer. When I asked him to stop he screamed at me. His words were slurred, I could barely understand him, and the look in his eyes . . ." She pressed her hand against her forehead, tears tracking down her cheeks. "What's wrong with him? Can you help?"

"We're working on that," Bailey said. She handed the woman a fistful of tissues. "But I've got to get more information. Where did your husband go this week? Did he travel out of town, for business perhaps?"

Sniffling, Patricia shrugged. "All he did was go to work in the city. He's an engineer. It was a totally normal week until this morning."

"What about last weekend?" Bailey asked. "Go anywhere?"

"We're homebodies, basically. We went to the town square last Friday night, but we almost always do. That's why we moved to

South Haven in the first place, for the sense of community. We like to do things here, there's always something to do."

"You watched a film at the Screen on the Green?" Bailey asked.

"Yeah." She nodded. "I don't remember the movie."

Bailey turned to Deacon. "This Screen on the Green event, how many people normally attend?"

"Several hundred," Deacon said. "I don't often go, but Jim does, and I've always got a couple of staff on duty there to keep things under control. Folks usually behave themselves, though. Someone might have a bit too much to drink but nothing serious has ever happened."

The doctor's large hazel eyes were bright. Deacon figured she was onto something, but he had no idea what it might be.

"Did you eat or drink anything at the event?" Bailey asked. "If so, do you remember what you and your husband consumed?"

"We both had tacos from one of the food trucks," she said. "I don't remember what we drank. Do you think something in the food made him sick?"

As Bailey started to answer, a loud shattering noise came from the house. Deacon shouldered open the shed door to get a better view.

One of the big back-yard facing windows had been broken. Shards of glass hung in the frame. As Deacon watched, another window exploded, and he glimpsed a shadowy figure swinging a blunt object inside the house.

The husband's doing a demo on his own house with a sledgehammer, Deacon thought.

Crying, Patricia pushed past Bailey and Deacon. "He's going to destroy our home. Can't someone do anything?"

"Without hurting him?" Deacon shook his head. "No, ma'am. Sorry."

"You can come back to the clubhouse with us," Bailey said. "It's safe there."

Shaking her head, eyes full of tears, the woman ran back toward her house, nearly fell on the wet grass, righted herself, reached the back door. She disappeared inside.

"She's putting her safety at risk going back in there," Bailey said.

Deacon heard the husband and wife shouting at each other. During his early days on the police force, he had handled his share of domestic disturbance calls, and the interaction he overheard between the woman and her frenzied husband sounded uncomfortably similar—and made him feel powerless to intervene.

"We can't stop her." Deacon shrugged. "She went back in by choice, she's staying by choice. You gave her an alternative."

"I know. But I feel as if we should do something."

"If he was going to hurt her, he would have done it already. It seems like some of these frenzied are obsessive, but they don't attack unless provoked. If his wife stays out of his way he might wear himself out eventually." He closed the shed door. "I saw a lightbulb go off in your eyes when you were questioning her. You figure something out?"

"Let's get back to the clubhouse," Bailey said. "I need to run an examination on a friend of ours."

"Who?" Deacon asked.

***

Back at the clubhouse, Jim paced in one of the conference rooms that the CDC had overhauled into a makeshift clinic. There was a narrow bed on wheels, and various monitoring devices sitting on tables and hanging from metallic stands. Deacon found it hard to imagine that only a day or so ago, someone had probably used this room to hold a discussion about catering a wedding reception. His life prior to today was beginning to feel like a dream—and Bailey wanting to run tests on Jim didn't help.

"You want to examine me?" Jim asked. Redness bloomed in his cheeks. "Why? I'm not sick, dammit."

"The doctor's got a theory," Deacon said. "Just hear her out, all right?"

"It's more of a gut feeling at this point, guys, to be honest." Dr. Bailey slid on a surgical mask and a pair of latex gloves, and began to set out a series of medical instruments on a stainless steel tray. "I suspect the Screen on the Green event that took place last Friday is the key to what's going on in South Haven."

"But I'm not sick!" Jim said again.

"I haven't determined exactly what happened there," Dr. Bailey said. "Was it a pathogen in the food provided by one of the food trucks? Was a person or animal infected with a virus and passed it on to others present? I don't know. But this event is the one thing that hundreds of residents recently attended, and there's a fair chance that if we look there, we'll find answers."

"Zack went last week," Emily suddenly said. She looked to Deacon as if she were on the verge of tears. "My boyfriend, Zack. I don't know if he's infected, I haven't been able to talk to him, but . . . he's not behaving normally."

"I think it's all horseshit, but I'll play along," Jim said. "What kind of tests do you want to do?"

"Let's start with a basic physical," Dr. Bailey said. She glanced at Deacon and Emily. "Can we get some privacy please?"

"Hell, let 'em stay in, I don't have anything to hide." Jim waved his hand. "I want to get this over with."

While Deacon and Emily watched, Dr. Bailey guided Jim through a physical examination. She had him step on a scale to note his body weight. Afterward, while Jim sat in a plastic chair, she measured his heart rate and blood pressure. She checked inside his ears with an otoscope, and then used a penlight to peer inside both of his nostrils.

She paused. "Your nasal cavity is inflamed. Do you have a cold?"

Jim shrugged. "No. And I'm not a cokehead, either, so don't get any ideas."

"All of the frenzied we've seen, they've got blood dribbling from their nose, like a slow leak," Deacon said. "I'm no doctor but it's something I've noticed."

Bailey asked Jim to tilt his head all the way backward so she could get a clearer look. Bending over him, she lifted the tip of his nose and peered deep inside.

Deacon and Emily glanced at each other. The anxiety in her eyes matched the uneasiness that curdled his stomach.

"You've got something attached to the lining of your nasal cavity," Dr. Bailey said.

"What?" Jim said, his Adam's apple bobbing. "That's bullshit."

"It's miniscule, barely more than a speck, but it looks . . . well, it looks like a bug."

Chapter 20

Alex walked to the meeting at the Sanctuary Book Shop.
Without question, it was the most bizarre walk he'd ever experienced during his forty-plus years on this earth.

The low, cloudy sky continued to shed a persistent drizzle. Alex had found a midnight-blue rain poncho in Wayne's hallway closet, and slipped it on before he left the house. He considered taking the Toyota Highlander parked in the garage, too—the keys hung on a hook in the kitchen—but even on a day as strange and violent as that one, when he had revisited some of his old ways, grand theft auto held no appeal for him.

So he traveled by foot. And, he saw things.

He saw a pack of dogs roam across the street, barely fifty feet away. There were over a dozen of them, comprised of various breeds, most of them wearing collars, all of them clearly infected with the same mystery illness plaguing many of the residents: eyes crusted with inflammation, blood dribbling from their nostrils. A burly, naked man walked with the dogs, like some dog whisperer from hell, leashes swinging from his thick neck like cheap necklaces. The man craned his head in Alex's direction, sniffed the air as if testing for his scent, and then turned away as though Alex held no interest for him and his canine horde.

Alex eased his hand off his pistol.

Farther along, he passed a man cutting the grass of a front yard. In the past, the spectacle of a man trimming his lawn while it rained would have been only mildly interesting—but this man was as naked as the day he was born. He pushed the mower methodically back and forth, rain slicking his diseased skin, inflamed eyes focused on the grass ahead of him.

Alex wasn't sure if the guy noted his presence as he passed by. He was oblivious to everything except his lawn.

Suddenly, Alex heard feet splashing through puddles behind him. He looked over his shoulder, hand reflexively moving to his gun.

It was a trio of young women. They were jogging in the middle of the road. All of them had the lean muscularity gained only from a rigid attention to diet and endless hours of exercise.

All of them were naked, too, their bodies mapped with festering lesions.

If he were another kind of man, he might have ogled the ladies, snapped a photo with his phone, but he found no pleasure in what he was seeing. Quickly, he moved out of their path and lowered his head.

None of the women paid him any mind whatsoever; he might have been merely a car parked on the street. But as they jogged past, bare feet slapping the wet pavement, he picked up snatches of their conversation.

"Mile another . . . feel so good the burn . . ."

"Wedding . . . lose pounds ten gotta . . ."

"Said I was fat . . . asshole . . . size zero here I come . . ."

Shaking his head, Alex kept walking.

He didn't understand what was going on with these people. Some of them boiled over in fits of uncontrollable violence, such as his wife, and the soldier. Others, like the man cutting his lawn and the jogging women, seemed harmless, but bent on mindlessly pursuing obsessive behavior.

But he knew one thing for sure: all of them were sick.

He wondered if he were sick, too.

He didn't have burning, crusted-over eyes, and his skin was normal, but he worried all the same that something terrible was happening to him.

***

Alex arrived on the scene a full thirty minutes before the announced meeting, but he didn't enter the Sanctuary Book Shop. Instead, he watched from inside his frozen yogurt shop, where he had parked a chair beside the large front window.

Before making his presence known at the bookstore, he wanted to get some idea of the nature of the gathering.

The town square was ominously quiet and empty for a Friday evening. Usually, even in rainy weather, the crowds would be out, armed with umbrellas and rain slickers as they trundled about the various shops. South Haven residents—those of them not sick anyway—must have opted to heed the emergency broadcast message to remain indoors.

Alex had dispensed a swirled heap of vanilla yogurt into the largest serving cup that his shop offered, decorated it with a drizzle of strawberries and whipped cream, and ate it with a spoon while he waited. He hadn't eaten anything in hours, and decided a blast of sugar and carbs would serve his body well.

It felt strange to be sitting alone in his darkened store. He felt out of place, less like the owner and more like an intruder who had found a door open after hours and decided to help himself to a treat.

After today, for multiple reasons, he would never again be able to go back to business as usual.

At a quarter to seven, people started to filter into the town square. From a distance, they looked normal, Alex noted with relief. They wore clothes and moved like regular folk. Many of them wore dust masks. Although the entrance to the bookstore faced the square, per the text message instructions, no one entered via the front door; they disappeared around the corner of the building, going to the back entrance.

Alex finished off his yogurt, left his shop, and crossed the street.

Standing at the end of a row of darkened storefronts, the front of the Sanctuary Book Shop was dark, too, the large windows covered with blinds. Alex went around the corner of the building, stepping around pools of water that had collected on the pavement.

There was an access road at the rear of the building that served all of the businesses located along that side of the town square. The back door of the book shop was propped open. A tall, barrel-chested man with a floppy fringe of white hair stood at the doorway. He wore a plaid shirt with the sleeves rolled up, displaying a pair of well-muscled forearms; rumpled jeans, and work boots. A holstered pistol rested on his hip. He also wore a dust mask and he was distributing them to those entering the shop if they weren't already wearing one.

Alex recognized him as the owner of the bookstore. Stan.

"Alex?" he asked when Alex drew near. Watching Alex closely, as if scrutinizing him for signs of infection, he nodded in the direction of Alex's shop. "You own the frozen yogurt shop across the way."

"That's me."

"Thanks for answering the call. Put this on." He offered Alex a dust mask. "Did you tell anyone about this meeting?"

"Everyone I've seen until now has been sick, so no."

Stan nodded gravely. "We're on the side of liberty. There may not be many of us but our cause is just. Head on inside and we'll get started in a few minutes."

Alex slipped on the dust mask and threaded inside the bookstore. About a dozen folding chairs had been arranged around a mahogany lectern, and most of them had been filled. Alex recognized several faces, in spite of the masks everyone donned. They were people who owned businesses in the community. Stan, he realized, must have sent his meeting invitation to a phone distribution list of business folk in South Haven.

Alex eased into a chair. There was little conversation amongst the group. Everyone looked exhausted, sad, or anxious. Alex wondered how many of them had lost loved ones, such as he had, to this strange illness plaguing their community.

A few minutes later, at seven o'clock sharp, Stan came inside and stood at the lectern. He pulled away his dust mask, letting it rest at the bottom of his blunt-edged chin.

"Thanks all of you for coming," Stan said. He had the deep, mellifluous voice of a radio show host. "Our time may be short so let's get down to business. People in South Haven are getting sick. It started yesterday as far as anyone knows. It seems to be some strain of virus, more on that later. Our children, our spouses, our neighbors—everyone knows someone who's been affected. We don't know why, but the virus is turning them into people we don't recognize. It's in their eyes, on their skin. Most of all, it's in their brains."

"Right," someone said.

"If there's a cure we don't know what it is. When you encounter someone sick the only sensible alternative is to get away from them. Not all of them are violent, initially, but they can suddenly turn homicidal with little provocation." He paused, and his blue eyes got misty. "I had to leave my wife because she tried to gut me with a wine bottle opener."

Alex thought about Melissa, coming at him with barbering shears, and felt his chest tighten with emotion.

"Now the CDC is on site: Centers for Disease Control and Prevention, as they call themselves." Stan paused, favoring them with a gentle jes' folks smile. "Don't be fooled by appearances and fancy acronyms, friends. This is an agency of the federal government. They are going to cage us inside South Haven with a federally-ordered quarantine. They will get full military support to enforce it. Anyone who tries to leave South Haven will be shot on sight."

There were a few gasps in the room, expressions of disbelief.

"But I'm an American citizen," a woman said. Alex recognized her as the owner of a barre studio on Main. Her hair was pulled back into a severe bun and with her red-rimmed eyes, she looked as if she hadn't slept in days. "They can't hold us here against our will and kill us if we try to leave!"

"Is that what you believe?" Stan shook his head sadly. "I promise you, friends and neighbors, once quarantine is declared, all of your precious rights as an American citizen will be promptly suspended. We will be under martial law."

"What are we supposed to do?" Alex asked. "From what you're saying, it sounds like we're stuck dealing with this, whether we're sick or not. Do you have an escape plan or something?"

"No." Stan shook his head firmly. "We don't run. We have businesses here, all of us. Most of us live here, too. We fight for our freedom. The government *created* this virus. It's a biologically engineered weapon they originally designed to infiltrate terror cells in the Middle East."

"How do you know that?" someone asked.

"Don't be a fool," Stan said, his voice booming. "That is what our government does. They spend billions of dollars annually on weapons R&D, like any other world power. I was in the Army, in my less-enlightened youth. I know how they operate. They've always wanted to create the perfect biological weapon. This virus is the handiwork of the government scientists."

"If you're right," Alex said. "How do we fight for our freedom against the military? We don't have the people, the weapons."

"We've got our minds." Stan pointed to his skull. "And our courage." He tapped his heart. "In times of civil unrest, the forces of resistance have always managed to prevail so long as they utilize their God-given strengths. I have a plan, friends."

Alex found himself leaning forward in his chair. In his peripheral vision, he noticed others were intensely focused on Stan's message, too. He wasn't sure he believed that the government was behind this, and Stan still hadn't supplied any evidence of his claim, but in the absence of any other theory, maybe they had to go along with it.

"What do you think we should do?" someone asked.

A smile flickered across Stan's face. He took a quick sip from a bottle of water.

Very slowly, he began to lay out his plan.

Chapter 21

"It's a tick," Hannah announced.

Hannah's CDC team, as well as Deacon, and the others, had gathered in the main conference room that they were employing as their command post. Most of the group stood, eager to hear her findings. Jim, bless his heart, sat on a chair in the corner, a towel pressed to his no-doubt aching nose.

She hadn't enjoyed using the speculum and the tweezers to extract the tiny tick from Jim's nasal cavity, and the arachnid had been tightly attached. It had required a determined—but delicate— effort to pry it loose. The bug's barely-visible legs had wriggled as she placed it on a glass tray, and Jim's nose had immediately begun bleeding from the puncture wound.

Other than the bleeding, Jim hadn't shown any signs of infection. Hannah was hopeful that they had removed the parasite before it had wrought any permanent damage to his nervous system.

She had placed the tick under a microscope and performed a rudimentary layman's analysis, combined with some quick reading of online resources, hoping for an instant explanation—which, not surprisingly, she hadn't found. In her line of work, solutions never came that easily.

"I don't have a strong background in entomology or parasitology," she said to the assembled gathering. "None of us do, which is why I'm working to find us an expert who can give us more information. But I know this much, and perhaps some of you do as well: a tick is an ectoparasite. They feed on blood, primarily from mammals and birds.

They move through four life cycles: egg, larva, nymph, and adult. In the larval stage, a tick will have six legs; it grows an additional two legs in the later phases. The tick we've found is a larva.

"Ticks transmit a range of diseases. Most of you are probably familiar with Lyme disease. Symptoms of Lyme disease? Fever, headaches, fatigue, eventually leading to joint pain, swelling, and other complications. Some of the same initial symptoms we've seen with the individuals in South Haven, but for obvious reasons, what we're dealing with here is different than Lyme disease. In my initial research, I haven't found anything like what we're seeing, and that's why we're going to talk to an entomologist who can tell us what we're facing."

Hannah paused. A mixture of hope and worry glistened in the eyes of the group watching her.

"Have we isolated the infection site?" a member of her team asked.

"Our working theory is that there was a social event in the community on Friday, July 8th, called Screen on the Green, in the town square. The town square contains about two acres of grass and shrubbery, and on the night of the event, I think the grass was infested with tick larvae. Larvae could have attached themselves to people and animals—dogs, apparently—unseen."

"We're talking about hundreds of these things, aren't we?" Deacon asked, raising his hand from the back of the room. "We treat common areas with insecticides pretty regularly during the summer. How the hell did the grass wind up crawling with so many of them?"

"We don't know," Hannah said. "We've got to answer that question. I'll need some members of our team to visit the town square and try to collect samples."

"A bug like this, that causes so much damage," Deacon continued. "Doesn't make any sense for it to suddenly show up, here, in a spot that's gonna be full of people one particular evening."

Hannah suspected where the security guard commander was headed with this line of reasoning, and she didn't like it one bit.

"Let's get more information before we jump to conclusions," she said. "We've yet to even determine exactly which species of tick is at work here."

"Fair enough," he said, and he thankfully left his thoughts unspoken.

Nevertheless, Hannah had known exactly what he'd wanted to say.

Someone had introduced this dangerous creature to South Haven on purpose.

***

Deacon couldn't remember the last time he had been so eager to work. Although it was past seven o'clock in the evening, putting his shift at over twelve hours for that day, and he should have been thoroughly exhausted, he was as charged as if he'd taken a double dose of amphetamines.

They'd finally had a real break in their case. Dr. Bailey's hunch had proved correct. While she worked with her team on identifying the exact classification of the arachnid, Deacon was going to figure out how the hell it had gotten there in the first place.

He didn't merely suspect malicious intent behind the arrival of the tick. He was convinced of it. This was a crime, and dealing with crime was a particular talent of his that had lain dormant for much too long.

After the meeting had broken up, he approached Jim. His partner continued to sit on a chair in the corner, looking miserable.

"You ready to roll?" he asked Jim. "We've got work to do."

"You aren't scared of me?" Jim dabbed at his nose with the towel.

"What the hell are you talking about?"

Jim scowled. "That goddamn bug was stuck in my nose. What if I'm sick?"

"Do you feel sick?" Deacon asked.

"No, but some creature hibernating in my nose, sucking my blood .
. . it had to have done *something* to me." Jim shook his head, his eyes
haunted. "I don't trust myself anymore."

"If you start to act like a whacko, I'll slap some cuffs on you and
throw you in the holding pen at HQ. I only ask that you don't strip
down to your birthday suit. I don't think I could survive the sight of
that."

"Right." A smile creased Jim's lips. "No way in hell you'll see
that, chief."

"Get your ass in gear then. We've got a job to do."

"Roger that." Nodding grimly, Jim rose. "Lead the way."

"My man." Deacon clapped Jim on the shoulder. Before leaving,
they approached Dr. Bailey, who was deep in discussion with members of her team.

Bailey was alarmed at their leaving, but agreed with the im-
portance of their task. She herself was dispatching two of her team
members to the town square, to gather additional specimens of the tick
larvae, and Deacon convinced her to hold off sending them out until
he got another of his security staff to provide protection.

He left Bailey with a walkie-talkie that she could use to reach them
in the event of an emergency. As he passed the device to her, their
fingers touched. Deacon felt a spark akin to a gentle ripple of electricity.

Was there a glimmer of attraction in her gaze, too? A lingering
look just a beat too long to be merely professional courtesy?

Regardless, it was definitely not the time for a love connection.
Maybe later. If nothing else, the possibility gave him something to
look forward to, a hope for the future.

As he and Jim headed for the doors, Emily caught up to them.

"Can I come with you?" she asked.

There was an urgency in her gaze that threw Deacon for a loop.

"Is this about your boyfriend?" he asked.

"I got a text message from him. He wants me to meet him at the pool."

"Isn't the pool closed?" Jim said. "Why's he asking you to meet him there?"

"I . . . I don't know." She nibbled her bottom lip. "I'm not totally comfortable about it, but I need to talk to him, if I can."

"I promised you earlier that I'd help out," Deacon said. "We're heading to HQ. The water park is on the way. Come on."

***

The South Haven aquatic facility was called Poseidon Park. It featured a towering, twisting, outdoor water slide that rivaled a commercial attraction, a large splash pad area full of colorful, nautically-themed fountains, play and leisure pools of various depths, and an indoor Olympic swimming pool.

During hours of normal operation, the outdoor lighting would have been activated, but when they arrived, every lamp was dark. As Deacon parked in front of the facility, he noticed a handful of people floating in the water in the leisure pool, their bodies shrouded in gloom.

He unfolded the South Haven map he'd been carrying in his pocket and circled the aquatic center, identifying it as another danger zone.

"The park's closed," Deacon said. "But it definitely isn't empty."

"Zack was on the swim team in high school," Emily said. "He was really good, actually, was named All-State. He likes to do laps in the pool inside."

"If he's in there now," Jim said, nodding toward the darkened building, "then he's probably sick, sweetheart."

"I have to see for myself," Emily said.

Deacon turned around in his seat and studied Emily. Her brown eyes were watery, but held a steely resolve. He would be wasting his time to try to persuade her to leave this alone.

Girl has spunk, he thought. But spunk or not, walking alone into a virtual horde of infected folks was foolish.

"If you're set on doing this, then I'll go with you." Deacon switched off the engine. "Jim?"

"I'll keep an eye out," Jim said.

Deacon and Emily climbed out of the vehicle. The drizzle had ceased, but the pavement remained wet, rivulets of water glistening in the glow of the nearby street lamps.

An eight-foot tall, chain-link fence encircled the entire property. As he and Emily moved toward the main entrance, Deacon saw someone crawl out of the wading pool, and from the distance it looked like a sea lion, but it was only a man. Morbidly obese, and completely naked, he waddled toward them on all fours, pressed his pockmarked face against the fence, and squinted at them with his inflamed eyes.

"*Not allowed kids . . . not allowed . . .*" he muttered in a gravelly tone.

Deacon had no clue what the man was talking about and suspected he probably didn't either. He looked away.

The glass double doors of the entrance were unlocked. Deacon drew his Glock, and gave Emily his flashlight.

They went inside.

***

Emily knew this wasn't going to end well. She knew that Zack was almost certainly sick, and that they might never find a cure for this condition that plagued so many of the residents. But she had to see this through.

None of the lights were on inside Poseidon Park. As she and Deacon stepped into the darkened lobby, she swept the flashlight beam back and forth.

She had been inside the facility many times, probably once a week, with Zack, who came there several times a week to put in his laps. She was a good swimmer, too. The familiar odor of chlorinated water, wafting on the air in the lobby, comforted her.

"This way," she said to Deacon, who kept pace close behind her.

The pool area was to the right of the lobby, past the entrance to the locker rooms. Floor to ceiling windows provided a view of the enormous swimming pool.

She shone the flashlight through the glass. She saw flashes of movement beyond the window: there were several people inside.

Her heart knocked. If all of these people were sick, would they attack? Or were they the merely obsessive ones, there to wade in the water?

"He's going to be in there," Emily said.

"I'm ready," Deacon said. "Let's turn on the lights when we get in there so we can see what's going on."

Emily pulled open the glass door. A blast of warm, chlorine-scented air rushed out. She stepped inside, her shoes squeaking on the wet tile floor.

To the right of the doorway, she located the bank of light switches. She flipped on one of them; pale light flickered into life.

Some of the people groaned, as if she had interrupted a sleepover. But they continued on with their activities, such as they were: floating in the shallow end, wading aimlessly, diving artlessly at the deep end of the pool.

It's like a zombie pool party, she thought.

Then she spotted Zack. He was in one of the roped-off swim lanes. He was performing a breaststroke, slicing through the water like a great, swift fish. He wore his favorite neon-blue swim goggles, and his hair was tucked underneath a black silicone swim cap.

"Zack," she said, and waved.

He continued to stroke through the water and showed no indication that he had heard her. Carefully, she navigated her way around the edge of the pool, Deacon at her heels.

"Folks aren't paying us much mind," Deacon said in a low voice edged with caution. "At the moment. We'll hope that holds."

Emily barely heard what he was saying. She didn't want to believe that Zack was sick. He was only swimming laps, right, like he often did each day. Why did that have to mean he was infected?

She reached his lane. She saw his cell phone on the floor, lying in a puddle of water. She picked it up. The screen was locked, but the display was full of text messages and notifications of unanswered calls, from her phone, and others, probably his parents.

Had Zack sent his message to her just before he had entirely lost his ability to function logically?

He was at the other end of the pool, cutting through the water with ease. How long had he been doing laps? Hours?

He reached the opposite end of the pool and flipped around, as if he were competing in a meet. Rapidly, he swam toward her.

"Zack!" she shouted. She waved her arms. "Please, Zack, I've got to talk to you!"

Zack drew near, bobbing up and down in the water, and as he did, she saw the lesions on his long, muscular arms, the reddened sores on his forehead under the edge of his swim cap. Her heart twisted, and she had to bite down on her knuckle to keep herself from screaming.

Zack swam to the lip of the pool. She noticed he still wore the silver necklace she had given him last Christmas. A matching silver locket was attached to the chain, the heart-shaped pendant containing a snapshot of the two of them in an old-fashioned shopping mall photo booth.

"It's me, Zack, Emily," she said. "I've got something important to tell you, please listen to me."

He paused, hands on the rim of the pool, goggles still in place. She needed to see his eyes, those beloved green eyes. She needed to see if he comprehended what she was telling him.

Kneeling, she reached forward to lift away his goggles.

"Hey," Deacon. "Don't do that!"

Snarling, Zack seized her by the wrist.

Emily screamed. "Zack, no!"

Zack yanked her toward him with savage force. She lost her balance and catapulted into the swimming pool.

Water rushed into her nostrils and poured down her throat. She gagged.

Zack wrapped his arm around her neck, in a virtual headlock. He paddled forward, legs kicking furiously.

She batted her hands against him. She couldn't get to the surface to get air.

He was her boyfriend, the father of her unborn child, and he was going to drown her before she could even share the news with him.

As if from a great distance, she heard a thunderous, muffled boom, and thought: *someone's shooting.*

And the water around her suddenly turned red.

***

Deacon didn't want to shoot the kid, but he didn't have any choice.

The boyfriend, Zack, dragged Emily under, and Deacon didn't know exactly what the kid intended, but he was drowning the girl. She was fighting to get away, to get up for air, and he just kept her head underwater while he swam away, like a shark departing with its prey between its teeth.

Deacon went for the headshot, and it was tough to get a good look because the guy kept bobbing up and down in the water. The first round he fired missed, causing a tremendous splash, water raining over Deacon.

The second round plowed squarely into the back of the guy's head. Petals of blood bloomed from the ruptured skull, and the kid's limbs went limp. Emily broke the surface of the water. She saw her dead boyfriend and let out a garbled scream that speared Deacon's heart.

I had no choice, he thought. *You've gotta believe that.*

The other frenzied in the pool area, a dozen or so of them, had stopped their obsessive behavior and taken notice of the struggle. Intense gazes shifted from the dead boy, to Deacon, to Emily, to the dead boy, back to Deacon.

Deacon got a sinking feeling in the pit of his stomach. Their muttered words washed over him.

". . . killed him . . . him shot . . ."

". . . execution . . ."

". . . cop dirty . . . "

". . . get him . . ."

In the pool, Emily cradled her boyfriend to her, a pinkish mixture of water and blood swirling around them. She was whispering to him. She had removed his swim goggles and was gently stroking his face.

"Emily!" Deacon shouted. "We've gotta get the hell out of here now!"

Weeping, she continued to whisper to her boyfriend. Deacon backed away from the swimming pool.

Moving almost as one, the frenzied began to clamber out of the water. All of them were naked. Deacon felt, bizarrely, as if he had stumbled into a nudists' pool party.

"Emily!" he said. "I am leaving!"

Finally, the girl snapped out of her fog and let go of her boyfriend. He floated away on a raft of blood, face tilted to the ceiling. She swam to the edge of the pool and pulled herself out of the water, her clothes dripping. Her face was reddened, eyes full of tears. A silver necklace dangled from her clenched fist.

By then, Deacon had retreated to the doorway. The frenzied gathered into a pack, as if drawn together by a single hive mind, people of various ages, all of them dripping wet, bare bodies mapped with sores, eyes crusted over but simmering with rage.

"... *get him* ..."

"... *pig* ..."

"... *execute* ..."

Emily ran to him, nearly slipped on a patch of water, and regained her balance in time to avoid a fall. She skirted the edge of the gathering mob, but they ignored her.

"I'm sorry," Deacon said. He didn't know what else to say.

She wiped damp hair out of her eyes. "Let's . . . let's just get out of here, okay?"

The mob roared, and charged after them.

Deacon led the way into the lobby. It was dimly lit from light spilling out from the indoor pool area.

But Deacon heard something. Someone was coming around the corner. He heard the quick patter of wet feet against tile, and saw a mass of shambling shadows on the corridor wall.

More of them, Deacon thought.

He hustled to the entrance, Emily close behind. Gun drawn, he whammed open the doors with his shoulder.

It was raining again, a violent downpour, as if gashes had been slashed in the sky.

Deacon flung water out of his eyes with his sleeve and yanked down his cap, rain dripping off the bill. He could barely see five feet ahead of him, but he could make out the hulking shape of the SUV, still parked at the curb, and that was all that mattered.

Behind them, the frenzied were bursting out of the facility's doors.

The people who, earlier, had been in the outdoor water play area had vanished. Deacon wondered if they had joined the growing mob of the infected, all of them unified in their intent to kill him.

Deacon and Emily raced to the vehicle, wings of water splashing from their feet.

Jim, God bless him, saw them coming and propped open the front passenger side door. He was hunched behind the wheel, wisps of smoke curling from the exhaust as the engine idled.

Deacon lifted Emily with one arm and swung her around into the passenger seat. He climbed in after her.

"Go!" Deacon said

But Jim had already hit the gas.

The Ford lurched forward, the sudden momentum causing the passenger door to swing shut and clip Deacon's foot as he dragged it inside. He barely felt the pain, his attention riveted on their pursuers.

The mob had gotten bigger, and it was coming.

Chapter 22

The bogeyman finally had a name.

"*Ixodes insanus*," the entomologist announced to Hannah and their team. His name was Dr. William McKee. When Hannah had sent out scanned, magnified images of the tick to the CDC's worldwide e-mail distribution list of specialists, McKee was the first and only one who had responded with a definitive answer. She promptly scheduled an emergency video conference call over an encrypted connection.

A tanned, bald-headed man in his seventies, Dr. McKee's profile filled the large flat screen TV in the clubhouse meeting room. The background behind the doctor was a brownish desert landscape that looked like a snapshot from a postcard; he was calling from his home in Mesa, Arizona.

"Or, in layman's language: the Peruvian Frenzy Tick," Dr. McKee said.

Hannah glanced at her team members who had gathered around the display. None of their faces registered any recognition of what the doctor had told them.

"We're not familiar with it," she said. "How common is this?"

Dr. McKee chuckled. "Not common at all, I'm afraid. To the best of my knowledge—and I would know better than anyone else in the world—*ixodes insanus* has never been found outside of its natural habitat. Its habitat, such as it is, amounts to only a thirty-four mile region of largely uncharted Amazon rainforest in southeastern Peru."

Hannah's mind reeled. Some exotic tick from the jungle had found its way to Atlanta, of all places. Deacon's theory of a deliberate infestation was sounding awfully plausible.

"But it's here now," Hannah said. "In metro Atlanta. We're developing our own theories, but I'd like to hear yours. Any feasible explanation of how it could have gotten here?"

"It's clear: someone brought it there," Dr. McKee said. "There is no other reasonable explanation. Understand, Dr. Bailey—*ixodes insanus* resides in an area of Peru inhabited exclusively by indigenous, *uncontacted* Indian tribes."

"Tribes isolated from outside civilization," Hannah said.

"Precisely. These tribes have dwelled there in the jungle for several hundred years. Many of the insects, creatures, and plant-life in this region have yet to be classified. We know about the Peruvian Frenzy Tick due solely to work I completed earlier in my career."

"You were there?" someone on Hannah's team asked.

"Indeed. It was a rare visit by outsiders, sponsored by an international health organization, and reluctantly allowed by the Peruvian government. I was there with colleagues and a guide for two weeks. We saw many unusual things. This rare species was the most remarkable of them all." Dr. McKee's blue eyes glimmered with something that approached awe. "We have the Australian paralysis tick, a species I've also studied, and which produces a neurotoxin that has damaging neurological effects, but there is nothing like this one I found in Peru."

"Do the indigenous tribes have immunity?" Hannah asked.

"I'm afraid not. The tick is revered amongst them and its venom is applied to blow darts and used against enemies. The venom may take several days to have an effect on the target, but once it does, the infected individual becomes a grave threat to his tribe. He may attack without provocation. He may engage in obsessive behavior that can wreak havoc in a close-knit community ruled by belief in superstition and magic, where odd activity can incite a panic.

"I learned these things through an interpreter, of course," he said. "But I did witness the tick's venom in action—we tested it on a rhesus monkey. In hindsight, it was an incredibly foolish, rash decision. The infected animal tore my arm out of its socket and to this day, forty years later, I still haven't regained a full range of motion." Dr. McKee touched his left shoulder and gently massaged it. "Naturally, we euthanized the animal, which in itself was quite an ordeal, even with a team of several of us trying to pull it off."

"Is there any treatment for someone infected by the venom?" Hannah asked.

"Regrettably, no," McKee said. "Shortly after the expedition concluded, my research project lost its funding, and no follow up studies have been conducted. There is no anti-venom. A heavy dose of narcotics may blunt the worst effects of the venom, but then you'd have to get near enough to the patient to sedate them in the first place. No easy task."

It wasn't what Hannah had wanted to hear. She tried not to let her disappointment show. Her team was still expecting her to put on a brave front and lead them, though this latest turn was going to take them to a place that most likely none of them had ever experienced firsthand.

"A widespread infestation of *ixodes insanus* will have a catastrophic impact on a settled community," Dr. McKee continued. "How many have been infected?"

"We've got about seventy confirmed cases," Hannah said. "But we are still working to determine the full extent of the infestation. We extracted the tick from the nasal cavity of a member of our group who hadn't shown any symptoms of infection."

"The effects of the neurotoxin are not always immediately apparent," McKee said. "It may take several days, a week, or perhaps longer. But this species loves to suckle the rich blood deep in the nose. That is its preferred feeding region in mammals—we hadn't determined why. Once a larva finds a host—which it can do quite easily by attaching to the tips of grass or shrubbery and extending its legs until something brushes past it—it will enter the nasal cavity and begin to feed. Generally it will nourish itself on the blood for about a week, and it's quite common for the host to have no awareness of the ectoparasite during this period. Once satiated, it injects the neurotoxin in the bloodstream, and then it detaches itself from the host. A slow flood of blood may trickle from the host's nose at this time."

"I've noticed," Hannah said. "The blood doesn't clot. The patients I've seen who are infected seem to have a persistent nose bleed."

"The neurotoxin appears to have some anticoagulant properties," Dr. McKee said. "Among its other effects."

"We know the neurotoxin leads to obsessive, violent behavior, but how long do the symptoms persist? Do they eventually subside?"

"The damage to the brain is irreversible." Dr. McKee blotted a film of perspiration from his bronzed forehead with a handkerchief. "We performed an autopsy on our rhesus monkey after we euthanized it. The structure of the brain's frontal lobe had been compromised— perhaps *changed* is a more accurate term. I suspect, if the subject had survived, its behavior would have continued to devolve and the baser instincts would have held sway."

"So they just keep falling lower and lower on the evolutionary ladder," Hannah said.

"The neurotoxin's effect on the frontal lobe will profoundly and permanently alter personality," McKee said. "Your assessment of falling lower on the evolutionary ladder, behaving less like a civilized adult and more like a subhuman savage, is unfortunately quite accurate."

Hannah and the other members of her team peppered Dr. McKee with more questions, and he freely shared what we knew, and promised to forward his research study notes, but Hannah ended the call feeling more pessimistic than she had ever felt before. There was no cure for the infected. They presented a grave danger to others. And death was inevitable.

She picked up her phone to call her boss.

It was time to commence the quarantine.

***

The mob of frenzied pursued them, but Jim left them behind, making a quick series of turns to throw the group off their tail and putting a significant amount of distance between them. Unless the infected communicated with one another via a psychic connection—the idea of such a thing didn't seem as far-fetched to Deacon as it might have yesterday—Deacon was willing to believe they were in the clear.

"Good work, Jim," he said. "I think we've lost them."

"What the hell happened back in there, chief?"

Deacon glanced behind him. Emily had crawled into one of the seats and curled into fetal position. She stared blankly out the window, her eyes red from crying. She clasped a silver pendant in her hands.

"We found her friend," Deacon said softly. "It didn't go well."

"I'd say," Jim said. "You go in alone and come out being chased by a whole band of those wild-eyed maniacs."

"I'm pregnant," Emily blurted. "Zack is—was—the father. I wanted to tell him . . . I *needed* to tell him."

She tightened further into a ball, as if wished to withdraw entirely into herself.

"I'm sorry," Deacon said. He didn't know what else he could say. There were no words that could ease the young woman's heartache.

"Yeah, me, too." Jim said. "What's going on here, it's an affront against humanity. A crime. Someone needs to pay for this."

"When we get to HQ we can start making that happen," Deacon said.

But as Jim drove them closer to their security headquarters and Deacon got a good look at the building, concern wormed through the pit of his stomach.

The doors were wide open; they were held open with a garbage can. As if someone had needed to make several frantic trips in and out.

They had three security specialists on duty at that evening hour: one was manning the gates, another patrolled the community as directed; the other was supposed to be on site at HQ watching the surveillance feed. What was going on?

"I don't like this." Deacon drew his pistol. "We've got trouble again."

"I'll take point." Jim parked. He pulled his shotgun out of the rack.

"Wait inside," Deacon said to Emily. She only nodded dully, as if she barely heard what he'd said.

They climbed out of the SUV. Light spilled out of the building's front doors. Moving carefully, they crept inside the building.

Shards of broken glass and potting soil from an overturned plant littered the floor.

"South Haven Security!" Jim announced. "If anyone is here, identify yourself!"

A thudding sound came from behind the front desk. Deacon found Carver Taylor, one of his regular night-shift guys, gagged with duct tape and bound at both wrists and ankles with plastic handcuffs. He lay on the tile floor in a mess of paper and glass splinters.

Carver's brown eyes widened when he saw Deacon had discovered him. He shouted against his gag.

"The hell is this?" Jim asked.

"Go check the armory," Deacon told Jim.

Deacon removed the duct-tape from the man's mouth and sliced away the restraints with a pocketknife. Groaning, Carver sat up. He gulped in deep breaths and massaged his abraded wrists.

"Oh, thank God you're here, man," Carver said. He was trembling, his uniform soaked with perspiration. He was only a kid, in his early twenties, working the night shift and going to college at Georgia State during the day. He was the nephew of one of Deacon's old buddies from the Atlanta police department. If something had happened to him Deacon would have felt terrible.

"I'm glad you're all right." Deacon put one hand on the man's shoulder, to steady him. "Tell me what happened."

"A group of them, three guys, they had on dust masks over their mouths," Carver said, touching his lips. "One of them had a shotgun. They didn't hurt me, but they tore up the place, and they took my keys, too."

Stepping over the mess on the floor, Deacon made his way to the bank of security monitors: his primary purpose for wanting to come there.

All of the displays were dark. Many of them had been smashed.

Someone had ripped the guts of the surveillance camera system's receiver out of the console, too.

Deacon's jaws clenched. This setback was going to complicate matters.

Jim rushed around the corner. "All of our weapons, ammo, vests, everything. Gone, chief. What the fuck happened here?"

"We were raided," Deacon said.

"The frenzied, you think?"

"Nope. This was a deliberate act. These guys knew exactly what they were doing. They don't want us spying on them and they took our weapons just because it was a good idea. Makes sense to me."

"But everything was behind lock and key," Jim said.

Deacon nodded toward Carver. "He had the key."

"Perfect," Jim said. "It's been bad enough dealing with those maniacs out there. Now we're fighting each other?"

"They seemed like regular folk, not trained robbers or anything," Carver said. He had gotten to his feet. "I don't agree with what they did, but there are a lot of scared people out there, now that the government is here."

"Anarchy is no excuse," Jim said. "People need to co-operate with one another. Now more than ever."

"Let's take an inventory of whatever we still have left," Deacon said. "We'll need two-way radios, Tasers, whatever we can find that they didn't loot."

"I'm on it," Carver said.

"What's the plan now?" Jim asked. "If we can't access the surveillance footage, we've got no way to find out what happened at the Screen on the Green last week, no way to find out how that bug got here."

"We aren't the only ones who monitor the video feed," Deacon said.

"Crap." Jim scowled. "You've gotta go see *him* again?"

"No doubt, Mr. Falcon will be happy to see me," Deacon said.

***

Emily didn't know what she was doing there.

She was curled in the backseat of the SUV, which had been parked in front of the building that served as the headquarters of the South Haven security team. It was full night. Pale yellow light glowed at the windows of the building and poured out of the propped-open front doors.

She barely remembered the drive there.

Ever since Zack had died in her arms, nothing had made any sense, life had been moving at a gelid pace, and she couldn't make any sense of what was going on, and had no idea what she would do next.

In the back most room of her mind, she understood that she was going through shock. But that logical aspect of her couldn't fight through the fog that had engulfed her brain.

Before she realized what she was doing, she had slipped out of the vehicle. The next thing she knew, she was at the doorway of the building.

The men were talking about various things. They didn't notice her. Something bad had happened, she realized, and they were planning their next move.

Unnoticed, she drifted away from the door.

She didn't get back in the big Ford. She didn't know where she wanted to go, but she didn't want to ride around with them anymore.

She began walking. It was raining. The cool water soaked through her clothes, and her sneakers got wet as she slogged through puddles. But she continued on.

She still had Zack's blood on her shirt, in spite of the pouring rain. The crimson stain was right above her heart.

She had slipped on the necklace she'd taken from Zack, too. The silver locket was cool against her skin.

Absently flicking damp hair out of her face, she kept walking. Damp grass squished underneath her shoes.

Eventually, the grass ended and gave way to wood chips.

She blinked, wiped water out of her eyes. She had reached the South Haven playground. It was an enormous space, lit by several ornately designed lamps, and lavishly appointed with all sorts of play equipment: various slides, a rock climbing wall, monkey bars . . . a set of swings.

Three children were on the swings: little girls, no older than six, all of them wearing identical frilly dresses. The girls swooped in large, rhythmic arcs, and their swings were closely synchronized, as if they were a team executing a stunt.

Triplets, Emily thought, and it was the first clear thought she'd had in a while.

She scanned the park benches—all of them were empty—and didn't see an adult nearby. How had three little girls wound up alone in the park at night, at such a dangerous time for anyone to be out-doors?

Emily headed toward them.

"Hi!" she said, and her voice came out weak; her throat was still clogged from so much crying earlier. She cleared her throat and called out with a wave: "Hello there!"

The girls kept swinging, but almost as one, their heads swiveled in Emily's direction.

Emily walked closer. Although it was rainy, and dark, the glow of a nearby streetlamp revealed their faces. Lesions spotted their skin. Rings of inflammation encircled their eyes.

Emily's heart twisted. They were clearly infected, but they were only children. She couldn't bring herself to turn away without trying to help them. Maybe she could get the girls to Dr. Bailey and her team could do *something* to heal them.

"Is your mommy at home?" she asked. "Maybe your daddy?"

The girls didn't answer. They swung, swung, swung.

Emily drew closer. "Come with me, sweethearts. I can take you to someone that can help you. Okay?"

The girls screamed.

"No!"

"No!"

"No!"

Their screeching was so high-pitched that Emily wanted to clap her hands over her ears. The girls suddenly launched themselves off the swings at the top of their arc, and dresses rippling, hurtled through the air and landed on the ground with a spray of woodchips.

Emily dragged in a breath. Their behavior had rattled her, but she reminded herself that they were only children, and could do her no harm.

The girls stood, and clustered together arm in arm.

"Let me help you, okay, sweethearts?" Emily said. "It'll be okay. I can take you to some people that will help you feel better. Promise."

". . . said . . . Mommy . . ."
". . . never . . . ever . . ."
". . . strangers . . . follow . . ."
"Yes, and that's good, but you're sick, and I promise to help—"
They shrieked again.

Their unified screams were like a spike splitting Emily's head in half. She put her hands over her ears and backed away from the triplets.

I tried, but I can't force these children to come with me, she thought. *I'm not going to abduct them against their will.*

Across the park, perhaps a hundred yards away, a large group had appeared on the edge of the grass. They must have been alerted by the screaming of the girls.

It looked like the roving mob from Poseidon Park. Except the group had increased in size. Before, there had been maybe twenty individuals. Emily didn't wait to do a full headcount, but at a rough estimate there were over thirty of them. Most of them were naked; those not nude were in various stages of undress.

Emily spun, and ran.

Chapter 23

E mily had vanished.

Deacon had been so busy plotting his next step that he didn't realize she had run away until he went out to the SUV to ask her if she wanted to come in and grab a bite to eat from the fridge in their HQ lounge before they headed out again. But she had left without telling anyone and leaving any clue where she had gone.

Deacon spat on the ground. The young lady was heartbroken, not thinking clearly, probably had wandered away in a fog of grief and shock. He felt partially responsible for what had happened, though he had only wanted to protect her and would have done the same thing again if given an opportunity.

He scanned the surrounding area, and found no sign of her. She could have gone back home; she could have gone anywhere. Given the present circumstances, he didn't have time to search for her. He'd have to assume that she understood the risks of wandering South Haven alone, and would take precautions to avoid trouble.

Nevertheless, it bugged him. He couldn't shake the sense that he had failed her, and that his failure had led to this sad outcome.

The two-way radio he wore clipped to his belt crackled. It was Dr. Bailey.

Hearing her voice instantly lifted his mood. "Hey. What's up?"

"Big news," she said, and began to explain the latest developments.

An entomologist—bug doctor, in Deacon's mind—had given them the rundown on exactly what sort of infestation they were facing, and the odds for the home team didn't look good. The quarantine was moving forward, and all signs pointed toward it being the sort of aggressive operation that fueled the bad dreams of government conspiracy-theorists: a full-fledged lockdown, with military support. Bailey urged Deacon to finish his investigation soon, because in a short period of time, their movements might be severely restricted.

"I'm on it," he promised her, and didn't bother to explain the raid of their HQ weapons cache. She had enough on her plate to worry about.

A few minutes later, Deacon and Jim were back in the SUV and driving away. Deacon called his father to check on him. Pops assured him that so long as he had his gun beside his bed and plenty of ammo, he was going to be fine.

"Don't worry about me," Pops said. "Stay out there and do your job, all right?"

"All right, Pops." Deacon ended the call with a smile.

"You think the rich douchebag is going to let us watch his precious video feed?" Jim asked.

"He told me to bring the 'haven' back to South Haven," Deacon said. "He ordered me to start acting like a cop again. All of this is part of that. We're conducting an investigation and he's got useful evidence."

"Something tells me the dirt bag knows what's going on," Jim said. "He knows everything that happens here."

"I don't know about that," Deacon said. "I'm just doing my job."

They reached the Falcon estate without incident, probably because Falcon lived on the outer perimeter of the community and it was possible to travel to his home without passing through the more densely populated residential areas.

Angie Falcon buzzed them in at the gate. She sounded tickled that Deacon had returned for the second time that day.

Here we go, he thought.

"Well, my Lord, sweet stuff came back to see me," Angie Falcon said, opening the front door. She wore a sheer red robe that left little to the imagination, and it looked as though she had just applied a fresh coat of matching red lipstick.

Then Angie noted Jim standing beside him, and her smile soured. "Oh, you brought the crusty old grouch with you."

"Nice to see you too, missy." Jim smirked. "Wow, you look ready for a photo shoot. Maybe a magazine spread."

"In your dirty little old man's fantasies, I'm sure." Angie tightened the belt of her robe and glanced at Deacon with annoyance. "Why'd you bring the garden gnome along?"

"He happens to be my partner, and we're working very hard here," Deacon said.

"Working on what?" Angie displayed only mild interest. She had shifted her attention to her cell phone, swiping the display with a long lacquered fingernail. She was playing some kind of colorful mobile game.

Deacon glanced at Jim, and he could read the same thought in Jim's gaze: *is this woman really that clueless?*

He realized the answer was: *yes, she is.* Angie Falcon and those of her ilk lived in a bubble, and the bubble was constructed of obscene wealth. It allowed her to ignore the concerns and fears of those on the outside, even those who technically lived in the same community. While others were dying in the streets, she was pouring herself another glass of champagne and playing *Candy Crush* or whatever the hell people were playing then.

"We're working on something Mr. Falcon asked me to do," Deacon said. "Is he here? We need to see him."

"Daddy left a while ago, sweetheart." She turned away from the door. "Got on that ATV of his and ripped out of here. You can wait around for him if you want, whatever." She drifted away, attention riveted on her phone.

"He's riding around South Haven on his dune buggy?" Jim said to Deacon and sneered. "Tell me again he doesn't know something, chief."

"We need to check the video feed." Deacon started to cross the threshold, remembered the box of shoe covers beside the door.

"Fuck it," he said, and stepped inside without bothering to put them on.

Jim grinned. "A man after my own heart."

***

Emily ran away from the roaming mob.

She didn't understand what she'd done to earn their malice, but as she'd seen many times that day, merely being in the wrong place at the wrong time was sufficient to wind up as the target of the violent segment of the infected group. She was exhausted with all of the running, and wondered why she'd left the warm and relative safety of the SUV near Deacon and his partner.

If she managed to survive this latest ordeal, she had to be more mindful.

Her sneakers swished through the wet grass, water spraying up and further saturating her already damp clothing. The playground, as expansive as it was, was only a component of a much larger outdoor recreation complex that spanned several grassy acres. Running away from the playground carried her to a circular jogging path. The jogging path ended at a baseball field, the baselines muddy in the pounding rain. A basketball court lay beyond the baseball field, nets dripping with water.

She ran at a brisk pace, thankful for the many years she'd spent jogging and riding her bicycle. Behind her, the mob had receded in the rain-tinged murk.

Emily passed onto the tennis courts. Someone was out striking balls with a racket, thwacking them into the opposite fence as he robotically practiced a serve. He wore a pair of low-cut white sneakers and a New York Yankees baseball cap but nothing else. Rainwater dripped down his naked torso and streamed from his slender legs.

Emily kept to the perimeter of the court, but he still screamed at her.

"Courts . . . off my . . . bitch . . !"

Shouting, he tossed a ball in the air and swiped it in her direction. She saw it coming and tried to zag out of its path, but he had served it with tremendous velocity. The ball smacked against the back of her head.

It felt as if a bomb exploded at the base of her skull. She cried out and fell hard to the concrete, her ankle twisting painfully as she collided with the wet ground.

The fall had knocked the breath out of her. Dazed, she stared at the dark, overcast sky, cold rain beating against her face.

She wanted to close her eyes and let the rain wash her away into oblivion. She was so tired of fighting. It would be so easy to give up for good . . .

You're pregnant, Em.

The thought penetrated the fog in her brain like a laser beam. *Pregnant.* A living creature that relied on her for its entire tenuous existence was forming inside her.

Get up, Em.

She couldn't give up.

Sucking in deep breaths, she pushed herself up into a sitting position. The tennis player was stomping toward her, with the look of a grizzly bear angered because someone had invaded his cave. He clutched the racket in his lesion-spotted hand, his crust-ringed eyes seething.

"Off courts . . . bitch!"

Deacon had given her a Taser earlier that day, but she wouldn't have time to draw it and depress the trigger before the tennis player would be upon her. She went for it anyway. Taking action of any kind was preferable to waiting to die.

Only a few feet away from her, the tennis player stopped dead in his tracks.

An arrow had punctured his throat, right through the center of his windpipe. Gasping, the tennis racket flipping out of his fingers, the man clawed at his neck. He sagged like a dead weight to the concrete.

Wildly, Emily looked around.

Someone wearing a helmet and riding on a four-wheel ATV roared toward the tennis courts, divots of grass and mud churning from the big tires. The driver steered the vehicle to the edge of the court, engine rumbling.

The stranger wore a full-face helmet with a darkly-tinted visor, a black leather jacket, jeans, and black boots. Although the stranger was seated, the tremendous size and musculature of the individual made it clear to Emily that her knight in shining armor was a man. He had a wicked-looking crossbow slung over his shoulder. Arrows bristled from a leather quiver attached to the side of the ATV.

The ATV was painted mostly black, and had a ferocious white falcon imprinted on the side panel. The metalwork was chrome, and glistened in the glow of the nearby street lamps.

She suddenly had the feeling that she had seen this guy before, or should have known his identity. But the answer danced out of her mental grasp.

The stranger hooked his thumb toward the empty rear seat of his vehicle.

Emily rose on wobbly knees. Her twisted ankle ached.

She didn't know this man, but if he'd intended to harm her, he wouldn't have rescued her, and with a bum ankle, she couldn't run anyway. The frenzied mob was still out there.

She climbed onto the seat. The movement made her slightly dizzy, and to stabilize herself, she hooked her fingers around a pair of handles that jutted from alongside the saddle.

The driver roared away from the tennis courts, leaving her would-be killer bleeding out on the pavement. The budding medical doctor in Emily despised the kill-or-be-killed world into which they had plummeted, would have preferred to strap that man to a gurney and work tirelessly to find a treatment to restore his health. That was the path she would have chosen. But her ideals wouldn't save her when someone was determined to tear out her throat.

The ATV thumped across the grass and splashed through puddles. Gritting her teeth, Emily held on tight.

"Please, take me to the clubhouse," she said. "There are people there that I've been helping. I need to get back."

Her rescuer didn't respond. In case he didn't hear her over the thundering engine, she repeated her request in a louder voice. He leaned forward and powered ahead. They tore onto a residential street, buzzed past parked cars and darkened homes. Water sprayed from the rolling tires, a mist wetting her face.

They had left the frenzied mob in the dust, but she worried the group would continue to roam the community, growing in size, like some sort of mutant amoeba.

They passed through an intersection, and she read the street signs. She thought they were heading in the general direction of the clubhouse, but she didn't want to ask him again. A man who would so casually let an arrow fly to kill another human being wasn't a man to be pushed too far.

But she needed to get back to Dr. Bailey and the CDC team. There was purpose for her there. Although the situation had long since spiraled out of their control, the group was working to find answers, and Emily wanted to be a part of that effort.

They careened around a corner. Emily noticed that a large leather satchel was hooked to the side of the vehicle, the top edge flapping in the wind. She peeled away the leather a couple of inches, to get a better look at the contents—and did a double take.

Suddenly, she couldn't wait for him to drop her off.

A short time later, he veered into the parking lot of the South Haven clubhouse. The ATV grumbled to a stop.

Emily carefully climbed off the seat.

"Thank you, sir," she said. "For everything."

Face still concealed by the helmet, he nodded curtly. He wheeled around and thundered away into the night.

The man hadn't spoken a single word to her, yet she was as positive of his identity as she was of her own name.

But why was Ronald Falcon, the multimillionaire developer of South Haven, transporting a bag full of dynamite?

***

The door to Falcon's office opened when Deacon twisted the knob.

Tension eased out of Deacon. Falcon could be so meticulous regarding security that Deacon had worried he'd need to break inside the room.

He went inside, Jim following close behind. Overhead track lights flickered into life, awakened by a motion-detection system.

"I've never been in here," Jim said, voice tinged with awe. "This room is bigger than the whole apartment that Linda and I lived in when we first got married."

Deacon headed to the bank of security monitors embedded in the far wall. All of the displays were dark, but the network server and computer terminal hummed, various indicator lights glowing.

Deacon settled into the desk chair and tapped the keyboard to access the terminal. Falcon's own surveillance system controlled a greater number of cameras than security HQ, but Deacon was hoping beyond hope that both systems utilized the same basic setup and shared user credentials. When the system asked him for an administrator username and password, he typed his own login information.

Access denied. Enter a valid username and password.

"Dammit," Deacon said.

"It's not letting you in?" Jim peered over his shoulder. "Try my info then."

"Give it to me."

Jim gave him his credentials and Deacon entered them carefully.

Access denied. Enter a valid username and password.

"He's got a totally different system here," Deacon said, shaking his head. "He's the only one who can unlock it."

"I can unlock it," a soft voice said from the doorway.

Both Deacon and Jim turned. Caleb, Falcon's teenage son, lingered at the threshold. Hands shoved deep in his pockets, he lowered his gaze to the floor and sucked in his bottom lip.

"It's all yours, kid." Deacon rose from the chair. He gestured toward the computer.

Caleb glanced at him. "Well, I was sort of hoping you guys could help me with something first."

"He wants quid pro quo," Jim said. "Christ, kid, do you understand what's going on here?"

"Let's hear him out, Jim," Deacon said, placing a hand on Jim's shoulder. "What do you want us to help you with, son?"

"Can you come up to my room?" Caleb asked. "Please? It might be easier if I show you."

Deacon glanced at Jim. Jim grumbled, but nodded.

"Let's go," Deacon said.

***

"I have a date," Caleb said, a blush settling deep into his pale cheeks.

The teenager had brought them to his bedroom on the second floor of the mansion. In Deacon's mind, it was less of a bedroom and more like a penthouse suite at a luxury hotel. It had a spacious sitting area with furniture and a gigantic flat-screen TV, a kitchenette, a Jacuzzi (which Caleb confessed he never used) an office area, and then the chamber with his bed. Computers and electronic gadgets were spread everywhere. A big poster of Albert Einstein hung on the wall near the computer desk.

"You have a *date*?" Deacon asked, certain he had heard incorrectly.

"Yes." Caleb glanced at his wrist watch, one of those expensive Apple Watch models. "It starts in about twenty minutes actually. It's a video chat with a girl from my school, sort of a getting to know you conversation. But I don't know what to talk about. I was sort of hoping you guys could give me some advice."

"Unbelievable," Jim said, shaking his head. "Son, you really need to get out of this goddamn house for a while. Get some sun, mingle with people out there in the real world. What you're talking about here is nuts, and your timing couldn't be worse. Do you know what's going on out there in South Haven?"

Caleb's blush deepened. He spun around in his swivel chair to face his computer display. He typed on the keyboard, fingers hammering the keys.

It was as if they had ceased to exist to him. Deacon happened to agree with everything Jim had said, though the delivery of the message was overly harsh. But the kid displayed the same blasé indifference to the outside world that his older sister did. The CDC was on site and a military-backed quarantine was coming down, and he was worried about a date?

Still, they needed the kid's help to crack the password. As Caleb withdrew into his comforting world of computers, Deacon felt their opportunity slipping out of their grasp. He nudged Jim aside, pulled up an ottoman, and sat next to Caleb.

"Listen, Jim's old and ornery, out of touch with how younger folks operate," Deacon said in a soft tone. "I know what you're talking about, and this date . . . well, I've never personally had a date like that but I get it. Have you ever had a girlfriend?"

"A girlfriend?" Caleb glanced at him and actually giggled, sounding like a much younger child. "God, no."

"How old are you? Fifteen, sixteen?"

"I'll be seventeen in August. And yes, I have my driver's license. And my own car, too—I got a Tesla for my birthday. It's so insane." He grinned.

I was born to the wrong set of parents, Deacon thought.

"All right, you're sixteen going on seventeen," he said. "It's an exciting time, I remember it well. You're developing a good sense of your own identity. You know some things you like, things you don't like. Sounds as though you like nice cars, and from the looks of your room, I'd say that you're into computers, too."

"Yeah." Caleb bobbed his head in agreement. "I wrote my first program when I was six. It's embarrassing to think now about how primitive it was, but I thought it was pretty cool at the time."

"What's the name of the young lady that you're having this date with tonight?" Deacon asked.

"Ava," Caleb said. "Ava Upshaw. We're in the same AP physics class."

"So she's an intelligent girl, obviously. What do you think she's interested in, for fun?"

"I have *no* idea!" Caleb says. "She barely uses her social media accounts. It's unbelievable."

"Jesus, kid," Jim started to say, and Deacon raised his hand. Thankfully, Jim lapsed into silence.

"That's okay," Deacon said. "It just means you've got more to share with each other when you chat. You *ask* her what she likes to do for fun. If she's slow to share that with you, then you start off by telling her what *you* like to do for fun. The conversation will flow from there."

"You think so?" Caleb asked. He laughed. "That sounds way too easy."

"You've just gotta be yourself, man," Deacon said. "That's my most important piece of advice to you. Be true to who you are, and don't worry about what others think. You've gotta be able to live with yourself and the decisions you make, and that's tough if you compromise your values and what's important to you. Be yourself, always, and things will take care of themselves."

"Be yourself." Caleb gazed at him, blue eyes shining. "Wow, do you have kids?"

"No, I don't. Why?"

"You should. I think you'd make a great dad."

"I've got two ex-wives who might disagree with you about that—but that's another story," Deacon said. "Are we square, Caleb? Jim and I really need to get back to work here."

"Oh, yeah, right." Caleb grabbed a Post-It note and scribbled on it with a pen. He passed the slip of paper to Deacon. "These are the administrator credentials. I set up the surveillance server, actually."

"Doesn't that just figure?" Jim muttered.

"Thank you," Deacon said. "This will help us a lot. We need to get to the bottom of who's behind what's hurting all the people who live here."

"Oh, that's easy, too," Caleb said. "Uncle Kent."

"Who the hell is Uncle Kent?" Jim asked.

Caleb shrugged. "My dad's younger brother. He and my dad basically hate each other's guts, even though they're both like old guys now. They've got a seriously epic sibling rivalry that's been going on since they were kids."

"You're sure he's involved?" Deacon asked.

"I'd bet all my computers that he is," Caleb said. "Uncle Kent lives here, too—in South Haven, I mean. But he's out in the forest part, with the nature trails and all that stuff. He doesn't like to be around other people."

"Appreciate the tip," Deacon said. "We'll look into that."

***

Back in Falcon's office, Deacon entered the login credentials that Caleb had given them.

"And we're in," Deacon said. Smiling, he glanced at Jim. "See, Jim. Try a little tenderness, like Otis Redding says."

"I'll admit it, I don't understand kids these days," Jim said. He sat on the edge of Falcon's desk. "Especially filthy rich ones who get Teslas for their sixteenth birthdays. I couldn't even afford to test drive one of those cars."

Deacon used the keyboard to scroll through the system menu. The surveillance server indicated that it had access to ninety-three cameras, many more than the HQ system could utilize. Deacon didn't understand why Falcon needed more cameras than his own security team employed.

As Deacon scrolled through the list of cameras, and selected them for viewing, a live full-color feed from each respective device popped up on one of the flat-screen monitors arrayed along the wall.

Some of the additional cameras were located on Falcon's private property—at his entrance gate, for instance. Another was nested in the upper corner of a chamber that served as the mansion's spa.

Deacon remembered, a few months ago, when Angie Falcon had lured him to the spa under the pretense of repairing the light fixtures. She had offered herself to him and he had resisted. Had Falcon been in his office the whole time watching the episode play out?

Two cameras in the system menu were tagged with the labels, "Deacon Apt. 1" and "Deacon Apt. 2." Frowning, Deacon selected each of them and looked up at the displays.

"Holy shit," Deacon said. "This guy has surveillance in my apartment."

"Surprised?" Jim asked. He looked ready to spit on the floor. "I keep telling you that he's an asshole. The jerk probably justifies it as 'protecting his investment.'"

One camera gave a view of the kitchen. The other camera watched the family room. The kitchen was empty, but the live feed of the family room showed his father awake, lounging in his recliner and watching TV.

Deacon's gut clenched. He hadn't any clue that surveillance had been installed in the apartment, and wondered how he'd been deceived.

He decided right then: If they managed to survive this ordeal, he was quitting this job, labor contract be damned. Falcon could sue him if he wanted. No job was worth this outrageous invasion of privacy.

Deacon returned to the menu. He found familiar labels for the surveillance positioned around Main Street, which bracketed the town square. He selected all four of them, and then drilled deeper, to footage history.

The footage was categorized by day, with each covering a full twenty-four hour period, and was further broken down into hour by hour segments. Deacon selected Friday, July 8—one week ago. The day of the "Screen on the Green" event during which they believed residents had come into contact with the deadly tick larvae. He started at five o'clock in the afternoon for the fateful day.

The selected cameras provided excellent coverage of the town square, from all four directions. At five o'clock, the four food trucks were parked along Main Street, and were already serving a trickle of customers. Some residents had set up lawn chairs and blankets on the grass, staking their claims well before the movie commenced.

"If these damn bugs were crawling in the grass looking for hosts, by this point in the day, they're already there," Jim said. "We need to find out who put them there. It must have been earlier that day, or maybe the day before."

"Agreed." Deacon scratched his chin. "This is going to take some time to dig through."

Chapter 24

Alex worried that they were going too far.

First, their group, led by Stan, had raided the South Haven Security headquarters. They had restrained one of the guards and looted all of the weapons, vests, and other valuables, and disabled the surveillance system. Alex had not participated in the raid, but he had been privy to the plan, and that made him an accessory. He'd understood the need to acquire weapons for self-defense, and the desire to prevent spying on the residents made sense, but none of it felt right, in spite of Stan's warnings that they stood on the precipice of martial law backed by the United States government.

To Alex, it was stealing, plain and simple.

He'd gone from a life steeped in crime in the cartel, to respectability as an entrepreneur, and had circled back to felonious deeds. Perhaps it was just in his nature to skirt the line.

Eres un chico malo, his mama had used to say to him. Mama had been perpetually disappointed by his choices, and had written him off for good when he'd joined the cartel.

The task he was about to undertake wouldn't have influenced his mother to think any better of him. Stan wanted Alex to infiltrate the CDC's base of operations at the South Haven clubhouse. Get inside, find out what the agency knew and what they were planning next, and report back to the group.

Which was how Alex wound up in the clubhouse parking lot that evening, making his way toward the facility. He had ridden a bicycle to get there, one that Stan had loaned him for this task. Although on the way there, Alex had passed several sick individuals and had even spotted from afar what appeared to be a mob of them, traveling like a herd of animals down the road, none of them displayed any interest in harming him.

Stan had a mission for him, but Alex had his own reasons for wanting to speak to doctors and scientists about what was happening—not only to the community, but to *him*.

Several utility vans bearing the CDC logo were parked near the building; a satellite dish bristled from the roof of one of the vehicles. Lights glowed at the clubhouse windows.

It was ironic. Before he'd made his escape and had started over, Alex had used to be an informant against the cartel, secretly feeding tips to the United States government. He supposed he knew all about serving multiple masters.

He approached the clubhouse's ornate entrance. He had expected a guard to be on duty at the doors, but there was no one there. Through the glass, he could see people hurrying back and forth, as if they were absorbed in their work.

Alex tried to go inside, but the entrance was locked.

He hammered his fist against the glass. "Hey! Can someone come help me?"

No one responded at first, but a couple of people did glance in his direction. He supposed he was quite a spectacle, with his rain-damp clothes and dust mask covering half his face.

He pulled away his dust mask and continued to beat on the doors.

After about a minute, a pretty young woman approached. She wore blue hospital scrubs, and her dark hair was pulled back into a ponytail. She looked familiar to him, and he guessed she was likely a community resident who had visited his store in the past. But if she lived in South Haven, how had she wound up helping the CDC?

She stopped at the doors but didn't open them.

"This is a restricted area," she said, her gaze unyielding. "The CDC is hard at work. They've asked everyone to stay in their homes until further notice. Did you get that message?"

"I need help," Alex said. "I'm not going to hurt anyone, but I don't feel right. Can you please help?"

"Please. Return to your home."

"I can't go back home, miss. My wife's there . . . she was sick." Emotion tightened his throat. "I only want someone to help me."

The woman's eyes softened. She hesitated for a beat, and then twisted a knob to unlock the door.

***

"Thank you," Alex said. "I won't get in anyone's way, I promise."

"Just stick with me, okay?" She looked around, lips pressed together. "All right, I can probably take you to one of the meeting rooms and do a quick exam."

He noticed that she didn't ask for him to relinquish his pistol, which he still wore holstered on his hip, though his jacket concealed the weapon. She wore what looked like a stun gun clipped to her waist. He didn't know why, but that gave him confidence that she understood what was going on.

"My name's Alex," he said. "I run the frozen yogurt shop on Main Street. I think I've seen you before."

"Emily," she said. "I thought I recognized you, too. I liked your shop."

Alex noted she said *liked*, as if the existence of his business had passed into ancient history. He wondered how much she knew about what was happening.

"How are you helping the CDC?" he asked. "Do you work for them?"

"Officially? No. It's a long story." She gestured for him to follow her. She walked with a slight limp. When he inquired about it, she revealed that she had sprained her ankle and recently wrapped it with a bandage. *Probably had been running for her life,* he thought.

They traveled through the lobby and down a wide corridor. As they walked, they passed a ballroom, the doors closed. Piano chords filtered from inside. It sounded as if a boisterous child were banging away on the keys.

"What's going on in there?" Alex asked, hooking his thumb toward the ballroom.

"Don't ask," Emily said.

They went past several uniformed members of the CDC; Alex saw the agency's initials on the badges they wore around their necks. He expected someone to stop them and question his presence, but they all appeared too busy to mind. Their gazes were intense, faces lined with stress. The place had an atmosphere of quiet desperation.

Emily opened a door off the main corridor and ushered him into a small conference room. She switched on the lights. The room was furnished with a round table and six padded chairs.

"Are you a doctor?" Alex asked.

"I'm starting my third year of medical school," she said with a shrug. "Take a seat, please. So you said your wife is sick?"

"She's dead," Alex said, and the words felt like stones in his mouth. "May her soul rest in peace. She went pure *loco*, like so many other people here."

"I'm so sorry for your loss," she said, and she sounded so sincere that Alex had to stifle a sob. "But Dr. Bailey and the CDC have discovered the cause."

"It's some government virus thing right? A biological weapon?"

"Umm, no." Emily frowned at him as if he had lost his mind. "Anyway, I don't know how much of this I'm supposed to share, but you're in here now, so I'll tell you. It's a parasite. A rare species of tick from Peru. It was in the town square a week or so ago, when we had the Screen on the Green event. The tick is so tiny you can barely see it, but they get into your nose." She touched one of her nostrils. "They release a neurotoxin that causes people to behave the way we've been seeing."

"Right," Alex said. It was an inadequate reply, but he didn't know what else to say. Stan's theory about a government-produced super virus had been almost laughably wrong—and called into question this entire covert "mission" that Alex had undertaken. "How did something from Peru get here?"

"That's what some of us are trying to find out," she said.

"Is there a cure?" he asked. "There's gotta be a treatment, right?"

Emily shook her head. "Quarantine is going into effect soon. I haven't heard anyone say this, but as far as the people who are already sick, I think they're going to let it run its course. Maybe they'll treat the entire community grounds with pesticides to try to kill any eggs and larvae that are still left over. I don't know exactly. But it's basically too risky for them to let anyone leave—you could be carrying larvae on your clothes. Imagine if this spread out beyond South Haven. Some of it probably has already since people from outside the community came to the movie event."

"That's a scary thought," Alex said.

"I know. But getting back to the exam I meant to do. If you can tilt your head back for a few seconds, I can have a look in your nostrils and let you know if you're currently a host or not."

Alex allowed her to check him out with a small penlight. She pronounced him parasite-free.

"What about a blood test?" Alex asked. "Can you do that, too?"

"That was my next step," she said. "I'll need to get a kit. Hang tight, okay? I'll be right back."

She left him alone in the room. Alex absently scratched his forearm. His mind reeled from what he'd learned so far.

His cell phone vibrated. He had a text message from the same phone number that earlier, had notified him of the meeting at the bookstore. Stan.

It read simply: *Update?*

Alex hesitated. If he shared his findings with Stan, he doubted the guy would believe him. The man was zealously convinced of his own theories and would claim that Alex had been turned by the government. Alex saw little point in returning to the group. With quarantine coming (which Stan *had* correctly predicted), the only sensible course for those healthy individuals left in South Haven was to find somewhere safe, and hunker down until the danger passed.

Alex didn't want to ignore him, so he replied: *Its not what u think.*

Stan shot back: *National Guard mobilizing outside gates. Expect to lose power and wireless soon. Come back to base or you're on your own.*

Emily opened the door. Alex quickly put away his phone.

"Change of plans," Emily said. "Come with me."

***

"I think I've got something, chief," Jim said.

After Deacon had spent half an hour digging through the feeds, he and Jim had switched places at the surveillance system terminal, in the hopes that a fresh set of eyes would yield results. Meanwhile, Deacon had been looking through the photographs on the desk, and on the walls of the expansive office, seeking family photos, and even more specifically, a photo of someone who might match Caleb's description of "Uncle Kent."

He had found only one that might prove relevant. An old black-and-white picture of three men: the eldest man—the father apparently—sat at a big desk, flanked by two young men, one at each shoulder. Deacon recognized the tall, broad-shouldered Ronald Falcon as one of

the brothers; the other son was shorter and wore bifocals, and he had
an intensely studious look.

Jim's announcement pulled Deacon away from the family snapshot.

"Sixth of July," Jim said, gesturing toward the four live monitors
on the wall. "Ten minutes past two o'clock in the morning. Who the
hell is this guy?"

The video footage had a greenish tint due to the infrared technology used to render the nighttime footage. But in the display that pulled
data from the east-facing surveillance camera, Deacon clearly saw an
individual enter the town square. His face wasn't visible, but he wore
dark clothing, and he carried a briefcase.

"Someone working late?" Deacon asked.

"Don't think so," Jim said. "He's wearing an overcoat that comes
down to his knees in freakin' July? It's been hot and humid all
month."

"Good point. Can we zoom in and get a closer look at his face?"

"Let's see if one of the other cameras gives us a better angle," Jim
said, and tapped the keyboard.

Jim paused the feed and zoomed in with the westward-facing camera, which offered a better frontal view of the stranger. The stranger
crossed the street.

Deacon's gut clenched. "What's wrong with his face?"

Squinting at the screen, Jim laughed. "Oh, that evil fucker."

Staring at the display, Deacon could make out a pale face, wide sly
smile, a mustache and a comma of a beard in the middle of the chin.
"It's a mask?"

"Oh, yeah. Not just any mask, either. A Guy Fawkes mask."

"Anarchy," Deacon said. "Cute."

Jim advanced the feed. The masked man proceeded to a bench at
the edge of the town square, opened his briefcase, and removed a cy-
lindrical object. He twisted the cap off the canister and began to

methodically walk through the grass, spreading the contents of the cylinder around him, like a man fertilizing his lawn.

"A deliberate infestation, like I thought," Deacon said. "Wonder how many eggs he distributed."

"Thousands?" Jim said. "I read up a little on ticks. Maybe ten percent of the eggs will hatch into healthy larvae. For us to see the several hundred people infected that we've seen, he must have dropped thousands and thousands of eggs."

"And two days later, they had hatched into larvae seeking hosts, just in time for the community event," Deacon said.

"Bioterrorism," Jim said. "Punishable by multiple life sentences in a federal prison."

"Why?" Deacon said. "Why would anyone do something like this?"

"Sibling rivalry, like that kid said, if it's really his uncle. Wants to fuck up his brother's whole deal? Who knows?"

"We've had this footage for several days and we're only seeing it now. Maybe it's too much to expect our graveyard shift crew to watch all of the monitors, but we blew it."

"Ah, you know how it is, chief. Two o'clock in the morning in South Haven? What the hell ever happens here? A whole bunch of nothing. Whoever we had on duty was probably catching up on sleep."

They continued to watch the recording. After spending about ten minutes distributing eggs throughout the grass, the stranger returned to the bench and packed up his briefcase. Briefcase in hand, he walked to the south side of the town square and turned the corner.

"Now let's see where he goes next," Deacon said. "Maybe he gets in a vehicle and we can identify the tags."

Jim brought up another view. The stranger walked at a brisk pace on the sidewalk along the south side of Main Street. There were no cars parked on the street at that hour.

He disappeared at the edge of the screen.

"Don't lose him," Deacon said.

"Relax, chief." Jim tapped the keys.

They had the man on the next camera feed. He had left the commercial district and roamed into the residential area.

"What's he doing?" Deacon asked.

"He's got that canister out again," Jim said. "He's like a goddamn Johnny Appleseed, isn't he?"

The stranger was distributing eggs into the lawns of the homes that he passed.

Deacon felt as if he'd been punched in the stomach. He sat against the edge of the desk.

"Busy as a bee," Jim said. He brought up another camera, which continued to track the masked stranger performing his nighttime misdeeds. "I really think he spread those things through the entire community."

They had assumed the town square was ground zero. As it turned out, the town square was merely a waystation for the infestation.

Deacon unclipped his two-way radio from his belt.

"I've got to tell Dr. Bailey about this," he said. "This is a game changer. Everyone who lives here could be infected."

Chapter 25

H annah had failed.

   She'd gathered her team in the conference room and announced the news her director had shared privately with her.
Their investigation was being shut down, effectively immediately.
The National Guard had mobilized at the South Haven perimeter, and
an Army helicopter was being dispatched to the clubhouse to collect
the members of her team.

None of her colleagues blamed her for the failure, but she blamed
herself. They had found the root cause of the sickness, but had discovered no cure, no treatment that could be effectively deployed to
help the community. In her opinion, that was failure. She was unable
to help the people she had been sent to save.

She wasn't accustomed to failure, in any form, certainly not in her
professional life. This experience was going to haunt her for a long
time.

After the meeting had broken up and her shell-shocked teammates
began quickly packing up equipment, Emily approached her. A Latino man that Hannah hadn't seen before hung at her side. Hannah
questioned how he had gotten inside the clubhouse, but at that point
the answer was moot.

"What about everyone who lives here?" Emily asked. "What happens to those of us who aren't sick?"

Hannah blinked away tears. "I'm sorry. I did everything I could to
help."

"What about us?" Emily asked again, fire in her eyes.

"You'll be left behind," Hannah said and found it difficult to meet the young woman's gaze. "No one will be permitted to leave. Beyond that, I really don't know what's going to happen, especially since . . ."

"Since what?" the Latino man asked. "My name's, Alex, by the way."

Nodding absently, Hannah dragged in a breath. "Deacon found evidence that the infestation was spread throughout the entire community, not only in the town square. He literally found video footage of someone distributing eggs."

"Who?" Alex asked.

Hannah shrugged. "Still unknown."

"I was sort of thinking that it had to be more broadly dispersed, too," Emily said. "There are just so many people roaming around out there . . . they couldn't have all been at the town square that night."

"I disclosed it to my director as soon as Deacon told me," Hannah said. "I don't know if that was factored into their decision to shut us down—I think they were going to shut us down anyway. But it doesn't bode well, Emily, I'll be frank with you. I'm scared for all of you now."

"You did what you could, right?" Emily offered a plaintive smile.

"Why can't they airlift the healthy people out of here?" Alex asked. There was a red tint in his eyes, which Hannah guessed was from extreme stress. He looked furious, too.

"If it were up to me, I would," Hannah said. "Logistically speaking, it's probably not feasible. I'm sorry. It's all out of my hands."

Hannah turned away from them. She couldn't stand seeing the hopelessness and fear in their eyes, and thinking that on some level, she was responsible.

She rejoined her team and assisted with packing their essential equipment—primarily, the electronics and blood and tissue samples—that they had been instructed to bring. Everything else, such as the gurneys and other lab items, were being left behind.

Their lone test subject, the solitary pianist, continued to work the keys in the ballroom. Her playing had become progressively worse, and was little better than a toddler's aimless hammering of a toy piano.

She realized she still had the two-way radio Deacon had given her. She owed the man a good-bye, but she couldn't bring herself to get in touch with him and tell him that they were being abandoned.

It would have been nice to get to know him better, she thought. *C'est la vie.*

She was about to track down Emily and hand over the radio to her, when she heard the familiar thumping of helicopter rotor blades outside. Her satellite phone chirped, and she answered it and spoke to a woman who tersely informed Hannah of what she already knew.

Their ride had arrived.

***

Hannah's team hustled outside via the clubhouse's front entrance and hurried into the vast parking lot. The nurse from the clinic, Jenn, rushed out there, too, though Hannah had promised a ride only to her team members. When Hannah called to her, the woman turned a vicious glare on her and gave her the middle finger.

Pulling her leather case over her shoulder, Hannah made her move to get out, too. Alex grabbed her arm.

"Don't go," he said.

"I have to." Hannah shrugged off his hand. "This is my only chance to leave. I'm sorry."

"Listen to me carefully, senora," he said. "There's a mob of sick people, they're out there roaming through the neighborhood like some kind of herd. The helicopter is going to attract them." He leveled his dark-eyed gaze on Hannah. "No one's going to make it."

A scream of terror tore Hannah's attention away from him. Hannah looked out at the dimly-lit parking lot.

"Oh, no," she said.

"They're already here," Emily said. She shrank away from the doorway.

The gigantic Black Hawk helicopter hovered about a hundred feet above the clubhouse grounds, blue marker beacon blinking, rotor blades spinning thunderously. The members of her team, hoping to evacuate, instead had been set upon on all sides by a rapidly growing crowd of infected residents, at least twenty of them, perhaps more. It was difficult to count them because their numbers grew by the second as they streamed into the area. The smart, dedicated people that she had been working with only a short while ago didn't stand a chance. Screaming, fighting futilely, they folded underneath the savage, mindless attacks of the seething mob.

Hannah's knees felt watery. She was their leader, and this had happened on her watch. The sense of failure immobilized her.

The infected residents shouted and bayed at the helicopter. Someone clambered on top of a CDC van and flung a brick at the craft that fell far short of its target. Another person hurled a shoe.

Hannah's sat phone buzzed in her hand, snapping her out of her daze. The same woman she had spoken to only a couple of minutes ago curtly informed her that unless the landing zone was cleared, they would be unable to extract anyone.

Hannah had failed her team, but she couldn't fail the last couple of survivors counting on her.

"Give us a few minutes, please," Hannah said, and turned to the others. "Can we try the roof?"

"Good idea," Alex said. "There's a maintenance room at the back of the building with a staircase that leads to the roof." He spun on his heel.

"How do you know that?" Hannah asked, but she had started to follow them down the corridor.

"I've catered a few parties here," Alex said. He added: "I have a frozen yogurt franchise on Main Street. Feels kind of like another life now."

Hannah found it difficult to imagine the cool, steely-eyed Latino as the purveyor of frozen treats, and decided there was more to his background than he had let on. But he might be just the kind of person they needed in a situation like this one.

They reached the door to the maintenance room. Hannah tried to open it, but it was locked.

"Stand back, everyone," Alex said. He had drawn a pistol. "May want to cover your ears."

He fired at the lockset. Orange sparks flashed, and the gun's report was like an explosion going off, making Hannah's ears hurt. But the door creaked open. Alex stepped forward and pulled the door aside, gestured for the women to enter.

The maintenance room was a damp, grey chamber full of humming machines and exposed ductwork. A concrete staircase on the far end of the room ascended to a door clearly marked, "Rooftop Access – Authorized Personnel Only."

That door was locked, too. Alex blasted open the lockset with his pistol.

"If you're trying to earn yourself a ride out of here I think you've done that," Hannah said to him. She glanced at Emily. "You, too, of course. I'll gladly vouch for all of you."

"Let's just get there," Alex said.

They hurried through the doorway. Beyond a small brick alcove, the shingles that served as roof of the building were slick with rain.

The Black Hawk hovered a short distance away. The rush of air created by the whirring rotor blades was like a hurricane.

Hannah clicked on her sat phone. She shouted into the speaker: "My team is on the roof!"

"Copy that, we'll move into position," the woman responded. "Stay clear until I give the order."

Five more minutes, and we're out of here, Hannah thought, clutching her bag against her. The past several hours in South Haven had been the equivalent of a bruising tour through Hell. She would never be the same after this; the faces of all those she had lost would haunt her dreams for years to come.

The Black Hawk drew closer. It was difficult to hear her own heartbeat over the chopping of the copter blades, but suddenly, Hannah thought she heard gunfire.

"Someone's shooting at the helicopter!" Alex said.

Of course they are, Hannah thought, and couldn't suppress a rueful smile. The frenzied were out of their minds, but some of them had firearms and other weapons and held no compunctions about using them.

Bluish sparks danced along the undercarriage of the helicopter.

"We're coming under fire!" Hannah's contact barked on the sat phone.

"Just get to us, please," Hannah said. "We're right here!"

Emily abruptly seized Hannah's arm. She pointed ahead of them, at the edge of the roof, and shouted in Hannah's ear. "Look."

A young man clambered like a monkey onto the roof. He had a scruffy beard and was completely naked—except for the rifle he had strapped across his chest. He planted his feet on the shingles and swiveled around, hands on the gun, seeking a target. Their group was partially concealed within the alcove and escaped his view, but Hannah knew that wouldn't last long.

Two more of the infected followed onto the roof, and Hannah figured there must have been a parked vehicle or other structure nearby that facilitated them reaching the top of the clubhouse. One man had a hunting knife clenched between his teeth. Another guy had a baseball bat, the meat of the bat broken off and the business end sharp as a hunting spear.

Moving like drones under the influence of a single hive mind, the frenzied trio began to roam across the roof. They moved slowly, their progress slowed by the tremendous rush of air currents the helicopter had created, but they were resolute, maniacally determined to find them.

Beside Hannah, Alex had drawn his pistol again, but he was the only one on their team who had a firearm or any sort of useful weapon.

Gunfire continued to hammer the helicopter. The copter bucked and swayed.

A tall, lumbering figure stepped around the corner of the alcove and seized Hannah by the throat.

Hannah was so shocked by her attacker's sudden appearance that she didn't even manage a scream before her air flow was cut off.

Both hands clamped around Hannah's throat, the attacker lifted her off the ground. It was a woman. Damp, matted hair hung in her eyes, and she was naked from the waist down. She wore a soaked-through pink tank top that had a message stretched across her large breasts: *Stop Staring.*

The woman snarled and uttered something unintelligible, but it sounded like it included the word, *bitch.*

Gasping, Hannah dropped the sat phone and used both hands to try to break the woman's grip, utilizing a technique she had learned from her self-defense training, but it was like trying to force apart a mechanically-powered steel vise. The attacker was supernaturally strong, rendering Hannah's training useless.

This is it, Hannah thought, her vision getting blurry. She thought about her parents and how she wished she could have seen them one last time.

Alex stepped forward and calmly shot her attacker in the head. The woman's hands fell away from Hannah, and her body collapsed like a robot's that had its battery removed. Freed, Hannah dropped to the floor. Someone caught her before she slammed her head against the alcove's brick wall.

"I've got you." It was Emily. "Take your time. Breathe."

Hannah sucked in short, painful breaths. She was dizzy, and her throat felt as if it were encircled with bands of fire. She was certain that the woman's crushing chokehold had left behind bruises on her flesh.

But she was alive. Air had never tasted so delicious.

Gunfire rang out, dangerously close.

The trio of rooftop hunters had spotted them.

***

Alex was terrified, but he had never felt so alive.

During his time working with the cartel, he had sampled various drugs, both legal and illegal. His favorite had been amphetamines. When taking on major assignments, he would ingest a liberal dose and be wired for days, able to plow through the cartel's dirty work at a breakneck pace.

He hadn't so much as sipped an ounce of beer since he had left behind that sordid life, but at that moment on the roof, he felt amped up on powerful drugs. All of his senses approached a sort of hyper-realistic clarity. He was as focused as a laser beam.

He wanted to stay on the roof and try to knock down the trio of hunters with his Beretta, but logic prevailed. There was a time to fight, and a time to flee and regroup. He could easily blow through all of his remaining ammo on these guys, and the night was still young.

As he urged the women to flee back inside, he looked over his shoulder and saw more of the crazy bastards climbing onto the roof.

Two of them looked like Wayne, and the ex-soldier he had helped Wayne tie up and confine earlier. They both were armed and utterly deranged.

So that's what happened to those guys, Alex thought.

He realized they would never make it onto the helicopter. The chopper itself was under fire from the armed maniacs on the ground.

The Army or whoever they were was going to say good riddance for this rescue mission and abandon them all to die in South Haven.

Dr. Bailey leaned against Emily as they charged down the staircase, back into the maintenance room. Alex brought up the rear. When they had all scrambled inside, Alex heaved the door shut behind them.

Closing the door wouldn't do much good to slow their pursuers. In order to get onto the roof in the first place, Alex had destroyed the lockset.

He pounded down the stairs.

"I dropped the . . . sat phone up there," Dr. Bailey said in a ragged voice. She coughed, one hand massaging her swollen throat, her eyes red with tears. "No other way to . . . get in touch with the . . . rescue crew."

"Forget about it," Alex said. "We can't go back up there, and we're not safe in here, either. They're coming through that door any second. I saw more of them getting on the roof, too."

"Okay," Emily said. "Where can we go?"

Alex thought fast. "Follow me. Move quickly."

He flung open the door to the maintenance room and rushed into the corridor beyond. The others followed on his heels.

Alex raced along the hallway, wet shoes clapping on tile. They were making a lot of noise, which bugged him, but at that point speed mattered more than stealth.

They reached the marble-floored lobby. Alex had a faint hope of escaping via the front entrance, but that idea was instantly dashed when he saw the maniacs had clustered around the doors and were pounding against the glass with their fists, weapons, and even their foreheads. The glass rattled in its frame, fissures spreading rapidly. Soon they would bust through.

"This way," Alex said.

He raced to the arched doorway for the clubhouse bar-and-grill.

228 · BRANDON MASSEY

The oak-paneled dining room was steeped in shadows, the only light filtering inside from the lobby beyond. All of the cloth-covered tables were set with flatware, napkins, and glasses, and the barstools were arranged at the counter, ready for patrons that might never visit again.

Someone in their group bumped against a table and sent a glass shattering against the hardwood floor.

"*Quiet*," Alex said tightly.

"Sorry," the guilty party muttered.

Footsteps clattered in the distance. Alex heard grunts, and yells.

The rooftop maniacs were in the building.

He pushed open a set of oak wood double doors to enter the kitchen. The doors swung open silently on well-oiled hinges.

The pleasant fragrance of a lemon-scented disinfectant wafted over him. The kitchen was a cavernous, darkened space, full of stainless steel appliances and gleaming food prep surfaces. Dim light issued from a bank of yellow fluorescents positioned above a large stovetop. A slice of weak bluish light also leaked from a massive open refrigerator standing in the corner of the kitchen.

A shadowed shape was wedged between the open stainless steel doors of the fridge. Alex heard the sounds of food being eagerly consumed: smacking, licking, tearing. It sounded as if a grizzly bear had wandered in from the woods and found a fridge full of select cuts of beef.

He glanced at the two ladies behind him, index finger raised in a *hush* gesture.

Kneeling, he edged behind a food prep counter and duck-walked across the tile floor, inching closer to the unknown intruder. Emily and the doctor followed, moving as he did. Thankfully, their shoes didn't squeak against the floor.

The late-night eater's back was to them as they drew into a position that provided a better view. It looked like a heavy-set woman. She wore only a bra and panties.

She held a tray of what looked like raw ground beef. She had her mouth literally buried chin-deep in the meat as she devoured it.

"It's the woman who was playing the piano," Emily said, whispering close to his ear. "She was harmless earlier."

Alex glanced at Emily. He had his doubts about how harmless she might be then, if she had left her perch at the piano and come in there to wolf down raw meat.

He pointed at the dark passageway beside the refrigerator. He whispered: "There's a service door down that way, it opens at the back of the building. It's our way out."

Behind them, distantly, Alex heard shattering glass, and bellows of rage. He would have wagered his right arm that the crazies pressing at the front door had finally broken inside, too.

How soon until they came to the kitchen searching for Alex and the others?

Alex looked at the woman standing at the fridge. In spite of the distant sounds of commotion, she was still intent on her food.

They needed her to keep eating. A noisy confrontation could alert the others to their location.

He gave the women behind him another *hush* warning, and indicated with a wave that they should follow him.

Silently, they lurked past the woman, keeping a row of counters between them. At the end of the aisle, Alex turned left. The refrigerator was barely five feet away from them.

About fifteen feet away, the passageway terminated at the service door, an "Exit" sign glowing red in the darkness.

The woman abruptly dropped something to the floor. Whatever it was, it splatted, and she uttered a grunt of dismay. She bent over to retrieve it, still standing inside the fridge doors. She muttered something so unintelligible that to Alex it sounded like pure gibberish.

"... *mushputta* ... *barnoop* ... *mutta* ..."

I don't ever want to wind up like any of them, he thought with as much conviction as he'd ever felt about anything. He would have preferred to stick a pistol in his mouth and pull the trigger.

As the woman fumbled to pick up the dropped food, he crept forward.

Someone behind him brushed against something on the counter. A metallic object clanged to the floor. The noise was thunderously loud in the kitchen.

Alex swore silently.

That's it, he thought. *We're done.*

The woman mumbled a confused, "Eh?"

Frantic, Alex reached up along the counter. His trembling fingers closed around what felt like a silver ladle. Without hesitation, he tossed it in an arc toward the other side of the kitchen. Over there, it hit something and rattled against the tile.

"*Mushputta* . . ." the woman mumbled. She left the refrigerator and shuffled away toward the sound.

Heart whamming, Alex hurried along the passageway to the service door. He mashed his shoulder against the long metallic bar at the center, to open it. The door swung out quietly into the rain-spotted night.

None of the maniacs had wandered to the back of the clubhouse.

But the rescue helicopter was gone.

Chapter 26

In Falcon's office, Deacon and Jim had discovered what they needed to know, and had passed along their findings to Bailey. There was nothing else for them to accomplish there as far as Deacon was concerned.

They shut down the surveillance server. The displays went dark.

Deacon allowed himself to enjoy a sense of achievement. They were finally making progress in this unofficial investigation. They had found out some bad things—the perp spreading the infestation through the entire community rated as about the worst thing that could have happened—but at least they *knew*, and it was a small victory.

"What's next, chief?" Jim asked, rising from the chair. "Want to bag Falcon's asshole brother?"

"If he's actually responsible for this crime, he needs to be held accountable," Deacon said. "We're still the law here. We'll do our jobs."

"Falcon's son said he's got a place out in the forest," Jim said. "Any idea where?"

Deacon crossed the room to a large colorful map of South Haven that had been affixed to the wall. He found the greenspace region in the East and tapped it with his finger.

"No, but we'll search. I don't care how long it takes."

"There were no surveillance cameras in that area, I looked for them before I logged off," Jim said. "If there are, they aren't linked to this network."

"That's about what I'd expect from a sibling rivalry," Deacon said. "Mr. Falcon's younger brother isn't gonna abide his big bro spying on him." Turning away from the map, Deacon slipped his cell phone out of his pocket. "Gonna check on my pops, and then we can move out."

His phone displayed the message: *No service available.*

"Jim, does your phone work?" Deacon asked.

Jim quickly pulled out his iPhone and tapped the display. "It's telling me, no service. Think we're in a dead zone?"

"Here in Falcon's castle? No way." He unclipped his two-way radio. "Dr. Bailey, are you there? Do you copy?"

She didn't respond. There could be various reasons for her lack of a reply, but coupled with the disruption in cellular service, Deacon was imagining the worst.

"Chief, take a look out here, will you?" Jim had parted the venetian blinds at a window.

Deacon stared outside. Falcon had built his estate on an elevated plot of land, to provide a panoramic view of his community, and there was no better view to be enjoyed of South Haven than the one from his office window.

The neighborhood beyond the estate was completely dark, as if covered by a vast black sheet.

"It's the quarantine," Deacon said. "They've jammed all cellular transmissions and they've cut electrical power, too. Falcon's estate must be running on an alternate power source, but as rich as he is, even he doesn't have his own mobile communications tower."

"Why the hell would they cut everything off?" Jim asked. He looked as shocked as if he'd been kicked in the groin.

"Why do you think?" Deacon said.

***

Glen couldn't avoid it any longer.

He *had* to get out of South Haven.

He rode his bicycle across neighborhood streets, his camo-colored backpack strapped across his shoulders. If not for the soft luminescent glow of the camcorder he gripped in his right hand, he would have had no idea where he was going.

South Haven had gone dark, in every sense of the term.

For a while, having a front row seat at the crisis that had been unfolding in the community had been thrilling. Glen was a full-time financial analyst but a part-time documentary filmmaker (sort of), and had been live-streaming everything he had seen going on around his townhouse. His social media feeds had exploded with traffic as he broadcast one scene of bloody mayhem after another. People he had known for years, folks who seemed normal and well-adjusted, were either killing each other for no apparent reason, or engaging in bizarre obsessive behavior, which was nearly as frightening: Ms. Stanfield, naked as a jaybird, was using a hula-hoop in the middle of the street, jiggling as if she were participating in a dance contest in hell.

Glen had been spooked, but couldn't stop filming.

This is how the apocalypse begins, he'd thought. *Someone needs to document this, for the good of humanity. Why not me?*

When the CDC had broadcast their quarantine warning over the community's Code Red system, Glen had kept taking video, undeterred. He hadn't truly considered leaving until later in the evening.

When all of the power went out, and with it, the landlines and the cellular signals, too.

He knew what those things meant. Showtime was over.

The military had pulled the plug on everything and was abandoning them, was going to let people kill one another with impunity. With everyone cut off from society, the feds could keep the imminent bloodbath concealed from the outside world.

Glen owned a battery-powered camcorder, like any self-respecting filmmaker would have possessed. He swept it across the neighborhood as he rolled down the road on his bike.

"I'm documenting my departure," he said into the device's microphone. "The situation here has become too unstable for me to risk staying. I know, that sounds funny because we probably reached that crisis point several hours ago, but in the name of performing my duty as a citizen I wanted to stick it out. With the cutting of all electricity, telephones, and cellular capabilities, I fear that the government has given up on us. I received confirmation from a neighbor that they're guarding the perimeter but I think I know a path out. I've got to try."

As Glen pedaled, he was mindful to avoid any deranged-looking residents who might attack, unprovoked. It had become easy to identify the crazies: look for anyone wandering around naked outside.

He saw a few of them, and had to either make a turn to steer away, or lower his head and increase his speed so he buzzed past without attracting notice. In that respect, the darkness that had fallen over South Haven was a benefit.

His route took him to a dead end, the termination of Magnolia Way. Beyond the road stood a grove of magnolia trees, and beyond that, a section of the stone wall that guarded the boundaries of the community.

"Here we are," he said into the camcorder. "Radio silence beyond this point."

He kept the camcorder running as he climbed off his bicycle. The bike was fashioned from carbon-fiber, and weighed less than twenty pounds. He figured he ought to be able to toss it over the wall, scale the barrier, drop onto the other side, climb back onto his ride, and pedal away.

But first, he needed to be sure the coast was clear.

The grove was dark, and quiet. A warm breeze sifted through the trees, carrying the sweet scent of summer blossoms.

He reached the wall and didn't hear or see any armed sentries, which was exactly what he had expected. South Haven was huge. It would have been implausible for soldiers to patrol every square foot of the perimeter.

He leaned his bike against a nearby tree trunk. The wall was about seven feet high, but Glen stood six-two, and he had long arms. After clipping the camcorder to his waist, he hooked both hands onto the top of the wall, and then pulled himself up, using the soles of his sneakers to get additional traction. As his head cleared the barrier, he looked around.

He didn't see anything past the fence, only a sparse collection of shrubs, but a loud buzzing noise came from the darkness beyond his range of vision.

"Alert, citizen," a computerized man's voice said. "Please return to your home. You are under Level Five quarantine."

Glen saw it then: a flashing set of red and blue lights floating in the blackness like malevolent eyes. The buzzing grew louder as the aerial craft approached.

Drone, he thought. *Holy shit.*

From the spinning lights, Glen could estimate the overall size of the thing: it was as big as a large falcon. Its whirring rotors generated so much displaced air that the nearby shrubs trembled as if caught in a strong breeze.

He realized the military wouldn't have needed to deploy soldiers to watch every inch of the wall if they had these robots flying around with infrared sensors, zeroing in on any suspicious movement they detected. He thought he saw mean-looking double barrels attached to the belly of the aerial device, too, but in the dark, it was hard to be certain.

"You are under Level Five quarantine, citizen. Return to your home immediately."

To hell with this, Glen thought. There was no time to go back for his bike. He levered himself over the wall.

The combat drone emitted a nerve-splitting siren, lights blinking more rapidly.

"This is your last warning, citizen. You must comply at once or risk severe injury."

Sweating, his eardrums throbbing, Glen dropped onto the dirt. He took off running, his camcorder bouncing against his waist, all pretenses at filming this experience forgotten.

The drone screeched, sounding remarkably like an enraged animal.

Glen lowered his head and pumped his legs as hard as he could.

He didn't get far.

Chapter 27

D eacon had a job to do. But before he could continue with any of it, he had to get to his father.

In Falcon's office, they booted up the surveillance server again. All of the cameras displayed the same status message: *Offline*.

It made sense, of course. The cameras were linked to the same power grid that supplied electricity to South Haven, and the grid had to be down.

Deacon tried to use the landline-based telephone to call his father's cell phone. He didn't get a dial tone. The line was completely dead.

Cursing, he slammed the handset back onto the cradle. Pops might have been okay, holed up in the apartment with his guns as he promised he would be, but with the recent turn of events, Deacon could no longer trust that he would be safe there on his own.

"No luck with the landline?" Jim asked.

"It's a full communications blackout," Deacon said. Unconsciously, he put his hand against his chest, rubbed as if trying to calm his heart. "It's necessary for what they're planning to do here."

"Which is what?" Jim asked.

"Let the epidemic run its course. Keep us all penned up until we kill each other off eventually or starve to death."

"You really believe that?" Jim sneered. "Christ, I thought I was the cynic in this partnership of ours."

"Think about it. Thanks to our stellar detective work, they'll logically assume that *all* of us are potentially infected." Deacon flipped off the lights in the office, and Jim followed him out of the room.

"There's no treatment for someone who's gotten sick, and anyone infected gets more violent, more feral, by the hour. Imagine a community of three thousand or so bloodthirsty lunatics with almost superhuman strength. They're going to contain the perimeter, I promise you that. No one will get out of here. Those of us stuck inside, who aren't infected? We're on our own."

"So total containment," Jim said. "Innocents be damned. In their minds, it's the less risky strategy."

"They had to cut the communications to keep people from posting more videos to Facebook, Twitter, e-mail, whatever the hell else folks have been doing. Black us out, and then start spinning damage control stories to the media. By the time it's all over, they'll say it was a carbon monoxide leak and that anything that claims otherwise is fake news."

"I want to know what happened to the big douche bag," Jim said. "Kind of funny how he goes AWOL before all this crap came down."

"I've wondered about that, too. He's got to be out there somewhere."

Out in the main corridor of the house, they saw Angie Falcon. She strode toward them, heels clicking on marble, the fabric of her flowing red robe swirling like flames around her. Anger twisted her cosmetically-enhanced nose and lips.

She thrust her iPhone toward Deacon. "What the hell is going on with my phone?"

"Lady, no one's phone is working." He gently pushed her hand aside. "Go read a paperback or something."

"But . . . but I need to use my phone!" Tears shimmered in her big blue eyes. "I was almost at level ninety-seven!"

Deacon didn't have any children, but at that moment, Angie Falcon brought to mind a child throwing a tantrum because she had been denied access to a toy. In a house almost as large as a shopping mall, full of every creature comfort imaginable, didn't she have some other way to entertain herself?

"We've got work to do, little miss," Jim said. "In case you hadn't noticed, the whole community's gone to hell, and now the military is here to clean up the mess."

"Who?" She blinked as if Jim had spoken in a foreign tongue. "The military?"

"There's a federal quarantine in effect," Deacon said. "If you just stay put in your gated mansion, you'll probably be fine."

"So that's why Daddy rushed out of here," Angie muttered. She ran her fingers through her long hair, frowned. "Crap. I need a drink. A gin and tonic would hit the spot. Care to join me, boys?"

Deacon glanced at Jim. Was this woman really so out of touch with reality that she thought they would take her up on her offer?

"Sorry, but we can't drink while we're on the job," Deacon said.

"Oh, whatever. Don't be a tight ass. I won't tell Daddy."

"Do you know where Mr. Falcon was going?" Deacon asked.

"He never tells me anything." She shrugged. "But he had his crossbow with him, like he was going hunting. I'd guess he was going to settle some things with my crazy-as-hell uncle."

"Why would you guess that?" Jim asked.

"Daddy had a look in his eyes like he wanted to kill someone, like seriously. Uncle Kent's the only one who really gets under his skin like that." Angie laughed. "Daddy's got his ways, but Uncle Kent is a certified psycho. He tried to blow up Daddy's car once, did you know that? Actually planted a bomb in it. Daddy figured it out before he started the engine or else he would've been a goner."

"What's this sibling rivalry of theirs all about anyway?" Deacon asked. "Your brother Caleb mentioned it's been going on for a long time."

"Money, power, the same pissing contest crap that you men always do," Angie said, and looked disinterested. "My granddaddy, may he rest in peace, died around last Christmas and left Daddy in charge of the so-called empire. Daddy finally cut off Uncle Kent's monthly allowance. He was *really* happy about doing that." She giggled. "I figure Uncle Kent did something to get revenge, and that's why Daddy stormed out of here looking ready to pin the tail on someone."

"All of you people are insane," Jim said. "It sickens me, it really does. Chief, can we please go now?"

"Hang on." Deacon put a steadying hand on Jim's shoulder, turned back to Angie. He tried to hide his eagerness with a casual tone. "Angie, you said Mr. Falcon left with a crossbow. Does Mr. Falcon keep other weapons here in the house?"

"Of course, he does, and I know the password to the gun safe, too." She smirked, batted her eyelashes. "What are you gonna do for me if I lead you to it, sweet stuff?"

"Good Lord, woman," Jim said. "Do you have *any* clue of the gravity of our situation?"

"It's critically important that we get our hands on more firearms," Deacon said. "Please. We don't have much time."

"I was only gonna say—you gotta have a drink with me, jeez," Angie said. "But fine, I'll take a rain check on that since you boys are in such an all-fire hurry."

He was willing to agree to almost anything in order to get his hands on more firepower.

"Deal," Deacon said.

"All right, then." She snapped her manicured fingers and spun around. "Follow me, boys."

***

Angie led them to a section of the mansion that Deacon hadn't seen during his prior visits. She took them down a winding staircase with a wrought-iron railing, to the basement level. There, she guided them past a room furnished with a pool table and old-school arcade games such as *Pac Man* and *Galaxian*, past an enormous wine cellar that looked like something you would see in an upscale steakhouse, around a corner, past a glass-walled cigar smoking room, and finally, to a large steel-fronted door that reminded Deacon of an entrance to a bank vault. An LCD display and numeric keypad above the door handle demanded a password for entry.

"I'm a little surprised that Mr. Falcon gave you access to this room," Deacon said.

"Think I tricked it out of him?" She winked. "You think I'm just some dumb, hot blonde, don't cha? Got this bootylicious bod but no brains?"

"Hey, you said it," Jim said. "Not us."

"Both of you are way wrong about me," Angie said.

She tapped in a series of numbers on the keypad. A short beep sounded, and there was the sharp click of disengaging locks, and the hiss of a depressurizing chamber.

Deacon pulled the door open, and they followed Angie inside. Motion-activated recessed lights flickered awake.

It was a large, windowless space with a concrete floor, and weapons. Dozens and dozens of weapons, mostly guns of various design. They hung from metal racks on the wall; several of them rested inside glass display cases standing on wooden pedestals. The room smelled faintly of oil, metal, and gunpowder. He also saw other gear such as hunting scopes, combat knives, boots, and gloves.

"Now this was unexpected," Deacon said. "You all could open a store."

"This is an original Colt 1911," Jim said, peering in one of the display cases. "Crap, it looks like it's never been fired."

"Pick two each, y'all," Angie said. "I'd suggest a hand gun and a rifle or shotgun, but it's your preference. We've got plenty of ammo for everything here."

Deacon blinked with surprise at her instructions. "Clearly, you're into guns."

"Daddy is a Marine," she said. "Learning how to handle a firearm is a requirement in this family. Heck, Caleb's a good shot, too, if you can believe that."

"I feel like a kid in a candy store," Jim said, lifting a Winchester hunting rifle off its rack.

Deacon picked out a Remington pump-action shotgun, and a Smith & Wesson .357, to go along with the Glock 17 he already wore. From a tall metal supply cabinet standing along one wall, he selected ammunition for all of the weapons, packing the ammo into a leather pouch that he slid across his shoulders.

"We need ammo for everything we've got," Deacon said. "You mind, Angie?"

"You're gonna owe me plenty, sweet stuff," she said. "Go ahead."

Jim settled on a rifle, and a Heckler and Koch nine millimeter semi-auto pistol. He also grabbed more ammo for the twelve-gauge shotgun he had left back in their vehicle.

While they geared up, Angie watched them with a bemused expression, as if they were a couple of kids getting ready to play war games with toy guns. Deacon still didn't think she understood the seriousness of their situation.

"Is there a panic room on the premises?" he asked her, once he had grabbed everything he needed.

She blinked. "Yeah. It's actually pretty darn nice, kinda like a penthouse suite. Why?"

"I think you should hang out in there for a while," he said. "You and Caleb both. Until tomorrow at least."

"So you *do* have feelings for me." She smiled and touched his arm.

He shrugged. "It's only a precaution. Between the military, and the dangerous, sick people roaming outside, it would be better for you and the boy to stay in a secure location for a while."

"If it makes you feel any better, then I'll do it," she said.

"Thank you. There's one more thing." Deacon motioned Jim over. "What can you tell us about your Uncle Kent? I know he lives on site, in the undeveloped greenspace, but I don't know exactly where. We need specifics on where he lives, *how* he lives, that sort of thing. We're gonna be paying him a visit soon."

"Oh, honey," Angie said, eyes twinkling. "You are so gonna love this."

***

They had escaped the clubhouse, which had been overrun by the frenzied, but in Emily's opinion they still weren't safe. It was full night, the darkness shot through with cold rain, and every pocket of blackness potentially hid someone eager to kill them.

After slipping out of the clubhouse by the rear service entrance, they had crossed a damp, grassy meadow, keeping low to the ground, and then reached a large Colonial-style residence flanked by pine trees. A blue and white sign in the front yard stated, "Model 3 – Open House on Saturday!"

It was the only house standing in the immediate vicinity. There were a few other lots nearby, each marked with a "Future Home Site" sign, but they were only empty plots of sodden land.

At the model home, all of the lights were off, inside and out, but the front door hung halfway open. Had someone already been inside?

Emily approached the threshold. "Anyone here?"

No response.

Moving silently, they filed inside to get out of the rain. The chandelier in the two-story foyer didn't respond when Alex flipped the switch, but Emily tapped the display on her cell phone and selected a flashlight app. Bright white light glowed from the LED flash on the back of the device.

Alex closed the front door. He scratched his arms vigorously, as if he felt bugs crawling across his flesh.

"Are you okay?" Emily asked.

"Let's search this place before we get too comfortable," he said, ignoring her question. He activated a similar app on his phone. "I'll look upstairs if you guys cover the first level."

Using the light emitted from their phones, Emily and the doctor conducted a quick search of the first floor. It was a spacious, elegantly furnished home, with generic landscape scenes hanging on the walls. As they moved from room to room, they attempted to switch on the lights and other appliances, but they were unresponsive. Either the power was disconnected in the home, or there was an outage.

Emily pulled open the door for the powder room, shone the light inside—and let out a short scream.

A body lay slumped against the toilet: it was difficult to tell who it had been because the head had literally been blown apart. A shotgun lay in the person's dead fingers, barrel resting against the blood-covered neck. Blood and bits of flesh stuck to the walls.

Emily stepped back a few steps, her stomach quivering.

"Jesus," Dr. Bailey said. "They just came in here to die?"

Alex hurried to them, eyes wild. "I heard a scream, what happened? The second floor's all clear."

Holding one hand against her mouth, her stomach threatening to heave its contents, Emily pointed at the corpse inside.

"Shit, that's a shame," Alex muttered. "But hey, we've got a shotgun now."

Alex knelt inside and plucked the gun out of the dead person's grasp. Then he checked the pockets of their clothing and found several more shotgun shells.

"You don't seem to be a stranger to this sort of thing," Dr. Bailey said with a narrowed gaze.

"Another life," Alex said with a shrug. He closed the door.

They gathered in the large kitchen. Emily placed her phone on the granite-topped island. The phone cast a narrow cone of light that still left most of the space drenched in darkness; the three of them clustered around the brightness like a tribe huddled around a camp fire.

Emily checked the refrigerator. She didn't expect to find anything, but there was a plastic tray containing about twelve bottles of water, and a six-pack of Coke. The beverages were still cold, which meant the power had only recently shut off.

"No beer?" Alex asked, and snickered. He scratched his neck.

"No food, either, unfortunately," Emily said. "I'm famished."

"Tell me about it, senora. I could slaughter and eat an entire pig right now."

While Emily distributed the water and soda, Alex checked the pantry and cabinets and found a box of unopened Ritz crackers. He tore into the box using his teeth, which Emily found disconcerting, and snatched out the packaged rolls of crackers.

"Going to share any with us?" Emily asked.

Alex blinked. "Oh, yeah. Sure."

For a little while, no one said anything, just drank their beverages and ate crackers as if they were enjoying a dinner in a five-star restaurant. To Emily, everyone looked exhausted and anxious, exactly how she felt, too.

"We aren't getting out of here," Dr. Bailey said, breaking the silence. "The helicopter is gone, and I've got no way to contact them since I lost the sat phone back there on the clubhouse roof."

"Can't you call them on your cell?" Alex asked.

"I'm not getting a signal on my phone," Emily said. "Guys, see if your phone works."

A minute passed while the rest of them attempted to use their cell phones. The muttered curses told Emily everything she needed to know.

"How can no one's cell phone be working?" Emily asked.

"Jammers," Alex said. "You can use them to disrupt signals to mobile towers. Illegal for private citizens to use, but the government would have them."

Emily looked at Dr. Bailey. "Is this normal procedure for a quarantine?"

"I don't know," she said. "But I can understand why they would want to restrict communications, especially considering the scenario here and social media these days."

"The power outage, too," Alex said, pointing at the ceiling. "Think that's part of it?"

"I'm sorry, but I don't know," Dr. Bailey said. "This is a military operation now. I don't know what they've done or what they've got planned."

"So we've probably got no power, and we've got no way to call out of here, either," Emily said. "Perfect."

"I still have this." Dr. Bailey showed them the two-way radio Deacon had given her. "I'd turned it off because we needed to stay quiet back there in the clubhouse, but I could try to raise someone on it now. Maybe Deacon . . ."

"Deacon?" Alex asked. "The South Haven security guy?"

Dr. Bailey switched on the radio and turned up the volume. Static crackled from the speaker. She held down the transmit button, identified herself, and asked if anyone was listening.

"Deacon here," a man said, and Emily wanted to cry at the sound of his voice. "Damn, it's good to hear from you, doc. Where the heck are you?"

Chapter 28

When he spoke to Dr. Bailey again, Deacon was more excited than he had thought he would be.

She was alive, and she was still there in South Haven. He would have preferred for her to be alive and *outside* of South Haven, but he was happy all the same.

She gave him the rundown on their situation, and while it wasn't good, it sounded as if they had found a temporary place of refuge. He asked her to sit tight until he could get to them.

Meanwhile, Angie Falcon had filled him in on quite a bit of useful intel on her nefarious uncle Kent. The woman was savvier than he had given her credit for, and he was inclined to re-evaluate some of his opinions of her. He was eager to get to Kent and force the man to face justice once and for all.

But first things first, he had to get to Pops.

Angie had suggested that he could bring his father back there to the estate, and he planned to take her up on the offer. Falcon's residence, with its back-up power generators and intricate security measures, was by far the most secure stronghold in all of South Haven.

She had also loaned them one of her vehicles, a 2010 Hummer, since the Ford Expedition had sustained a significant amount of damage. Although the Hummer was several years old, the truck was practically brand-new, with only nine thousand miles on the odometer.

"I thought I'd drive it more often," Angie had said. "But it's too darn big for a petite little thing like me."

Equipped with their new weapons, plenty of ammo, and a new vehicle, they drove away from the mansion, Deacon behind the wheel and Jim quite literally riding shotgun. The Hummer's headlamps sliced through the rain-drenched darkness.

It was a quarter past eleven o'clock at night. It had been a brutally long day, and Deacon had enjoyed little rest and eaten only a turkey sandwich and an energy bar a few hours ago, but he was more energized than he had felt in years.

Jim, too, looked invigorated. He clutched the shotgun, head swiveling back and forth to survey the area.

"I've gotta admit, you've a touch with the ladies," Jim said. "You had Miss January eating out of your hand. She'd have probably cooked us dinner if you'd asked."

"Don't hate the lady because she's got good taste in men," Deacon said. "Besides, I think she sees how serious we are about all of this. It's human nature to want to help out."

"But she's not concerned about any of it personally."

"The ultra-wealthy are different than you and me," Deacon said. "Hell, think about what we've learned about Ronald Falcon and his brother Kent. It's looking like everything we're seeing, all this mayhem and death, is because of a sibling rivalry."

"We're pawns in their game." Jim smiled sourly. "Until I shove this nine millimeter up his ass."

"I heard that." Deacon laughed. "Hey, I know it's way past your bedtime, man. I appreciate you sticking with me on this."

"Past my bedtime, hell." Jim barked a laugh. "I barely realized the time. I don't even feel tired, chief. I feel like I'm twenty again."

"Your wife has to be worried about you, now that the phones are down."

"She was a cop's wife for thirty-five years," Jim said with a shrug. "She knows some of these things come with the job. I'll have a helluva story to tell her when we get outta here, won't I?"

"No doubt," Deacon said, though he wasn't convinced any of them would be getting out of there anytime soon. If the military had set up a blockade, an escape attempt would come with a fatally high price. They would have to find an alternate route. But that was a problem they could deal with when the time arrived.

As Deacon steered through South Haven, taking an alternate route back home that he hoped was clear of the frenzied, he spotted lights blazing against the cloudy sky in the general vicinity of his apartment.

His stomach cramped into a tight knot. He levered his foot harder against the accelerator.

"What's wrong?" Jim asked.

Deacon didn't answer. He drove faster. He took a corner so rapidly that the Hummer nearly tipped on its side, and Jim braced himself in his seat, mouth open in surprise.

Please, Deacon thought. *Don't let it be what I think it is.*

The air had become corrupted with the acrid smell of smoke, but it wasn't coming from underneath the hood of the truck. When he cut around the corner at the next intersection, he saw the root cause was exactly what he feared.

The apartment building was on fire.

An army of flames marched across most of the roof. Fire and black smoke fluttered from multiple shattered windows. In the parking lot, at least half a dozen vehicles spat orange flames.

A group of naked people danced and leapt around the burning cars and building, like drunken revelers at a giant bonfire.

Frenzied, he thought, and felt a surge of almost crippling rage. *They did this.*

At the edge of the parking lot, he slammed the brakes so hard that the tires screeched. He grabbed the shotgun and flung open his door.

"Chief, hold on," Jim said. "I'll back you up, we'll get your old man out of there."

Deacon turned away from Jim in time to see a large, naked man running toward him, belly jiggling, eyes crusty and crazed. Deacon pumped the shotgun and blasted the man directly in the chest, and the attacker rocked backward as if snatched away by a great wind.

He pressed on into the parking lot. He didn't wait on Jim. He wasn't going to wait on anyone. Hot currents of fury sizzled through his blood, and the twelve-gauge shotgun in his hands felt like a natural extension of his own limbs, an instrument of unbridled rage.

The heat from the conflagration warmed the sweat on his face. More cars were ablaze than he had thought at first glance. Flames rippled across his own car, a late-model Jeep Grand Cherokee. Technically, it was Falcon's vehicle, loaned to Deacon as a perk of his employment, but the destruction infuriated Deacon nonetheless.

In the apartment complex, something exploded and blew out a window.

He saw the window of the ground-level unit he shared with his father. It was dark but intact, no flames guttering from it, but that meant nothing, as the fire was on a path to devour the entire complex.

Two frenzied came at him from opposite directions. A man and a woman. He blasted the man, the closest one, in the chest, swung around to drop the other one, but she moved fast and was right in his face in a blink. She sliced at him with a chef's knife. The blade slashed across his neck, barely missing the jugular vein. He shoved the shotgun barrel in her stomach and squeezed the trigger.

She collapsed at his feet with a sigh.

Blood trickled from the gash in his neck. He put one hand against the cut, felt that it wasn't deep, and moved on.

On the ground, he saw a red gasoline can, a trail of flames leading from it to various vehicles in the parking lot. One of the frenzied, in one of their bizarre obsessive fits, must have thought it was a bright idea to dribble gasoline all over the place and take a match to it. He was certain that the flames consuming the apartment building were borne of the same pyromania.

He stepped around a flaming truck. A couple was copulating on the ground. Like dogs. Their skin glistened in the firelight. The man noticed Deacon and sneered. Deacon swung the shotgun and whacked the man full in the face with the butt of the weapon, and heard the crunch of the guy's teeth cracking.

He reached the alcove of the apartment building. This close, the heat was intense enough to singe the hairs on Deacon's face.

He hurried down the corridor. Wraiths of black smoke billowed along its length. Deacon coughed, but kept moving. The exterior hallway hadn't yet been touched by the spreading inferno, but flames glowed at the top of the staircase that connected the three floors of the building.

As he neared his apartment, he saw the door was already open. Black smoke poured from the doorway.

No . . .

His knees got weak.

Maybe Pops got out, he thought. *Maybe the door is open because he escaped.*

Deacon charged inside. He screamed: "Pops!"

Smoke and flames were everywhere. The smoke stung his eyes, brought forth tears. His chest burned.

He was at risk of poisoning himself with smoke, but he pressed on.

He didn't see his father in the living room. He rushed down the hallway. A tongue of flames slowly lapped across the ceiling. He swung into his father's bedroom. The bed was empty. Flames danced on the bedsheets and pillows. Fire crawled across the ceiling and walls.

His father's wheelchair stood next to the burning bed. Empty.

"Pops!" Deacon shouted, hoarse.

A muffled cough. From across the room. The closet.

Deacon moved so fast he wasn't conscious of crossing the distance. In the next heartbeat his hand was on the doorknob of the closet. The brass knob was hot, and scalded his fingers, but he barely felt the pain as he flung open the door.

His father was crumpled in fetal position on the floor, half-hidden underneath a pile of old clothes. He coughed weakly.

His gaze found Deacon. His eyes looked watery and red.

"Fell . . . asleep," Pops wheezed. "Fell asleep . . . woke up when everything . . . was burning . . ."

Deacon dropped to the floor and gathered his father in his arms.

"Hold on to me," Deacon whispered, but his father was too weak to comply. Deacon slung his father over his shoulders in a fireman's carry position.

He staggered out of the bedroom.

Behind them, the ceiling collapsed with a boom.

In the hallway, Deacon paused. The route to the doorway was impassable. The flames had advanced. He couldn't see his way through them.

He swung around and stumbled to the end of the corridor. A bathroom on the left, his own bedroom on the right.

He turned into his room.

Fire slowly chewed through the space, and smoke churned through the air, but the path to the large window on the opposite wall was clear.

Deacon moved toward it. It was a short distance, but it felt like a mile, like a scene from a nightmare in which a hallway keeps lengthening no matter how fast you run. The smoke was getting to him, making his throat and lungs ache. His father felt as if he weighed five hundred pounds, a ton.

The bed was calling him. He could drop his father on the mattress and lie beside him and they could lie there together and let the flames and smoke fold over them . . .

Grimacing, he kept on.

He reached the window. He blew a hole in the glass with the shotgun, used the barrel to knock away jagged shards.

Come on now, Pops . . .

He heaved his dad off his shoulders, and pushed him through the window. His father offered no resistance or support. It was like shoving a bundle of laundry down a chute. His father dropped into the bushes outside the glass.

There was a crackling noise behind him. Deacon turned. All around him, the bedroom ceiling was falling apart. The smoke had gotten thicker, more toxic. The heat inside was tremendous—Deacon was completely saturated with sweat.

He reached forward to climb out and a blood-streaked hand thrust toward him. He was about to raise the shotgun when he heard a familiar voice.

"I've got you, chief," Jim said.

Deacon clasped his hand, and his partner pulled him outside.

Fresh air had never tasted so good. Sucking it in, Deacon was overcome by a painful fit of coughing. He doubled over. His lungs felt as if they were full of shattered bones.

"Get Pops . . ." Deacon gasped, but Jim was already on it, had lifted his father over his broad shoulders.

Jim moved his father out of harm's way, near an elm tree in the courtyard. His carefully placed him on the ground.

"Jesus, he's not breathing," Jim said.

Deacon stumbled toward them. He dropped onto the ground next to his dad and shoved Jim aside.

His father's eyes were shut. His face was ashen, and slack.

No, no, no, no, no . . .

Deacon began to administer CPR. He put his hands on his dad's frail chest and pushed hard and fast.

"Wake up, Pops," Deacon said in a raspy voice, pushing. "Hey, old man! Wake up!"

He pinched his dad's nose shut, covered his mouth with his, blew in twice, and then started pushing on his chest again. Pops was unresponsive.

"You're missing all the fun, old man!" Deacon said. He laughed, hot tears streaming down his face. He was crying and couldn't stop. He was trying to bring his dad back and couldn't stop. His father had never given up on him, even when he had given up on himself. "Come on, Pops! Pops! Get your ass up and let's get down to business! You've got work to do, old man! Pops . . ."

Behind them, the apartment building sizzled and smoked, while the frenzied danced and rutted around the flames.

Chapter 29

A fter she had connected with Deacon via the two-way radio and gotten word that he was coming their way once he picked up his father, Hannah dared to relax for a spell.

She had found some plain white candles and matches in a drawer beside the refrigerator, lit them, and placed them around the kitchen, trying to strategically eliminate as many dark pockets as possible. The group sat around the circular wooden table in the breakfast nook, eating crackers, sipping water and soda, and talking about everything except what was going on outside the walls of the house.

The mystery man, Alex, was the only one who wouldn't sit still. He paced the stone tile floor and circled the large granite island like a mouse trapped in a maze, scratching his arms and neck as if phantom insects swarmed over his skin. He had eaten his share of crackers and kept eyeing the food the rest of them were still consuming; he looked as if he desperately wanted to steal their portions and was struggling to control himself.

He kept looking at Hannah and Emily directly, too, with long gazes simmering with desire. Hannah imagined that he was undressing them in his mind and fantasizing about what he could do to them. Like most women, she was accustomed to similar looks from other men, but the searing heat in his eyes took her aback.

Then, Alex abruptly left the kitchen, muttering under his breath. She heard him stomping upstairs.

Hannah looked at Emily. The young woman's face was crinkled with worry.

"There's something wrong with him," Hannah said. "I know you see it, too."

"He saved our lives back at the clubhouse," Emily said. "If he hadn't been there to guide us, we wouldn't have made it out. He saved *your* life, doctor."

Hannah would never forget the Amazonian woman who had nearly choked her out on the roof. She had the purple-black bruises on her neck to remind her.

"His skin is clearly irritated, his eyes are beginning to look inflamed," Hannah said. "We both know what those symptoms indicate."

"What do *you* want to do about it then?" Emily asked. There was a challenge in her gaze.

"I'm not the enemy here," Hannah said. "Neither is he. I'm only saying, he's not well, and we need to be cautious."

"Fine." Emily got up and went to the counter island, where they had placed the shotgun Alex had taken from the dead man in the bathroom. She brought the shotgun to Hannah. "Here you go. Stay on high alert."

"You keep it. I don't know how to use a gun."

"Of course you don't." Emily placed the weapon back on the counter. "Maybe it's time you learned something useful, *doctor.*"

"Girl, what the hell is wrong with you?" Hannah rose from her chair, arms crossed over her bosom. "What's the deal with all the attitude you're throwing at me?"

Emily sneered—and smacked Hannah in the face. The blow was hard enough to snap Hannah's head sideways. Her cheek stung, tears blurring her vision.

I don't believe this girl hit me, she thought. *Has she lost her mind?*

Emily grabbed a fistful of Hannah's hair. "You were going to let us die here, you bitch! You were going to leave us!"

Shifting her weight, Hannah broke Emily's hold on her. She expertly wrangled Emily around, got her off balance, and tossed Emily over her hip, a perfectly executed hip throw. Emily crashed against a chair, knocked it over. Sitting on the floor, she looked dazed.

"I don't know how to use a gun, true, but I know how to use my hands quite well," Hannah said. "Cool out, girl, or I will *make* you cool out, believe that."

Shrieking, Emily rushed her. Hannah sidestepped, got her hands on Emily, and hip-tossed her again, sending her hurtling against the cabinets.

She didn't want to hurt the girl, but she had to let Emily get all of this out of her, or else they wouldn't be able to move forward.

Emily was as tenacious as a bulldog, though, she would give her that. The girl got up again and came at her, flailing, and Hannah easily grappled her into a submission hold of pure dominance: Emily's arms pinned behind her back like a pair of chicken wings, Hannah bracing her against the edge of the counter.

"You're hurting me!" Emily said.

"You started this, now I'm finishing it." Hannah didn't relinquish her hold. Instead, she tightened her grip a notch.

"My arms . . ." Emily whimpered, her body shuddering.

"I am a judoka, Emily," Hannah said calmly. "I've trained since I was six years old. I could easily dislocate both of your shoulders right now—it would be like breaking breadsticks to me. I've done it before. I do know a *few* useful things. Don't ever raise your hand to me again. Are we clear?"

"Let me go!" Emily wailed.

"Wrong answer." Hannah applied slightly more pressure, and Emily let out hiss of agony. "I said, are we clear, Emily?"

"Yes . . . yes . . . clear, clear!" Crying, Emily bobbed her head.

Hannah let her go. Sniffling, gently rubbing her shoulders, Emily set upright one of the knocked over chairs, and slumped into it. She cast a glance at Hannah. Her eyes held a little fear, but mostly, they reflected a newfound respect.

Hannah closed her eyes for a beat. She felt worn out, physically and emotionally. She hated that this had happened between them. She hated everything that was going on, to all of them, and figured stress was pushing them to the breaking point.

"I'm sorry for what happened at the clubhouse," Hannah said. "You were right, I was going to hop onboard that chopper and go on my merry way. It was selfish and wrong. I never should have agreed to the extraction in the first place, not without a plan to help those who are healthy."

"You were only here to do a job, right?" Emily asked. She brushed hair out of her face. "Your job was over, doctor."

"Please, call me Hannah, okay? I think we're well past all the formalities now that we've tried to beat up each other like a couple of boys on the schoolyard."

"Beat up each other?" Emily smiled through a faceful of drying tears and rubbed her shoulders again. "That was a pretty lopsided fight. I had no idea you knew how to handle yourself like that. Wow."

"It's not something I discuss often. I'd rather let someone underestimate me."

"I'm sorry about slapping you and calling you a bitch," Emily said, cheeks flushing red. "I'm not a violent person. That's so unlike me. I don't know what got into me."

"We're both under more pressure than we've ever felt in our lives," Hannah said. "But we can't ever turn against each other. We've got to have each other's backs."

"We've got enough enemies out there already, for sure," Emily said.

"So." Hannah indicated the shotgun on the counter. "It sounds like you know how to use this?"

"Zack is—was—sort of into guns," Emily said, and looked sad for a moment. "He took me to the firing range with him every now and then."

"Mind teaching me?" Hannah asked.

***

Alex felt seriously ill.

His head hurt. His mouth was dry. His skin itched, and felt hot, as if he were under the constant glare of a heat lamp.

And he was starving. Famished.

He couldn't bear to be in the room with the two women, not while they were eating. He had to restrain himself from snatching the crackers out of their hands and licking the crumbs off the floor.

What most disturbed him was the way he was beginning to think about the women, too.

In the glowing candlelight, both of the women looked absolutely delicious, Emily with her smooth olive skin and Hannah with her honey-brown complexion, both of them clearly exhausted but still unbelievably attractive. He kept imagining them naked. He saw himself running his tongue across their fine bodies.

He saw himself taking a bite out of them.

Taking a bite out of them, what the hell am I thinking?

He couldn't handle being near them, and fled the kitchen, wandering upstairs to the darkened second floor. He groaned.

I'm sick, I've got that shit they all do, the bug neurotoxin or whatever it's called . . .

He had long suspected he was sick, ever since he had awakened in a cage in crazy Wayne's house and found evidence that the man had injected some of his diseased blood into his bloodstream. A tick had never crawled into his nose. Apparently it hadn't needed to; someone else's bad blood was sufficient to do the trick, given enough time.

He stormed into a bathroom. Using the flashlight on his phone, he examined himself in the big mirror above the dual-vanity.

He was beginning to look like one of *them*.

"Ay dios mio!" he said.

He smashed the butt of his Beretta against his reflection. The mirror broke, blades of glass clinking into the sink.

He heard a commotion from downstairs; it sounded like the ladies were arguing. Someone screamed, and there was the crash of what might have been overturning furniture, and a shriek of rage.

Let them fight, he thought. *Let them kill each other. Better for them to kill each other than for me to go down there and tear into both of them.*

He moaned. He pressed his hands on either side of his skull, squeezing, as if he could apply enough pressure to eventually force these murderous thoughts out of his head.

I am not a killer. I don't want to hurt anyone.

But how many people had he killed during his life? Dozens? He had been an assassin for the cartel for much longer than he had ever done anything else. How could he claim that a talent—an urge—to kill had not been in his nature all along?

He stumbled out of the bathroom, into a large furnished bedroom. The room should have been darker, as there was no visible light source, but he was able to clearly make out lines of furniture, shapes of artwork hanging on the walls, as if he'd been granted a measure of night vision.

Was that a symptom of the affliction? The enhancement of nocturnal predator traits such as being able to see in the dark?

He didn't want it. He didn't want any of it.

He had to end this.

Gnashing his teeth, he levered the barrel of the Beretta against his temple. His finger inched to the trigger.

Do it, while you still have some dignity left, Alex.

Then he heard laughter downstairs. The women, who apparently had been battling like tigers only a short while ago, sounded as if they were sharing a joke.

The music of their laughter broke his resolve. He imagined them smiling. Eyes sparkling. Skin so gloriously smooth and tasty.

His mouth watered with hunger.

He tore off his shirt.

And left the room.

***

Emily didn't consider herself a weapons expert by any stretch of the imagination, but she was able to instruct Hannah—it was tough to call the doctor by her first name, but she insisted on it—in the basics of using the shotgun. How to load, hold, and fire it; just as important, how to reload it. Zack had taught her well during their numerous trips to the local firing range, and though she had merely tolerated those visits at the time, she appreciated the lessons now. They could save her life.

Hannah was a quick study, too, but whether she would be capable of pulling the trigger on anyone was another matter entirely. Emily wasn't sure she would be able to do it, either. Her entire focus in life was to become a healer. Could she draw a weapon on someone if she had to? Thus far, she had been spared that difficult choice.

"You're a good teacher," Hannah said. She carefully placed the shotgun on the kitchen counter, and lined up the extra shells. "I feel as if I'm prepared for anything."

"Sure thing," Emily said. "You'll have to teach me some of those judo moves sometime."

"Of course. Every woman should know how to defend herself. I'd be happy to show you a few things."

They exchanged a smile. Emily was embarrassed when she reflected on their altercation, but they had clearly progressed beyond that incident, thankfully. It was beginning to feel as if they were developing a genuine friendship—sort of a big sister, little sister bond—

and the idea excited her. She had a handful of friends, but they were all people her age, hyper-focused on school and positioning themselves to launch successful careers. It would be refreshing to hang out with someone like Hannah, a woman who—

The sound of approaching footsteps diverted her thoughts. She turned.

It was Alex.

He shuffled into the candlelight. He had stripped off his shirt. Elaborate tattoos decorated his skin: one around his neck that resembled a rosary; another on his arm of a robed skeletal figure holding a scythe; yet another on his chest of a horned, demonic visage.

Emily had once watched a cable documentary about Mexican drug cartels. The ink on Alex's skin marked him as a member—a former one, no doubt—of that deadly fraternity.

But fresh crimson sores mapped his body, too. His deep-set eyes, ringed with inflammation, seethed like glowing embers.

A blade of tension twisted through Emily's chest. Hannah had been right about him. Emily had known it, too, but she hadn't wanted to accept the truth.

Beside her, Hannah tensed.

"Alex?" Emily asked. "You don't look well. How are you feeling?"

"I . . . can't help it," he said in a voice as coarse as sandpaper. "Help . . . can't . . . I . . . so delicious . . ."

Gaze shifting between Emily and Hannah, he licked his lips.

"So delicious," he said again. "Bite . . . wanna . . ."

"We're your friends, Alex," Hannah said in a tremulous voice. "You don't want to hurt us."

"Friends," Alex said, as if the word were alien to him. He squeezed his eyes shut for a beat. A grimace contorted his face. "Dios lo que está mal conmigo?"

Emily had taken several units of Spanish during high school, but that had been years ago. She thought he had said, *what is wrong with me?*

"Estás enfermo," Hannah said. "Usted debe estar. Nosotros nos encargamos de usted."

Hannah was trying to persuade him to rest, Emily realized. Trying to convince him that they would care for him.

Moaning, Alex clasped his head between his hands. Emily edged closer to the counter where the gun lay. She met Hannah's gaze. Hannah seemed to understand Emily's intent, and nodded.

Emily closed her fingers around the butt of the shotgun. She quietly dragged the weapon toward her.

Alex uttered an unintelligible sound of primal anguish, as if he were being devoured from inside out. A shiver coursed through him—and then he drew his pistol with the quicksilver speed of a gunslinger. He swept it across both of them, back and forth. Sweat streamed down his face in fat rivulets.

"No," Hannah said, raising her hands. "You don't need to do this, Alex. Por favor."

By then, Emily had both hands on the shotgun, but she had no chance of getting off a shot before he did.

"*Dios perdoname,*" Alex whispered.

He jammed the pistol in his mouth and pulled the trigger.

***

Both Emily and Hannah screamed.

Alex collapsed forward. His head struck the edge of the granite island. Blood and dark bits of flesh seeped from the ragged exit wound at the top of his skull. A final death spasm jittered through his body, and the movement sent him sliding to the floor, where he hit the tile with a lifeless thud only a few feet away from Emily.

"Oh, God," Emily said. Her heart felt as if it had lurched into her throat. Shock had flash-frozen her in place.

Hannah, too, stood as still as a wax figure, one hand raised to her mouth, teeth clamped over her thumb.

"You tried to talk him down," Emily said, finding her voice. "I know he didn't want to hurt us."

"Yeah." Hannah lowered her head and let out a deep sigh. "We should move him somewhere. Leaving him on the floor like this, it's not right."

"He deserved better," Emily said.

"Help me lift him, okay?" Hannah bent to grasp his ankles.

"Wait, what was that?" Emily had heard a banging sound, close by. At first, she thought it was another gunshot. Then she heard heavy footsteps in the foyer, and realized the initial noise was an opening door.

Front door, someone's inside.

She tightened her grip on the shotgun. Perspiration trickled into the corners of her eyes.

"Do you think that's Deacon?" Hannah whispered.

"Not sure," Emily said.

The roaming footsteps sounded as if the walker was barefoot: Emily picked up the squishy noise of bare flesh slapping against wood.

Naked, she thought. *That means it's one of them.*

She edged backward. Hannah had sensed it, too. She sidled along the island, retreating from the vicinity of the doorway.

The door banged again, and more footsteps clapped inside. A woman cackled, a sound that sent a chill coursing down Emily's spine.

The gunfire had attracted them. Probably, it was the same frenzied mob they had eluded at the clubhouse only a short while ago. They were winding through the streets, seeking out those unlike them, eager to tear and destroy for reasons they no longer understood themselves.

Something shattered in a front room of the house. A man let loose a stream of pure gibberish.

Emily caught Hannah's gaze, and they communicated without verbalizing a single word: *Let's get the hell out of here.*

Together, they raced across the kitchen, opened the patio doors, and plunged into the night.

Chapter 30

The buzzing of Deacon's walkie-talkie summoned him back to the world.

Deacon didn't realize he had dozed off. He had been dreaming about Pops, a dream of a beloved childhood memory. When he was five, on Saturday mornings, Pops had begun taking him to a local barbershop to get his hair cut, and in the beginning, Deacon would squirm in the chair as the barber buzzed the clippers across his scalp. *Boy's a little jumpy, but he'll settle down,* Pops told the man. After getting his hair cut, Pops would usually take him to the park and shoot baskets with him.

When Deacon came to he found he was in the passenger seat of the Hummer. Jim was behind the wheel, but they weren't moving. They were parked somewhere dark and quiet. Rain dribbled on the roof.

He reeked of smoke, and his mouth tasted like ashes. His throat ached, too, but his heart hurt most of all.

Pops is gone, my daddy is dead . . .

He wanted to dive back into the comforting womb of unconsciousness, but the two-way radio was buzzing.

"Gonna get that, chief?" Jim asked. He lifted his head; he sounded as if he had slipped into slumber, too. "Might be the girls calling. We still have a job to do."

Moving as sluggishly as a sleepwalker, Deacon activated the walkie-talkie. "Deacon here."

"It's me," Dr. Bailey said. "Listen, where are you?"

The urgency in her voice pulled him up in his seat. Clearing his throat, he looked around at where they had parked, and didn't immediately recognize the area, but his brain was still foggy.

"Memorial Court," Jim said softly.

"We had to leave the house," Bailey continued. "Alex is . . . dead. We ran into some infected."

"Where are *you*?" Deacon asked. "We're on Memorial Court—that's the street name. We're parked in a cul-de-sac. We're in a black Hummer."

"Hang on," Bailey said. Deacon heard Emily's voice in the background. Bailey said, "Hey, that's literally right around the corner from where we are. We've been hiding out in someone's backyard gazebo."

"Finally something goes our way," Deacon said, and his voice nearly broke. A wave of grief had risen in his heart, threatened to pull him under. He bit his bottom lip and blew out a breath. He could not grieve. Later, there would be time to properly mourn his father, but right then, he had people counting on him, and he couldn't let them down. Pops would have wanted him to do that—stay focused on the job, regardless of what was going on with him personally.

Jim had twisted the key in the ignition. The vehicle awakened with a rumble. Jim steered out of the cul-de-sac and crept along the road.

"Sit tight, but stay on the line and keep talking to me," Deacon said. "We're coming to get you."

***

The women had given them the address of the residence where they had hidden in the gazebo on the property. Jim pulled the Hummer in front of the house; it was an elegant Colonial, utterly dark. Both Dr. Bailey and Emily emerged like shadows from the back yard. They dashed to where the truck idled at the curb.

Deacon got out of the vehicle to receive them. He pulled both of the ladies into an embrace. He and Dr. Bailey were still holding on to each other after Emily had slipped away and climbed into the backseat.

Dr. Bailey clutched him tightly, her head buried against his chest. She felt good in his arms. She felt *right.*

Or perhaps, after what they had experienced in the past twelve hours, they both simply craved a good hug.

"Sorry, Doc." He released his hold on her. "I'm suffocating you here."

"It's Hannah." Her eyes glimmered. "No need to apologize. I think I could get used to that, in fact."

Her smile was like a promise of the future, one that he desperately hoped could arrive soon. A future beyond the hellhole of South Haven, somewhere he could laugh and love again.

He held open the rear passenger door for her, and then got back into the shotgun seat.

"Where's your father?" Hannah asked. "You were going to pick him up?"

"It didn't work out," Deacon said.

"Oh." Hannah reached from the backseat and touched his shoulder. "I'm sorry."

Deacon didn't elaborate—he couldn't talk about his father without falling apart—and thankfully, neither Emily nor Hannah pressed for more details.

"Where to folks?" Jim asked. His fingers drummed the steering wheel.

"Let's pull into the driveway of this place and cut the engine," Deacon said. "We've found a pocket of quiet here, but it's best to lie low until we're ready to move. We need to discuss some things."

Jim maneuvered the big SUV into the driveway under the sodden boughs of an elm tree. Once he shut off the vehicle, the only sound was the relentlessly thrumming rain. The neighborhood was dark as a forest, not a single light burning in any of the homes.

"All right." Deacon shifted in his seat to face the women. "Fill me in on what went down. You said this guy Alex is gone?"

"Alex was infected." Emily dragged her fingers through her hair. "He tried to fight it, but he couldn't. He took his own life."

"Damn," Deacon said. "I knew him, not well, but I was acquainted with him. He had that frozen yogurt shop over on Main. Seemed like a good guy."

"We wouldn't be here if it weren't for him," Hannah said. "But after he was gone, we ran into more of the infected. Their numbers are growing, and they're wilder than ever as crazy as that sounds."

"Fighting them isn't our priority, we only need to steer clear of them," Deacon said. He unfolded his marked-up community map. "Our priority—mine and Jim's anyway—is getting to Kent Falcon. He's the criminal, and he's going to be held responsible for what he's done to us, and everyone else who's suffered here."

***

"He lives in that old mine off the greenway?" Emily said. "I heard about that place but obviously never went in there since it looked like it was off-limits to everyone. I thought it was shut down?"

"We all did, but that's where Kent Falcon has been hiding out, according to his niece," Deacon said. "Most important, she says he's got his own service road that he uses to travel in and out of there, and it takes him beyond the perimeter of South Haven."

"In other words, it's our only way out of the community," Hannah said. "Since the military clearly has established a blockade at the fence and the gates. If we could get into the mine and find this service road, we could slip out under their radar."

"Right." Deacon studied the faces of the women. They looked exhausted, but resolute. Nevertheless, he said, "You don't have to go through any of this with us, you know. I'm sure Angie Falcon would let both of you wait it out at their estate. They've got a panic room."

"*No*," Emily and Hannah said in unison.

"We don't know what we're going to run into in the mine," Jim said. "But we keep hearing that this Kent asshole is crazy as hell. Both of you girls up for that?"

"Going there is as much my job as it is both of yours," Hannah said. "My boss might have shut down my investigation, but I've still got a responsibility to uphold."

"And I've got personal reasons for going—things I've lost," Emily said, eyes shimmering. She clasped a silver locket she wore around her neck. "Hiding out isn't an option. I have to see this through."

"Sounds like we're all in, then." Deacon looked from the women, to Jim. "Let's divvy up our gear, and head over there."

Chapter 31

Deacon was grateful Angie Falcon had loaned them the Hummer. It did a more than adequate job of transporting them through the night-swept woodlands of the South Haven Greenway. Off the paved path, the land was bumpy, rife with clumps of grass, dense shrubs, and towering pines, elms, and magnolias. Jim plowed the Hummer across the wilderness as if it were an Army tank, mowing over weeds, crunching past tree branches, ripping through vines.

It was a rough ride, and Deacon's head had banged against the ceiling a couple of times, but they made it to the fenced perimeter of the old mine all in one piece. Rusty barbed wire bordered the top of the seven-foot-high fence like rows of miniature teeth. A faded sign warned: *Private Property - No Trespassing.*

A shiny ATV stood outside the open gate. Elaborately detailed images of falcons adorned the vehicle's body. Deacon could only shake his head.

"As expected, Mr. Falcon beat us here," Deacon said. "Nice of him to leave the gate open for us, too."

"Think he's already taken care of his shithead brother?" Jim asked.

"If so, he's done us a great service." Deacon glanced behind him at the two ladies. "Ready to roll?"

"Let's do it," Hannah said, and Emily nodded.

The women had brought along a twelve-gauge shotgun they had picked up in their travels, and plenty of ammo. Emily kept the weapon, and Deacon had given his fully-loaded Glock 17 to Hannah along with a spare magazine. Deacon kept the .357 revolver and the Remington shotgun he had taken from Falcon's arsenal.

He climbed out of the Hummer. The rain had kept up a steady, maddening drizzle. The only light came from the headlamps of their vehicle.

"You can kill the engine," he said to Jim. "If all goes as planned, we're not coming back here."

Jim shut off the engine, and the headlights died. Darkness rose, and surrounded them like a broad cloak.

Deacon approached Falcon's ATV. His hope was that Falcon had left behind something that might come in handy, but a quick search of the vehicle yielded nothing of use.

"He had a bag of explosives," Emily reminded them. "He must have taken it with him."

"I would think we would have heard dynamite going off," Hannah said. She shrugged. "But we've admittedly been preoccupied."

"The mine looks intact." Deacon peered ahead, squinting against the raindrops. The entrance was about a hundred yards away, a dark passage embedded in the craggy hillside. "We're not going to know what's happened until we get in there."

He realized they didn't have anything that would have qualified as a master strategy. Their objectives were simple. Get inside the mine. Track down Kent Falcon. Interrogate him using any means necessary. Grab evidence proving his crime. Get out of the mine, and hopefully, out of South Haven without alerting the armed guard on the community perimeter. It was a straightforward plan, but there were so many unknowns that everything could go catastrophically wrong.

They were about to proceed through the gate when Jim halted.

"Hey, hear that?" he asked in a near-whisper. He cocked his head, eyes narrowed to slits.

Deacon listened closely. Under the ceaseless patter of the rain, he heard it, too: distant barking, growing louder. Cold dread stirred in his gut. "Dogs."

"Crap," Emily said.

"If it's that same pack of 'em we've seen, we can't outrun them," Jim said. "They'll get in here and tear us to shreds. We've gotta close this gate."

"I'll stay behind with you," Deacon said. "Emily, Hannah—I think both of you should go on ahead and figure out how we get inside the mine."

"Are you sure?" Hannah asked.

He nodded. "Go."

Emily and Hannah hurried ahead, their shoes sloshing along the muddy dirt path that led to the entrance. Deacon turned to Jim.

"Let's get it done."

In only a minute, the dogs' barking had grown much louder. The darkness in the woods was so thick that he couldn't see anything. He brandished his tactical flashlight and swept the beam across the woods beyond. He saw only trees, but the light had a limited range of perhaps ten yards.

"Cover me, chief." Jim raced outside the gate.

"You're clear." Deacon drew the .357 and held it at a low-ready position. He clutched the flashlight in a reverse grip, allowing him to scan the area with the lamp while keeping the firearm prepared for a quick shot.

"Shit," Jim said, tugging at a piece of metal. "It's got a post keeping it in the ground, and the mud's got it all clogged up down in there."

"Take your time," Deacon said, though his heart slammed and he wanted nothing more than for them to finish this, asap.

He light-scanned the woods again, found nothing, but from the sound of them, the dogs were closing in fast.

"Got it." Jim snatched the post out of the earth, the metal screeching. Gripping the handle, he strained to pull the gate shut. The rusted hinges creaked.

Deacon stepped forward to help him. In the backsplash of the flashlight he spotted a dog running at them, like something out of a bad dream. It was the St. Bernard that had nearly ripped out his throat that morning. Emerging from the darkness, the infected dog looked impossibly huge.

Deacon fired. The hollow-point round drilled the monstrous dog squarely in its massive chest, and it staggered to a stop and collapsed on the grass.

"Move it, Jim!" Deacon shouted.

Cursing, Jim struggled to pull the heavy gate shut. Another hound leaped out of the shadows, a German Shepherd with feral, inflamed eyes. Deacon went for center mass again and blew a round into the animal. It wobbled to the ground.

But plenty more were coming. The woods were alive with furious howls and barks.

Jim swung the gate into the closed position. Deacon grabbed a piece of the gate and held it while Jim drove the post into the fence's metal sleeve, snapping it in place.

"There's a padlock by the ATV." Jim pointed.

"Forget about it," Deacon said. He rattled the gate, once, and it held firm. "This'll do fine."

As he spoke, the rest of the pack thundered out of the woods and gathered at the fence. The group was larger than what they had seen earlier; there were over two dozen dogs, varying in breed and size, but all of them marked by the same symptoms of illness. The canines snarled, snapped, and slobbered, their snouts poking at the chain-link barrier.

A couple of them tried to chew their way through the fence, teeth breaking on the metal.

"Let's get the hell out of here," Jim said.

They backed away from the gate.

Where's the dog walker? Deacon thought. Earlier, a young man had been steering the pack through the community like some demonic version of the dog whisperer. It was unlikely that the dogs had tracked them to the mine on their own.

Someone yelled what sounded like a battle cry. Deacon looked up and saw a large shape hurtling toward them, coming from the elm tree boughs that nearly overhung the perimeter fence.

"Jim!" Deacon raised his handgun.

The dog walker launched himself off the tree, over the fence, and on top of Jim. Jim collapsed under the weight of the big man like someone flattened by a falling safe, his head rapping against the hard earth with an ugly thudding sound.

Wild, damp hair obscuring his face, rain glistening on his nude body, the dog walker seized a fistful of Jim's mane and slammed his head against the ground. Jim twitched like a sputtering live wire. The dog walker shouted incoherent words, leashes swinging like strange talismans around his neck.

Deacon fired the .357 from a range of barely ten feet. The round penetrated the attacker's chest, knocked him back a few feet off Jim's body. Another shot in the head dropped him for good.

Beyond the fence, the dogs howled.

Jim wasn't moving. He lay on the ground on his stomach, head twisted to one side, arms spread-eagled.

Deacon's knees felt as if they would buckle. He rushed to Jim's side.

Please, God.

He panned the flashlight across Jim's face. Jim blinked, his eyes unfocused and glassy.

This close to his partner, with the bright light in his face, Deacon noticed that Jim's eyes were outlined with a faint crimson hue, and the telltale lesions had begun to develop on his forehead. That tick they had found in his nose must've gotten some of its poison into his bloodstream before they had extracted it.

Maybe going out fighting like this is a blessing, Deacon thought.

But he wasn't ready to give up on Jim.

"Can you walk?" Deacon asked. "Talk to me, buddy."

Jim's lips moved, but Deacon couldn't hear him. Carefully, Deacon pulled him into a sitting position. Jim offered no resistance or help. His limbs felt limp, like a broken doll's.

"Leave me . . ." Jim whispered. He wheezed. "Can't . . . move . . . can't . . . breathe . . ."

Cervical fracture, Deacon thought, his heart plummeting. The impact of the attacker crashing onto him from an elevated height, and hammering his head against the ground, had literally broken Jim's neck.

It might not have been safe to move Jim, but he couldn't leave him there to die. Gently, Deacon cradled his arm underneath Jim's neck, to support his head. He got his other arm beneath Jim's legs.

"No . . . chief," Jim whispered.

Deacon ignored him. Groaning from the effort, Deacon lifted him in his arms. The strap of Jim's rifle slipped off his shoulder, and the weapon dropped to the ground. Deacon left it behind and focused on his friend.

"Whoa, you're heavy, man," Deacon said. "You need to lay off those donuts, buddy."

Jim uttered a wheeze that Deacon interpreted as a laugh, but the light in his eyes had dimmed. He didn't want to believe that Jim would fail to pull through this. Jim was a tough old bird. He would pull through—he *had* to pull though. Deacon had already lost his father that night, a wound so deep and fresh he couldn't bear to think about it. He couldn't lose Jim, too.

He carried Jim to the mine entrance, where Hannah and Emily worked at opening the door.

By the time he reached them, the light had already faded from Jim's eyes.

***

A roll-up metal barrier, like the kind used to secure storefronts in shopping malls, protected the mine entrance. While Emily panned the flashlight around, Hannah located the hand crank at the side of the doorway that controlled the enclosure. She was cranking it, slowly raising the door—the mechanism was rusted so it was a tedious effort—when Deacon shuffled to them cradling Jim in his arms.

"Oh, no." Hannah felt a weakness come over her.

"What . . . what happened?" Emily had dropped the flashlight.

Deacon didn't say a word. Kneeling, he carefully placed Jim against a small mound of rocks piled beside the entrance. He propped Jim upright.

Jim's head drooped against his chest. Hannah didn't need to check his pulse to know that he was gone.

"I'll have to call his wife, if we ever get out of here." Deacon searched Jim's pockets and removed his partner's cell phone. He also took Jim's pistol and two-way radio.

Hannah touched Deacon's shoulder.

"I'm sorry," she said. "Jim was a good man."

Deacon pressed his lips together, as if to seal in all the emotion that Hannah knew he was struggling to contain. She wanted to hold him, but he was keeping in constant motion, in no mood to be comforted.

"We've got work to do," he said in a flat tone. "Let's get back to it."

"Should we say a few words, a prayer or something?" Emily asked. She sniffled, tears leaking from her eyes.

Deacon pulled in a breath. He shook his head.

"Let's just get this door open," he said.

Emily looked crestfallen. But Hannah understood. Probably less than an hour ago, Deacon had lost his father. Now, he had lost a good friend. He couldn't bear to slow down and grieve. It would destroy him, and without him, they would all be lost.

Hannah returned to the hand crank. Emily picked up the flashlight. Deacon grabbed the bottom edge of the door with both hands.

Working as a team, they lifted the door, and scrambled inside.

***

The mechanism that should have allowed the door to remain locked in an open position was broken. As soon as they clambered inside the entrance, the door clattered down behind them and hit the ground with a rattling boom that echoed off the stone walls.

It's like being sealed inside a tomb, Emily thought, and admonished herself for the idea. But she was in a grim mood, what with leaving behind Jim, who had been such an indispensable ally.

A mélange of odors swirled around them: dust, old oil, the pungent aroma of raw earth. She swept her flashlight around the area. Thick wooden columns and wide ceiling brackets supported the tunnel structure; the distance from floor to ceiling was about eight feet. Three rusted mine carts stood on a track, looking as if they hadn't been used in decades. The track twisted ahead and dwindled into darkness. The stone walls glistened with wetness.

Beside the entrance, a small area had an old wooden table piled with assorted junk: a cracked yellow hard hat, and various tools.

There was also an elevator. A badly-rusted gate was pulled across the shaft. Emily shone her flashlight through the metal grate and saw an ancient-looking set of pulleys so frayed the slightest weight would snap them in half.

The interior of the mine was much cooler than it was outdoors, perhaps sixty degrees. The drop in temperature, combined with her rain-sodden clothes, made it feel as if she had walked into a refrigerator.

"Only one way to go," Deacon said. "We follow the track forward. I'll take point. Hannah, stay behind me. Emily, you bring up the rear.

We keep a few feet of spacing between us, but we stay together no matter what."

Listening to him, Emily felt good about their chances. Deacon sounded as if he had done something like this before, though she knew he hadn't.

Deacon gave her the two-way radio that he had taken off Jim.

"We've all got a flashlight, a weapon, and a radio," Deacon said. "Call out to the group if you see anything, hear anything, smell anything. Are we good?"

"Good as we'll ever be," Hannah said.

Emily started to answer but stopped. She thought she had heard something, a distant echo.

"I just heard a noise," she said. "Did you guys catch it?"

Hannah shook her head.

"What did it sound like?" Deacon asked.

She shivered. "It sounded like a scream. I'm not sure it was human. Hard to tell."

"I'll take that as a good sign, then," Deacon said.

"Someone—or something—screaming is a good sign?" Hannah asked.

"It means we're on the right track," he said. "Someone is in here doing bad things. That someone has to be the man we've been seeking."

They advanced into the darkness.

As Deacon led their group, the track sloped deeper into the earth. Fine pebbles and dust, displaced by their shoes, skittered ahead of them.

Although Emily had reported hearing a distant scream, Deacon hadn't heard much since, only the sounds of their shoes crunching across the faded, rock-strewn track. He continuously panned the flashlight back and forth, but so far had found nothing of interest.

If he'd been inclined toward claustrophobia, he would have been suffering a panic attack right about then. The stone tunnel was about eight feet high and ten feet wide, but there was a strong sense of isolation, as if they were traveling into the uncharted depths of a forgotten civilization.

There were lamps spaced along the wall, the bulbs shielded in wire cages, but none of them were in operation.

About a hundred yards in, the main tunnel branched into three different passageways. At the juncture, Deacon shone his flashlight along each corridor, searching for a clue to point them in the right direction.

"Pick a number?" Emily laughed uneasily. "It's like standing in front of three closed doors in some old game show. Guess which one holds the prize."

Deacon grunted. "If Mr. Falcon came in this far, he left behind footprints. I'll check the middle tunnel. Both of you, check the others. Don't wander more than ten feet away. That's far enough to find any footprints, and we can't afford to get separated."

"Good idea," Hannah said. She took the branch on the right.

Deacon got on his knees. His joints popped. His muscles ached. He was so tired, his motor running solely on fumes . . .

No. Gotta stay focused.

Using the flashlight, he crept forward, scanning the ground. Falcon was a large man, and would have left behind sizable footprints in the mixture of dust and rocks.

Deacon duck-walked roughly ten feet without finding any clear indication that Falcon had traveled this way. Straightening, he swept the flashlight ahead one more time.

Something passed through the light. A shadow, quick and low to the ground. It had moved too fast for him to accurately estimate the size.

A chill coursed along his spine. He rested his hand on the .357.

It's an abandoned mine, he reminded himself. *Anything might be in here. Bats, snakes, all kinds of things.*

The conclusion, while true, didn't make him feel any better. He panned the light around once more, but saw nothing.

"Guys!" Hannah said. "I've got something!"

Deacon backed along the tunnel to rejoin the group.

***

While searching the tunnel that lay to the far right of the others, Hannah had not only located Falcon's footprints, she had discovered something better: the leather bag he must have left behind.

She felt fortunate that she had spotted it. She had been creeping along the ground, mindful of straying no more than ten feet into the tunnel, and found a trail of footprints that clearly belonged to a large person. That would have been enough for her . . . but slightly ahead of the limited radius she had intended to cover, she had noticed a more significant difference in the ground.

The bag lay in a section of the passage that had partly collapsed. Old slats of rotted wood had been placed underneath the rail track, for support, and a couple of those boards had broken in half. The back pack was nestled about six feet down, in a pile of shattered wood.

"That definitely belongs to Mr. Falcon," Emily said. "He had it with him earlier when he gave me a ride on his ATV. It had dynamite in it."

"So we know he came this way." Deacon panned the light ahead, but Hannah saw only the continuing rail line. "He had to know where he was going. We go in this direction then."

"Why do you think he left behind the bag?" Hannah asked, pointing. "Isn't that strange?"

"Dropped it down there by mistake, maybe?" Emily asked.

"If I drop a bag full of dynamite that I went through the trouble to bring inside," Hannah said, "I'm going to try my best to retrieve it."

"He might have been attacked." Deacon glanced behind them as if worried. "Dropped it in the melee and couldn't come back to get it."

"Dynamite could be useful to us," Hannah said. "If he thought it was worth bringing in, he must have had a purpose for it."

"I know." Deacon peered into the collapsed section with his flash-light. "But it doesn't look too stable down there."

"I'll go get it," Emily said.

"I don't know if that's a good idea," Deacon said.

"I'm the smallest and lightest of all of us," Emily said. She glanced at Hannah. "No offense."

Hannah shrugged; Emily spoke the truth. But she shared Deacon's concerns about the stability of the piled wood shards where the bag lay.

"All right," Deacon said. "Be careful."

"Always. Give me some light, please."

Emily put down the shotgun she'd carried. Both Deacon and Hannah shone their flashlights into the shattered section of the tunnel.

Emily picked her way down there slowly. Wood groaned and shifted under her weight.

Hannah was holding her breath.

"It's okay," Emily said. "It's holding up fine."

"You can do it," Hannah said. She clutched the flashlight in both hands. Her palms were clammy with perspiration and dirt.

Emily was perhaps two feet away from grasping the bag's strap when Hannah heard a crack. She gasped.

"Get out of there!" Deacon said.

As Emily turned, the fragile structure supporting her collapsed with a calamitous crackle of breaking wood.

No, Hannah thought. She stepped forward, but too late.

Screaming, Emily plunged into the dark depths below.

***

First, Pops. Then Jim. Now this sweet, firecracker of a young woman, Emily.

Deacon refused to accept it. He dropped to the ground and crawled to the edge of the hole into which she had disappeared. Dust and grit swirled into his face, and he had to cover his mouth with his hand.

He stuck the flashlight down there and tried to see. It was like peering into an abyss.

He shouted: "Emily! Can you hear me?"

"Emily!" Hannah had gotten on the ground next to him. "Make a noise if you can hear us! Emily!"

Nothing. A few remaining shards of broken wood fell into the shaft, creating faint echoes as they dropped into the blackness.

The collapse had taken away Falcon's bag, too.

Instinct had warned him that agreeing to Emily's attempt to retrieve the bag was a bad idea. But he had let her do it anyway. Now she was gone.

Deacon closed his eyes. *I let this happen.*

Groaning, he rolled onto his back. Water trickled from the ceiling and onto his cheeks, feeling like cold tears on his skin.

Beside him, Hannah sobbed quietly. In their short time together, the two women had forged a bond. Deacon felt bad for her, too, responsible for her pain.

It was nothing but bad news for them, all around. This half-baked plan of his to bring Kent Falcon to justice was an unmitigated disaster. Perhaps the wise move was to get up, lick their wounds, and take their asses back to Falcon's estate to hide out until everything blew over. Stop trying to be heroes. Trying to be heroes was killing them one by one.

He shifted to face Hannah. "We should go back."

"Go back?" Hannah raised her head, stared at him. In the back-splash of the flashlights, her dark eyes were like darts. "You mean, quit?"

"Jim . . . now Emily. We're losing this, Hannah. I don't see a way forward that ends well for us."

"No." Hannah wiped her eyes with her thumb, clearing away tears and grime. "I'm not going back. With or without you, I'm finishing this."

As he gaped at her, she pushed to her feet with a determined grunt. She gathered her flashlight and the shotgun that Emily had left behind.

Deacon got up, too. "You're serious, aren't you? About going on alone?"

"Welcome to the story of my life." She brushed dirt off the lens of the flashlight and played the beam across the wood-patched section of the corridor floor. "I'll be careful. You take care of yourself, too."

She turned away from him and inched forward. The wood creaked beneath her footsteps, but held firm as she reached the other side.

She didn't even look back to see if he were coming.

Deacon dragged his hand down his face. He spat in the dirt.

Then he picked up his flashlight, and followed her.

***

They didn't speak for a while as they navigated the tunnel, moving nearly shoulder to shoulder, the beams of their lights guiding the way. A couple of times, they ducked to avoid rocky outcroppings that almost nailed them in the head. As they traveled, they passed a series of rusted tools that littered the walls and ground: a pick-axe, a wheelbarrow, long spear-like items that Deacon assumed were old drill bits, left behind from the mine's operational days.

"Sorry for that back there," he finally said. "I lost my way for a minute."

"You of all people don't need to apologize," Hannah said. "What you've been through today . . . well it's amazing that you've come this far. I couldn't do it."

"You gave me the kick in the ass I needed. Thanks for that."

"Sure, that's me, you know. Dispensing kicks in the asses whenever they're required."

A chuckle slipped out of him.

"It's funny," he said. "My cardiologist says I need to be careful with my heart, not exert myself too much. That's why I left the force after I took a round in the chest, and accepted the job here. Security guard commander in a ritzy neighborhood? No problem. I thought every day would be a cakewalk."

"If only you had known, right?" Hannah laughed.

He decided that he liked the sound of her laughter, musical and pure. Like him, she had seen terrible things in her line of work, but she still had a perspective that allowed her to take a step back and see the humor in the world. A woman with such a quality was a rare find.

Maybe, he thought. *Maybe, we've got something good here, something worth exploring if we can get through this night alive.*

"Look at that," Hannah said. She focused her light on an object on the floor.

It was a large crossbow, painted in camouflage colors.

"That belongs to Mr. Falcon," Deacon said. "We're definitely heading in the right direction."

"He wouldn't have left it behind intentionally," Hannah said. "Just like the bag of his."

"I don't think things went as planned for him, either." Deacon scanned the immediate area. On the rock wall not far from the discarded crossbow, he saw a crimson smear that looked like blood. He touched it.

"Still wet," he said.

"He can't be far," she said.

Deacon knew what she meant. She expected to find Falcon's body, soon. A man bereft of weapons and tools, leaking blood from wounds, could not have made it much farther in this tomblike place.

They followed the tunnel around a bend in the rock. Ahead, an old mine cart stood in the center of the track.

There was more blood, too. It covered the inside of the cart, and droplets spattered the ground. A couple strips of a torn shirt lay on the dirt, too.

"Falcon was in this cart," Deacon said. "But he got out. Possibly he bandaged his wounds with his shirt."

Hannah whistled. "Tough guy, huh?"

They continued on. Ahead, dim light glowed at the edge of the corridor. They hurried forward, their footsteps echoing.

They found themselves in a large, cleared out area. Along the far wall, a glass-fronted chamber stood, light glowing within.

"It looks like a lab," Hannah said in a soft, awed voice.

Both of their two-way radios crackled.

"I'm okay, guys," Emily said.

***

Emily told Hannah and Deacon that she was fine, but she wasn't, not really.

She had fallen down a shaft for an indeterminate distance, perhaps twenty feet. It wasn't a free fall—she had bounced against some stones along the way. Bumping against the rocks had broken what could have been a deadly fall, but her head had banged against an outcropping, and she had blacked out.

When she awoke with a pounding headache, it was so dark it was impossible to verify that her eyes were actually open. The blackness was like a solid material surrounding her.

Coldness seeped into her bones. She was lying in cold water. It had a depth of a few inches. She heard the persistent trickle of running water nearby, sounding like a broken toilet.

By touch alone, she located the flashlight clipped to her belt. She thumbed the switch.

The light flared on. The contrast of the electric whiteness against the extreme darkness stung her eyes.

Blinking, she sat up. A dozen pain points throbbed throughout her body. Slowly, she panned the flashlight around her.

She had fallen into some sort of cavern. It was a small space, with a low, jagged ceiling, and a dirt floor covered with rocks and shallow pools of still water. Rivulets of water streamed down the walls, feeding the pond.

The strap of Falcon's bag was twisted around her ankle. The discovery made her chuckle, but laughing aggravated the pain that throbbed throughout her muscles and joints.

She pulled the bag toward her, unwinding the strap from her foot. A check inside confirmed it held six units of plastic-wrapped explosives.

She was lucky that the tumble down the shaft hadn't set off a detonation. Perhaps all of them were lucky.

She grabbed the walkie-talkie Deacon had given her, which she'd clipped to her waist. She told Hannah and Deacon she was okay—banged up, but fine, though she honestly felt like total crap. They wanted to know where she was, but she couldn't tell them exactly. She promised to keep in touch and urged them to move forward with their plans.

"Now to find a way back," she muttered.

The ceiling was so low that couldn't stand up. She had to crouch. As she shone the light around, she located various miniature tunnels in the rocks, large enough for small animals but much too small for her to fit through.

But the stream of water flowed toward a small passageway near the floor that might have been promising. It was small, too, reminding her of a tunnel on a children's playground.

She got on her knees, water drenching her legs and hands. She shone the light into the aperture.

Small creatures with dark, leathery bodies shifted away from the light with a rustling sound. She lowered the flashlight.

Wonderful, she thought. *I've got to crawl through a tunnel full of bats.*

She pulled in several deep breaths. She pulled the hood of her sweatshirt over her head.

When she lifted the light again, the bats had shifted toward her. Their marble-like eyes were blood-red, swollen with infection.

Oh, God, no . . .

Screeching, they funneled toward her.

***

Deacon and Hannah hurried toward the lab like kids on Christmas morning rushing toward a tree surrounded by gifts. Deacon wanted to believe that, finally, momentum had shifted in their favor. Emily was alive. They had discovered this laboratory. They had to seize advantage of the run of good luck.

"After me," Deacon said once they reached the glass doorway. Beyond the door, he saw several wire cages, of various sizes, clustered inside. Computer equipment stood on a small desk.

He drew the .357. The door lever yielded, and the door swished open with a soft gasp.

Nothing rushed out at them. All of the cages were empty.

"The smell in here is god-awful." Hannah coughed. She went to the laptop computer, began tapping the keyboard.

Deacon tried to ignore the cocktail of malodorous odors. A stainless steel door stood at the opposite end of the room. He crossed the space, opened the door.

An overhead light flickered on, and it was like a horror show back there: three perfectly preserved human cadavers lay on morgue-style steel tables, each of them in various stages of dissection, like test subjects in a gross anatomy class. Their disfigured faces rendered them unrecognizable. Deacon saw glass jars standing on wire shelves, packed to the brim with extracted organs floating in preserving fluids: hearts, brains, livers, kidneys, eyes.

Disgust roiled Deacon's stomach. What in the hell had Falcon been doing in here? Had he deliberated infected these people and then run his experiments on them?

The only thing that didn't inspire disgust was the large glass terrarium in the corner. Exotic-looking plants thrived inside the sealed environment. Deacon read the label on the case, "Warning – Do Not Open!" and wondered about the terrarium's contents.

A thick black cable snaked through a small aperture on the floor at the corner of the room. Deacon surmised that all of the equipment in the lab—the computer, the lights, everything—was hooked to an alternate power source.

He headed back to Hannah. She was hunched over the laptop, fingers racing across keys.

"Find something?" he asked. "Because I've got a thing or two to show you in the back room."

"Say hello to Kent Falcon." She turned the computer to face him.

Deacon wiped his face with the back of his hand, and gazed at the laptop display.

A man in his early sixties stared back at him. He had a lean, long-ish face, a wooly white beard that flowed down to his neck, and thick white hair drawn back into a man-bun. He wore wire-rim glasses that framed piercing blue eyes.

From those eyes alone, Deacon knew he was looking at Kent Falcon. He and his older brother shared those penetrating baby blues.

The date of the video recording blinked at the upper right corner of the media viewer application: May 4th. Over two months ago.

"I am Dr. Kent Falcon," he said into the web camera. He had a soft Southern accent; he sounded a bit like a genteel professor, some-one who might have taught a lit class on Faulkner. "This is the first in a series of video log entries that I'll be recording for Project Wilding."

"Project Wilding?" Deacon said, and Hannah shrugged.

"I don't imagine that anyone else will ever view these journals," Falcon continued. "That's irrelevant to me. This work—this *manifes-to*, if you will—is for my own edification, not posterity. I intend to watch these from time to time. Sometimes I like to be reminded of my own genius in laying bare the ills that plague our species."

"Clearly, humility isn't a character trait of his," Hannah said, shak-ing her head.

"Humanity is a cancer upon the earth," Falcon said. "We've raped the planet, all in the name of industrial advancement, technological mastery, and corporate greed. Unimaginable amenities are at our beck and call. Climate-controlled homes. Genetically-modified foods. Mobile phones that are the modern equivalent of supercomputers. Automobiles that virtually drive themselves.

"The average American has no survival skills whatsoever. They're estranged from nature. Who among them, if abandoned in the wilderness, could select edible plants? Who could locate drinkable water? Kindle a fire without matches and other artificial tools? Gather raw materials to construct a place of shelter that keeps them safe and warm? Hunt for food without a firearm?"

"Sort of has a point there," Deacon said.

Falcon leaned toward the screen, his eyes afire as he warmed to his subject.

"We must be re-introduced to our feral natures," he said. "We must strip away the accoutrements of our cluttered, pointless modern lives and recapture our connection with the planet, with the animal kingdom, with one another. We're lost, and we must be found. I've discovered a vehicle to facilitate this transition back to the wild, for all of us. It will not be without pain. There are side effects that must be considered. But the overall benefit to our species, to our planet, outweighs any disadvantages . . ."

"He's insane," Hannah said. She clicked to another log entry: there was a list of perhaps forty files, arranged chronologically.

In the next journal, Kent was ranting again, his cheeks flushed cherry-red.

". . . my elder brother, Ronald, is one of the most disgusting capitalists the world has ever seen, a man obsessed with profit and self-aggrandizement to the exclusion of all else. He erects glittering monuments to his own ego on each of his environment-destroying properties. This travesty of a community, South Haven, was erected out of a misguided sense of nostalgia, and serves as nothing more than a walled-off, artificial paradise for one-percenters who worship at the altar of materialism . . ."

"No love lost between the two of them," Deacon said.

"It'll take days for us to comb through all of these videos," Hannah said. "He's a man who loves the sound of his own voice."

"We'll just take the computer with us, then. It's evidence."

"And this." Hannah flipped through paperwork stashed in a manila folder next to the computer. "These papers are mostly related to inventory, shipments."

"For experiments?" Deacon said.

"Clearly, he was deliberately infecting animals with our friendly Peruvian tick," she said. "Presumably, he was conducting tests before he dispersed the eggs throughout South Haven."

"What kind of animals was he using?" He was thinking about the largest cage he had seen.

"Several chimpanzees. Raccoons. Bats. Mice. Coyotes. A black bear."

"A black bear." He didn't want to think about the possibility of such an immense creature, infected with the neurotoxin, roaming in the mine. "Let me show you what's in the back."

She rose from behind the desk and followed him. She grimaced at the sight of the corpses and stored organs, but the terrarium intrigued her the most.

"I'm not going to open that case," she said. "Because I'm willing to bet dollars to donuts that it contains live specimens of *ixodes insanus*."

Deacon stared into the sealed case but couldn't see a thing except the colorful plants. "Kent Falcon would have had the resources to do it all on his own. His family's real estate empire spans the globe. Going to Peru, throwing some cash around and picking up a rare specimen like this? Just another day for our boy."

"Still incredibly risky," Hannah said. "Risky and stupid."

"So Kent brings the tick here," Deacon said. "And like a mad scientist, he begins running tests on animals, and soon moves on to people."

"Which he happens to do in his brother's prestigious real estate development, South Haven," Hannah said. "A brother he obviously despises. It's a perfect environment for him to exercise his anarchist theories, this Project Wilding."

"Forcing people to become feral again," Deacon said.

"Which is working, more or less. The infected are stripping off their clothes and howling and generally behaving like a sub-human species, minus the nasty side effects, which includes wanting to rip out your neighbor's throat."

"We got what we wanted." Deacon patted his backpack. "We're taking the laptop with us, along with any other paperwork that supports our case. Once we get out of here, we go public. Anyone involved in this needs to go down."

"Kent Falcon most of all," she said. "I can't wait to watch the rest of those videos."

"Yeah," Deacon said, and unconsciously slid his hand to his gun. "And I can't wait to meet him in the flesh."

***

As the infected bats converged on her in a dark, screeching funnel, Emily bowed her head and protected her face with her arms.

Their tiny teeth and claws tore at her exposed hands, like little razors ripping into her flesh. Screaming, she swung the flashlight like a baton. The metal thwacked a couple of the creatures and sent them smashing against the rocks. They collapsed with a whimper.

Charged with adrenaline, she gripped the flashlight in both hands and kept swinging. Another bat fell, skull crushed against the edge of the lens.

Hair hanging in her eyes, she whirled around, taking on all comers. Light panned wildly throughout the chamber as she fought. Water splashed around her feet, and blood dripped down her cheeks, like tears.

She eventually realized that nothing else was biting her. The crushed animals littered the floor, or squirmed weakly in the water.

At some point she had stopped sobbing, too. But she was breathing so hard her lungs ached.

Blood smeared the flashlight lens. She rinsed it carefully in the water, wiped off the lens with the edge of her jacket.

Her hands burned as if from a hundred cuts. Although the infection could not be transmitted via a bite or scratch, she nonetheless wanted to disinfect her wounds. She rinsed her hands in cold water, but needed something to kill any bacteria festering in the injuries.

She slung Falcon's bag over her shoulder, and crawled toward the narrow, low-hanging tunnel, lighting her way with the flashlight. There were no more bats, but the pathway was so tight she worried she would be unable to squeeze through, that she might be stuck in there and forced to use the explosives to free herself—which seemed like suicide.

By crawling on hands and knees, her belly scraping against the dirt, she made it through the tightest section of tunnel, a length of nearly ten feet. She reached a wall. But it was a wall that felt and looked like a panel of wood, not rock.

Like the back of a piece of furniture, she thought, heart knocking.

She pushed against it with both hands. The object yielded, the bottom grinding against the stone floor.

When she had created an opening large enough to accommodate her, she crawled through, and into a more expansive area. Rising, she shone the light around.

She was in a bedroom.

"I must be dreaming," she said, aloud.

The walls were made of rock, and the craggy ceiling was well over ten feet high. A queen-size bed stood against the far wall, sheets and pillows precisely arranged. A metal nightstand stood on one side of the bed, and held various items: a lamp, a sixteen-ounce bottle of water, a digital clock, a bottle of medicine.

On the other side of the bed, she saw a waist-high machine that looked like an industrial-grade air purifier. Farther away, against a wall, stood what looked like a large portable-toilet, the lid snapped shut. A small metal table near the toilet held a four-pack of toilet tissue and a tall bottle of hand sanitizer.

"All the comforts of home." She laughed at the absurdity of it all.

A large, weathered storage trunk had blocked the tunnel she'd used to enter the room. She lifted the lid and panned the light beam inside. The trunk held men's clothing: shirts, khakis, undergarments. Everything was neatly stacked and folded.

Kent Falcon's clothes? It really floored her that the man had apparently *lived* in here, deep in an abandoned freakin' mine. That fact alone qualified him as insane.

She crossed the chamber, rocks crunching under her soles. She turned the power knob on the lamp.

White light blazed from the bulb, chasing away the darkness.

Some sort of tiny lizard stood next to the water bottle. The reptile regarded her with beady eyes. Emily braced herself for an attack, but the animal appeared more interested in the water.

"Sorry, buddy, I'm taking this," she said. She twisted the cap off the bottle. The water was as cool as if it had been stored in a refrigerator, not surprising because the temperature in the room bordered on chilly. She consumed most of the water in three gulps.

The bottle of medicine was store-brand ibuprofen. She chased down four tablets with the rest of the water.

The bed was inviting, but if she stopped to rest she worried that she wouldn't get up for hours. The digital clock flashed 1:37am, way past her normal bedtime.

She had to keep moving. She needed to find a way back to the others.

The electrical cords of both the air purifier and lamp were connected to a thick, rubber-coated power cable that snaked along the floor, and wound through a wide doorway on the other side of the chamber. She headed through the door.

The next room was larger than the sleeping area, with a higher ceiling. She found a lamp on a small table, and flipped it on.

The power cord led to a panel hanging on the wall; a single cord from the wall panel fed into a power generator, the machine humming softly in the corner. A couple of tables lined with various items occupied the space, a swivel desk chair standing between them. Another doorway yawned on the far side of the chamber, the area swathed in blackness.

She also found a portable sink, and a mini-refrigerator. Her stomach growled as if activated by a switch. She made a beeline to the fridge.

As she went to open the door she remembered the wounds on her hands; the blood had clotted but it looked as though she had dunked her hands in a bucket of red paint. Bacterial infection was a legitimate concern.

Although her stomach ached with hunger, she stepped to the sink, instead. The faucet provided a weak trickle of lukewarm water, but it was enough to wash away the blood.

In the cabinet underneath the basin, Kent had stocked a literal medicine cabinet of products: more ibuprofen, a first-aid kit, anti-bacterial ointment, and more. After carefully drying her hands with a paper towel, wincing at the pain, Emily applied a liberal coating of the ointment, and covered the wounds with Band-Aids.

Finally, she returned to the mini-fridge. A small stack of canned goods stood on top: various types of soups, vegetables, a couple cans of Spam. The refrigerator contained about a dozen bottles of water, but no food.

She tore into a can of Spam and ate the meat with her fingers. She was so hungry that it might have been the finest filet of Kobe beef. She tilted the can and let the remaining contents dribble into her mouth.

Satiated, she took stock of the rest of the room. Random items were organized on the tables, mostly equipment that one would have used to navigate the dangerous depths of the mine. A hard hat with a mounted lamp. A compass. A pack of AA batteries. A twelve-pack of chemical light sticks. A loop of rope. She took the light sticks, as they were potentially too useful to pass up.

But the finding that most interested her was what appeared to be an old, hand-drawn map of the mine.

The mine evidently spanned three levels, a section of the map devoted to outlining each level. Key areas were indicated by neat handwriting in blue pencil.

Emily's heart knocked. She removed her iPhone from her fanny pack—the device had survived her fall down the shaft with barely a scratch—and snapped several pictures of the map. She couldn't wait to share her discovery with the others.

It was exactly what they needed to find their way out of there.

***

Soon after leaving the lab with the evidence they had found, Deacon had no clear idea of their next destination. They were following the trail Mr. Falcon had left behind, which, thus far, had worked well for them. It had led them to the lab. Presumably, Falcon knew where to locate his renegade brother, too.

But after a few hundred yards, the tunnel they had followed away from the laboratory split again. A shallow pool of cold water blanketed the floor of both passageways, fed by a steady trickle streaming down the rock walls.

"The water here is masking Falcon's trail." Deacon played the light along both tunnels; they looked nearly identical. "Any idea where to go next?"

"Split up and explore a bit, see what we find?" Hannah asked.

"Don't like that idea. We're already separated from Emily. We need to stay together."

"Flip a coin?" She bounced her flashlight from one tunnel to the next. "Honestly, I've no idea either."

"Then we go right," Deacon said.

"Why right?"

"Gut instinct." He shrugged. "Not scientific but that's how I sometimes roll."

As they started along the path, their radios buzzed. It was Emily again. She had found, incredibly, a map. When they gave her an approximate idea of their current location, she confirmed that they were headed in the correct direction.

The other path, the one they had not taken, led to an alternate exit from the mine.

Deacon trotted back to the tunnel intersection. Using one of the ancient drill bits he saw lying against the rocks, he scratched a small "x" on the wall to mark the exit tunnel.

The tool splashed in the ankle-high water when he dropped it on the ground, the echoes reverberating over them.

"You hear that?" Hannah asked. She cocked her head.

"What was it?"

"Sounded like a scream . . . distant, though. Maybe my ears are deceiving me."

"I doubt it. Let's get moving."

According to the map Emily had found, the mine had three levels. Currently they were on level one. The plan was to rendezvous with Emily at the juncture of level two—where she had found Falcon's bedroom—and the third level. In Deacon's opinion, if Kent Falcon were to be found anywhere there, it would be in the deepest, most remote region of the mine—an appropriate hiding place for a murderous coward.

And once they found him, he was going to answer all of their questions, whether he wanted to or not.

***

Following Emily's directions, they traveled from level one, all the way down to the juncture of levels two and three. As the paths sloped ever downward, the air grew cooler. Deacon could see his breaths frosting in front of his face as he scanned the flashlight ahead of them.

More old mining equipment was scattered amongst the walls. Water dribbled from the rocks in an unending trickle. Several times, they had to find their way around rusted mine carts that lay overturned on the tracks.

There were worrisome weaknesses in the wooden beams, too. In some sections, paths off the main tunnel had collapsed completely, the weight of the rocks winning the battle versus the wooden supports.

"This old place," Hannah said, "is held together like a house of cards."

"Keep that in mind if we've got to shoot something," Deacon said. "Don't want to bring down the whole place on our heads."

They continued on. Soon, reddish light glowed around the bend, just ahead: Emily's marker. She told them she had found a pack of light sticks and would use one of them to communicate her position.

"Our girl's right up there." Deacon increased his pace, water splatting as his shoes slapped across the wet floor.

Before they hit the curve, Emily lunged out of the shadows and grabbed Deacon's arm.

Deacon let out a gasp of surprise, but shut his mouth fast. Emily had brought her index finger to her lips in a "hush" gesture.

The three of them huddled in the small alcove where Emily had waited. With sufficient brightness cast by the nearby light stick, Deacon and Hannah doused their flashlights. The stick's red glow gave all of their faces a crimson tint.

Emily looked like hell, Deacon thought. She had bandages wrapped around her hands, like a boxer after a bruising fight. Tiny cuts peppered her forehead and cheeks.

But she wore Falcon's leather bag slung over her shoulder, the prize of her ordeal. He wondered about all the details of what she had endured, but hearing the story would have to wait for later.

Hannah spoke in a whisper. "What's wrong?"

"There's an elevator shaft, around the corner." Emily gestured with her thumb. "Right before you guys got here, I heard something moving in it. Like something climbing up."

Deacon glanced at Hannah. He didn't need to speak a word to know that her thoughts matched his. She had seen the empty cages in the lab, too.

"We'll check it out then since it's on the way." Deacon gave the shotgun to Emily and cocked the trigger of the .357. "We've got to keep moving."

He clicked on his tactical flashlight again. As he took point, they crept out of the alcove and edged around the corner of the tunnel. The intersection of the converging passageways—one leading to level two, the other down to level three—was a broad space strewn with shattered rocks, splintered wood, and a rusted wheelbarrow. Wooden beams crisscrossed the ceiling, the boards broken in multiple sections.

"The ceiling in this area is weak," Deacon said. "Based on your map, is there another way back up to level one if it all comes crashing down on us?"

"I think so." Emily nodded. "Back the way I came, past Falcon's bedroom."

Nodding, Deacon turned to the elevator shaft Emily had mentioned. It occupied a large section of the wall. The metal door had been twisted off the hinges and lay on the floor in a puddle of water. From the looks of it, it had been that way for many years.

From a distance of perhaps ten feet, Deacon honed his light beam on the shaft. He saw only a pair of frayed cables dangling from a rusted pulley system.

"Not hearing anything," he said. "Not seeing anything, either."

"I *know* I heard something in there," Emily said.

"Wait, the cables are moving," Hannah said. "See?"

Deacon grunted. He noticed it, too. Gun held in the ready-position, light aimed ahead, he stepped forward.

"Hey, be careful," Hannah said.

"I'm not going to go any further looking over my shoulder," he said. "We settle this here."

In spite of his tough words, his stomach had doubled up into a knot. He inched to the edge of the shaft. He panned the light downward.

A chimpanzee hanging from the cable bared its teeth. Its inflamed eyes seethed with fury.

Deacon's response was automatic: he fired the .357. The gun boomed like a cannon in the enclosed space, and the shaft's walls shook, rocks tumbling free.

But the primate had already scrambled out of danger. It clambered up the cable with ghastly speed and leaped out of the shaft, out of Deacon's immediate range.

Behind him, Hannah and Emily screamed.

Deacon was going to swing around and fire, but he heard something else climbing up the cable. It was up the shaft and coming at him fast.

He stepped back, heart feeling lodged in his throat.

It was another frenzied chimpanzee. The primate snarled in his face. It was about four feet tall, maybe a hundred and twenty pounds. Twice as strong as a human under normal circumstances. Deacon remembered a story on the news a few years ago, of a woman mauled by an angry pet chimp. She had needed hours of surgery and a face transplant to look even remotely human again.

Wired with neurotoxin, the animals would be as powerful as monsters from the deepest regions of hell.

Can't miss.

The chimpanzee charged him. He fired, and missed. The animal vaulted to the ceiling and grabbed onto one of the wooden cross-beams. It glared at Deacon.

Somewhere behind him, Emily screamed. Her shotgun boomed. The other primate screeched. Wood chips and bits of stone rained down on them. Shifting rocks groaned.

Other noises were coming from the elevator shaft, too. Scrabbling sounds. Screeching. The cables swung.

In a matter of seconds they were going to be engulfed by a mob of creatures of all sizes, all of them united by murderous rage.

"Shoot the ceiling and run for the tunnel!" Deacon shouted.

As he barked the words, he fired a round at the chimpanzee that scrambled above him. He missed the primate, but hit a crossbeam, blowing a chunk out of it. The wood buckled, and smashed rocks as large as his fist dropped to the floor with a bone-rattling crash.

Behind him, Hannah and Emily were unleashing firepower at the ceiling supports, too, guns booming like fusillades of thunder, muzzles flashing. As they fired their weapons, animals poured out of the elevator shaft. Raccoons. Another pair of chimpanzees. The infected animals howled and thrashed in the storm of falling rocks.

Deacon retreated into the passageway. A hunk of rock smashed against the back of his head, and he nearly passed out from the blunt force of it, his knees wobbling. Someone—it sounded like Hannah—screamed at him to follow them, and the terror in her voice kept him from losing his grip on consciousness. He staggered away, focusing on the sound of her voice.

Behind them, the section of mine they had damaged collapsed with a roar, the screams of the dying animals echoing in the dusty blackness.

***

Emily was hurt. Deacon shone his flashlight on her when she protested that she had to stop running.

"One of those crazy chimps took a bite out of me." Grimacing, she lowered herself to the ground. She touched her leg, appeared to choke down a cry.

Deacon looked at her wound and winced. She had a big, nasty bite on her left thigh, the spreading bloodstain on her jeans as large as a grapefruit. She was a tough one. If he'd had a wound like that he would have been hollering like a choleric baby.

"We've got to disinfect it," Hannah said. She reached for the leather bag Emily had brought. "Is there anything in here we can use?"

"I brought a first-aid kit I found in Kent's bedroom or whatever it was."

"Good thinking." Hannah tore open the bag and rummaged through the contents, carefully avoiding the explosives, Deacon noticed. She glanced at Deacon. "You took a hit on the head, too. I'll check you out in a sec, okay?"

"Sure, doc," he said. "Can you give me one of those light sticks, please? I want to see what's going on around here."

He snapped in half the chemical light stick Hannah gave him and placed it on the ground nearby. Soft, greenish light pushed away the shadows. Turning around, Deacon saw that an impregnable heap of rocks blocked the corridor they had left behind, like stones dumped from a giant wheelbarrow. Ahead of them, the tunnel stretched into nondescript darkness.

It felt like the most remote location on the entire planet. Deacon's sense of isolation was so strong, actually, that they very well might have *been* on another planet.

"I really hope you were right about there being another way out of here," he said to Emily.

"Promise." Emily gasped as Hannah cleansed her wound. "I snapped a pic of the map with my phone. Every level was designed with at least two paths going up or down."

"Have you seen this alternate route with your own eyes?" he asked.

"It's on the map."

"Can we trust a map of a mine that hasn't operated in decades?" he said. "There might be paths indicated but who knows if they're still passable? This place is falling apart."

"It's too late to worry about that now, isn't it?" Hannah said. She applied a bandage to Emily's wound. "I don't know, Em. I did my best here but I think you're going to have some serious mobility issues."

"I can manage, thanks." Emily tried to stand. Although Hannah helped her rise, her leg buckled under her weight, and she clamped down her teeth, holding back a cry of pain. "Shit!"

"I'll help you, it's okay," Hannah said.

"It's not okay. We're going to have to haul ass at some point and I'm limping along with one good leg." She sighed. "Just . . . just leave me here and come back and get me afterward."

"No one gets left behind," Deacon said. "I'll carry you on my goddamn back if I have to."

"I'm only going to slow you guys down," Emily said. "Look at what we just dealt with, all those sick animals attacking us. How much worse do you think it will be if we ever find Kent Falcon?"

"We're not leaving you alone, injured," Deacon said. "Out of the question. Period."

"I'm not going to put you guys at risk," Emily said.

"All right, let's end the stalemate." Hannah shifted her gaze to Deacon. "Deacon, I'll stay with her."

"What?" he said. "No. No way."

"We aren't going to sit here knitting afghans," Hannah said. "You continue down to level three and find Kent Falcon, while Emily and I verify this alternate route out of the mine system. We keep in touch with our radios."

It was tough to argue with her logic. That was a major part of what made her so appealing to him. She had a knack for cutting through the crap and focusing on the important details.

"Okay, let me check out those explosives you found," Deacon said. "Depending on what I find down there, I want to be prepared to use them."

***

Deacon was on his own.

Hannah had examined the knot on his head, where the falling debris had struck him. She had wanted to apply a bandage, but he declined and asked for some ibuprofen instead. His body had suffered a multitude of aches and bruises. Anything that could dull the pain for a bit was all he needed.

When this was all over, he was going to sleep for a week.

They'd parted ways at an intersection of three tunnels. Hannah and Emily took the branch that Emily was convinced would lead back to the upper levels. Deacon's decision was easier: of the other two corridors, one was impassable, water streaming over the stones, rusted drill bits mingled in with the rocks. He followed the only passageway left to take. Emily's map indicated that it would plunge into the mine's deepest level.

He had the bag full of explosives strapped across his shoulder, the pump-action shotgun, the .357, extra ammo for the firearms, his tac-light, and his two-way radio. Everything else—light sticks, the laptop they'd looted from the lab, and other items—he had given to Hannah.

He'd purposely avoided an emotional good-bye. Hannah, too, had kept her cool, and he liked that about her. They were heading off to complete separate tasks—that was how he chose to view it. They would see each other again when their work was done.

The truth was, if he'd pulled her into his arms like he wanted to, he wouldn't have been able to let her go.

Sweeping the flashlight ahead of him, he followed the mine track as it sloped deeper into the earth. The only noises were his boots crunching across shale, the ever-present trickle of water dribbling down the walls, and his labored breathing.

The light didn't reveal any signs of whether Ronald Falcon, or anyone else, had come this way. He saw only scattered, ancient-looking mining tools, like artifacts left behind by a lost tribe.

Was there anyone actually down at this level, except for the infected animals?

Small tunnels branched off the main passageway. He glanced at them, but kept to the widest path, as Emily had assured him that there was one primary artery that would take him to the deepest level. All he had to do was stick to it.

The echo of a scream cut through the darkness. It was the rough-edged howl of a man in agony.

Ronald Falcon, he thought.

He quickened his pace. The satchel bounced against his ribs.

The tunnel twisted to the right. He followed the path, his breath roaring in his ears, heart pounding.

Two more passageways split off the main tunnel. But flickering light came from up ahead. He stayed the course.

As he advanced, he noticed paintings had been scrawled on the stone walls. He panned his light across them. They were crude chalk drawings, reminiscent of cave artwork done in prehistoric times. One depicted a stick-figure with flowing hair, gripping a spear. Others dramatized a man leading a herd of wild animals of various sizes; two stick figures copulating on the ground; someone setting fire to a tall building, torch held high.

Another drawing showed only a man's head, hair standing on end like spikes, pupils dilated and mouth peeled open in a scream.

Was this Kent Falcon's work? What strange compulsion had driven the man, supposedly a PhD, to scribble on the walls like a child?

The corridor emptied into a vast chamber, some sort of materials processing area. Mine carts and old drills and pumps were heaped along the walls. The jagged rock ceiling was perhaps twenty feet high, crisscrossed with wooden beams. A series of bonfires spat and sizzled throughout the area, casting flickering light, throwing wriggling shadows on the walls.

In the bonfire glow, he discovered Ronald Falcon.

Wrists bound in rope, Falcon hung from the support beams, his feet dangling above the floor. Most of his clothing had been torn away. Blood streamed from various cuts and dripped to the ground, as if he were a hog being butchered in a slaughterhouse.

His butcher paced the ground in front of him: Kent Falcon.

***

But Kent Falcon wasn't in the state that Deacon had expected.

In the video journal entries Deacon had seen, Kent was professorial, intense but soft-spoken. The kind of man who might have found it inappropriate to take off his shirt in public.

But there, deep in the mine, he was completely naked. Oozing sores mapped his body. He moved on all fours, like an ape. He clenched a large, blood-streaked knife between his teeth.

Frenzied, Deacon thought. *More than anyone else I've seen.*

There were lots of others in the room, too. Assorted animals licked and sniffed the floor where Ronald's blood had collected: Rats, dogs, cats, possum, chimpanzees . . . a thick cluster of creatures moving as if controlled by a single hive mind.

Ronald Falcon lifted his head at Deacon's entrance. Blood streamed down his face and bare chest. It looked as if Kent had cut deep into his brother's chest, as though intent upon carving out his heart.

But those piercing blue eyes of Ronald Falcon's located Deacon, and they glinted with something approaching pride.

Kent Falcon turned and noticed Deacon, too. The quantity of hair and sores that covered his face almost entirely concealed his swollen eyes.

He pulled the knife from between his teeth. He snarled.

"Umlaut tukok!" Kent shouted in a hoarse voice, spittle flying from his cracked lips. "Thwack do!"

There would be no forced confession of his crimes, Deacon realized. No contentious debate about the evils this man had produced. This Kent Falcon, his brain blitzed by parasitic neurotoxin, was about as coherent as a prehistoric man would have been if one had been strapped into a time machine and transported fifty thousand years into the present.

Almost as one, the mass of infected animals took note of Deacon. Dozens of crimson eyes simmered with primordial bloodlust.

Deacon brandished the bundle of dynamite.

He had already set the fuse afire. The flame crawled toward the blasting cap. Once the blasting cap exploded, it would ignite the nitroglycerin and bring down the whole room.

"Did my job," Deacon said, and glared at Ronald Falcon. "Paid in full."

Ever so slightly, Falcon nodded.

Kent Falcon roared. He surged forward, his assembled mob of creatures flanking him.

Using what last bit of strength he had remaining, Ronald Falcon lifted his long legs and wrapped them around Kent's neck in a scissor hold, trapping his brother with him. He grinned as Kent struggled in vain to slip free.

Deacon tossed the dynamite toward them.

And ran.

***

Emily was right.

Her confidence in the map she'd found paid off. They discovered an alternate route back up to level one of the mine.

Hannah's only concern was ensuring Deacon would be able to follow their path. She had left behind a breadcrumb trail for him: a chemical light stick at each key juncture, each one placed to indicate the direction he should travel.

If he survived—*no, he will survive,* she told herself—he should find his way to them with no problem.

As she and Emily picked their way along the service tunnel, Emily leaning against her for support, Hannah scanning the flashlight ahead of them, Hannah heard what sounded like a distant rumble of thunder. The ground trembled, a thin hail of rocks and dust falling from the ceiling.

"Dynamite," Emily said. "Wow, he really did it."

Hannah felt a laugh bubbling at her lips. She hadn't had much to laugh about throughout this entire hellish adventure, but the thought of putting all of this behind them, of seeing Deacon again, lifted her spirits to euphoric levels.

She needed to hear his voice. She unclipped her two-way radio and tried to raise Deacon. He didn't answer.

"He's probably running out of there, can't hear it for all the noise," Emily said.

"Right," Hannah said, but a stone had rolled over her heart. "I'm sure he's on his way."

They shuffled along in silence for a few paces. The worst of the trembling had subsided, but smaller disturbances rippled through the mine, like the aftershocks of a major earthquake.

"You two make a beautiful couple, you know," Emily said. "You'd have gorgeous children."

"I think you're getting ahead of yourself, girl." Hannah smiled. "We aren't dating."

"Promise to invite me to the wedding, okay?" Emily said.

"You're only being silly," Hannah said.

"Hey, what's that?" Emily lifted her own flashlight.

Hannah saw it, too. A vehicle parked ahead of them in the tunnel: a black Chevy Silverado, the back panels splashed with whorls of red clay. It had a Georgia plate. The truck's lights were off.

"Kent's pickup, you think?" Hannah asked.

"Let's check it out. It would be nice to drive the rest of the way out of here."

They drew closer to it. The driver's side door hung open a few inches. Emily reached for the handle.

"Wait," Hannah said, struck with a premonition of danger. Why was the door open? Kent wouldn't have left it that way, would he?

But Emily was already swinging the door open all of the way. "It's all right . . ."

Inside the cabin, something shrieked. Emily screamed, too.

A chimpanzee leaped out of the truck. It bounded onto Emily, its long, powerful arms wrapping around her torso.

It's the same one that attacked Em earlier, Hannah thought, in a flash. *It's come back to finish her off.*

Hannah had, in that instant, a terrifying vision of how it could all play out. The enraged chimp would rip a plug out of Emily's neck. Meanwhile, she would fumble the pistol Deacon had given her because she was really no good at using guns anyway. The infected animal would move from Emily and jump onto her and tear her apart as if she were made of confetti paper.

But that flash of thought was overcome by sheer survival instinct. She already had the pistol in her other hand, had never relinquished her grip on it. She lifted the gun, took aim at the primate attacking her friend, and pulled the trigger one, two, three times.

The sick animal dropped to the ground, tried to get up again but didn't have the strength.

Hannah took no pleasure in killing the chimp, wished it hadn't been necessary. The animal had been only a pawn and hadn't deserved its fate.

"You okay, Em?" Hannah went to where Emily huddled on the ground.

"Yeah." Emily nodded. "It didn't bite me again, thank God. Came awfully close, though."

Hannah helped her to stand. Together, they examined the pickup truck. The interior was spotless, and had that new-car smell that Hannah had always found appealing.

Emily found the key fob nestled under the sun visor.

"Not as though he would have expected anyone to steal his truck down here," Emily said.

Emily offered to drive, and clambered behind the wheel. The engine started with a rumble. The fuel tank gauge indicated it was three-quarters full, head lamps carving away the darkness ahead. Hannah couldn't see the exit out of the mine, but she saw nothing stopping them from progressing.

"Wait for Deacon?" Emily asked.

"He'll be here soon. I'm sure of it."

Hannah twisted around in the passenger seat and stared out the rear window, at the empty blackness beyond the red glow of the tail lights.

Don't make a liar out of me, Deacon, she thought.

***

The mine was collapsing.

Deacon dropped everything except for the flashlight and the shotgun, and ran pell-mell down the tunnel. The ground shook beneath his feet. Rocks fell from the ceiling. Dust got into his eyes and mouth. The sound of destruction was like nothing he had ever heard—it sounded as if the earth itself were falling apart.

But he kept running.

He hit a curve in the tunnel, a turn he remembered taking earlier, except from the opposite direction. He was confident so far of finding his way back, up to a certain point, but Hannah and Emily would need to come through for him if he were to escape the mine entirely.

As he hustled down the passageways, whipping the flashlight back and forth, the most destructive tremors eventually subsided, but rumbles and rattles continued. He became aware, however, of another set of noises echoing along the tunnel: rapid, heavy footsteps.

Someone—or *something*—was following him.

Swinging around, Deacon shone the light in the tunnel behind him. He saw nothing but veils of dusty darkness, rippling like curtains.

But the noises of something stalking him were unmistakable. Whatever it was, it had weight. It would be bigger than him—it would be something they hadn't seen before.

He flashed back to all of those empty cages in the lab, and the largest enclosure of all, and had a strong sense of exactly what might be out there looking for him.

The shotgun had a mount large enough to accommodate his tac-light. He slammed the light into the slot. It wasn't a perfect fit, but it would serve fine for his purposes.

He tightened his grip on the gun and resumed moving.

A roar of pure rage washed over him, echoes assaulting his ears.

Cold sweat coated Deacon's hands. He steadied his grip on the gun.

Keep moving, keep moving, keep moving . . .

Bluish light glowed ahead near a juncture of the tunnels. One of the light sticks Hannah and Emily had left behind for him, pointing the way to freedom. He plunged ahead, past the intersection.

As he passed through, he caught lumbering movement, on his left, something immense coming out of the shadows, a giant killing machine that could be only one thing, a creature from his most terrifying nightmares.

The black bear bellowed in murderous fury.

Deacon kept running. He didn't look back. He kept the shotgun aimed ahead to light his way. His boots kicked up shale and dust. Random pieces of debris continued to pelt him as the mine rumbled and pitched.

He heard the bear gaining on him, massive paws splashing through pools of water.

He'd watched a nature documentary some time ago and remembered that bears could run up to thirty miles an hour. The animal on his heels couldn't travel that fast in a shifting tunnel full of debris. But it still held a substantial speed advantage over him.

Doesn't matter. Run. Run for your life.

The animal's roar reverberated all around him as it closed the gap. As if from far away, he heard a tinny voice, Hannah's voice, issuing from the walkie-talkie riding on his hip. He couldn't spend time responding, but hearing her calling for him, wanting to know if he was okay, stirred something in him, a sudden compulsion to fight back instead of running, to face the beast on his heels and let loose with buckshot until the shotgun clicked on an empty chamber.

Deacon swung around, and the bear was so close that he could smell its rank breath, could see the whites of its crimson, swollen eyes in the glare of the mounted flashlight.

He started shooting—at the already weakened support beams bracketing the tunnel ceiling.

The shotgun leapt in his grip. Chunks of wood fractured and flew like shrapnel. Roaring, the bear surged forward and swiped at him with its mighty paw.

Feeling as if he'd been flayed open like a fish, Deacon went down.

The tunnel came down, too.

***

Sitting in the passenger seat of the truck, Hannah checked her watch for perhaps the tenth time, and looked out the rear windshield again. She was starting to feel sick.

She had tried to raise Deacon several times on the two-way radio, with no luck.

"He'll make it," Emily said, but she had begun drumming her fingers on the steering wheel.

"Maybe he missed one of our markers," Hannah said. "Maybe debris from the explosion covered up one of them and he's lost."

"Or maybe he's almost here." Emily touched her arm.

Hannah shrugged off her hand. "I'm going to look for him. Wait here."

She got out of the truck before Emily could talk her out of it. Emily meant well, and she appreciated her quiet faith in a positive outcome, but Hannah couldn't sit there and hope that this man made it back to them, she had to do *something*.

The glowing tail lights brightened the tunnel for a radius of perhaps ten feet. Beyond that range, darkness came down like a solid wall.

Hannah realized she had left behind her flashlight in the truck. She was so distraught she wasn't thinking clearly.

A noise, close by. A groan of exhaustion, pain.

"Deacon?" Heart leaping, Hannah hurried forward.

Deacon crawled out of the darkness and into the light.

He was covered in blood, but he was alive.

"Let's get out of here," he said.

Chapter 33

It was all over the news.

Two days later, lying in bed in an ICU room at Grady Memorial Hospital in downtown Atlanta, Deacon flipped through various news broadcasts on the flat-screen TV positioned above him. All of them repeated the same fabricated story: a carbon monoxide leak isolated to the upscale live-work-play community of South Haven had resulted in a tragic loss of life. The area was under strict, federal government quarantine for an indefinite period.

Social media, however, told a much different story. Before the military's jammers had disrupted wireless communications, dozens of community residents had sent texts to friends and family, and posted videos of what had really happened within those gilded walls.

The room's glass door whooshed open. Emily and Hannah came inside, laden with paper bags.

"Hey, ladies," Deacon said. His stomach grumbled, and he adjusted the bed into an upright position. "Is that real food I smell?"

Emily lifted a bag from a local deli. "Just what you ordered."

"Appreciate that. If I had to eat another cup of applesauce, I was gonna shoot somebody."

"I'm sorry, but I had to eat the pickles on the way here," Emily said. "I've picked up these weird, pregnant-lady cravings."

Emily had spent some time in the hospital, too, to get treatment for her wounds. She'd gotten multiple stitches to address the bites from the frenzied chimps, and she'd been vaccinated for rabies and tetanus.

None of it was expected to impact her pregnancy, a blessing for which all of them were grateful.

Hannah placed a leather laptop carrying case on one of the wing chairs, and came to the bed. She grasped Deacon's hand, kissed him on the lips.

"You're looking better," she said. "How're you feeling?"

"Better than could be expected, considering that a black bear on steroids tried to rip my heart out—thank God for Kevlar body armor." He squeezed her hand. "Better now that you're here, too."

Hannah sat next to him on the mattress; they still held hands.

"I finished reviewing Kent Falcon's video journal, all forty-six entries," she said.

"And?" he asked.

"He isn't an anomaly."

"Tell me about it. He was a psychopathic douchebag. The world is full of them."

"It's more complicated than that," Hannah said. "He was a leading member of some sort of underground order. A secret network of anarcho-primitivists who want to push back the advances of modern technology by any means necessary. Remember Ted Kaczynski, the Unabomber? He was another one, who acted as a lone wolf, but Falcon's group seems much more organized. Extremely well-connected, too."

Deacon sighed, rested his head against the pillow.

"Did he give names?" Deacon asked.

"Only aliases." Hannah watched him, her gaze expectant. "We'll need to decide what we're going to do about it. This isn't over."

Deacon glanced at the television, at the media outlets dispensing fake news, whether they realized it or not.

"Give everyone the truth." He looked from Emily, to Hannah. "My dad, Jim, all of the others we lost, we owe them that, it's our duty. We give everyone the truth."

"My thoughts exactly," Hannah said. Emily was nodding, too.

"But that's a task for tomorrow," he said, and pulled Hannah into his arms. She fit perfectly in the circle of his embrace, as if all along, throughout the ups and downs of his life, she and she alone always had been meant to be there next to him, and he to her. "I want to enjoy this day, this moment, before we face the rest of the world."

Emily gave them a knowing smile and quietly slipped out of the room. Their faces so close their noses nearly touched, Hannah laid her palm against his heart, and he put his hand against hers, too, felt the slow throbbing beneath his fingers.

"Promise not to break it?" she asked.

"Only if you promise not to break mine. It's taken a lot of damage already, not sure how much more it can handle."

She traced her hand upward, to his chin, guided his face even closer, and gave him a teasing, feather-light kiss, then another, and another.

"I think I can work with that," she finally said.

Get on the Mailing List!

Enjoy this story? Visit www.brandonmassey.com now to sign up for Brandon Massey's free mailing list. Mailing list members get advance news on books, the chance to win autographed copies, and much more. Sign up now!

Also by Brandon Massey

Novels

Thunderland

Dark Corner

Within the Shadows

The Other Brother

Vicious

The Last Affair

Don't Ever Tell

Cornered

Covenant

In the Dark

Collections

Twisted Tales

The Ancestors

Dark Dreams I – III

About Brandon Massey

Brandon Massey was born June 9, 1973 and grew up in Zion, Illinois. He lives with his family near Atlanta, Georgia, where he is at work on his next novel. Visit his web site at www.brandonmassey.com for the latest news on his upcoming books.

CPSIA information can be obtained
at www.ICGtesting.com
Printed in the USA
LVHW092258200920
666611LV00001B/104